I0823961

GODS BENEATH the ICE

TITLES BY ALEXANDRA KENNINGTON

◆ ◆ ◆ ◆ ◆

THE BLOOD & SOULS DUOLOGY

Blood Beneath the Snow

Gods Beneath the Ice

GODS BENEATH the ICE

ALEXANDRA KENNINGTON

ACE
NEW YORK

ACE
Published by Berkley
An imprint of Penguin Random House LLC
1745 Broadway, New York, NY 10019
penguinrandomhouse.com

Book design by Daniel Brount

ISBN: 9780593820148

An application to register this book for cataloging has been submitted to the Library of Congress.

First Edition: February 2026

Printed in the United States of America
1st Printing

The authorized representative in the EU for product safety and compliance is Penguin Random House Ireland, Morrison Chambers, 32 Nassau Street, Dublin D02 YH68, Ireland, https://eu-contact.penguin.ie.

For my mom, who has championed my writing
from the very beginning.
And for those whose anger is a shield.
I hope you allow it to become your sword instead.

AUTHOR'S NOTE

This novel contains heavy themes and topics that might not be suitable for all readers. I hope the following list will be helpful in allowing you to decide whether reading this novel is in your best interest. Whether you choose to continue reading or not, I'm grateful you took the time to pick up this book. Take care of yourself, friend.

This book includes the following: anxiety; death; depression; domestic violence (past, brief mentions); drowning; explicit sex scenes, all consensual; grief; intrusive thoughts of a dark nature; mentions of ableism (past, off-page); murder; strong language; and violence.

GODS BENEATH the ICE

Prologue

Søren

THE NORTHERN WASTES OF BHORGLID WERE THE LAST PLACE I wanted to be, but I hadn't exactly given myself much of a choice in the matter.

Our feet crunched as we arrived and Mira took her hand from my arm. In the three weeks since the battle here, the snow had melted slightly in the afternoon sun and frozen again as night descended. The endless cycle created a preserved graveyard of Kryllian soldiers, their blood smeared across the white.

I slid my helmet on, latching it into place, and saw the scene through the eyes of a monster.

Mira frowned. "There's no one here." As if concealing my identity was the only reason to wear the wolf skull's visage over my own. As if showing any minute expression, any beginnings of emotion would not lead to my downfall.

My carelessness had already destroyed me once. I would not allow it to do so again.

But Mira was not privy to the swirls of my dark thoughts. She did not—could not—understand what it all meant for me. So instead, I quipped back, the voice distortion taking hold of my words, "You're here."

She rolled her eyes. "Yeah, and I know what you look like already."

I ignored her. Mostly because I didn't feel like talking, especially considering what I had come here to do. But also because she was unaware of the truth.

We were not alone.

"General."

The word was half whisper, half plea. It sent a shudder down my spine, the way the voices always did. I forced myself not to turn my head—if I did, I would be face-to-face with . . . him? Her? Them? Whichever soldier was still here, clinging desperately to the last vestiges of life. The spirit of a Kryllian fighter who had died under my command mere days ago.

A ghost here to haunt me.

It didn't matter if they knew my face. After all, there was no one for them to tell. No one else who heard or saw them.

But at least this way I could pretend not to hear them. Avoid looking directly into their eyes while they begged me to acknowledge them. The mask was another layer to hide behind.

The first whispered word multiplied until a chorus sounded. It took every effort not to flinch. This was not a lone soldier waiting here in their death-place for a familiar sight. It was a contingent of them, their number impossible to discern without acknowledging the secret I held so tight to my chest—that I could see the souls of those who had passed on before they departed for the next life.

Mira was still complaining, and I forced every taut muscle to relax and focus on her words. "—is out doesn't mean she won't return and find us gone. What's your plan for that?"

The Queen of Kryllian was away on an errand today. It was the only reason we were able to sneak away to the wastes for a few hours.

She had been venturing out for longer and longer periods of time ever since the Trials. Even Mira wasn't sure where she was going.

"She's leaving at other times, too," Mira had reported, her fingers fidgeting nervously. "I know it. There's at least one other teleporter working with her, and she hasn't mentioned it."

"Where is she going?" I'd asked, frustrated. "Where is she having you take her?"

"The wastes, mostly."

"Bhorglid?" I'd wracked my mind but was unable to find an answer to the puzzle placed before me. We had some of the pieces, but not enough to form a picture.

I was certain the queen was up to something, though I wasn't sure what.

I turned my thoughts back to the matter at hand. "You're not staying. You'll go back and then come retrieve me in two hours."

Mira scuffed her boot in the snow. It hit me suddenly how young she was—barely eighteen. War had changed us both, and I tended to forget just how little she'd experienced outside the confines of the front lines and the Kryllian palace. "I don't want to leave."

I softened slightly. "I know. But someone needs to be on guard back at the palace. In case the queen returns early."

"Do you think you're clever?" Mira's retort had bite, and I frowned. "I know exactly what you're doing. Exactly who you're looking for. You know you won't get redemption from her, right?"

"Yes." The word tore from me, harsher than I intended. Mira's reaction was immediate, her nonchalant expression twisting into annoyance. She glared at me—at the Hellbringer. Anyone with eyes could recognize she hated Revna, though I didn't understand why. Maybe because Mira and I had both been punished for leaving the Trials early.

The Queen of Kryllian had not appreciated her general—her obedient pet—cutting corners. But she'd said to watch the Trials, said to go without my mask and sit right in the front, said to ensure Revna knew she was watching.

I did what I was asked. Held my tongue while her prick of a brother used his knife to slice into Revna's face. Sat still and unmoving as he prepared to kill her. Watched with a satisfied smirk as the last brother died at my princess's hands.

Even in the face of death, even as I watched her struggle for survival, she was beautiful. She was everything. And thinking of her expression when she'd locked eyes with me after her win killed me a bit inside. She hated me for what I'd done.

I didn't blame her.

"I am not here to try and be redeemed," I told Mira. "Whether or not Revna could possibly forgive me doesn't change the fact that this is the right thing to do."

The teleporter stood quietly at my side for a long moment. She'd been assigned to my regiment, a small number of elite Lurae soldiers, three years ago. I'd taken one look at her and seen my younger self shining in her defiant eyes. Despite her youth, Mira fought for her country with a quiet aptitude most would never realize she possessed. She was an asset I used often, one I couldn't afford to lose—neither to death nor lack of trust. I thought of her like a younger sister, and taking her loyalty for granted would be a mistake.

"You love her." Mira said it so softly I almost didn't hear.

I didn't answer. Perhaps she would think I missed the declaration, lost in my thoughts. "Keep watch. Notify me if the queen returns early."

She was gone in the next instant.

◆ ◆ ◆ ◆ ◆

THE SPIRITS HERE WERE NOT HAPPY WITH ME.

As I scoured the landscape for any trace of a head of red hair, they followed. Their demands were incessant, their insults worse.

"You're the reason we're dead," they hissed, paying no mind to my personal space. I was grateful spirits didn't keep their death wounds in their ghostly forms; they all appeared as human as they were when they'd served under my command. "You knew the royals were coming and you didn't warn us adequately."

And something about the voices of the dead pierced straight through my flesh to chill my bones. Listening to them was almost painful. It was another reminder of my loneliness, my cursed Lurae.

"Don't you know I have a family back home? Don't you know that my children will never see their mother again, that my spouse will spend an eternity grieving me?"

Everything about this place was unrecognizable now. I nudged bodies with my boot, wondering if maybe a Kryllian soldier had fallen over him, covering him from view. And the whole time, I thought of Revna—the way she'd looked as she pushed to her feet, bloody knife in hand, and turned to the audience with a scream that resonated from deep within. This was for her. Dealing with every one of these loud spirits would be worth it if I could just—

"You're the reason we're stuck here, on the plains of a foreign land for eternity, not even granted peace in our deaths—"

"Enough!"

I whirled on the crowd of spirits amassing behind me, my shout echoing across the wasteland. There had to be at least fifty now, all astonished to discover I could see them. I stepped to the closest one and got directly in her face. "There are hundreds—thousands—of deaths on my hands. Yours isn't one of them. The Bhorglid royals who wielded their blades and their Lurae killed you. Not me."

She blinked at me. It was a common enough scene, one I was all too familiar with. No one else even knew spirits existed, so why would the dead think anyone could see them? For all they followed me around, they often didn't truly realize I was paying attention. Until my control snapped.

But I saw them all.

"The only reason you're still here is because you've chosen not to pass on," I continued. "Don't pretend. I know how this works far better than most. If you really want your peace, you'll head through the archway you see, the one you're all ignoring, the one you're all afraid of, instead of harassing your former general."

I sighed and stepped back from the soldier's spirit. If my mask were off, I would run a hand over my face. Instead, I curled my hand into a fist, hoping it would soothe my restless impatience. It was nearly impossible to reason with the dead, especially the ones who stuck around—their fear encompassed them like shrouds. They didn't want to venture down the path some had described to me before. They wanted someone to blame. They wanted their lives back.

Even I couldn't give them that.

Relishing their stunned silence, I turned back to the endless expanse of snow in front of me. Perhaps this entire endeavor was futile. If I couldn't find a single dead body with bright red hair against a backdrop of pure white, then maybe it wasn't meant to be. Maybe there was no way to atone for my sins, no way to cut the leash the queen held wrapped around my throat. Maybe I was destined to remain a monster after all.

When the spirits didn't return to their clamoring, I glanced back.

They were gone.

With a frown, I looked around for them. Surely they hadn't—

"They didn't move on, but you're pretty terrifying. They'll keep their distance for the time being," a laughing voice said.

The spirit stood on my left, staring out into the distance. I wondered, not for the first time, how he and Revna had come from the same parents. They looked hardly anything alike, though they did have the same eyes.

I sighed. "Frode. I've been listening to them harass me for twenty minutes while I dug around for your body. And the entire time, you were right there? Unwilling to be helpful?"

"Helpfulness isn't my best quality," he offered. When I made no attempt to reply, he continued, "It was actually because I was so curious about the seeing-spirits thing. I'd wondered if that's what was happening when we were fighting and I was listening to your thoughts—but I wasn't entirely sure. Thought I'd let you wander around for a bit while I observed."

"And you're Revna's favorite sibling . . . how?" I asked. Gods above, this man was frustrating beyond belief.

"Not like she had many better options." But at the mention of his sister, he lit up. "How were the Trials? Those were a couple of weeks ago, right? I've been trying to keep track of the time, but it's been difficult. Everything feels a bit warped without a body. Did she win?"

"She did." I attempted to keep my voice level, but a hint of pride slipped through. "They immediately launched into a rebellion. I didn't stay for that part, but they were successful. The priests have been run out of Bhorglid."

Frode visibly relaxed. "Thank you. For training her."

I hummed noncommittally. "She's only alive because of you."

He shrugged. "I know."

Neither of us made another move to acknowledge what had happened here a short time ago: the terrible choice I'd been forced to make, the clear solution Frode had offered at the expense of his own life. He might be annoying, but he bought me enough time to continue searching for Sonja—to avoid making the impossible choice between the life of my sister and the life of the woman I loved.

Love.

I knew Frode couldn't read my thoughts anymore, but his shit-eating grin made me wonder. "I'm here for your body. Do you know where it is?"

He led me to a shallow crest in the snow, identical to all the others around it. Crouching down, I began digging. By the time his unseeing eyes stared up at the sky, my fingers were numb, wetness seeping through my thick gloves.

"I'm almost afraid to ask what you'll be doing with it."

I rolled my eyes before remembering he couldn't see it. "Taking you home. Burying you next to your brothers."

His face fell. "Jac?"

"Wasn't at the Trials. Deserted."

Frode's expression somehow conveyed both confusion and frustration at the same time. "That bastard. He left Revna to fend for herself?"

I shrugged, reaching down to haul his body up by the armpits. He was far too light, and I recalled Revna telling me about the food shortages Bhorglid was facing. "Seems like it."

"Have you told her yet?" When I remained silent, pretending not to know what he was talking about, Frode sighed. "You haven't explained to her what happened out here?" He swept his arm out, gesturing to the icy remains of the battle we'd fought.

"No."

I hoisted his dead body out from the snow, resting it in my arms. Out of the corner of my eye, I watched Frode fidget. He had something to say about my decision, and I had no interest in hearing it. "My teleporter will be back any minute," I said. "You should go. No point in staying here any longer."

"But why?" he said, exasperation obvious in his words. "Why haven't you told her? She would understand."

I scoffed. "And then what? We live happily ever after, the queen and the monster? No. It's easier if she hates me—kinder to her, even. She deserves far better than me anyway."

"Hjalmar's tits, you're depressing."

Gods above, Mira needed to get back here now. "I'm well aware.

Do you plan to pass on, or sit around staring at the snow for the rest of eternity?"

Frode glanced out at the wastes. "I stayed hoping someone would come back with news about the Trials. I wanted to know whether Revna won before I moved on. But I heard you mention an arch and . . . well, the archway disappeared shortly after I arrived here." Worried eyes met my own. "Should it not have?"

"Disappeared?" I couldn't hide the incredulity in my voice. "I don't know. I've never been able to see the archway, only the spirits. Maybe you're not looking hard enough."

Frode glared at me. "Hellbringer. I'm not talking about a tiny little thing anyone could misplace. It was right there."

He pointed, but the landscape appeared unchanged to me. "I don't know what to tell you. There's supposed to be an archway, and once a spirit goes through it, they leave this life."

"And I'm saying there was an arch, but now it's—"

A resounding *crack* echoed across the wastes. I turned to face Mira. "Finally. Let's—"

At the expression on her face, I froze. Mira was rarely afraid, but terror was written in her every feature. "You have to come back to the palace. The queen is looking for you, trying to get into your quarters."

"My *quarters*?" Fuck, the queen had never once come to my quarters before. There was always someone lowlier to do that for her, to summon me to the throne room. If she was searching for me there . . .

"When I left, she was screeching about finding someone to bust down the door." Mira shook her head. "She's in one of her moods."

I held in a groan. I knew exactly what the queen's moods meant: more assignments for me, each more difficult to accomplish than the last, and harsher punishments when I wasn't able to perform them exactly to her specifications.

I hauled Frode's body over my shoulder. There was no time to make a stop in Bhorglid to drop him off until I could return there to bury him; he would simply have to come to Kryllian. I grabbed Mira's outstretched arm. "Take me."

Frode's cry of "Hey, wait!" rang in my ears as we landed with a thud in my living quarters. Without a second thought, I dropped Frode's frozen body onto the bed. Thank the gods for insomnia. It would give me a chance to have the bedding washed before I made my next poor attempt at sleeping there.

Mira hadn't been lying. A fist hammered incessantly on the door, accompanied by a screeching voice I rarely heard without a semblance of composure. When I turned the knob, Mira was already gone.

I peered into the hallway. Besides the queen, her normally perfect hair disheveled, her eyes gleaming with madness, and her clothes soaked through with blood, the passage was empty.

"There you are." Her grin was manic. "Let me in."

I froze, grateful for the helmet obscuring my features. "In my quarters?"

She pushed past me into the space.

The queen was petite, smaller than Revna. It would have been impossible for her to overpower me, and yet . . . with every demand she made, Sonja's face flashed before my eyes. I knew the queen better than I knew my own sister at this point. And I knew my monarch would not hesitate to slide a blade along the throat of every person I loved until there were none left. The fear was her efficient way of keeping me docile and obedient.

So I allowed her inside. The same way I allowed her everything.

I waited for her to see Frode's body and pounce—after all, the bed was in her line of sight, pushed up against the wall. There was no canopy to hide him, only the hand-carved wooden frame adorned with my early attempts at whittling, an adequate mattress, and dark sheets.

But she made no comment about Frode. When she began to pace, hands moving wildly in front of her as she muttered to herself, I studied her more closely.

She was dressed in fighting attire instead of a gown; an infrequent but not uncommon occurrence. What truly concerned me was the blade sheathed at her hip, clearly designed for someone twice her height. The hilt was unique, made of gold and fashioned elegantly. And even beyond the unfamiliar weapon—

"Why are you covered in blood?"

She laughed, as if the question was ridiculous. But she stopped pacing, her icy-blue eyes connecting with my own as she fired back her own query. "Where were you when I knocked?"

I stiffened. Her calm, collected composure was back, as if she hadn't been nearly manic mere seconds ago. It was unnerving. "I was here. When you knock on the Hellbringer's door, the Hellbringer has to answer. Not Søren."

"Take off the mask," she demanded.

I swallowed my protests, swallowed my fear. Often, I'd wondered if sensing emotion was the queen's Lurae. No one knew what her true power was, but she was overly adept at noticing my tells: the slight tremor in my fingers, the pale red flush in my cheeks. I reached up and removed the mask, setting it gently on the side table next to the door. If I faced the bed, she wouldn't see the corpse when she looked at me. Her frenetic energy was unusual, but perhaps I could use it to my advantage—distract her from the dead body of my lover's brother resting there like a morbid doll.

The queen studied my face while I stared straight ahead, refusing to make eye contact. I'd learned long ago there was no point in trying to understand what she was looking for in my expression. But it was difficult to fight the terror so deeply ingrained from when she'd studied me in the past.

I may have been a monster, but the queen knew better than anyone how to make me feel like a frightened child again.

"Your sister is well," she said without preamble. "I received a report from my spies earlier this morning."

I kept my face carefully blank. The queen knew exactly how to get under my skin, exactly how to manipulate me. And the reminder of Sonja was the perfect way to do it.

Because I had no idea where Sonja was. Five years ago, Sonja had escaped the prison beneath the Kryllian palace and run away, leaving the queen—and me—behind. But the queen was no fool. She had Sonja followed by spies and kept an eye on her whereabouts from that day forward.

All it would take for her spies to kill my sister was a single slipup from me.

Maybe Sonja had found her freedom. But she'd tightened the queen's leash on me even more by fleeing. Despite my complicated feelings on the matter, my sister's life meant more to me than a life outside of the mask.

I stared straight ahead when I said, "I'm glad to hear it."

"Prepare for the Bhorglid delegation's arrival tomorrow," she ordered. "And supervise the returning troops as they arrive in the ports."

I bowed my head. "Of course, my queen."

Despite my confusion and my worry for Revna, a glimmer of hope swelled in me. The queen moved for the door behind me, reached for the knob. She hadn't seen the body. Perhaps one thing would go right today.

And then she turned for one last glance at my quarters and her greedy eyes lit with excitement.

Doorknob forgotten, she strode to the bed as dread set into my limbs. "And who might we have here?"

"I—" Any truthful answer I gave would be used against me; used against Revna. But she spoke again before I could fumble my way into a suitable lie.

"The brother." My heart sank. Not only had she discovered him, she recognized him. "The one you killed in her stead. You thought his death would appease me when I had ordered hers."

Silence encompassed the space around us, filling my lungs like smoke.

"We both know how that went," she murmured, tracing a finger down Frode's pale cheek. I was grateful his spirit was tied to the place he died and not to his body—no doubt he'd have excessive commentary about this interaction. "You've become sentimental, Søren. We'll have to work on that. You're lucky that this time, your sentimentality has proven useful. Go back to Bhorglid. Bury him with the rest of his family. Remain unseen."

My mind whirled. Had I been any less shocked by her orders, I would have needed to bite my lip to keep from snarking back at her. *Remain unseen while burying a body. How simple.*

She strode to the door, throwing it wide on her way out. I shut it quickly behind her. Perhaps the queen didn't care for the secrecy of my identity anymore, but I knew the risks of anyone seeing my face and identifying the man behind the Hellbringer mask.

I took my time dressing in plain clothes. For this job, I wanted to be myself. Revna—and Frode—deserved as much. Mira reappeared, and I knew from her expression that she wanted to discuss my interaction with the queen. But she didn't say anything as she transported me away, back to Bhorglid with Frode's body once more. *It's for the best,* I reminded myself as the world went dark for a moment. *Revna is better off without you.*

At least Frode would get the burial he deserved, I supposed.

Only as I shoveled in the darkness and blisters formed on my palms did I stop to wonder whose blood the queen had been covered in.

1

Revna

I LOOKED OUT AT THE CROWD OF EXHAUSTED SOLDIERS, TENSE Nilurae, and scowling citizens and clenched my jaw as my thoughts told me again what I already knew to be true: *every person here today hates you.*

My eyes caught Freja's where she stood, just in front of the temple steps. Her foot tapped a steady, anxious rhythm against the cobblestones and she tried to muster a smile. It was a poor attempt—the result was far more grimace than anything else. I swallowed down the lump in my throat and tried not to think about how much *more* she would hate me tomorrow, when the treaty with Kryllian was officially signed and I told her the full truth of everything I'd been hiding.

The thought was another chip out of my carefully constructed, utterly porcelain armor. I winced as the slipup of my thoughts avalanched into something far worse.

Music.

My mother's lullaby was never far from the surface, but today, I'd shoved it down as far as possible. Now, of all times, was not an option for breaking. It was too late, though. The thud of my own heartbeat in my ears was now echoed by dozens, hundreds more as thin threads, invisible to everyone but me, stretched from my chest outward to latch my Lurae to everyone present.

Start the speech, I told myself, shuffling the papers in front of me on the podium we'd had carted down in front of the temple dais. My face itched, but I didn't scratch. The scars left by Björn three weeks ago were nearly healed now. That didn't keep them from pulling the skin of my cheekbones and forehead taut, leaving me constantly aware of the way my features were now mangled. *Focus on the people. The Nilurae. You're here for them.*

I opened my mouth. Words emerged, the product of nothing more than hours upon hours of rehearsing until I knew the speech better than I knew the foreign magic that was somehow a part of me now. But even as I spoke, the song of my Lurae crooned in my ears, and I heard none of what I said.

As I continued to read, more rote than anything else, I scanned the crowd again until I saw Volkan. My ex-fiancé stood at the back, arms crossed over his chest, brow furrowed with concentration as he listened.

My thoughts hissed, unwanted. *How long until he looks disappointed in you again? Or worse—afraid?*

My hands gripped the edges of my notes hard enough to nearly crumple them. I kept speaking, allowing the memorized words to flow from me. Platitudes about peace and community despite our differences, congratulations to the soldiers for their valiant efforts in the war against Kryllian. The latter rang false, I was sure of it. Volkan had insisted on putting them in.

And still, the familiar melody in my mind had hold of me. My Lurae crept over my skin with every shuddering breath, desperate to grasp the threads gathered in front of me and pull until the bodies in the crowd were broken and lifeless and—

"As we readjust to life without a looming battle around every corner, only generosity and a willingness to see each other as equals will allow Bhorglid to become the blessed land it longs to be. Thank you."

The end of the speech was so rushed, I would be amazed if anyone could decipher it. But it was over. I stepped down, away from the podium, and into the shadow of the temple rubble. Behind me, I heard the murmurs of the crowd grow louder as everyone chatted and caught up with their friends and loved ones who'd returned from the front.

The song quieted a bit, but it was an ever-present grip along my spine now. There was no ridding myself of it. I allowed myself to rub my fingertips softly over my scars, easing the itch slightly, and looked up at the towering statue before me.

Aloisa. She was the only remaining statue from the pantheon of gods our country worshiped at the command of the priests. Ironically, her statue had refused to fall when Halvar and the other rebels took hammers to them all.

Before the Trials, Aloisa was the only deity I related to at all. I'd wondered whether she was lonely, the only woman in a room full of men. Even my freshly forged sword, only a couple of months old, was named after her.

Now, though, I found myself looking to the statue for any small semblance of comfort more often. Loneliness didn't even begin to cover the gaping hole living inside of my chest, caving in more and more every day. Once, it had been filled with purpose, with anger, with my mind-reading older brother and his endless jokes.

"She's not real," I whispered to myself as the crowd continued to disperse behind me. I knew some of the Nilurae had set up shopping stalls around the courtyard, hoping to capitalize on the returning soldiers' hunger for familiar fresh-baked goods. Plenty of people would linger. I straightened my shoulders and shoved a new piece of porcelain over the spider-webbing crack forming in my fragile armor.

"Everything okay?"

I turned as Volkan approached, his face carefully unreadable, and offered him a tight smile. "Good enough for now."

He hummed, hands in his pockets, and a bit of a wry note took residence in his voice. "I'm sorry to break it to you, but there's no prize for giving the speech as fast as possible. Even if you likely broke your own personal record."

A huff of laughter escaped me. "Maybe we can race next time. Start the speech simultaneously and see who finishes first."

Freja joined us on the dais, far less amused. Next to her was a woman around our age—early twenties. Her black hair was cut just above her chin, and her eyes radiated wariness. She rubbed one of her hands against the opposite wrist, and I noticed the grooves dug into the skin there. Only years of being handcuffed frequently chafed in such a way.

I knew exactly who this woman was. My shoulders tensed and the song in my head perked up with awareness, eager to latch on to another instance of conflict between Freja and me. But I took a deep breath and forced my voice to remain calm when I turned to her, lowering my voice as I said, "We talked about this."

Freja crossed her arms. "No. I talked and you argued. How else are we going to get to the Kryllian palace in the morning? If we were going to travel on foot, we needed to leave three days ago. A teleporter is our only option now."

I clenched my hands into fists, nails digging into my palms. I reminded myself that the square was still full of people—all of whom wanted to watch me fail, all of whom were waiting for me to slip up. I was no longer magic-less enough for the Nilurae, the people I'd fought for. And my Lurae abilities manifesting so late marked me as an impostor to the pompous upper class of Bhorglid. My taut leash on my magic was stretching thin, and the melody of my mother's lullaby twisted on a sharp note that made my ears ring.

Freja waited until now to ambush you with this, my thoughts whispered. *She knew you weren't going to agree otherwise, and this is her revenge for your decision to bring the army home despite her arguments against it.*

"And," Freja continued, lowering her voice and stepping closer to me, "we can't afford to waste our time on logistics tomorrow. Not when we know Queen Anja wants something from us, but we aren't sure what it is."

I stiffened. "I'm well aware." It was all we'd talked about over the last three weeks: her, Volkan, and me running over the possibilities again and again, trying to parse what we had to offer Kryllian to persuade them a treaty was worth it. None of us understood why the queen had put so much effort into securing my spot on the throne.

Volkan stepped up next to me and smiled at the woman, who had said nothing but was studying us all intensely. He extended his hand. "My name is Volkan. You're Astrid, right? Freja has told us a lot about you."

Indeed she had. Freja had spent more than six weeks in prison while I trained with the Hellbringer in the northern wastes and my family continued fighting the war against Kryllian. But her time in a cell hadn't been lonely. She'd been released with new friends—namely Valen, a Seeing One, and Astrid, a Lurae woman locked away for refusing to fight in the war.

I hadn't realized until a few days ago just how close Freja and Astrid had grown. When I'd mentioned we probably needed to find a teleporter loyal to our cause to ferry us to the upcoming treaty negotiations, Freja had volunteered Astrid immediately.

Astrid shook Volkan's hand quickly, but pulled back. I waited for her to speak, but instead, her hands moved as she signed her response. Blinking, I attempted to follow what she was saying, but it had been years since Halvar had taught us the basics of sign language to communicate without alerting the priests to our plans. Over time, we'd stopped using it as consistently, but Freja and I had been nearly fluent for a while.

I managed to catch a few words. *War. Lurae. Deaf. Loyal. Queen.*

Desperate, I waved my hands and she paused. "Slow down?" I signed. "Please?"

A half smile and a nod as Astrid acquiesced. "The war was wrong. I did not want to fight. If I was a soldier, my needs would never have been accommodated. My Lurae peers made my childhood miserable. Prison was a luxury, one I accepted happily."

There was nothing disingenuous about her movements or her body language—it all spoke of sincerity.

Still, I was wary. After the Trials, after the betrayal, I had to be.

My Lurae hummed at the thought of my brother's body frozen in the snowy wastelands, the melody of my mother's lullaby dancing tantalizingly just out of reach. I imagined myself pulling it back, strangling it, squeezing the life out of the magic.

I could not afford a mistake. Not here. Even now, I felt eyes on me from all sides. People watching, waiting for me to show weakness.

I studied Astrid for a long moment. Her gaze remained sharply on mine, never wavering for a second to ogle my scars.

My gut instincts? They told me she was trustworthy. But my instincts had done irreparable damage to me recently—the sting of the Hellbringer's betrayal still flooded my mind every time I allowed my thoughts to wander. And with everyone in the country calling for my head on a pike, trusting a Lurae was not an easy task.

Trusting *anyone* was not an easy task.

But Freja and Volkan were right, as much as I wanted to deny it. The meeting to sign the treaty between our warring nations was tomorrow, in the Kryllian palace. We needed a teleporter to get there on time. I didn't want to bring another person into my small circle of trust. But there was no other option.

I signed, stumbling over my words, "You must be loyal. Sharing secrets . . . not allowed."

A smile cracked across her face, brightening her features. She nodded enthusiastically.

"The war is over," I continued. "We plan to make the Lurae and Nilurae equals. We need a teleporter to join our cause."

"I will do it." Her jaw set with determination, and something like excitement grew behind her eyes. "Just tell me what—"

Her attention flickered past me, to the desecrated remains of the temple.

Astrid lunged for me, wrapped her arms around my middle, and threw me to the ground. I may have been suspicious of her, but I was fully unprepared for her to tackle me. The back of my head slammed against the ground, and black spots danced in front of my eyes. Astrid's entire body weight pressed me into the ground. Freja was screaming something unintelligible, and cries of shock echoed across the buildings, bouncing back and forth to twine with the song of my Lurae.

My magic woke with a vengeance, moving without my permission. It latched on to Astrid and tossed her off me. She landed heavily with a grunt and a groan but didn't move. I spared half a thought to feel guilty, but my head was spinning.

When I sat up, my dress was covered in blood. Wounded. I was wounded. *Shit.* I ran my palms down my front, searching for the open gash I couldn't feel. Was I in shock? There was no other explanation for why I couldn't—

Freja's voice solidified. "Volkan! Help her!"

My best friend knelt beside Astrid, whose hands clutched her abdomen on the right side. The hilt of a dagger peered out from them, and I realized suddenly that it had been meant for me. Astrid had seen the danger and attempted to push me out of the way.

I stood and the world swayed around me. *An assassination attempt.* I wanted to laugh, but my head throbbed so painfully I almost collapsed again. The perfect timing for a true test of Astrid's loyalty—one she'd passed with flying colors.

The song of my Lurae swelled, taking over until I could hear only the melody. It moved in tempo with my rushing heartbeat. I watched Volkan run over to Astrid, kneel beside her. The threads stretching from me *yearned* to move closer. *There, there, where the blood is pooling on the ground—*

I steadied myself. I couldn't look out at the crowd of once-friendly Nilurae and returned Lurae soldiers, not when I already knew the variety of expressions that would face me. Instead, I focused on Freja's tear-strewn face, Volkan's concentrated expression as he ran his hands over the wound. He grimaced when he grabbed the blood-slick hilt and wrenched the dagger from Astrid's flesh. She groaned, the sound making its way straight to me.

Someone had tried to kill me. To remove me from the throne permanently. And in the process, they'd hurt an innocent person instead.

The song in my veins rose in a crescendo.

Distantly, I heard my friends calling my name. They told me to slow down, to stop, to come back. But I had no interest in listening. Not when the assassin had fled into the rubble. They could not be allowed to walk free.

I moved with purpose, the gasps of the fearful crowd fading behind the lullaby. My dress caught against the jagged edge of a soot-stained wall and tore. Freja would scold me for that later, I knew.

I didn't care.

The threads of my magic that had stretched into every person around me earlier had solidified into one solid string connecting me and the would-be assassin. It stretched out, winding around corners and over piles of crumbled rock. The white stone of the temple faded as I followed it into the Nilurae side of town, where the buildings were closer together.

More shadows—easier to hide here. But as the hum of my mother's voice sounded in my ears I followed the anchor that led me true. I ground my teeth, my vision tunneling to only the path ahead. And I felt the end of the thread tethered to my chest hitch and begin to reel itself in.

I was no longer hunting a killer. I was dragging him back to face his penance.

My breath stuttered, but I didn't stop moving. *How am I doing that?*

The song escalated, tempo rushing now. The magic was ravenous, clamoring for control. Working without my permission. It had clawed its way to the front of my mind and seized its chance to end this in blood.

I should have minded. But I didn't—not when I arrived in front of the Sharpened Axe and the man at the other end of the thread stumbled to his knees in front of me. He'd used red paint to draw a familiar symbol on his forehead: an eye, dripping blood in three dots down the bridge of his nose.

He panted, hands and knees scraped raw. I hadn't seen what happened, but I'd felt it. When my mind succumbed to the Lurae, only my cold, calculating self was left. She knew the exact paths an escapee would have taken through these familiar streets. Her magic had grabbed hold of his body, his will, and pulled him stumbling back the way he came. Had dragged him on his hands and knees to me here.

I crouched down beside him. He snarled.

"Who are you?" I asked. "Lurae or Nilurae?"

The daggers in my sheaths trembled. One pulled itself free and thudded to the ground, then spun in place and launched itself at my throat.

I leaned to the side. In one swift movement I pivoted, using my body weight to swing myself around and follow the path of the blade as it scraped over the edge of my neck. My hand shot out and latched around the hilt.

I tucked it back into its sheath and secured it there. “Lurae, then.”

“You don’t deserve the throne,” he snarled through gritted teeth.

My Lurae tensed along with my shoulders. It wasn’t an uncommon sentiment, but this was the first time anyone had taken it so far. “My father didn’t deserve this throne either.”

Footsteps sounded behind me, frantic on the cobblestones. Volkan’s voice called out, “Wait, Revna! We need to question him.”

And my shoulders notched higher, my Lurae wrenching control from me for a brief moment. The thread between myself and the would-be assassin fluttered, and a full-body shudder traveled through him.

The dark whisper of my thoughts pulsed in time with the high notes of my mother’s lullaby. *Volkan doesn’t trust you.*

I shook my head, trying to dislodge the thought.

They know what’s happening to you, how out of control you’ve become.

I inhaled sharply.

And the attacker hissed, “You and all Nilurae scum deserve to die. You’re not even worth breeding.”

He spat in my face.

By the time I blinked, my hand was wrapped around his throat. Fury fell like an avalanche, burning through me with icy fingers. The song increased to a frantic tempo as my hand shook, as the gasping man clawed at my skin until he drew blood. It occurred to me that I could crush his windpipe with nothing more than my own strength. He had no real training—had relied on his Lurae long enough that when it was rendered useless, he was, too.

Dimly, I heard shouting behind me. Heard him choking for air.

Through his gasps he managed to eke out his final words: "Long . . . live . . . Callum . . ."

My song knew what I craved, what I so desperately desired. And so it flowed through my fingers until every pound of his heart resonated in time with the music. Until the threads that bound his life to his body were directly in front of me, poised and ready for the quickest mental *tug*.

The symphony ended with a loud *crack* as his neck twisted until it snapped. The only applause for the performance was the hollow thud of his lifeless body hitting the ground.

When a hand came down on my shoulder, I whirled. The world around me was colored red at the edges, my teeth bared in a snarl. But when I recognized Freja had been the one to reach out, I backed away.

The world began to return to itself. Freja's face was pale. Neither of us wore a cloak, and her teeth chattered in the cold. "Revna," she said slowly. "Are you all right?"

With every heartbeat, my magic receded and my awareness came back. Every muscle in my body shook. The scratches on my right hand from the assassin's struggle stung, and nausea rose in my stomach. Volkan stood behind Freja, running a hand through his hair as he watched the scene. Astrid huddled against the tavern wall, her arms wrapped around her midsection. She was deathly pale.

And through the windows of the Sharpened Axe, more horrified eyes stared at me. Silence and stillness had swept through the building, rendering everyone a perfect witness to my crime.

I wondered if the building itself wished it could shrink away from me. If it remembered the last time I'd spilled blood on its floors, the last time I'd left someone for dead within its line of sight.

"He deserved it." The words I spoke felt far away, a desperate attempt to cover my lack of control. I turned to Freja again. "Did you hear what he said? About me? About *you*?"

Freja took a tentative step closer. "I know. I know."

"He did deserve it," Volkan said quietly, stepping close enough that no one watching from a distance could hear. "But Revna . . ."

I couldn't look at him as he sighed, his disappointment a nearly tangible thing. He continued. "Now we can't question him. We have no idea if he was working alone or with a group. Whether an attack like this will happen again."

Astrid caught my attention and signed, "I've never seen magic so powerful."

I swallowed down the scream threatening to burst from me. Turning away, I brought my eyes to the crumpled body lying in the snow in front of me. Blood dripped from his mouth and nose. *Long live Callum,* he'd said. Surely he meant the man who had created Bhorglid and the Holy Order of Priests hundreds of years ago—the leader who had declared Nilurae were less than their Lurae counterparts. A strange sentiment, considering Callum had been dead for nearly four hundred years now.

But I'd never know what the assassin meant, because I had killed him.

Panic clawed at my throat, the truth sinking in. How had this happened? How had my awareness, my ability to reason, slipped so forcefully that I was unable to keep from killing him? How had my magic twisted my emotions and my thoughts until there was no path left but violence?

He didn't deserve to live after he said such horrifying things, part of me cried. *Before you won the Trials, every Nilurae in the city would have celebrated to know you'd killed such a horrible excuse for a person.*

But I was queen now. The familiar dread that lodged in my chest like a permanent stone returned in full force, its weight suffocating.

And the sight of the body, broken and lifeless, brought back the memory of another body much the same. With every blink, the scene in front of me changed. The dead man wasn't an attempted assassin but my mentor, the closest thing I'd had to a real father. I wasn't wearing this dress, but one ragged along the bottom from where Volkan had used a knife to saw off the blood-soaked fabric, to hide my crimes during my coronation.

"Revna. Breathe." Freja's hand was around my bicep, and I resisted the urge to scream, to pull away from her, to prove I was ripping at the seams, because she still didn't *know*—

A familiar figure stepped out of the Sharpened Axe, lumbering over to join our small party. When he scratched his beard, eyeing the body with a hint of disgust, I had to swallow the vomit burning up the back of my throat. Of course he would arrive now, when I was thinking of his death at my hands.

Halvar raised an eyebrow at me. "Looks like you've got a bit of a mess here."

2

Revna

AS WAS THE CASE EVERY TIME I SAW HALVAR DURING THE PAST three weeks, I repeated the truth over and over in my head. I could not afford to forget, to let my guard slip. Not now, when everything was held together so fragilely, determined to break if I so much as considered it.

Halvar is dead. I am the one who killed him.

The words became a chorus, accompanying the contented hum of my magic, sated now with blood.

I continued the refrain unceasingly as our small party made the trek back to the castle, leaving the Sharpened Axe—and the scene of my crime—behind. The conversation was heavy, as usual. Once we'd left the city behind and begun walking up the mountain path, Halvar—the impostor, the fake, the fraud—spoke. "I don't know that the Nilurae will be content for much longer. They aren't feeling the results of any of the changes that have been made so far." His eyes turned to me, an apology written in them. "They are frustrated about the army returning despite there being no official treaty signed yet.

Most Nilurae would have preferred to leave them up there to freeze for as long as possible before allowing them back home."

Volkan adjusted his hold on Astrid, who had an arm looped over the prince's shoulders. Freja, who was interpreting the conversation for Astrid, piped up, signing while she spoke aloud. "Have you told them about the plans for the festival?"

Before the war began, Bhorglid had celebrated the arrival of spring with a festival each year. There were food and games and dancing late into the night. Of course, the Nilurae had never been allowed to participate except to sell goods and provide services. When Freja had realized the usual time of the festival would arrive a few weeks after we traveled to Kryllian to sign the treaty, she suggested we hold the celebration again. This time, everyone would be part of the enjoyment.

I'd agreed, though my memory of doing so was fuzzy. It was only a few days after the Trials. My scars had still been scabs, were still radiating pain and itching like mad so soon after the infliction of the wounds. And I'd finally noticed that the song of my powers echoed in my ears almost constantly.

The festival quickly became Freja's pet project. She spent all her free time working on it. And why not? It would increase morale, at the very least.

Halvar rubbed a hand along the back of his neck and grimaced as he walked. "You know I have. But the festival is three weeks away. We need something to tide them over now."

"Invite a key Nilurae with influence in the community to attend the signing in Kryllian with us tomorrow," Volkan suggested. "Another witness that we're doing what's best for *all* the people. They won't have any duties, they'll simply be there to observe. They can bring back a report of the event that the Nilurae trust. Hopefully that will ease the tensions enough until the festival."

"Sure. I'll come up with a few names," Halvar said.

Who? I wondered. *Because you don't know the Nilurae the way Halvar truly did. Will the person you choose raise suspicion in Freja? In the other Nilurae whose good graces I so desperately need?*

I rubbed my temple, a poor attempt to relieve the headache blooming there. The thought of bringing a stranger with us to Kryllian, an unfamiliar place where we'd be negotiating with a foreign ruler, grated. But no one here was looking to me for an opinion—rightfully so, after the spectacle we'd left behind us.

I swallowed the lump in my throat. "I know it doesn't seem like we're doing much, but giving the Nilurae equality is my highest priority. It's like balancing on the edge of a blade—the moment I step too far in one direction, I risk a coup from the other party involved."

Halvar shrugged, and his voice sent a shudder through me. "There are two fundamentally opposed groups of people here. The solution to this will not come overnight."

"But it would come far quicker if you were willing to find a tutor," Volkan said. I locked eyes with the prince, whose face held no humor or sympathy. Only exhaustion and frustration were left there. "You must learn how to use your Lurae before it grows more volatile."

Shame flooded my cheeks, the heat a telltale sign of the red on my face. The feral, uncontrollable gift lurking just beneath the surface skittered, and I tensed, trying to keep from jolting.

I still wasn't used to the many sensations of magic living inside me. At first, it had been merely the hum of song in my ears, a tune no others could hear. Hypnotic, it called to me, finally snapping into place after I won the Trials. The music carried the thump of heartbeats to my fingers, stretching invisible threads from me to the lifeblood of everyone nearby.

It gave me the courage to kill my father, and then my mother after him. When the Hellbringer had dared to watch me sleep as I recovered, it granted the opportunity to prove myself his equal. And for a moment, I felt like everything I wanted was finally possible.

But only for a moment.

"Give her time." Freja's voice snapped me back to the scene before me, but staring at Halvar, whose eyes remained firmly on the path in front of him, made my pulse rise to my throat, my breaths shortening as if a vise were clamped there. "Most Lurae have had their entire lives to master their magic by the time they're Revna's age. She's had three weeks. You're not being fair, Volkan."

The prince's hands curled. "Not being *fair*? Do you think the unrest will dissolve itself? That the Lurae and Nilurae will spontaneously decide to get along? We do not have the *luxury* of time, Freja. And if she does not get her Lurae under control"—Volkan's voice shook with barely suppressed anger—"then fairness will be the least of our problems."

We stepped into the courtyard. Volkan beckoned Freja, handing Astrid over to her. Then, without another word, he stormed into the castle. The door slammed against its hinges.

This is my fault. The realization struck me, not for the first time. *I am destroying us all.*

Freja laid her free hand on my shoulder. "Let's focus on getting the treaty signed. Once that's done, we can take care of the rest."

I nodded, unable to respond. She supported Astrid, helping the teleporter ease her way into the castle. She had nowhere else to stay, so Freja had offered to clear the empty bedroom next to the one she occupied for the teleporter.

And then only myself and a ghost remained.

When I closed the door to my father's office behind me, my head throbbed. The only benefit of losing my control with the assassin was that now the song was quiet. Resting in the back of my mind, preparing to return with more vengeance than before.

My shoulders slumped.

But even the weight of the day's events wasn't heavy enough to numb the arrow to the heart of Halvar's voice behind me. "I can't do this anymore, Rev."

I turned to face Jac as the transformation melted away, leaving my only surviving brother hunched over the desk, Halvar's too-big clothing hanging from his lanky frame.

"Just a few more days," I begged, my voice low. Even now, the thought of telling Freja the truth made me nauseous. How did I confess to my best friend that I'd killed the closest thing we both had to a father?

I couldn't. So when Jac had returned to Bhorglid less than twenty-four hours after my coronation, I'd asked him to help me with the impossible.

My older brother had taken pity on me. I knew he regretted it now.

"A few more days might not be possible," Jac replied, arms crossed. He kept scratching at his chin, like the ghost of the beard was impossible to ignore. "My Lurae has limits. The Nilurae have endless concerns about your rule, and they bring them to me at every hour of the day. I can't even afford to drop my shifting while I sleep."

"So come to Kryllian with us. You can sleep in my room and I'll make sure you aren't disturbed. Claim you aren't feeling good and you'll even be able to rest during the day." I pushed down the uncertainty threatening to drown me, the surety of my mistakes. Was there a single negative emotion I hadn't felt in its fullest since the Trials? I was beginning to doubt it. "Things *must* begin to settle before I tell anyone the truth. Halvar is—*you* are essential to this transition of power. We can't do it without you."

Jac's expression was exhaustion and blatant pity. I wanted to punch him, force him to stop looking at me like that. "Revna. You don't know whether you can do it without Halvar because you haven't tried. It might be possible, but if this charade continues, then we will never know."

I swallowed the harsh words threatening to escape me. I *did* know. Jac was foolish if he believed admitting the loss of the Nilurae's most outspoken leader was a good idea. He assumed I was asking this of him only to assuage my own guilt, to hide my wrongdoings from my friend.

No. I was the only one who could see both sides of this conflict. The only one who knew how influential Halvar was to ensuring the Nilurae supported my rule.

He continued. "I have to stay in the city. Everyone knows how close you and Halvar are. If he's the Nilurae sent to observe the treaty proceedings, then they won't believe anything I bring back."

"Who will you send then?" I asked, dreading any answer. "It will be ten times harder to put on a mask of indifference in front of a stranger if the negotiations begin to go wrong. And if there's a fight of any kind, that leaves an innocent Nilurae vulnerable. What if we can't protect them?"

"I'll figure something out," Jac said, rubbing the bridge of his nose between two fingers. The nails were short, to the quick, and ragged. He chewed his nails only when he was incredibly stressed, and a spear of guilt lodged in my chest.

With a shake of my head and a sigh, I steeled my expression, my emotions, and my thoughts. "We will return from Kryllian with a signed treaty by the end of the week. Can you hold out until then?"

His mouth twisted. I didn't need Frode's Lurae to see what he was thinking. He wanted to say no.

There was only one solution.

I allowed my shoulders to slump, the true weight of the day's events—and the overexertion of my magic—easy to slip into. "I'm sorry, Jac. Everything has been so overwhelming since the Trials . . . I was nearly assassinated today. I don't know what I would do if . . ."

My voice trailed off, and I let out a shuddering sigh. It was a performance in some ways, but the words rang true. It was part of what made it so effective.

The other part was knowing how Jac felt about what had happened at the Trials. I was the one who had pushed him to desert, told him to disguise himself and run away to Faste. But he carried all the guilt of leaving me behind after we'd agreed to be allies in the arena. I'd overheard him and Volkan exchanging a whispered conversation about it shortly after Jac's return—the prince was the only one who knew what I had done to Halvar, and what my brother was doing to hide the damage.

Using my knowledge against him in this way probably made me a monster. But I already was one anyway.

Jac groaned, and I risked a glance at him. My brother had put his face in his hands and was muttering something under his breath. I made out "fucking *fuck*" before he straightened with a deep breath and stepped up to grip both of my biceps.

"Sign the treaty, and then this is over. Promise me."

I nodded. "Of course. The moment the ink dries and Astrid teleports us back, we'll end this."

He released me and stepped back, rubbing at his eyes. I watched as the shift took over him slowly. His arms became broader, his hair lengthened and curled slightly at the ends, and the dark circles beneath his eyes were now accompanied by crow's-feet. Jac shook out some of the tiredness from his limbs and forced a smile.

"I'll head back to the tavern then. There will be someone to join your party waiting for you in the courtyard tomorrow morning."

He left, closing the office door behind him, and I sank into my father's chair, the heaviness of the day's events serving as a reminder of just how much bloodshed had been required to take the crown in the first place.

3

Revna

IN THE DARK OF NIGHT, I PAID MY PENANCE.

Sleep was hard-earned since the Trials. Most nights I lay awake, staring into the darkness and wishing the song would silence for long enough to allow me some rest. When I did succumb to unconsciousness, vivid dreams haunted me. Tonight was no different.

My feet were wrapped in layer upon layer of fabric, but it still wasn't enough to keep out all the chill of the ice beneath my soles. A set of fishing poles rested on my shoulder and heavy mittens covered my hands. The sun was just beginning to peer over the mountains.

The body I occupied didn't frown, but mentally I did. We were in the wastes, but that mountain range looked familiar. Where had I seen it before?

I tried to turn my head, but it didn't move. Instead, I shifted the bag of supplies that rested on my other shoulder. "We should be out far enough now," a voice said from next to me. "Let's get set up."

I turned to see a boy, probably sixteen, setting down his own handfuls of supplies atop the ice. He was bundled as heavily as I was, covered from head to toe in furs wrapped with leather straps. His blond hair fell over his face, strands whipping back and forth in the wind. He scrunched his nose, pink from the cold.

I looked down at the ice. I knew I should be studying it, like the person I dreamt was. But my attention caught on the fuzzy reflection there. Long red hair tumbled down from the hood I wore, secured with strips of leather at the base of my skull and then at four-inch intervals all the way down. My lips were thinner than usual, but the focused expression on my face was eerily similar to the one I saw in the mirror every day.

Who am I?

A loud *crack* sounded in the distance, and I gasped as I turned in that direction. "A crack in the ice? It's the dead of winter. How is that possible?" My voice was high-pitched, and I wished again that I could frown.

The boy waved a gloved hand. "Not a crack. That's normal. The ice shifts sometimes since there's water beneath it. We're fine."

But I shot a nervous glance toward the shore. It was indistinguishable from the lake, considering everything was covered in a thick layer of snow, but a figure sitting on the edge waved from afar. In my dreaming state, I couldn't navigate through my mind enough to put a name to the face of the girl watching us from a distance, but I knew her safety mattered more than anything.

I waved back, my breath steadying again. If the boy said we were fine, then we were fine. He came fishing out here every day in the winter. I'd trusted him with my life plenty of times before, and he'd always kept me safe.

Time passed in a blur as we set up two little stools and a few buckets, then baited our hooks. I watched as my friend grabbed a small chisel and a saw from the bags of supplies and started to chip away at the ice.

Another rumbling *crack* resounded in the distance. Louder than the last. My shoulders tensed. I could swim—my mother had insisted

I learn from a young age, even taking my younger sister and me south during the summers to find bodies of water to practice in. But no one else in the village could.

Including the boy next to me.

He hadn't even looked up. He continued chiseling away, then shoved the thin saw into the ice's opening, putting his whole weight on the handle to force the blade beneath.

He didn't see when the movement turned the ice to spiderwebs below him.

I gasped, the frigid air scraping my lungs. In the space of a heartbeat, the rumbling returned, this time with a creaking groan so unearthly I wondered briefly whether a monster lived below the surface of the lake. By the time I opened my mouth, the cracks had spread, their long fingers stretching around him. Water shoved its way through the gaps, greedy in its arrival.

"Callum!" Instinctually, I scrambled backward. The boy's wide eyes imprinted in my memory as I watched him push to his feet.

But the redistribution of his weight was too much for the steadily crumbling ice.

The water pulled him under in the blink of an eye. I screamed.

A gust of wind slammed the shutters over my window, startling me into consciousness like a cold bucket of water poured over my head. My heart thudded as if I'd been running. I sucked air into my lungs, rubbing my chest. A phantom ache from breathing the cold air of the wastes nested there.

Unnerved, I pulled my braid over my shoulder, examining it in the moonlight. Still dark as ever. I shook my head and sighed, collapsing back into bed.

It wasn't the first time I'd had an unsettling dream, and I doubted it would be the last. Each one was the same: I left my body behind to become the red-haired girl I didn't recognize. The dreams were vivid and memorable each time.

The one consistency between myself and the woman I transformed into in my dreams was the heavy weight of terror we both felt as we watched our lives crumble beneath our feet. I'd recognized the true reason for the dreams easily enough. My mind had turned to stories to cope with the endless loss I felt during my waking hours.

This time, though, the dream felt more ominous than before. The boy who fell beneath the ice . . . I'd called out for him. *Callum.* The same name my near-assassin had invoked when I caught him.

Coincidence, I told myself. *I thought about it too much this morning, and it showed up in my subconsciousness. Nothing more.*

Moonlight streamed through the window, the curtains left open out of a compulsion I couldn't identify. The first night after the Trials had been the one when I woke to find the Hellbringer sitting at my bedside, unapologetic in the face of his betrayal. Perhaps I feared the same thing would greet me when I woke and knew the moonlight would allow me to see him.

Or perhaps I feared the other monsters that flourished in the darkness these days.

Lying in bed, wide awake, my thoughts descended like vultures to prey on my mind.

Volkan is angry with you, they whispered. *He has shielded you at every turn, and in exchange, you allow your magic to run wild. To ruin everything he's trying to help you build.*

The lump in my throat was never far these days, and it rose again as I desperately tried to keep my breathing steady. Panicking was the fastest way to bring my unruly magic to the surface—even now it hummed my mother's lullaby in my ears, a song that no longer brought anything but anxiety. Soul-crushing, bone-aching loneliness covered me like a shroud at all times.

My thoughts paid little heed to my desperate need for peace, though.

Tomorrow, the treaty will be signed. Freja will discover the truth.

And then she will leave you—just like the Hellbringer, just like Frode, just like Volkan wishes he could. And it will be all your fault.

I pressed the heels of my palms into my closed eyes, colors blossoming in the dark. The amorphous blobs whirled without a care, twisting until they shaped Björn's face taut with pain and surprise as he realized my dagger was buried in his chest. Then they morphed into my father's limp and broken body sprawled in the sand. My mother's still pulse. The assassin's broken neck.

I sat up, my breathing heavy. There would be no more sleeping tonight. When my thoughts grew restless and insistent in this way, there was only one solution that could distract me.

My fighting clothes were draped across the chair in the corner. I pulled them on, wondering when my mind would allow me peace again. When everything was sorted, when the truth had been revealed to Freja, when Volkan had finally given up on me and returned to Faste, when the Lurae and Nilurae were no longer at each other's throats?

Admit it, my mind taunted as I strapped on my belt and sheathed my sword at my hip. *You have everything you dreamt of and it isn't enough.*

The worst part, I decided as my footsteps echoed in the empty halls, was that I knew exactly what would bring me peace again. Or rather, who.

Søren's face—*no, the Hellbringer's face,* I chided myself—swam in my vision. Pushing open the castle doors and stepping into the freezing night did nothing to dim the heady mixture of longing and grief and fury that ripped through me at the thought of his dark hair, his gray eyes, his soft lips.

Despite the coming spring, frost covered the grass in the courtyard. It crunched beneath my boots, the faint sound grounding me.

No matter how I felt about him, I would see the Hellbringer tomorrow. I had no doubt.

When the Queen of Kryllian and I began correspondence after my coronation, she'd extended an invitation to host our party in her palace while we negotiated the terms of the treaty. There was only so much that could be accomplished via letters, after all. And it wasn't like Bhorglid was in any fit shape to host a foreign delegation.

Knowing we were laying the terms of peace didn't make me feel any better. This was nothing more than another power struggle, albeit one fought with words and subtle moves instead of blades. And who would show up to a battle without their most powerful general at their side?

The queen had seen to it that I was able to win the competition against my brothers for the throne. She'd been the one who ordered the Hellbringer to train me in combat. But even now, with the kingdom under my power, I still couldn't figure out *why*. How did it benefit her to see me on the throne? What was the purpose of it all?

And that question didn't touch on the even more difficult one: How had the Queen of Kryllian known I had a Lurae, even when it hadn't manifested yet?

The uncertainty of it all made my head throb.

I couldn't keep my gaze from the graves as I walked by them. Five headstones, four plots of freshly turned dirt. My parents and two of my brothers, Erik and Björn, were buried here. Frode's body was somewhere in the wastes, left for the scavengers and the snow. The thought made my heart ache.

Ahead, nestled in a cleared spot beside the armory, was the small section of the courtyard I'd had outfitted with training dummies and targets, so anyone could train throughout the day. Mostly me. Despite reminding me of the Hellbringer, the heft of my weapon in my hands soothed my most frantic thoughts and kept my magic at bay. The glide of one form to the next took the shrill tones of my mother's lullaby and eased them to a manageable octave.

Even now, as I pulled the weapon from its sheath, the song of metal sliding against its counterparts echoing in the silent darkness, the tension in my shoulders eased slightly. This was familiar. I was good at this. My sword, the one I'd forged into being with my own hands, would not fail me the way others had.

I adjusted my stance, breathed deeply, and began.

As my muscles warmed, his voice echoed like he was standing next to me.

No, move your foot back. Just like that. These stances aren't about fighting or winning—they're about muscle memory. Your body needs to know these positions so deeply that it's physically impossible for you to forget them. Then, when the moment really counts, you will find yourself with the upper hand.

I moved to the second position. My mind cleared steadily. The voice in my head held no distortion; it belonged to Søren, not the Hellbringer. Tears pricked my eyes at the thought of him. Three weeks of not seeing his face, not being able to pull him to me when I needed grounding. He would stand behind me while I tried to stitch a country back together. He would understand all the difficult choices I was making. He wouldn't hate me for being a monster.

Never fight angry.

As I swung into the next position, the memory of his words made me huff with annoyance. How many times had he said that to me? The first time had been when I threw my freshly forged weapon to the ground in a fit of rage after he'd corrected me one time too many. The words had felt so poignant. When I stared at the mask, I felt like he saw past the rebellious Nilurae everyone else thought I was and looked straight to my core. Right where the raw hurt sat.

Because that's what my anger had been, back then. Hurt.

What is it now? The voice in my head was no longer a memory, but my imagination. And I knew him well enough to know it's what he would ask if we were having the conversation.

I slid into the next position, my muscles aching from the strain.

I'd come out here and run these same drills every night for the last three weeks. I didn't know how to answer the Søren in my head. And I wasn't sure if I wanted to.

So instead, I thought about what it would be like to see him in the morning.

Reminded myself that the mask hid a murderer, the man who killed my brother. The man I'd loved was gone now.

He wasn't coming back. He might never have been real to begin with—an illusion, a second mask the Hellbringer wore when he wasn't fighting. A façade.

I trained until the pitch-black sky turned indigo, then sheathed Aloisa once more. I would need to bathe before we left, which would add time to my preparations. But before I stepped around the armory to head to the castle doors, a sound stopped me.

A faint scratching carried through the courtyard.

I frowned. We kept no guards, not when any Nilurae would be annihilated by a Lurae attacker who intended true ill will. I couldn't ask them to put themselves in harm's way. And trusting the returned soldiers to keep me safe was a laughable choice. No one should have been puttering around the castle at this time of night.

I wrapped my hand around Aloisa's hilt. My Lurae song trilled, alert. A thread stretched around the corner, ending somewhere beyond my sight.

I don't know what possessed me to observe stealthily before charging in, weapon drawn. Perhaps my exhaustion had worn down my brashness for the day. But when I poked my head around the side of the building, my heart plummeted and left me frozen.

Someone was digging at Frode's grave.

I don't know how long I stood there, still as stone, utterly shocked, before watching the person stumble slightly with their next strike of the shovel and nearly twist their ankle trying not to fall into the pit they'd dug. "Shit." The hissed expletive carried across the near-silent courtyard.

I knew that voice.

"Fucking ground is half frozen," Søren muttered, wiping sweat from his brow. He was dressed plainly, no mask in sight. I couldn't even tell whether he carried a weapon. "Pretty sure six feet is typical, but the best you're getting is three. We can argue about it later."

Who the hell was he talking to?

My hand remained tight on Aloisa's hilt. But I didn't move.

He set the shovel down, his form still swathed in shadow. Stepping past the mound of dirt next to the hole, he leaned down and picked up . . .

I swallowed, throat tight. He carried a body wrapped in white cloth. *That doesn't make any sense,* I told myself. *It can't be Frode.*

But logic had no place here. My chest ached as the thought hit me: my brother's body was returned home. Offered a proper burial. The peaceful resting place it deserved, far from the front lines of the war he'd hated.

It wasn't enough.

As Søren gently laid the body in the grave, the song in my mind soared to new volumes. My hands shook. Breaths came in ragged gasps.

Don't. I forced it back, willed the thread to disappear as it grew brighter, more visible. *If he knows you're here, you'll have to talk to him. You'll have to look him in the eye and hate him at the same time.*

I pressed my back against the wall, the cold shocking me to my senses as I sank down, pulling my knees up to my chest. The emotions cycled viciously. Grief to loneliness to sorrow to anger to ice-cold fury. How dare he bury the brother he'd killed only a few weeks ago? Was this some kind of trick—an attempt to sway the negotiations in Kryllian's favor tomorrow? Did he think I could possibly forgive Frode's murder with the simple act of laying him to rest?

I'd planned to bury him myself, once everything calmed. Once I'd had the chance to return to the wastes and seek out his body. And now I wouldn't get the opportunity.

The song turned shrill. I covered my ears with my palms, attempting to block it out. The threads seemed to pull at my limbs, whispering that I should stand and confront him. Hurt him.

Part of me wanted to. The other part of me wanted to collapse in his arms and cry. And I wasn't sure which part would emerge if we stood face-to-face.

So I sat and forced myself to breathe and think of anything but *him*. When the thread finally slackened its hold and I peered around the corner, the shadowed figure was gone. All that remained was a freshly dug grave covered in smooth dirt.

◆ ◆ ◆ ◆ ◆

"HOW DO I LOOK?"

I turned back to see Freja and Astrid emerging from the castle doors. Freja's lilac dress was sleeveless, the fabric starting just below her collarbones to leave her shoulders and neck bare. It clung to her figure, accentuating her curves and wrapping around to tie at her waist. A matching shawl covered her arms. Freja clutched it tightly, hunching in on herself. Snow fell from the sky in lazy spirals. The wind was frigid. We were all dressed for Kryllian weather.

I offered her the brightest grin I could muster. "Beautiful."

Astrid stood next to her. She was not dressed as formally as Freja and I—where we wore dresses, Astrid had chosen functional garb with light armor overtop. She'd followed me around like a bodyguard since saving me from the assassin yesterday, ignoring Volkan's pleas for her to rest while she finished healing. Her chin-length hair was braided back on one side and pinned behind her ear, showcasing the sharp line of her jaw. A thin line of dark makeup stretched her narrowed eyes into a cat-eye shape.

I noted the expression on the teleporter's face as she studied Freja. There was something awed there, the kind of emotion friends were unable to muster for each other. I had wondered yesterday, when the two spent more time at dinner absorbed in their own conversation than in anything the rest of us signed, whether there might be more behind Astrid and Freja's shared camaraderie from being imprisoned together. Now it seemed obvious.

"What do you think?" I signed, catching Astrid's attention. My gestures were still slow and clumsy, but even one day of practice had brought back much of the sign language I had forgotten. "How does Freja look?"

Astrid's face flushed.

"Beautiful." There was no hesitation in her response. "Freja is always beautiful."

I stifled a grin. Oh, how oblivious I'd been.

But Freja's widening eyes and long blink told me perhaps I was not the only one.

Volkan emerged from the castle then, dressed in neutral colors. While Freja and I had chosen to honor our hosts by wearing Kryllian purple and gold, Volkan had opted to show no true allegiance with his clothing alone. "Can you imagine if my parents thought I was trying to initiate an alliance with Kryllian?" he'd scoffed when we discussed our attire a few days ago. "I've been 'forbidden from making any political moves' since our disaster of an engagement."

Now he smiled, though I could sense his anxiety beneath the expression. He looked me over. "That dress is stunning on you."

I grimaced. I didn't feel beautiful. I'd spent far too long staring at myself in the mirror this morning, wondering if I'd made a mistake when I asked Volkan not to heal my face and prevent it from scarring. "You're sure it isn't too revealing?"

Even as I asked, goose bumps skittered over my bare arms and up my legs. The violet fabric fell in a loose skirt down to my ankles with a long slit up each side that ended over my hips. The bodice consisted of a single piece of the cloth that started on one side of the waistband, crossed up and over my chest on the opposite side, and then wound over my neck to go down the other way and secure itself on the waistband once more. Another band of material was stitched to the fabric on either side of my breasts, winding across my back to prevent any unfortunate, revealing slips.

It was gorgeous. It was meant to stun, to draw attention to me. I tried not to shudder at the thought of every eye from the Kryllian palace slinking over my form.

"Not too revealing," Volkan said, raising an eyebrow. "But you need to believe it, too. Otherwise, instead of confidence, you'll project insecurity."

I sighed. "I know."

"Where is Halvar?" Astrid asked.

I shook my head, the weight of my secrets bearing down on me once more as I remembered my conversation with Jac yesterday. "He said he isn't coming. He was supposed to send someone else but didn't say who. I assumed they would be here by now."

"I am here," a voice called from behind me.

My entire body stiffened, a chill that had nothing to do with the weather cascading down my spine. I turned slowly, hoping desperately to be wrong.

Arne stepped up to our group and surveyed me from head to toe with a disgusted expression on his face. I reached for my blade instinctively, but it wasn't there. Volkan had insisted we pack all weapons in our baggage, lest we look like we were leveling an unspoken threat against the Kryllians.

"Arne," Freja said, an air of anxious cheerfulness in her voice. She stepped up to him, pulling him into an embrace. When he stared at me over her shoulder, I rolled my eyes. "It's good to see you again. Are you *certain* you want to come with us, though?"

He pulled from her embrace. "The Nilurae want someone trustworthy on this trip. Someone whose interests match their own, and not your *Lurae* queen's."

I wished Jac was here so I could chew him out for this. Why, of all the Nilurae in the city, had he chosen my terrible ex-lover? Arne had made it incredibly clear when I saw him again at the war front that he thought I owed him love. He was bitter and jaded because I made choices that didn't center around him.

Astrid stepped up beside me. She had been allowed to keep two small knives on her person, since she was technically my bodyguard. She narrowed her eyes at Arne, pulling one of the blades from its sheath.

The Lurae song thrumming in my ears picked up its tempo. I waited for the anger simmering beneath the surface of my skin to ignite and flare out, catching everyone here in its blaze.

But when the fury reached its breaking point, building up to an explosion, it faltered. Instead, the exhaustion of the last three weeks came rushing in like an avalanche. *I just want my friends to be safe,* I thought. It took all my effort not to let my shoulders slump. *I want them to be safe and happy and then I want to sleep. But rest is too much to ask for, it seems.*

And I couldn't ignore the other half of my thoughts either: the ones reminding me that Jac was the best strategist among my brothers during the war. Arne had been vocal about his mistrust of the crown—of me—ever since our argument on the front lines.

If a mistrusting man, a soldier even, witnessed the treaty signing for himself and returned with the truth, then the people would believe him. Far easier than they would believe me.

"Did you bring clothing suitable for a ball?" I asked, meeting his glare with a steady gaze. He nodded stiffly. "Then go change. Yesterday you were a soldier in Bhorglid's army. Today, you are a diplomatic guest in the home of our future allies. Leave your uniform here; then stow your sword and scabbard with the other weapons."

For a long moment, everyone was still and silent. I waited for Arne to snap back and refuse my order. Instead, he merely scowled and grabbed his bag before storming into the castle.

When the doors closed behind him, Freja turned to me with wide eyes. She signed, "Does Halvar not know what happened between you?"

I clenched my jaw. "He knows perfectly well. This was a strategic decision. A good one, unfortunately."

Astrid replaced her dagger in its sheath. "What's the likelihood of him attempting to assassinate you?"

Freja and I glanced at each other. At this point, she likely knew better than I did. Arne had been hostile when we clashed on the front lines, but as far as I knew, he was still dedicated to the Nilurae cause. And while the Nilurae might hate to admit it, they were better off with me on the throne than anyone else.

I settled with, "Not very likely. I hope."

Arne returned, dressed in a black tunic and matching pants. His were plain compared to Volkan's, but we didn't have time for a wardrobe overhaul. "Time to go," I said and signed as one. "But remember—be on high alert. Snubbing the Kryllians will end this treaty before it begins, but we must discover why they want to ally with us. Otherwise, we risk walking into a trap."

Everyone nodded. Freja, Astrid, and Volkan all wore expressions that told me they understood the gravity of this moment. Arne simply glared, and I ignored it.

Silently, I reminded myself of my other motive during the negotiations: doing whatever I could to discover how Queen Anja had known I was Lurae before I did.

I looked to Astrid. She nodded, her mouth set in a determined line as she grabbed my wrist and Freja's and teleported us away.

4

Revna

I ADJUSTED THE CROWN SITTING HEAVY ON MY HEAD, TOOK A deep breath, and schooled my face to impassivity as we rode our mounts—teleported with us from Bhorglid—onto the grounds of the Kryllian palace.

The building's spires stretched thin, pointed fingers into the blue sky. It surprised me to see the sharp lines contrasting against slopes and curves in the architecture. The castle in Bhorglid was modeled after this one, but ours was certainly less magnificent. Here, the stone was not stark white but a pearlescent cream color, shot through with veins of gray in some places. Ornate patterns were carved into the marble and gilded with gold.

I sat up straighter, grateful our estimations of the weather had been correct. We'd barely been here for fifteen minutes and already the chill in my bones had nearly dissipated entirely. I hadn't realized how much I missed the warmth of summer until we arrived, appearing in the forest that bordered the palace on the east side so we had a moment to mount our horses and arrive as a unified group.

The figures standing on the steps grew in size as we approached.

I led the way, the four others behind me. The Queen of Kryllian stood front and center, the Hellbringer next to her. Two nobles stood on her other side, and a contingent of guards stretched out behind them.

The first thing I noticed was that he was masked.

Of course he is, I chided myself. *Did you think Søren was going to be on the queen's right hand, the same man you cared for?*

I knew better.

I forced my attention to the queen as we dismounted. She was the only one of importance today—the Hellbringer was nothing more than a distraction. Freja, Astrid, and Volkan stepped into careful bows and curtsies on either side of me.

When I turned a commanding stare to Arne, he clenched his hands into fists. After a long moment, he offered the queen a shallow bow as well.

My heart thudded in time with the song in my head. It was only a matter of time before we committed a slight against the Kryllians, especially if Arne was feeling particularly rebellious.

With a serene smile, the queen moved to stand directly in front of me.

"Your Majesty," I said. She was at least four inches shorter than me, but despite her stature she radiated confidence. Her blond hair was woven into a braid and wound around her head. She wore a golden dress with no sleeves and a plunging neckline. With the matching crown atop her head—far more delicate than the one I'd liberated from my father's study on the day of my coronation—she exuded poise and control. I noted a sheath belted around her waist, a blade secured there. One of her hands rested on the hilt.

She couldn't have been older than my own mother. Her delicate features showed few signs of aging. The occasional line on her brow, the beginnings of crow's-feet. Her face held a smile, but when I looked into her eyes, they were emotionless. A fortress of stone.

I kept my face schooled with politeness. My feelings would not escape me either, then. "Thank you for inviting us to your home. We are thrilled to be here."

The queen's gaze, a sharp blue reminiscent of the coldest blizzards, flickered to the members of my party. "You may rise," she said. "We are grateful you deigned to travel to us. I am sure you must be busy, as a new ruler."

I refused to let my smile slip, even as a dark-clothed figure moved down the steps to stand at his monarch's side. "Signing the treaty and ending the war peacefully is my highest priority. There is nothing more important."

For a long moment, Queen Anja studied me. The silence was broken only by the warm breeze, which rattled the leaves of the forest trees behind us. And of course, my mother's lullaby strummed in my ears. That, I ignored.

"Allow me to introduce you to the trusted members of my court. The lord and lady"—here she gestured to the two nobles who had moved closely behind her—"are representatives in my court. Lord Agard watches over the city of Vandsted, a booming locale on the coastline. And Lady Dahl oversees the capital city in ways I alone cannot."

The blond man and dark-haired woman both bowed, and I lifted a hand to bring them back to standing. When I glanced at the queen again, her serene smile had formed an edge sharper than a blade. Was she smirking at me?

"I believe you are more than acquainted with the general of my armies."

She gestured to the Hellbringer, and I was forced to look him in the eyes for the first time in three long weeks. The wolf skull helmet covered all of his features, obscuring him from anyone's true gaze. His hands rested in front of him, one wrapped around the wrist of the other. His sword was sheathed along his waist, and his cloak—*fuck, don't think about the cloak right now*—fluttered in the wind.

The Hellbringer was entirely unchanged from when he'd sat in my bedroom, taunting me.

I wanted to kick him in the balls.

Queen Anja must have seen the slight narrowing of my gaze because she visibly brightened. "How lovely to witness such a heartfelt reunion."

It took everything in me not to roll my eyes. The man before me had once said I was incapable of hiding my emotions, and I wasn't about to prove him right.

It seemed laughable that he'd been in Bhorglid, unmasked, just a few hours ago. If he hadn't been wearing gloves, I would have tried to steal a glance at his nails to see if any dirt remained beneath them.

It doesn't matter if he buried Frode, I reminded myself. *He's the one who killed him.*

"There will be time for pleasantries later," the queen said, turning and beckoning us to follow her to the palace doors. "My servants will show you all to your rooms and then we'll reconvene for a meal in the gardens."

The Hellbringer walked quicker than the rest of us. He was the first to escape through the doors, and the queen let out a quiet chuckle. I was so focused on lifting the hem of my skirt that I almost missed the queen's murmur. "It's easy to see why he was so taken with you."

I stopped so suddenly that Freja ran into me. I didn't apologize, simply stared at the queen. The smaller woman leveled a sharp smirk in my direction. Hesitantly, I resumed our walk. The song in my mind skittered like a prey animal making a desperate escape. Still, I kept my face impassive.

"I have no idea what you mean," I said smoothly. Could she hear the catch in my voice, the fear living there?

Søren's own words echoed back in a wave of memory. *No one*

can know. This thing between us . . . if the queen found out, she would use it against us both.

But who had told her? Had the Hellbringer regretted our relationship so thoroughly that he ratted himself out? Or had someone else learned the truth of our time together and told the queen, allowing her to tighten Søren's leash, too?

It was impossible to know.

"Don't bother lying, child." She raised a brow. "We're just getting started."

◆ ◆ ◆ ◆ ◆

I DIDN'T TELL FREJA AND ASTRID ABOUT THE QUEEN'S ACCUSAtions.

As the servants showed us to our rooms—all in the same corridor, thankfully—they chatted cheerfully, and I was loath to bring down their good mood. Arne also walked alongside us every step of the way, though I couldn't tell if it was because he was afraid to get lost in the palace's never-ending hallways or because he wanted to make sure we didn't say anything out of his earshot. Arne and I were over, but discussing my once-romantic relationship with the Hellbringer in front of him would light a fuse we couldn't afford right now. Not when everyone needed to be on their best behavior.

Freja, Astrid, and I shared three rooms that were each connected to the one next door by a shared bathroom. I'd been directed to the middle one, which was the largest, but promptly switched places with Astrid. It was easy to see she wanted to room next door to Freja, but she was reluctant.

"Think of it this way," I signed to her. "Anyone who tries to assassinate me will find my most loyal bodyguard there instead."

Her grin was unparalleled.

While they freshened up, I lay back on the bed and stared at the ceiling. The queen had flaunted her knowledge of my relationship with the Hellbringer. She hadn't brought him to stand on the steps with her because he was formidable—she'd done it because she knew it would make me uncomfortable.

And that meant these were hostile negotiations.

I'd suspected as much, but the confirmation simmered in my chest. From the moment the Hellbringer kidnapped me, Queen Anja had been in power. She was willing to help me claim the throne because our goals aligned. But what was her goal?

And how did she have so much knowledge about me? For a moment, I wondered whether she was a Seeing One, secretly able to see visions of the future. It was possible, but those with the ability joined the Seeing One caravans from a young age, becoming wandering people.

I turned the pieces of the mystery over and over in my mind. The Hellbringer had told me during our time together that the Kryllian army could have annihilated our people and ended the war years ago. Yet the queen insisted on continuing to fight, never pressing their advantage.

Now, when I sat on the throne, she was suddenly willing to negotiate peace. But what did she want? And why did she believe I was the one who could offer it?

When a pair of guards arrived to escort us to the gardens for dinner, Volkan raised a questioning eyebrow at me. I wasn't sure what emotion showed on my face, but I shook my head and held my hand low in front of my stomach to hide it from the others while I signed, "Later."

The gardens were magnificent. It was still early evening, but I realized the sun hadn't set as far as it would have by now in Bhorglid. Instead, it cast the sky in purples and pinks, a pastel canopy above budding bushes, bunches of lavender swarmed by lazy bees, and beds of tulips. Between the bright foliage grew different produce—

strawberries were beginning to turn slightly red instead of pink and many of the trees shading the area bore fruit.

"It's beautiful here," Freja signed. Her expression was almost wistful.

Volkan just shrugged. His sign language was still slow and haphazard, but he managed to communicate his sentiment regardless. "It's warm. Winter ruins everything."

We stepped into a clearing within the garden, surrounded by plants on all sides. One long table was set, covered in a purple cloth. The queen stood at the head and gestured to the plates laden with food, steam rising in the cooling air. "Please, sit."

Volkan had walked me through the precise politics of where to sit. The right-hand side of the queen was occupied by the Hellbringer, which meant I was sitting on the left. Directly across from him.

The lullaby began playing again in earnest. It had receded for much of the afternoon, but no longer.

When everyone was settled, I raised my glass of wine. "A toast," I offered, hoping my effort toward goodwill would erase the unspoken leverage hovering in the air, waiting for the queen to use it like a weapon. "To peace between our nations."

Everyone, including the queen, raised their glasses and repeated the words before taking a sip.

Except for the Hellbringer.

He couldn't drink with the mask on. Fine—this much, I would grant him. But my jaw tightened when the chatter of casual conversation didn't include his dark and distorted voice. He made no attempt to speak or put anyone at ease.

No. He merely sat and stared straight ahead.

I shouldn't have been surprised. The Hellbringer complied with his orders, but he'd never once attempted to make anyone feel comfortable. Least of all me.

Volkan stared directly at the Hellbringer while the food was served, like he was trying to communicate silently with the general. Arne sat on Volkan's left, as far from Anja as possible. Out of the corner of my eye, I watched him toy with his food, eating only a few bites here and there before devoting more of his time to glaring at the Hellbringer. The queen observed it all, her careful eyes catching every movement.

It had to have been Søren who confessed the true nature of our relationship to her, I decided as we began to eat. Clearly hungry, the diners were nearly silent for several minutes—leaving me with ample opportunity to mull over this second betrayal of trust. The meal tasted like ash on my tongue. And who else would have told her what they knew? Mira might have guessed, but she never saw proof. The goodbye note the Hellbringer had left for me to find only hinted at what our relationship had become.

Had I truly once believed that the Hellbringer was on my side? That he cared for anyone other than himself? That once the war was over, I would figure out a way to free him from his shackles as the queen's general?

I wanted to chide my past self. Find her and smack her upside the head. Only a fool would have believed the promises of her enemy.

He hadn't uttered a single word since we had arrived. Was his face unchanged beneath the mask? Or if I lifted it, would I find the same dark circles beneath his eyes that graced my own features? If I dared to look directly into his eyes, I knew with certainty he would see it all—the way I hated him with every fiber of my being. The way I longed for his comfort so desperately.

All he'd done so far was walk near me. And still, I was hyperaware of his every movement.

My magic churned. Was it following the path of my emotions or guiding them? The woman I'd been before the Trials was angry and passionate and decisive. She wasn't twitchy or paranoid or incapable of control.

Since the moment I became queen, I'd been spiraling. And the Hellbringer's presence made that more obvious. Still, I couldn't help the thought that had followed me into sleepless nights and guilt-ridden shadows.

This would all be easier with Søren at my side.

"There is a member of my court most excited to meet you," the queen said between her next bites.

"Oh?" I wasn't sure where she was going with this, but my magic tightened in my chest like a vise and I waited with bated breath.

"A scholar of sorts. He studies Lurae and magic, so when I told him of your extraordinary new abilities and your fascinating experience coming into your magic so late in life, he told me he simply had to meet you." Her smile was knowing, and I couldn't shake the feeling I was missing something obvious.

Whatever it was, it didn't come to me. But the idea of a scholar asking me about my magic . . . I suppressed a shudder. Scrutiny was the last thing I needed now, when the treaty was so close to being finalized and my magic was still so raw and untamed.

"He plans to attend the ball we're hosting in honor of your visit tomorrow evening," she added.

"I look forward to speaking with him." I hoped the platitude was enough to ensnare her goodwill for now. Every word felt like a careful step over thin ice, the possibility of falling to my doom a constant companion. I had expected the trip to be complicated, demanding, emotional. I hadn't expected that the queen, who had bargained so much to train me to win Bhorglid's throne, might be hostile. No weapons had been drawn yet, but words were their own blades when wielded right.

Swallowing another tasteless bite, I attempted to steer us toward small talk. "Does Kryllian have many scholars?"

The queen's eyes lit with venomous excitement. "Of course," she said with a laugh. "The history of the Fjordlands is so rich, and we are dedicated to uncovering it. Those who held the Kryllian throne before me cared little for history, but I feel the past is the key to enlightening our future. So much of the origin of magic has been lost to time, and our scholars have taken great care to bring the stories back to the present day."

"The origin of magic?" Freja spoke for the first time since the meal began. My friend had not been idle, though—I'd noticed her painstakingly interpreting every word of the conversation for Astrid, who sat next to her. "You have this history . . . uncovered?"

The queen's glance was pitying. "Of course we do. Bhorglid's dependence on the Holy Order of Priests to keep their history oral instead of writing it all down means much has been lost to time. You've wasted generations worshiping false gods."

Even I tensed at the abrupt switch to callousness in the queen's voice. My Lurae sensed it, and the song in my mind screeched a discordant note, the tempo galloping faster. My hands tightened on my silverware, but before I could manage a retort, Volkan stepped in. "You may call it history, Queen Anja, but there are many who would disagree. I've heard your wild tales before, and many of these stories come from conjecture—not fact."

"Call them what you want, little prince," the queen said, her voice pitched to reflect feminine demurity. "But there are three countries in the Fjordlands, and only one harbors the truth. Bhorglid's priests were closer than most, certainly. And Faste . . . well, choosing to ignore history doesn't make it any less real."

"If you're truly so enlightened," I said, forcing my muscles to relax despite every instinct telling me to let my hackles rise further, "then why don't you share this history with us?"

I noticed for the first time the heavy silence ringing the table. The only person whose head wasn't swinging back and forth between members of the verbal sparring match was the Hellbringer. He had his arms crossed, reclining slightly in his chair. I wondered if the front feet of his perch were off the ground, and turned to nudge Frode with my mind. His typical seat was next to the Hellbringer, and he didn't mind causing a political scene. There was no one better to knock the general off balance and straight onto his—

My eyes found Astrid in Frode's seat. It was like time stuttered. A wave of grief shuddered over me, so strong my chest ached. Absentmindedly, I rubbed a palm over my heart.

"Once," the queen began, "a young girl lived in a village in the middle of nowhere—my scholars speculate it may have even been in Bhorglid's northern wastelands. When the girl was sixteen, there was an accident. She and her friend were ice fishing on a lake and they went out too far, to where the ice was thin. It broke and the young man who accompanied her fell through. He could not swim, and quickly began to drown. The woman had a savior complex worse than any I've seen or heard tell of since—and of course she dove in after him.

"Neither of them died that day. And the girl? She became something *more*. When she emerged from the depths of that lake, she had a Lurae. The first Lurae.

"The girl's name was Aloisa."

That's the dream I've been having, I realized. *The boy falling through the ice and his friend jumping in to try to save him.*

The knowledge unsettled me. I managed to keep my composure, though; there was no more than a heartbeat of silence before I scoffed. "You can't honestly believe Aloisa was a real person."

"Most legends are born from the truth." She didn't look at me, instead studying the food on her plate. I realized most of it was untouched. "Your pantheon is six gods and one goddess, yes? Aloisa and her husband had six sons together. It's theorized that once Aloisa received her Lurae, the rest of the population began discovering their own magic. It would make sense if, long ago, someone took the story and twisted it to believe she was the cause of magic."

Astrid waved a hand, calling our attention to her. She signed and Freja interpreted aloud, "Where did the magic come from, then? If it wasn't gifted by the gods and it wasn't something she was born with, how did Aloisa get her Lurae?"

I realized I was leaning forward, resting my elbows on the table as I waited to hear what the queen would say. I pulled myself back, putting my mask of disinterest back on. But . . . I hadn't been born with magic either. Volkan had never even heard of a Lurae manifesting after the age of nine. Yet here was a story from across the sea that felt oddly familiar.

A girl desperate to rescue her friend. A girl forever changed afterward.

The queen sighed, running the pad of one thin finger around the lip of her wineglass. "Our scholars are the best, but despite it all we do not know everything. If the story is true, then something must have happened when the pair were underwater. It's not as if we were there, after all."

I leaned back in my chair as Volkan added his own opinion to the fray. The queen was small in stature, unassuming when she wanted to be. I had no doubt she was used to being overlooked and underestimated. She likely expected us to treat her similarly.

But she didn't know I was already familiar with her game. I didn't trust the Hellbringer anymore, but like the queen herself had just reminded us, the best stories came from the truth. I did not doubt that Anja was willing to manipulate those who stood in her way.

And this story? The entire direction of our conversation? It felt off, somehow. Even though I'd been the one to ask for the history lesson.

But I was utterly lost as to how her story about Aloisa and her sons might push us closer to the queen's end goals.

And though I hated to admit it, I liked the idea of Aloisa being a powerful woman, not a true goddess. The knowledge slid smoothly into place alongside my other beliefs. After all, I'd never truly embraced the idea of gods, especially ones who thought of me and my friends as less-than.

Hearing my name brought my focus back to the conversation at hand. "Whether we believe it or not is irrelevant. Revna is queen and the priests have been banished from Bhorglid. She will decide whether their religion is allowed back into the country again." Freja folded her arms as she finished speaking and signing.

The queen turned her bright gaze to me once more. I interjected before she could speak. "And decisions regarding such will be made after the treaty is signed. This peace between our countries has been a long time coming—I'd love to hear what motivated your people to seek the end of the war, Your Highness."

Volkan sat forward in his seat next to me, squeezing my hand approvingly beneath the table. He'd been training me in political small talk all week, helping me learn how to rephrase my typical blunt questions into more palatable ones. Before I wore the crown, I'd have held my dagger to the queen's throat and demanded she tell me why she'd wanted this alliance to begin with. Why she'd forced the Hellbringer to kidnap me and train me to win the Trials, even when he so clearly hadn't wanted to.

But queens did not threaten their future allies. And they certainly didn't ask for the information they wanted outright.

"Quite simply, I was tiring of dealing with your buffoon of a father." The queen laughed, but there was no humor in it. Once again, my Lurae song came alert. I had been the one to kill my father. There was no love lost between us. But her tone spoke of a hidden insult to me as well. "I had a vested interest in seeing a woman on the throne, taking the power she deserved. And look at you now."

She'd woven her answer as deftly as I'd spun my question. My fingers itched for a weapon I didn't have. There was more she wasn't saying, and it made me want to scream.

My mother's lullaby happily took up the cause, tempo and volume rising until I couldn't hear myself think. We'd come here for answers, for the chance to solidify an alliance, but the queen had no interest in telling us the truth. It gave her an easy advantage, one she would use to manipulate us without hesitation.

You're helpless, my mind whispered. *Perhaps you once triumphed on a bloody battlefield, but here? You cannot protect your friends or your people when you're useless in a political arena.*

"Indeed." I managed to keep my voice level even while the song in my head screamed, twining with my thoughts. "Look at me now."

"And how has ruling been so far? Everything you've ever dreamt of?"

I held my tongue, biting back the truth—that I'd entered the Trials to help make a change only for nothing to make a difference; that now I found myself floundering with unfamiliar magic and no true purpose; that I would give up the throne and my new Lurae if it meant things would go back to normal.

But every time the thought crossed my mind, I remembered that normal had been terrible, too.

"It's been excellent," I told her, taking a sip of wine. "Incredibly busy, as I'm sure you're aware. There is much to be done when filling the void left by a dictator-led theocracy."

"And your people?" The queen leaned forward in her seat. It was a subtle move, but I was on high alert already. "How are they taking to new leadership?"

Warning bells sounded in my head—I didn't need the nearly imperceptible headshake Volkan sent me or Freja's narrowed gaze to tell me the queen was fishing for weakness. "Change is difficult for everyone. It will be some time before all have adjusted to the new ways things are done in Bhorglid."

Out of the corner of my eye, I saw Volkan relax slightly. The

Hellbringer uncrossed his arms to lay his palms flat on either side of his place setting. His right index finger tapped lightly against the wood there.

"You misunderstand," the queen said. "I mean to ask whether there is civil unrest among your people. Do they accept your rule, or are you challenged?"

The silence following her invasive question felt eternal. I was certain the queen already knew the answer. Søren had been a spy in the city once. Surely there were others. My thoughts whipped through my mind. The threads of my Lurae appeared, stretching between myself and everyone at the table—my friends. The one connecting the Hellbringer and me was thicker than the rest. Did it recognize our past, intertwining so unmistakably because of the connection we'd once shared? Panic surged, immutable, as the image of Halvar's body in a pool of blood joined my thoughts.

Desperately, I grasped for a coherent response and heard myself say, "I'm not sure why that's any of your business."

Volkan looked like he had swallowed a bug. Freja chewed her lip, eyes darting back and forth between myself and Anja. Astrid pushed her plate aside and pulled out a small, thin dagger, which she spun in lazy circles on the surface of the table. Even Arne tensed visibly.

The Hellbringer's finger stopped tapping.

To her credit, the queen didn't laugh. I would have understood if she did. With a single sentence, I'd confirmed everything she wanted to know.

"It is, sadly, very much my business. If I am to sign a treaty with your nation, then it is important to know whether that nation may see another quick change in power shortly thereafter, in which case I'd wake to find an army on our doorstep." She'd settled back into her chair, lounging casually now while still managing to look regal.

It was a threat. She hadn't even bothered to veil it in pleasantries. We'd come all this way to negotiate a treaty, and now she planned to pull the rug out from beneath me.

For a single, brief flash of time, I hated her. Hated that she had been a monarch for so long that she knew exactly how to play this political game. Hated that despite her machinations to put me on the throne, all to end the war, she was still holding the treaty just out of reach, using it to her advantage in every way. Hated that no one in her country opposed her rule enough to try to assassinate her.

Was this all a ploy to catch us off guard so Kryllian could win the war?

"Of course there is civil unrest," Freja spat. I frowned, surprised she would speak up—and with an anger that sounded nearly equal to my own. "For generations, Bhorglid has been a kingdom run by extremists. And now, after three weeks, you expect Revna to have somehow turned the entire population in her favor? If you're such an adept queen, then you should know the kind of finesse required to make change without inciting violence. Are we here to sign a treaty? Or for you to toy with us before you pull it from our grasp?"

"What Freja means to say," Volkan cut in smoothly, before the queen, the Hellbringer, or soldiers standing throughout the gardens could erupt in outrage, "is that Queen Revna's goals are lofty. She has faith in her people and their ability to change for the better. Unfortunately, these kinds of changes do not happen overnight. There is civil unrest, yes. This is to be expected when power changes hands so drastically. We are taking every measure necessary to ensure the people are taken care of and the dissenters are dealt with quickly. I, for one, have no doubt things will return to peace shortly."

Well, at least one of us actually knew how to talk like a politician. I spared a brief thought of bitterness for my father, who had never bothered teaching any of us how to navigate political waters. Why bother when he could strong-arm every other country into subordination?

The queen turned to me. "Does the young prince speak for you now, Your Highness?"

It was impossible to miss the demeaning nature of her tone. Her cool and calm persona was gone now, replaced by an air of superiority. I straightened. "Volkan is one of my closest and most trusted advisers. When he speaks, it is with my permission and with the best interests of Bhorglid at heart."

She huffed a laugh. "My, my. Some people are raised for a throne, and it's clear to me you weren't one of them."

A distorted voice interrupted before I had the chance. "Was winning the Trials not enough?"

The entire table, including the queen, froze. The only movement was the gloved fingers of the Hellbringer's right hand, which all tapped a steady rhythm against the table now as he observed us.

I knew exactly what expression he wore beneath the mask, and I hated myself for it. His lips pursed in disapproval, a single brow raised. If he took the helmet off now, his hair would be mussed along the top and sides. I wondered if it had grown out since I last saw him, then shoved the thought back down, down, down into the depths of my mind, where it would not find the light of day again.

This was the difference between Søren and the Hellbringer—one was a loyal protector with a smile that lit the room; the other was a predator who watched everyone around him, searching for cracks in their armor where he could strike.

But why would he strike at his own queen?

He continued with that deadly voice, so casual we all knew it was dangerous. "You were the one who ordered me to train Revna for the Trials. You wanted her on the throne, enough that you sacrificed the time and attention of your general on the battlefield to do it. If you required more from the new ruler of your potential allies, perhaps you should have sought another instead."

I couldn't tell if he was insulting me or not.

Either way, he'd come to my defense and . . . my Lurae was twisted up in the knots of my emotions, the strings between me and him begging to be pulled. When I used my magic to tug at the threads holding a person together, they were thin. Nearly imperceptible. But my connection to Søren—the Hellbringer, I corrected myself internally—was different.

The anxiety of the day was wearing on me, the high stakes of current conversation sending me back and forth across the spectrum of fear, anger, and uncertainty faster than I could account for. My heartbeat pounded in my ears, and my rogue Lurae, sensing my weakness, lunged for control.

In one instant, three things happened at the same time. I stopped breathing, holding all the air tight in my lungs like it would stop my Lurae from escaping. The thread between me and the Hellbringer lurched wildly, like I had tugged sharply on it from my side. And his hand, which had moved to toy with the stem of his untouched wineglass, jerked toward me, spilling the dark red liquid all over the white tablecloth.

He pushed away from the table, standing back to keep the wine from staining his dark uniform. The queen rose slowly and turned to me, an unreadable look in her eyes. "We will reconvene for negotiations in the morning. It's late—rest will help us all come to the table with clear heads."

The sky had indeed darkened while we spoke, the warmth of the wind now rescinded into a chill. I wanted to demand she sit down, demand we hammer out the specifics of the treaty now, under the moonlight if we had to. But my Lurae was ready to snap again and I couldn't allow it to do so. Couldn't put my friends in the way of my pride.

So I nodded. "We'll speak in the morning."

5

Revna

ARNE HAD THE DECENCY TO WAIT UNTIL I'D CHANGED INTO my training clothes before pounding on my door.

I paused reaching for my belt. Aloisa lay on the bed next to it, ready to be sheathed at my hip. I'd missed her familiar, comforting weight at dinner. I gathered myself, knowing my slight reprieve was over, and twisted the knob.

Arne forced his way in before the door was open even an inch. I stumbled, snarling, the threads spinning once again.

"You trained with the fucking Hellbringer?" he demanded, pacing back and forth. His eyes wouldn't even meet mine.

"Do you have a problem with that?" I asked, straightening slowly.

"Of course I have a problem with it!" he shouted. "I knew there was someone else, I *knew* it and you know what? Maybe I would have gotten over it. But *him*? Not only have you been a liar this entire time, you've been sleeping with the enemy—"

"Enough."

My hands shook with the force of my fury, and I stepped closer to Arne, hoping to stop my Lurae from pulling him toward me. "Did you put your life on the line for the Nilurae?"

His mouth pressed into a thin line. "I fought in the war."

I shook my head. "Because you were forced to. Not because you wanted to. Not because you had any interest in making a difference. Hell, you couldn't even bring yourself to help Freja and me when we'd commit our acts of . . . what was it you called them? Petty rebellion?"

"At least I didn't spend weeks cozying up to the man who killed more of our people than any other," he hissed. "At least I wasn't fucking the man who murdered Freja's father."

He stormed out. I managed to pull my threads back, to allow the feral scream building within me to escape as nothing more than a low growl and a muttered curse. When I turned around to grab my sword once more, I instead locked eyes with both Freja and Astrid, who watched from the doorway of the connected washroom.

"What?" I snapped.

Neither of them answered. I buckled my belt and sheathed my weapon. The silence weighed heavy, and against my better judgment I signed, "Do you agree with him?"

"Yes."

My heart sank. Finally, I forced myself to look at Freja. I knew my expression and the movements of my hands held all the hurt I felt when I replied, "You never said anything."

She pursed her lips. "What was I supposed to say? You were in love with him. And there were far more important things to focus on."

You knew it was a mistake to tell her how you really felt about the Hellbringer, my thoughts taunted. I clenched my teeth, remembering the night shortly after the Trials when Freja had walked into my father's office to find me crying. I'd been desperate for her friendship, desperate to ease the crack in my soul. I told her everything—

confessed the truth of my relationship with the Hellbringer. Up until then, I'd left those details out of the story of my capture.

Freja had comforted me. Reassured me. Told me she understood. Now I knew the truth.

She had lied to me.

The realization turned my Lurae hostile. Threads twisted and tangled as my breaths shortened. My tenuous hold on my control frayed. If I stayed here any longer, someone was going to get hurt. I walked out the door, leaving the two women behind, desperate to put some distance between us.

There were two guards stationed at the end of the corridor where our rooms lay. I didn't spare them a glance as I walked by, and they made no attempt to stop me or offer an escort.

The gardens were my destination. I could train there, and they were far enough removed from the palace that my threads wouldn't be able to hurt anyone inside. Gods, I needed the weight of my sword in my hand, the rush of swinging a blade through the air. Especially now, when the whole world was against me.

You're the only one who wants this alliance to succeed. The words were stark laughter against the backdrop of my mind. *Your friends accompanied you here because they pity you, not because they want what is best for Bhorglid. The queen herself is waiting for you to slip up so she can send her armies back to the northern wastes.*

I shook my head violently, as if that would dislodge the muttering and the lullaby. The two twined as one until they were nearly indistinguishable.

The hallways were decadent, elegant gold filigree spiraling up to the ceiling. They were also nearly identical. When I turned one corner, then another, then another without arriving at the front doors of the palace, my chest tightened.

Lost.

No guards even, to ask for directions. "Stupid," I mumbled

under my breath, unsure whether I was speaking of the situation as a whole or myself as a person.

The sound of a latch clicking into place on a door came from ahead. I jogged forward and turned, hoping to catch someone before I grew even more turned around. But when I saw the figure striding purposefully away, I hesitated.

Søren ran a hand through his hair, the Hellbringer mask and armor nowhere to be seen. He wore an outfit unlike any I'd seen on him before. A simple, cream-colored tunic tucked into a pair of nice pants. A purple jacket with gold embroidery rested on his shoulders. Finery in place of his usual armor.

It felt like a lie just looking at him. A façade. *Maybe this is the truth,* I reminded myself, *and the version of Søren you knew is the lie.*

I followed him without thinking.

He strode casually through the palace corridors, hands in his pockets. I stayed far enough back to remain unseen, but I was curious where he could possibly be going. I'd seen the Hellbringer in public spaces plenty of times. But until now, Søren had existed only in the abandoned prison—to me, at least. It was odd to acknowledge that other people knew his face, his voice, his mannerisms.

Especially when I could clearly tell he was attempting to act more casual than he felt.

His stiff shoulders and frequent glances to the left and right told me this was more than a simple nighttime stroll. Maybe he was off on an errand for Queen Anja. Perhaps it even had to do with the negotiations. My suspicion grew as he continued walking.

Where was he going at this time of night?

When the palace front doors came into view, I ducked behind a statue. He greeted the guards, who both merely nodded. As he reached for the door handles, he looked back.

My breath caught in my throat. His face was the same—dark hair framing high cheekbones and full lips, gray eyes searching as ever.

The thought ricocheted without permission. *I miss him.*

He didn't notice me, hiding in the shadow of the sculpture, and he left without another word to the guards.

I straightened, counted to ten, and then went to the doors myself. The guards once again made no comment as I exited the same way Søren had. The stars shone and a cool breeze tossed the wisps of hair that had escaped my braid.

In the distance, a shadowed figure continued out the gates surrounding the palace. I glanced in the direction of the gardens. Training would wait until tomorrow night. Whatever nonsense Søren was up to demanded an investigation. I had an obligation to follow him. Who knew what kind of trap he and Anja might be laying for me and my friends?

I jogged after him.

◆ ◆ ◆ ◆ ◆

ROSKILDE FELT VERY SIMILAR TO BHORGLID'S CAPITAL IN SOME ways. In others, though, it felt entirely different.

Nice buildings and shops on the edge of town closest to the palace quickly gave way to tiny cabins with moderate-sized pastures as Søren and I moved further into the village. Abandoned homes in varying states of decay and ruin hid within the trees on the far end of the small town. I followed Søren from a distance, surprised he didn't turn around and catch me at any point. I was used to the general—brilliant war strategist. Perhaps here, the Hellbringer could relax without fear of retaliation.

Small fenced areas for keeping livestock surrounded us on either side. As he approached one, a horse whinnied. Søren's hand flew to his opposite forearm, where a sheath concealed a dagger. He froze. I did too, wondering if this was the moment he would catch me.

But he simply shook his head and continued on.

Strange.

Søren passed through quickly, not stopping until he reached the outskirts of town. Dilapidated buildings were scattered amid the towering oaks. He stepped up to the front door of a small home and knocked quietly.

The shadows were deep, but the moon was out and full—its light illuminated the dirt roads. I swore underneath my breath. The knock on the door had been barely audible, and there was no way I'd be able to hear the conversation that followed.

And I was correct. A man in his thirties with dark blond hair in a ponytail stepped out of the house. He seemed confused but joined Søren on the road. I watched them speak. Søren ran his hand through his hair multiple times before finally sighing and pulling out a bag of coins to hand over.

Even from a distance, I could tell it wasn't light.

The man accepted it, went back into his house, and closed the door.

Only I would have taste terrible enough to ensure I dated both the general of Kryllian and *an illicit goods smuggler.*

By the time the thought was finished, I realized Søren was headed back in my direction. And I'd done a shit job of remaining hidden, curious as I was about the exchange. His glare was locked on me, eyes wary and brow furrowed.

I straightened when he drew near. He reached out, as if to wrap a hand around my upper arm, but I leaned away. For a moment, we regarded each other in silence. Then he said, "Come on."

We didn't speak again until the city was far behind us, the trees our only companions. I stepped in front of him so he would stop walking.

"What are you doing out here?" I asked finally. I wasn't sure what kind of mask I needed to wear for this conversation. Anger still simmered low in my gut, fueled by the knowledge that he'd told the queen about our relationship.

He smirked, and it rankled at me. "Not exactly any of your business, is it? What were you doing following me?"

I scowled. "You looked suspicious. And I know the kind of damage you're capable of."

My words struck true, and he winced. The movement of his face was so slight, anyone else might have missed it. "Why don't you just kill me now, Princess? Get it over with."

Now I laughed. What a joke. Did he think I was an idiot? "Sure, and play right into the queen's hands. We'd be prisoners, never to return to Bhorglid."

Despite my own protests, I acted on instinct, pulling my dagger from its small sheath at my hip. We were too close for me to draw Aloisa, and the dagger felt better in my slightly shaking hand anyway. I pointed it at his chest.

Maybe I should kill him. The thought was far more ambivalent than it had any right to be, the apathy like a drug. *Would Arne and Freja forgive me if I did?*

"Playing into the queen's hands?" Søren repeated my words slowly, studying me. "You know what she's planning, then."

I inhaled sharply, hoping my surprise didn't show on my face. Of course we didn't know—but this was confirmation that Søren did. "What is she planning?" I pushed the dagger against his skin, feeling it give slightly. He hissed, the linen of his shirt darkening in the moonlight as it streamed down between the leaves. "*Tell me.*"

"I don't know," he snapped. Søren took a step back, out of range of my dagger. "I was hoping you did, because it's driving me up the wall trying to figure it out."

I rolled my eyes, belatedly realizing he likely couldn't see it in the darkness. I didn't believe him for an instant. "You're telling me the general doesn't know the queen's plans?"

"Hush," he hissed. "Did it not occur to you that the point of a secret identity is to keep it a secret?"

"We're alone."

"You can't know that." He glanced around, eyes wide. "The queen is certainly planning something, but I'm no closer than you are to discovering the details. She doesn't trust me these days."

Lies. All of it, lies.

I decided to pull on the single thread I knew might have some give in this tangled web. "How did the queen know about my Lurae?"

"I don't know."

"Of course you know," I hissed. "You're the one who argued with me about it in the prison!"

"I told you then, and I'll tell you again," he said, "she didn't answer any of my questions about the source of her knowledge."

"You're lying," I said through gritted teeth.

"I'm not." His whisper was harsh. "She believed me when I came back and told her you didn't truly have a Lurae. But . . ."

I waited a moment, but he didn't continue. I stepped forward again, this time leaving the tip of my blade a few centimeters from his chest. "But *what*?"

Now when he met my eyes, his face awash in moonlight and shadows, there was something hesitant there. It made me want to run, to escape before whatever it was caught up with me.

"You deserve to know," he finally said, and it sounded like he was trying to convince himself. Was I imagining the tremble in his voice? "Why I did the things I did, that day in the wastes. I owe you the truth, at least."

I inhaled sharply and pressed the knife to his chest once more. My heartbeat pounded in my ears, a thunderous accompaniment to the lullaby's accelerating tempo. Did I want to know?

No, part of me screamed—the part that sounded suspiciously like my Lurae. *You hate him. You know enough already.*

"You *need* to know," he said, whispering this time. I froze when he wrapped a hand around my own, pulling the blade slightly away from his chest. "And after, you can run your pretty blade through my decaying heart. I promise."

I didn't move. If I did, the risk of crumbling was too great. Because part of me desperately craved the missing pieces of what had happened the day Frode died. The same part of me that lay awake listening night after night as it screamed, *What could I have done differently? What if I could have saved him?*

"You and I had a fight," Søren said finally. His fingers around mine were steady. An anchor in the storm. "You'll remember the one—I accused you of hiding a powerful Lurae, and you told me the truth. That I was an idiot."

I did remember the fight. But most of what still haunted me about it wasn't the fight itself. It was our conversation afterward, when we'd imagined what life might be like if we'd met under normal circumstances. As two people at the market, and not the Nilurae princess and the Kryllian general.

The question of what could have been often threatened to overwhelm me.

He continued, "I knew you were telling the truth. Shortly after I returned you to your family, I made a report to the queen, who demanded to know what state your magic was in. I told her you didn't have any and . . . she believed me. I was shocked, considering how adamant she'd been. And then, of course, she declared you useless to her plans." Søren shook his head, eyes unfocused, like he was remembering the moment. "She said the next time I saw you, I was to kill you."

My hand shook, something I noticed only when I blinked back to awareness. Part of me had been listening, and another part of me had been far, far away—alone on the wasteland plains, covered in snow and blood. But what Søren said confused me. "After you spent so much time training me . . . she ordered you to kill me?"

"That's what I told her, too," he said with a sigh. "At the very least, it was such a waste of time and potential. But she didn't care. Said it had to be done.

"I hoped you'd win the Trials before we saw each other again. But when we caught Jac in camp that morning, I knew exactly what was happening. If I didn't obey the queen, she would kill my sister—the threat she's held over my head every single day for the past seven years."

I swallowed as understanding took hold. Søren had seen me on the battlefield and been faced with a decision: me or Sonja. Only one of us could live.

"I couldn't kill you, Revna. But I couldn't make a decision that would kill Sonja either." The shadows cast over his face, darkening his expression. "I didn't know what to do. I panicked. I told myself I had to do it, I had to end your life. I could have, too. But . . . it would have broken something in me, I think. My thoughts were chaos, and I was desperately trying to think of a solution, of a way out.

"And then I found myself wondering . . . whether killing another heir might be enough to satisfy the queen."

Horror and dread in equal measures suffused through me. The lullaby, which had been absent since I began following him, chimed. I wanted to scream, but the only noise that emerged from me was a pitiful whimper. "You killed Frode—killed my brother—rather than let your own sister die?"

It was simple to see the desperation on his face. "I didn't want to kill Frode. I knew how much he meant to you. I thought maybe I would have time to get to Erik, or even Björn. Because that would have at least been helpful to you in some way.

"But every time I looked over, it was the three of them standing back-to-back: Erik, Björn, and your father. Killing one would have been a possible substitute the queen would allow. I could play dumb to a certain extent. But all three? No. She would have known, and the consequences would have been the same. There wasn't time to get all the way to them, kill just one, and then leave with my soldiers. Because they were dying in droves as well. I had to retreat lest the innocents under my command lose their lives while I tried to make my choice.

"Frode heard my thoughts. Do you remember what he said, right before he died? That he understood? That's what he meant. There was no other way. Not that I could see."

Was there a knife in my chest? Surely that had to be why I hurt so damn bad. Like the grief of watching Frode's sightless eyes was fresh all over again. Like I was the same woman screaming for Erik to put me down so I could bring Frode's body back with us.

The lump in my throat refused to be dislodged. I swallowed again and again, as if it would make a difference.

"Revna?"

I thought about laughing. Had the fierce Hellbringer ever sounded so tentative before? Would he ever sound so tentative again? Or would this be the final extent of whatever vulnerability I seemed able to pry from him on occasion? "Tell me what you're thinking, Princess."

"I hate you."

The words flew from me, impossible to take back once they'd been said. I couldn't look at him, couldn't bear the ripping and tearing in my chest I knew would follow. So instead I stared past him at nothing, like it would ease the pain.

How had I managed to fall into an unfairness so deep it was a wound? Søren's sister got to live, but at the cost of my brother. At the cost of my best friend, the truest companion I'd ever known.

Once, I'd thought perhaps Søren's companionship could rival the way Frode knew me. But what the Hellbringer and I had was built on lies, and lies were always destined to crumble.

Søren's hands curled into fists, his knuckles whitening. He took several deep breaths and slowly relaxed his hands before he said, "I know."

The other things crowding my mind threatened to escape. *I should kill you for what you've done. Maybe, when our countries are finally at peace, I will. Maybe I'll end your life like you ended his. You would deserve it.*

But here, alone in the woods . . . anyone could be listening without my knowledge.

Even this short conversation was a risk. What if someone was hiding in the shadows? It was entirely possible. The alliance—what little possibility of an alliance was left, at least—would crumble if the right ears overheard this conversation. If someone from my party discovered the Hellbringer's true identity. If a passerby loyal to the queen returned to her with news of Søren's tiny rebellion in the wastes.

With every second I remained, the risk grew. I pulled my blade away, unwilling to carve the final mark on him. Not now. Without another word, barely holding on to any semblance of control, I walked away.

Back to the Kryllian palace.

Back to my rooms.

To my solitude, where I was destined to remain.

6

Revna

"YOU'VE RUINED YOUR OUTFIT IN THE MOST PREDICTABLE WAY."

I turned to see Freja and Astrid closing their respective bedroom doors and striding down the hall toward me. I couldn't muster a smile—especially not now, when I knew Freja had been keeping her opinions about my training with the Hellbringer hidden—but I raised an eyebrow in question. My best friend nodded to the sword and sheath belted at my waist. She signed, "Do you really think a ball is the right place for weaponry?"

I managed to huff a laugh as I replied, "We're still at war with the very people hosting this event. I'd say this is the best place to be armed."

Astrid didn't appear amused. "Revna is right," she said. "We've been ignored all day; the queen could be preparing to make a carefully coordinated attack tonight."

Despite promising that negotiations would begin early this morning, we had not been summoned to meet with the queen. When I'd finally demanded one of the guards standing at the end of the hallway explain what was happening, he'd simply said the queen had decided to postpone negotiations until after the ball, in light of new information she'd received.

The cold chill that ran down my spine hadn't warmed since then. I'd tried to distract myself by training, but every time I managed to slip into the ease of my sparring forms, my conversation with Søren from the night before returned to me.

Frode was dead. For *nothing.*

Now the guards had the decency to escort us to the ballroom. Freja walked on Astrid's other side, the teleporter standing between us. A strategic decision, so my bodyguard was within reach? Or a slight, after the admissions of last night? There was no way to know.

"Where's Volkan?" I signed as we arrived in front of a set of grand doors, the gold etching on them glinting in the lamplight.

"He left early," Astrid replied. "Said he wanted to get a feel for things before you arrived."

"And Arne?"

She shrugged. "No idea. He was gone when I knocked on his door to see if he wanted to walk with us."

Music drifted around us, and I steeled myself. It felt the same as when I'd stood on a hillside and watched Bhorglid's army descend into the arms of the Kryllian soldiers waiting there. This was likely my last chance to convince the queen to reconsider signing the treaty. If tonight went poorly, war would reign once more.

And this time? Kryllian would win.

I wasn't optimistic.

The doormen moved to announce us, but Freja held up a hand to stop them. "Is your Lurae under control?"

My mind ran rampant with nothing but a single question. *She doesn't trust you not to ruin everything the moment you start speaking. Just like dinner yesterday, when you admitted to the civil unrest because you didn't think it through. And if she distrusts you now, imagine how much she'll hate you when she learns the truth about Halvar.*

Every muscle in my body went taut as I took a breath to shove my Lurae down, down, down, ignoring its siren song as golden threads began to spin to life around me. I gritted my teeth and signed a blatant lie. "Yes."

My hands were restless. I straightened my dress, a dark red piece that draped along one shoulder, with golden embroidery over the bodice, and adjusted my father's crown. I'd insisted on wearing it tonight despite it not fitting—it was the one I'd worn to my coronation, and whether or not the alliance went through, I was a queen.

Freja's shoulders relaxed. "Good. Maybe this isn't as hopeless as I thought, then."

I had barely enough time to prickle with defensiveness at Freja's response before she gestured for the doormen to let us into the ballroom.

The music softened, and we looked out into a wide space as elegantly decorated as the rest of the palace. It was packed with dancers dressed in finery, couples spinning round and round in dizzying loops. A group of musicians played in one corner. On the opposite side of the room from us was a dais where the queen sat on a throne made of twisted gold.

The doorman announced Freja and Astrid, and the two linked arms before entering. I swallowed down the knot of unidentifiable emotion at the sight.

I was next. The doorman raised his voice once more and called, "Revna of Bhorglid, the Bloodsinger Queen."

All eyes turned to me, like I'd known they would. It surprised me when the partygoers slowed, descending into bows and curtsies to offer me the respect I'd earned. As I stepped through the crowd, I took a deep breath to slow my heartbeat.

This was already going better than expected. None of us had been murdered yet.

Are they looking at the crown? my thoughts taunted as I passed dozens of beautiful nobles. *Or are they staring at your scars?*

I willed my shoulders to relax as the hum of a song only I could hear started up once more. Thinking about the scars made the skin on my face feel taut.

I reminded myself of the truth: I'd chosen to keep my scars, chosen to give my people a visual reminder of my right to the throne. Perhaps they were ugly. Perhaps they marred whatever sliver of natural beauty I'd possessed before. But now was not the time to grow weary beneath their gazes.

"Rise," I commanded. The crowd obliged, the musicians began strumming once more, and because today was determined to be as terrible as it possibly could be, my eyes locked directly with Søren's.

For the span of a heartbeat, his stare bored into me. I managed to pull my own gaze away. Now knowing exactly what had happened the day my brother died, I wouldn't—*couldn't* look at him. Just because I recognized his features didn't mean I knew the man underneath the mask.

A fact he'd proven when he admitted to murdering Frode in an attempt to save his own sister.

Why was he unmasked for this event? I had expected the queen to want him at her side constantly, as a show of power.

I pursed my lips as we began to weave through the throng. This was no show of good faith. If Søren was here as himself and not the Hellbringer, there was a purpose to it—a firm reason.

The hair on the back of my neck stood up, prickles of awareness from his careful observation of me. Besides the scars, I knew I looked stunning.

I hoped he hated it.

I wanted to bare my teeth and snap at him. How dare he? Staring at me in public, like I was an object and not a public figure worthy of his respect—no, his *fear.*

Freja sidled up next to me, her hushed whisper bringing me back to myself. "Six guards along the west wall and eight along the east. Two next to the dais, and then . . ." She frowned. "Who is that speaking to the queen?"

Yesterday, I would have told her exactly who was speaking to the queen, a soft smile on his face—one I knew was fake. Søren didn't smile like that. But today, with the heavy knowledge that Freja disapproved of my alliance with the Hellbringer and thought I shouldn't have fallen for him . . .

"I don't know," I said. The words felt too true, and they sank like a stone in my gut.

When I turned to discreetly observe the guards Freja had mentioned, I noticed Astrid. Walking casually behind us, she had drawn a dagger from one sheath and was steadily flipping it end over end to catch it in her palm while she stared directly at anyone who appeared to be eavesdropping.

The song ended, and as another began, I moved forward again. "Let's go make our pleasantries."

The dais was only a few steps off the ground, and in moments I stood face-to-face with the queen. I wasn't the only one who had come to the ball armed. Anja had her decadent sword balanced across her lap, hands cradled protectively over it. I wondered why it mattered to her so much that she'd bring it to an event like this; she had plenty of guards willing to fight and die for her.

"Your Highness," she said. "Glad you could join us."

"As am I," I replied, using all my strength to keep my voice steady. "The event is beautiful—the perfect way to celebrate peace between two once-warring nations."

An empty throne sat next to hers, and I sank into it, crossing my legs and leaning back. Volkan's admonishments from earlier this afternoon still rang in my mind. *Be confident, act like the alliance is a sure thing. We may be in a foreign palace, but you are ranked just as highly as she is—pretend you own the place.*

Søren faced away from me. A good thing, considering the queen knew exactly what this moment meant. I was relieved to have stumbled upon him the night before. Otherwise, the heaviness of seeing him unmasked might have shattered me. Freja and Astrid remained at my side, Astrid now polishing her blade with the edge of one sleeve.

The queen hummed. "Peace has been proposed, but not finalized."

"I'll grant you that," I said with a nod. I should have left it there, but hadn't Volkan urged me to be confident? The rest of my thoughts slid into words with no resistance: "Hard to finalize a treaty when the opposing country's leader declines to negotiate with you, though."

Søren was utterly still, waiting.

But the queen did not rise to the bait. "It became clear after our dinner that there is more at play than originally thought. I'm grateful for your patience, but rest assured—by the end of the night we will have made a decision."

Out of the corner of my eye, I watched Astrid's knuckles go white where they clutched the hilt of her blade. Tension radiated from Freja.

Before I had the chance to reply, the queen continued. "Yesterday, I mentioned one of our most prestigious scholars was interested in meeting you, to learn more about your Lurae and its unprecedented manifestation. I've invited him here tonight to meet you."

I wondered if there was ever again going to be a time when an unplanned introduction did not send dread through me with the precision of a practiced archer. Because I had a suspicion I knew exactly who this scholar was. It would certainly explain the mischievous glint in the queen's eyes.

"Queen Revna, meet Søren Anselm. The finest scholar Kryllian has seen in generations."

Søren turned to face me, finally. He still wore the same fake smile, one of docile curiosity. He bowed low at the waist, another act that made me want to cringe away. Who was this man? Certainly not the Søren I had known.

"Your Highness. Pleased to meet you."

"Rise," I said. No matter how much delight the queen would take in my acting, Freja and Astrid could not know his true identity. I kept my voice even. The song raged within all the while. "Lovely to meet you as well, Søren. Her Highness made mention last evening of the rich history of the Fjordlands that you and your fellow scholars have gathered over the years. I'm eager to learn more about it."

His fake smile slipped into a smirk. "Perhaps you'll do me the honor of a dance later this evening and we can both share our unique findings."

"We'll see whether the time allows."

Volkan stepped up to the dais, offering me his hand as he bowed. "Would you do me the honor of a dance, Your Highness?" When he glanced up at me, his expression was clear—this was an offer to escape.

Thank the gods. "Of course."

He escorted me to the dance floor, ever the gentleman, and we began to waltz—Volkan had insisted that I know at least one formal dance now that I was queen, and I'd held my memory of doing the same steps with the Hellbringer in the prison behind my gritted teeth while the prince taught me. The past few weeks had lent themselves to many a dance lesson, and I fell into the muscle memory, allowing him to lead. The steps were far different from the traditional dances

I'd grown up with and learned by heart, but my body was experienced with intuiting rhythm and moving with it.

I caught sight of Arne glaring in my direction from across the room, nursing a glass of wine. It was easy to brush off his displeasure. My friends were already upset with me—but Arne was not my friend any longer. His opinion was the least of my concerns, so long as he behaved himself while we were here.

For a moment, it was peaceful. I forgot about Søren, about the treaty, about the secrets I was keeping from my friends. Twirling in the prince's arms, I thought of what it would be like if every day were like this, if every event was full of laughter and ease instead of—

Volkan's lips migrated to my ear. "You know how badly Bhorglid needs this alliance."

I did my best not to stiffen visibly. Mother's lullaby began to pick up tempo, overlapping with the musicians. "No one understands that better than I do, Volkan."

"I know." He sighed. "She has something up her sleeve. Something more she wants. I've been puzzling over her refusal to start negotiations all day, and it's the only thing I can think of that makes sense. She had a motive when she ordered you trained, and it hasn't turned out the way she planned."

"The only unexpected part of the Trials was my Lurae," I said, careful to keep my voice low. "But she suspected I had a Lurae from the beginning. So that can't be it."

"I don't know what it could be. But I do know this: she's going to ask more of you because she *can*. Even if it isn't anything she needs. I've known the queen a long time—have sat in on diplomatic meetings with my parents and Anja since I was a child—and while she puts on an arrogant act, she's also clever and conniving in ways no one anticipates."

We turned with the dancing crowd, and exhaustion threatened to suffocate me. "What do I do, Volkan? My father spent my whole life using me as a pawn—making an example out of me, proving he wasn't afraid to punish any Nilurae because he punished me. Am I doomed to that fate? Forced to dance for these rulers if I don't want my people to suffer?"

For a long moment, we spun in silence. As the final bars of music played, he said, "You're queen now, Revna. As a princess, you had far more freedom. You could think about yourself and what you wanted. You didn't have to marry me because you didn't want to. Now? You carry the fate of a country on your back, far more than you ever did before.

"When you won the Trials, you didn't win your freedom. You're on a leash now—one held by the people. If you allow them to fall, then they will take you with them. Are you prepared to tumble over that ledge?"

The couples around us began to separate, Volkan's words a dagger to my heart. I wanted to draw my blade and shove it through his ribs. I wanted to collapse onto the floor and curl into a ball while the people I loved wrapped around me like a shield.

"You have always been a pawn," he said quietly, lifting my frozen hand from his shoulder. "And if you care about your people at all, then you will become one again in order to keep them safe."

A deep voice interrupted us. "May I have this dance, Your Highness?"

I turned to see Søren's outstretched hand, accompanied by a raised eyebrow. There was nothing I wanted less than to dance with the man who killed my brother, who broke my heart until the pieces were too fine to be put back together. But Volkan's reminder made it clear—there was no room left to think of what I wanted anymore. If this dance might help solidify an alliance we desperately needed, then . . .

"Of course." I took Søren's hand.

When the music began again, I ignored the swooping in my stomach as he pulled me tight to him and led me to the beat.

I waited for him to say something, but we moved in silence.

I swallowed. It took all my strength not to notice every inch of our bodies touching now. Not to notice the warmth radiating from him, a comfort against the cool air filling the room. I spared a brief thought of gratitude that this song was not a waltz and therefore required every ounce of mental energy to follow the steps without stumbling. Otherwise, I wouldn't have been able to ignore Søren's pine and fresh snow scent.

Had he been to the wastes recently? Is that why he smelled the same as he had in the prison? He must have, if the body he buried two days ago was truly Frode's. I wanted to ask him, instead biting my tongue until the taste of iron spilled.

"This is going far better than the last time we danced." Søren's voice held a hint of humor, but his shoulders were stiff. The fake smile had returned, a mask far different from the one he wore on the front, but a mask all the same. "You haven't stepped on my toes once."

We turned with the crowd of fellow dancers. The ballroom was full to the brim, and I saw Freja's worried expression amid the gathered citizens. My emotions, scattered and intense, strummed the strings of an instrument I couldn't see; one only I could hear.

My response to Søren was automatic. "Wasted opportunity," I replied.

"Has Volkan been teaching you?"

"Who else?" Before he could speak again, the words spilled out of me. "What kind of game are you playing?"

I couldn't force myself to look into his eyes, but I saw his jaw clench. "You'll have to elaborate."

He released his hold on my waist and spun me, the skirt of my dress flaring out. A bloodred stain against the nearly white stone floor. "I mean," I said as I caught my breath, his hand settling against my hip once more, the pressure from each of his fingers sending a bolt of lightning through me, "the treaty. You spent six weeks holed away in the wastes, complaining about your duty. Why is the queen so hesitant to commit now?"

"I told you last night—I don't know."

He moved his other hand to my waist as well, then lifted me off my feet while he spun. I gasped, clutching his shoulders. Now, though, I was forced to look into his eyes. They were as deep and familiar as I knew they'd be. I held my breath. It was the only way to keep from falling into the comfort of his presence.

"I still think you're lying." A thread fizzled in and out between us, thicker than the ones connecting me to everyone else in the room.

I heard the smile in his voice. "I don't lie, Princess. Remember?"

How much of an unmendable scandal would it cause, I wondered, *if I kneed him in the groin right now?*

On the next spin, my eyes caught with Volkan's. Thinking of the prince's reaction was enough to put me off.

The music slowed to a close and I stepped away quickly. My palms tingled from where I'd been touching him. I curled my hands into fists to keep them from shaking. "I remember everything."

◆ ◆ ◆ ◆ ◆

I RETURNED TO THE DAIS NEARLY AN HOUR LATER, WHEN THE ball had just passed its midpoint.

Exhaustion clung to my limbs. While all the Lurae in Bhorglid were afraid of me, the Kryllians instead seemed fascinated by my unprecedented power. I'd been dancing with men and women alike since leaving Søren behind on the dance floor. My vision was beginning to blur with flickering strings, and I knew if I didn't sit down, my fragile hold on my Lurae was bound to snap.

The queen hadn't left her seat all evening, only speaking briefly to those who came to her. A few minutes ago, she'd instructed a page boy to fetch Søren. He now stood to the side of her throne, speaking to her quietly.

When I came into earshot, she held up a hand to silence him and turned to me. "I have decided," she said, voice calm and cheerful despite the edge to it, "what I require in order to proceed with the treaty."

I froze. So much for sitting down, then. The string tying me to her was vivid. I refused to let myself envision how good it would feel to pull it taut until her bones gave way beneath my power. "Do tell."

She leaned forward, her voice barely a whisper but still managing to cut like a blade. "Demonstrate your Lurae."

"What?" I couldn't keep the surprise from my face. If I tried to use my magic purposefully right now, would it even listen to my commands? Or would it do what it had always done and consume without mercy? I scrambled for an excuse. "My Lurae is dangerous. And you must know it's rude to ask for such a display."

"Of course it is. But nonetheless, I insist." She looked at Søren. "I'm sure Søren here would have no qualms about being held captive by your Lurae for a few moments. It wouldn't be the first time."

So she knew what had happened when he visited me after the Trials as well. That moment had been private—only the two of us in the room. No one but Søren could have divulged the intimate details of it.

My heart sank. He *was* the one who'd told her about our relationship.

You thought you loved him, and he has betrayed you in every possible way, my thoughts whispered, their deadly steadiness whipping my suppressed Lurae into a frenzy. I tilted my head, hoping the stretch in my neck would distract me from the gold blurring the edges of my vision, the string between him and me growing tauter with each second. *Every sacred moment between the two of you, handed directly to his master. Her perfect lapdog.*

Søren's hand twitched, and panic sliced through me. Was it a muscle spasm or an accidental tug of my magic? There was no way to know. But if I tried to unleash it for a demonstration, someone in this room packed full of innocent civilians would die. Most likely Søren, if he was the target my Lurae latched on to. I thought back to the body of a would-be assassin, bloody in the cobblestone street.

I hated Søren. *Hated him*. Maybe even enough to want him dead.

But not right now. Not at the hand of my Lurae.

If I'm going to kill him, I thought, *I will accept only the satisfaction of my sword through his gut. Nothing less will do.*

I studiously ignored the twinge in my stomach at the lie.

"No." The word settled into the air of the room, and for the first time since we arrived in Kryllian, I breathed easily. "I do not oblige petty requests to demonstrate my magic for all to see. You invited us here to sign a treaty—so sign it. Or don't. Either way, our delegation will depart in the morning."

She laughed again. "So much fire in you. I will not sign any treaty with a girl masquerading as a monarch." The words hit like a slap to the face. "Only with a queen. And a queen can use her magic in any way she pleases—so why won't you?"

"She can't."

Søren's declaration sent a chill up my bare spine. I turned to face him. "Excuse you?"

His expression was unreadable. "I said you can't use your magic," he repeated. He pitched his voice low, unable to be heard by those dancing and milling about. "Or you can, but you aren't able to control it."

"That's not true."

"But it is." His gray eyes snapped to mine, and I wondered how he managed to see through my façade every time. Still, after all the hatred I was desperately cultivating around him. "I didn't lose my grip on that wineglass at dinner last night—my hand was yanked by something I couldn't see. Your Lurae is untamed and untaught, a dangerous combination."

The lullaby was echoing in my ears. I barely heard it when the queen said, "As I suspected."

Meanwhile, I was attempting to hold myself together. Everything was falling apart around me—like the moment when an avalanche is no longer a sound in the distance but a visible downpour of snow devouring everything in its path.

The treaty. We were only supposed to sign the treaty. Instead, the queen was poking holes in the careful mask I'd constructed before arriving here. I wanted to fold up into a ball on the floor and cry. Or maybe sleep forever.

All she had to do was *sign the damn treaty*.

Instead, she continued. "We cannot ally with you and end the war unless your magic is controllable. I hope you understand—the point of removing your father from the throne was to work with a leader who didn't destroy on a whim. Your Lurae, to be frank, threatens that.

"Which brings me to a proposed solution. In three weeks, I will visit Bhorglid. Demonstrate your magic for me then, after spending that time with an experienced teacher. He will teach you how to wield your Lurae and take control of it. If, when I arrive, you are fully able to keep yourself under control and can use your magic how you like, then the treaty will be signed. But until then, we cannot move forward, unfortunately."

The ringing in my ears was dissonant against the familiar notes of my mother's lullaby. The question forming on my lips filled me with dread—I suspected I knew the answer already. "And who, exactly, is this great Lurae that will be teaching me to use my magic?"

My heart pounded a steadily increasing tempo, so hard I wondered if it might bruise. The queen smiled serenely.

"Søren, of course."

For a long, long moment, everything was still. The only way to save my people from impending starvation, years more of war, and eventual conquering by our enemy nation was to let the Hellbringer instruct me in how to use my magic.

The scream building in my chest, the one that had sparked when she first threw the knowledge of our relationship in our face and burned to a blaze over the course of two long days, escaped.

And the ballroom exploded beneath my rage.

7

Revna

THREADS ERUPTED FROM EVERY BODY IN THE VICINITY—Søren's brighter, thicker, more visible than all the others. I felt my awareness stretch further, too. I could sense everyone in the room. If there was blood, there was a connection.

Mother's lullaby screamed in my ears. So did the voice of the magic, in words that were not words but *feelings*.

Look at her, it hissed. I couldn't blink, and when my vision centered on Kryllian's leader once more, she was frozen. Her pupils darted back and forth, her body under my deadly thrall. *She dares to make demands for her entertainment instead of for anyone's good. She dares to speak down to you. She treats you like a child. Like Father did. She makes you look* weak.

A breath hissed out from between my teeth. I knew what came next—pulling on her threads until they *snapped* like her neck. Only with her lifeless body on the floor would we be able to make real progress. Otherwise, the threat of looming war would sow unrest in Bhorglid until the Lurae started a coup and attempted to overthrow me.

I was the savior of the Nilurae. Even if my people didn't want me—they would have me. And allowing the queen to live after betraying her promise of a treaty so quickly would be a stain on Bhorglid's white snow.

Snow that was stained red enough already.

Kill her, my Lurae cooed, and the idea sounded so satisfying. The song in my ears accelerated to the tempo of my captives' heartbeats, which grew faster with every passing second.

Before I could pull the string, a hand landed on my shoulder. "Your Highness."

I wanted to scream at the audacity. To call me by my title when once we'd been—

Nothing, my Lurae screamed. The words choked me. *You were nothing to him.*

"Before you continue," Søren said, "you might want to take a look around you."

The suggestion was so reasonable that I obeyed without thinking, twisting over my shoulder to cast my eyes over the scene. And I saw what I'd missed in the throes of my rage.

Around me, every person in the ballroom stood frozen, incapable of movement. The queen and her guards . . . and the partygoers. Even my friends. Astrid and Freja were still as stone, Freja's hand wrapped around Astrid's wrist. Volkan was mid-step, facing the dais. Even Arne was motionless, his eyes wide with fear.

Only Søren and I remained in motion.

No. I stumbled back, away from the queen. My breaths came in ragged gasps. *No, no. Not again. Not the people I love.*

Fearful eyes flickered between me and the scholar at my side. I tried to pull back only the strings grasping the innocent, but the effort was far too monumental.

Sweat broke out across my forehead. I could let them all go or cut every lifeline together. There was no in between.

For a moment, I considered it.

The thought of leaving this room as the only one standing filled me with a sickening sense of relief. There would be no Kryllian queen to press her boot to my throat and force me to obey. No threat of Freja discovering what I'd done to Halvar and abandoning me. Volkan would no longer look at me with eyes full of disappointment and regret.

I would abandon the throne, in that case. And then . . . no Lurae to persuade of my worthiness. No Nilurae to act as if I'd been corrupted when I had no choice in my magic. I could leave this place and walk away. Step into the unfamiliar forests of a foreign country and never return.

It would be far easier than the alternative.

When Søren stepped close, the warmth of his breath brushing against my ear, I felt a single tear slide down my cheek. "Princess," he whispered, so softly I knew no one else was privy to his words. "This battle cannot be won by a single show of power. It may feel like your Lurae is offering the simple solution, but it's not. Your magic is trying to control you. Show it your strength."

My hands, fingers splayed and palms stretched out in front of me, shook with the effort of holding back. One of the noblemen closest to me jerked unwillingly, and a surge of panic made my heart stutter. Fear radiated through the air, filling the space like an impenetrable fog. The haunting lullaby wove in and out, like my Lurae had taken on a life of its own and was wandering around the space, observing its work.

"I can't." The words pushed through my gritted teeth. One wrong move and every neck in the room would snap.

"Start by forcing your jaw to relax." Søren's voice was quiet, but it held no trace of the false smile he'd given earlier. When I glanced at him, my eyes wide, he tilted his head slightly, his gray eyes serious.

"Relaxing won't make you lose control. Tightening your hold on your Lurae will be your downfall. Now *relax*, Princess."

I didn't trust him. Didn't even want anything to do with him. But his advice was the only thing available to me now, so I obliged. When I opened my mouth wide and inhaled a deep, steadying breath, then circled my aching jaw, the lullaby ticked down its intensity by a notch.

Søren noticed. "Good. Now the rest of your face." A few moments later, "Now your shoulders."

We continued in that manner for what felt like an hour—Søren instructing me to relax a part of my body slightly and me obeying. There was no room left for the shame I knew would flood me later. Right now there was only relief. I'd managed not to kill anyone yet.

When I relaxed my toes, the threads disintegrated. It reminded me of Erik's bones—charred into ash by Björn's bright, burning fire.

Despite being free now, the entire room remained motionless for a single moment. Then, like a simultaneous release of breath, everyone moved.

The guests ran for the doors, filing out and casting fearful glances back over their shoulders. My friends—Volkan, Freja, Astrid—only stared at me, stunned. They made no move to come to my side as the partygoers fled. Arne's expression of disgust reminded me of Halvar's, when the tavern keeper had called me a liar on the morning of my coronation. It was like a knife to the heart.

"Søren."

The queen's voice echoed with her footsteps as she approached, and it was like the scholar had been doused with cold water—he stepped away from my side faster than I imagined was possible. For the briefest moment, I wondered if her Lurae was mind control. I dismissed the thought quickly. If she was truly that powerful, she could have deposed my father and put me on the throne without even bothering with the Bloodshed Trials.

Something ugly rose beneath my rib cage. My lips curled back from my teeth when I said, "Your demands have gone too far, Your Highness."

The queen didn't even blink. "And yet I am not the one who put helpless civilians in danger tonight."

If my magic had not been depleted already, I would have killed her then. I rubbed my thumb over the hilt of my sword as I considered doing it the simpler way.

She continued, "I presume you've made your decision regarding my offer."

I thought of every subtle threat she'd levied at me over the past day. Of the way she'd toyed with us and left me in suspense, wondering if tomorrow would bring peace or war again. Of how she'd learned about my relationship with the Hellbringer and chosen to use it against me, to not only give a wound but rub salt in it. She enjoyed making me squirm, of that I had no doubt.

But her purpose had been accomplished. After today, I knew exactly what kind of manipulation she was capable of. The woman was as honed as a blade, a sharper predator than even the Hellbringer. If we went to war again, if my people were left at her mercy again . . .

Nothing would remain when she was through.

"I accept your offer." My voice was dull, as beaten as I felt. For a moment, I wished for the cold of my home. Few things grew in Bhorglid. Few things would grow in my heart. Only weakness lived there. "I will train with your scholar."

"Excellent. Søren will return with you in the morning. And I will travel to Bhorglid in three weeks' time, at which point we will discuss the treaty once more."

She walked away, Søren following. The silence reigned absolute. Everyone was gone. Including my friends.

I stood alone in the solitude my hands had wrought and wondered if it was worth living another day.

8

Søren

MY BEDROOM WAS ONE OF THE FEW PLACES IN THE KRYLlian palace that was utterly devoid of ghosts.

I pulled off the tunic I'd worn to the event tonight, balling it up and chucking it in the corner. Was I grateful for the silence, or did I hate it? My mood lived in a constant flux, indecisive as I was about the solitude.

I rested my forehead against one carved bedpost and sighed.

The memory of the ball, which had ended in disaster less than an hour ago, tasted like sandpaper. I grimaced. I wanted to force the queen to tell me what she was thinking, making such an offer to Revna—even more, I wanted to know why she hadn't told me beforehand. Hadn't I deserved to know she was tossing me to the wolves? No, apparently not. And now I needed to pack for three weeks in Bhorglid.

Three weeks living in the same space as the woman I love. The one who also hated me.

I'd followed the queen down the halls and around endless corners in silence before finally opening my mouth to ask her what the hell she'd been thinking. But she'd held up a hand to silence me. "Do not question me, Søren." Her voice had an edge to it that I rarely heard, one reminiscent of when she'd caught me with Frode's body. Then, she'd been utterly manic. Now, she vibrated with something I couldn't define. "You are not privy to my mind. And know this—for every secret you try to pry from me, your sister will suffer."

Shoulders taut, I let her go. What was the point of following her if she wasn't going to tell me what she was thinking anyway?

Absentmindedly, I ran my left hand over the scar on my opposite shoulder. I wondered whether the villager I spoke with had left to search for Sonja yet. He'd told me his contacts had brought him word of a traveling caravan of Seeing Ones in Faste, of all places, that included a woman who might very well be my sister. It had taken a bribe more significant than any I'd paid before to convince him to depart this morning to confirm his suspicions.

It's probably not her, I told myself. *You're likely wasting all your money hoping to cut the collar around your neck only to be disappointed.*

But now, even if he did locate her, I wouldn't know. Not until I returned from Bhorglid. The man made a living searching for missing people. He traveled frequently. Would he even be in the village when I returned? Or would I find myself waiting weeks more for news of my sister?

The queen was sending me on a petty errand, one she knew would eat away at me—she'd made that clear when she let slip how much she knew about my relationship with Revna during our time in the prison. Maybe she was trying to distract me. Occupy me with training the princess so I would stop digging for answers about her motives.

She continued to leave for days at a time, always to Bhorglid—per Mira's knowledge. She carried her new sword everywhere with her, fingers running up and down the hilt, caressing it like a lover.

But who had she killed for it? And why did a weapon matter? Especially one that wasn't even made to Anja's specifications?

At least I'd been successful in keeping my search for Sonja under wraps thus far.

I collapsed onto the bed, still half dressed. There would be no sleeping tonight. A regular occurrence, but I'd been hoping to get at least a few hours before leaving for Bhorglid.

My mind spun. Revna hated me. I'd spent the last three weeks trying to force myself to come to terms with it and yet . . .

Seeing it on her face was different. Sharper. Far more capable of causing me to bleed out than when I could push it to the back of my mind and live in the memories and dreams of our short time together instead.

This is the price you've paid for Sonja's safety.

After all, wasn't her safety the reason for everything I did? The thing that made every bad decision worthwhile?

Revna despises you now, I thought. *Are you so sure a fruitless search for your sister is worth every sacrifice you've made?*

I rubbed my palms against my face. It wasn't often these days that I was able to play the scholar instead of the general. I enjoyed the time I had without the mask pressing against my forehead and nose, making it difficult to see and obscuring the world in a haze of gray. My helmet and the light layer of armor I donned while fulfilling my Hellbringer duties on the front lines were tucked deep in the closet, behind a hidden panel. The entire contraption was locked, the key secured on a chain around my neck.

I would need to bring it all with me to Bhorglid. Just in case. I knew the queen would demand it of me anyway—if she decided she needed her Hellbringer at her beck and call, Mira would arrive to retrieve me from Bhorglid and whisk me away without delay. There would be no time to return here and grab the armor from its hiding place.

My mind drifted. Revna had been understandably furious when

the queen proposed her ultimatum. I doubted she had any interest in seeing me, much less training with me.

Even though she desperately needs the help.

I supposed that left me with nothing but thoughts of her in that decadent red dress, looking lovely and pissed off all evening. I suppressed a chuckle. Power suited her. Maybe in another life, one where she forgave me, I could stand behind her. Help her hold on to that power, kill anyone who tried to take it from—

A knock sounded at the door.

Stifling a groan of annoyance, I forced myself off the bed. At least I didn't have to change back into the Hellbringer's uniform. The room had two entrances, one on the west wall and the other on the east, to give the illusion of the Hellbringer and Søren occupying two separate living spaces. The knock had come from the door to my right—Søren's door—so whoever was knocking would expect my face.

But who could possibly have need of a scholar in the middle of the night?

For the briefest flash of a second, I allowed myself to imagine it was Revna on the other side of the door. Her face set in cool determination. I'd let her in and she'd thank me for helping her tonight.

She would tell me she understood my actions that day on the front. And then she would forgive me for my choice.

Another rap of knuckles against the wood called me back to reality. "Coming," I called, careful to keep my voice pleasant. Søren the scholar was thrilled about the chance to travel to Bhorglid. Utterly delighted to study the magic of the Bloodsinger Queen.

Gods, even the thought made me want to run myself through with my own sword.

Instead, I straightened my shoulders, decided it wasn't worth putting on a shirt just to spare whatever servant was there from seeing my bare chest, and opened the door.

I got a single glimpse of Revna's furious features before she drew back a fist and punched me in the jaw.

"*Fuck*." The word was out before I stopped myself, my mask of calm quickly replaced by the Hellbringer's growl as pain exploded. The force of the blow and my surprise sent me stumbling back a step, just enough for her to slide through the doorway and kick the door shut behind her before lunging again.

But her next strike wasn't fast enough, and I reached out a palm to catch her curled hand. My chuckle was genuine. When was the last time someone had managed to make the Hellbringer feel like an eager child?

I knew the answer: three weeks, four days, and one hour ago. When this same woman had truly defeated me in training and I'd known she was ready to win the Trials.

This, I mused as she tried to yank her wrist from my grasp, *is better than the daydream I was having before I opened the door.*

Sparring was nothing but foreplay between her and me. The decision to drop her hand came from a feral part of my brain, the part that couldn't stop imagining all the ways I could pin her down. Ways to make the battle between us last longer, stretch it out another few seconds so I could savor it more.

And gods above, she still wore that sinful red dress. My mouth watered.

The words slipped from me before I bothered to stop them. "I've missed you, too."

She growled, her face set in an expression I knew well on her—hatred. A flurry of blows followed, and despite her speed, I managed to avoid most of them. "Have you been training?" I asked her. "You're faster than when we last fought."

The glare sharpened and I realized my mistake. Our last fight had been on the battlefield shortly before I killed her brother.

She lunged for me again.

We slipped into the dance of war like it was an old, familiar friend. Revna's strikes were precise, and I decided to make it a game—how long could I dodge before she was able to land a blow? She was here to hurt me, make me suffer. I wouldn't let her do me harm, but I had no intention of striking back. Not when we'd already wasted so much precious time fighting.

Besides. I was suffering plenty without her help.

Now well into the center of the bedroom, she pulled a small dagger from an arm sheath—a familiar weapon, one of the pair I'd made for her—and lunged for me again, teeth bared. *Even her rage is beautiful,* I mused, twisting and barely missing the bite of the blade. It was the first time since returning from the front that I'd been calm. She focused me, forced my energy to align myself.

I wanted to spar with her until we both collapsed from exhaustion.

At the thought, I knew it was time to end this. Only one of us was enjoying it, and the rage radiating off her in waves only served to remind me of the things I'd done. The ways I didn't deserve her.

The next time she reached to trip me with her foot, I let her do it, tumbling to the ground as she straddled my ribs and held the knife to my throat. The hem of her dress was torn and it bunched up around her waist, leaving her legs enticingly bare.

We were both breathing heavily, the warm weight of her settling on me and . . .

Well. I missed her in the soul-deep way of her understanding me better than any other person alive, but also in a vividly physical way, a fact becoming more obvious by the second thanks to my now-tenting trousers. I thanked whatever deities were out there that she hadn't straddled my hips instead—if she had, that beautiful fury simmering in her would have turned to disgust.

I could bear her hatred. But her disgust would destroy me.

Her free hand pressed into my shoulder, holding me down. The other trembled, and I wondered vaguely whether the silver had drawn blood yet. "Going to kill me, Princess?"

For a long, long moment that stretched out before us, she stared at her weapon against my throat. I waited for her to snap back, to remind me she wasn't a princess any longer. But a retort never came.

She watched her weapon tremble on my skin, but I knew when her eyes glazed over that she was seeing something different. "Every single part of this," she whispered, "is *your fault*."

I had nothing to say to that. She was right. The queen had kept her plans from me, but Revna wasn't just talking about the next three weeks. I knew she didn't want to hear my excuses, though, so instead of retorting I took the moment to survey her.

Again.

My focus had been locked on her from the moment her delegation rode up to the palace yesterday afternoon. Her hair was still pinned into its elegant style from the ball, though a few strands had escaped. A bead of sweat trailed down the side of her face, and I had the intrusive thought to push up slightly and lick it off—blood from the knife on my throat be damned.

You can't, I reminded myself. *You made your choices and she made hers. And she will never forgive you.*

I thought back to the ballroom. When the bright fire of her anger had dimmed, when her Lurae had released its hold on her, I'd seen what she was hiding. Emptiness. Fear. Desperation. Exhaustion.

Something inside her had snapped. I wondered when it had happened, whether it was my fault or someone else's. I thought about offering to kill them for her, if it was someone else, but held back. More likely than not, I was to blame—and I couldn't fall on my own sword until I'd found my sister, at least.

The same yawning chasm of devastation was beginning to open in her eyes again now. I could see it as her hand shook.

"I must say, this dress isn't as fun as the one you wore yesterday."

I let the words linger as I spoke them, taunting. "I enjoyed seeing so much of you on display."

Revna growled and a spark of anger returned to her gaze.

That's my girl. The thought slid, unbidden, into my mind. *Fight back. Don't let it bury you.*

The knife bit into my neck, and I inhaled sharply at the sting. *That* had most certainly drawn blood. "You planned this," she snarled, leaning closer. "You asked her to let you train me so you could rub it in my face."

I blinked, surprise keeping my face expressionless. "No."

"You're *lying*."

All right. Enough of this.

She was angry and, as I'd told her over and over again, an angry opponent is a sloppy one. It took no more than three seconds to grab her wrist, twist it until she inhaled sharply and dropped her knife, and push her over, rolling until I was the one holding her down.

With one hand, I pinned her wrists above her head as she thrashed. She was strong, and I found myself grateful that training had been the only thing capable of distracting me from thoughts of her after that fateful day on the front. She seemed surprised, like she hadn't realized I was letting her take control of the situation earlier.

Still, the feeling of her body beneath me stirred the desperate *want* I'd barely managed to force behind bars. Especially when her eyes flicked down my bare chest and then back up. So quick I could have imagined it—but I knew I didn't.

Do not, I ordered myself, *think of the last time you had her in this position.*

"I have told you many times," I said, allowing a hint of something deadly to creep into my voice. "I am not a liar."

"Maybe not," she snarled. "But you're certainly an excellent lapdog."

Now she wasn't the only one who was angry.

I released her and stood, crossing my arms. "If you're only here to toss insults around, then go. Despite your insistence that I'm lying, I want this arrangement as little as you do."

Her answering laugh was cold. "You think I'd ever believe that? You're going to turn me into a monster. Again."

Ah. So that's what this was really about. I watched her move to her feet. "You didn't mind the monstrousness, as I recall." I stepped closer to Revna, until she was forced to tilt her head back to keep my gaze. "Is your country not worth your destruction? If you won't become a monster for them . . . then what was the fucking point of winning the throne?"

She shoved me away, her jaw grinding, and I saw the shine of tears in her eyes. *Damn it. You swore you weren't going to hurt her again. That you were going to soften your sharp edges for her.*

Stepping back, I ran the fingers of both hands through my hair, tugging at the roots. It grounded me a bit. "You're backed into a corner, Princess." I glanced toward the door, double-checking it was shut. "The queen is not an easy person to get along with. She is the one with the power in this scenario. You're a new ruler, dealing with civil unrest and a brand-new Lurae."

"One you told her was out of control." Her jaw tightened.

"It wasn't like you were keeping it hidden," I said with a shrug. I'd certainly seen the obvious signs. The queen must have been thinking it too, considering she'd halted all negotiations after the disastrous dinner.

Like this—back to the wall, dagger hanging limply at her side—Revna was a shadow of herself. This was not the Revna I knew. The fiery princess determined to save her people was gone, replaced by a defeated shell.

I did this to her. The knowledge ate at me.

She frowned, and her gaze moved to me. "You don't know the queen's plans. You don't know how she discovered my Lurae. Am I to assume you also don't know about the prophecy, then?"

I wanted to laugh. The exhaustion of endless nights without sleep was getting to me, and I suddenly felt it weighing down my bones. I sat heavily on the edge of the bed, elbows on my knees, and gestured to the chair beside my desk. "Will you sit? I haven't heard anything about a prophecy."

Revna hedged, glancing back and forth between the door and the chair. Finally, she stepped forward and took a seat. My shoulders relaxed. Hers remained taut.

"There was a Seeing One released from prison in Bhorglid, after the Trials," she said. "Their name was Valen. They said they had a vision that you and I were going to fulfill the very first prophecy together."

When she lapsed into silence, I prodded. "And? What does that mean?"

She glared. "If I knew, I would tell you. The first prophecy was lost to time—the only people who have heard it were the Seeing One who gave it and Arraya. It was hundreds of years ago."

"Arraya?" I frowned, searching my memories of endless history book pages for why the name was so familiar. "She was the wife of that revolutionary, wasn't she? The ones who founded Bhorglid."

"Yes. She and her husband, Callum, were the first to believe that Lurae and Nilurae should have different statuses. Most of what the priests taught came from them." She shrugged. "Valen said she kidnapped the first Seeing One—Tam—and kept them locked away until they revealed the prophecy to her. At which point . . ."

"She promptly killed them." It's what I would have done. "I had no idea there was any kind of prophecy about us."

Revna exhaled deeply and slid back, closing her eyes and tilting her head to the ceiling. With her face turned toward the light, the dark shadows beneath her eyes were plain to see.

Had she been sleeping? Or were her thoughts as turbulent as mine?

I traced my gaze across her face. The bottom edges of her scars touched just past her cheekbones. They were still a dark red, clearly not finished healing. I hadn't seen them before yesterday—when I'd sat a silent vigil in her room three weeks ago, waiting for her to wake and either confirm or deny her new powers, they had been covered in bandages.

Somehow, the scars made her more beautiful. Testaments to her ferocity. Surely Volkan had offered to heal them for her. That they existed meant she'd refused him. She'd chosen to let the Trials leave marks.

Upon closer inspection, her dress was tighter around her waist than I'd expected. It hugged her curves, which were smaller than I remembered. Not sleeping or eating well, then. One of her hands twitched, then curled into a fist. That was a familiar movement. I forced down a fond smile as I watched her mouth and, just as I expected, she began chewing on her lip.

Predictable as ever.

Slowly, she opened her eyes and stood. "If you have no useful information, then I'll be going."

"And if I do have useful information?"

She glared. "Then stop being an asshole and speak up."

I fought a smile. Now was certainly not the time for it. Especially not when I had an idea. "There may be a way to learn what this prophecy said. I've found mentions in books about a place that's . . . well, magical is the only way to describe it. It holds memories, ones entirely lost to time. Whether or not it truly exists is debatable, but on the off chance it does, it's our best bet at hearing exactly what Tam said about our futures."

“Where?”

“Deep in the northern wastes.”

Surprise flitted across her face almost imperceptibly. She rubbed a hand over her forehead. For the first time, I wished my Lurae was mind-reading.

After a few moments of silence, she stood and crossed to the door.

“Revna.” She paused with her hand on the knob but didn’t look back. “The queen is not kind. The cost of this alliance is high—but you do not want her as an enemy.”

My princess scoffed. “If you really cared, you would do more than offer useless words of advice.”

She slammed the door behind her as she left.

9

Revna

WE RETURNED TO BHORGLID WITH LITTLE FANFARE.

Our small delegation stood in the courtyard of the castle silently. Søren lingered on the edge of the group, unwilling to step between us. The events of the night before weighed heavy on everyone, and I refused to make eye contact with my friends.

I knew what I'd find on their faces. Fear. Disgust. Things I couldn't bear.

Arne finally spoke up. "Allowing him to stay here is a bad idea."

Søren clenched one hand into a fist. He had a bag of his things slung over one shoulder. I wondered if the mask was in there or if he'd left it at the Kryllian palace. Surely he remembered who Arne had once been to me—he'd been spying on us at the Sharpened Axe the night we discovered Arne had been conscripted.

The urge to use my Lurae to humble my ex-lover was surprisingly distant. I hadn't slept at all the night before, my mind turning the explosion of my magic in the ballroom over and over until there was nothing left but my grief and shame. And when I needed relief, I'd instead been assaulted by memories of Søren's body beneath me while I held my knife to his throat.

Maybe I should have killed him last night, I thought. But even that brought me only exhaustion. I had chosen to let him live, and I'm sure I would regret it later.

I spoke aloud and signed, "You're right. It's only fair if one of our people stays in Kryllian for three weeks, too. I take it you're volunteering?"

He glowered. Astrid huffed a laugh, and I thought I caught the hint of a smirk as it disappeared from Søren's face. Freja waved a hand to catch our attention. "None of us are happy about this, Arne. But unlike our previous monarch, Revna is actually doing what's best for the people. Including you."

"He's a spy!" Arne was growing incensed now, his anger spilling from him. "He's here to report back to his queen on what he learns about our plans, our people. So that when she decides to bring her army in again and truly decimate us this time, we won't have any hope of resisting."

"Maybe you're right," I snapped, my patience fraying. "But our options were war right now, *today,* or the possibility of war in the future. If you enjoyed your time on the front lines so much, you're welcome to go back to the wastes."

His lip curled. "You're responsible for everyone in Bhorglid now. And you'd rather take your power and reign supreme than make the smart choice."

"Go home, Arne," I said. Threads began to wind their way through the air, and I blinked, hoping they would disappear. No luck. "I don't need your gratitude or your understanding, much less your approval. I earned this power when I killed my brothers."

He shook his head. But as he started walking away, he called back, "Your throne means nothing if the people don't want you sitting on it."

"That," Volkan sighed, "went about as well as I expected." He readjusted his bag and clapped Søren on the shoulder. "Let me show you to your room."

When the two were out of earshot, Freja turned to me. She wouldn't meet my eyes either, and I kept my own gaze glued to her hands while she signed. "Arne is right—the scholar is probably a spy."

I thought about laughing, but couldn't muster the energy. "Of course he's a spy."

I'd like to see you choose, I wanted to scream. *Train again with the man you thought you loved or send your people to war. I'm in an impossible position, and the only way to save us all is by sacrificing my own heart.*

Freja just said, "Be careful. Don't tell him too much."

Silently, I gathered my own belongings and stepped toward the castle doors. Freja wouldn't believe my assurances, but she had no need to worry.

I didn't plan on telling Søren anything.

An hour later, when he knocked on my door, calling for me to join him to start training, I stared at my ceiling and said nothing.

⬩ ⬩ ⬩ ⬩ ⬩

FIRELIGHT LIT THE DIM SPACE. WHEN I LOOKED UP AT THE CEILING of the cave, wiping sweat off my forehead, the hole in the rock gave space to the starry night sky. Exhaustion weighed down my bones, but this wasn't any typical tiredness. Sleep would not be enough to solve it, I knew.

Shaking my head, I went back to the task at hand. Metal glowed on the table in front of me, and I adjusted my grip on the knife I held. With a deep breath, I sliced across my forearm until blood pooled and then dripped onto the hot metal with a sizzle.

Distantly I knew—I was dreaming. This wasn't real. But I had no control over the motions of my body. Who was I? And why was I in the forge the Hellbringer had brought me to during our time together?

I bandaged the wound and pulled on heavy, heatproof gloves. Then, I hefted a hammer and began to shape a weapon. The blade came together over long hours that felt like minutes. When it cooled, I studied it with a sigh.

"A blade to slay an immortal," I murmured aloud. Morning sunlight glinted on the sword. "A Soulcleaver."

Internally, I paused. I'd seen that blade before. It belonged to the Queen of Kryllian.

Was I dreaming of the queen?

Three pounding knocks against my door startled me awake. I sat up in bed with a gasp, sweat pouring down my face. The percussive beat of the sound sent throbbing pain through my skull in time with my Lurae song. Threads spiraled out in every direction, coating the whole room in gold. "Revna!" a gruff voice called. "Open this gods-damned door!"

My hands trembled. No time to think over the dream, only to reassure myself: it wasn't real, I was safe in the castle. I shook my head, as if it would dislodge the sight of the cave behind my eyes. The only thing it truly accomplished was making a few threads disappear while the others blurred together in a tangled mess.

"Coming," I called, startled by the hoarseness of my voice.

Quickly, I threw on a tunic and pants, stepping into my boots but not bothering to tie the laces before I opened the door. It caught on the chain lock. I'd installed it myself after waking up to find the Hellbringer watching me while I slept. Had installed them on all the doors in the castle, actually. Something to keep my hands busy while my Lurae ate away at me from the inside.

Halvar glared at me from the hall. "Let me in, Revna."

The dread that made its home in my stomach reared its head,

accompanied by Mother's lullaby. Talking to Jac was the last thing I wanted to do right now—especially when I knew exactly what he was going to say. But it was impossible not to hear the threat underneath those words, one he intended to follow through with if I didn't oblige him now.

I swallowed and unlatched the door. The moment it closed behind him, Jac shed Halvar's skin. The disguise dripped from him quickly, erasing inches of height and broadness in moments. "I can't do this anymore. You have to tell her the truth."

"I can't." I didn't meet Jac's eyes. We'd been back from Kryllian for four days. I'd spent most of those hiding in my room, ignoring everyone who knocked or pandering with poor excuses. Jac knew what had happened in Kryllian, knew of the queen's ultimatum. He wasn't happy about either. "I promised you this would be over when the treaty was signed."

His hands curled into fists, and it was almost relieving. Anger was a swift, sharp blade. It wasn't the dull, never-ending pain of disappointment or sorrow. I roused a bit in response to it.

"You're a coward. The only reason you haven't confessed is because you can't stand the idea of what Freja will think of you. This isn't about the good of the Nilurae anymore. In fact, I wonder if it ever was."

"You weren't there that night," I said, forcing my voice to stay calm. My Lurae rushed under my skin, held back by sheer force of will. "Can't you see it in Freja's and Volkan's faces? In Arne's face? They *fear* me. Without Halvar on my side to convince the Nilurae they can trust me, we might as well set the treaty on fire right now."

Jac ran his hands roughly through his hair, pulling at the roots. "Arne is suspicious, Rev. He knows something strange is going on. He can tell I'm not Halvar."

"What?" My chest tightened. "That's . . . Has he said something?"

Jac shook his head. "Not yet, but he's been asking questions. Constantly wants to reminisce about the past, about things he and Halvar did together. But he's testing me. Waiting for me to slip up. Freja hasn't figured it out, so I doubt he has either, but it's only a matter of time." My brother's anger faded faster than it had arrived. "I don't want to do this anymore. This isn't what I came back for."

I swallowed the guilt tightening in my throat. "I swear to you, this won't be forever."

He laughed, a harsh, vicious sound. "Won't it? Because you've had a magic tutor sitting in our library for four days. One whose sole purpose is to train you to use your Lurae. And how many times have you worked with him?"

I looked away, unable to meet his eyes. More than anything, I wanted to tell Jac who Søren was—why I was really avoiding him. But no one could know. It was dangerous for Volkan to know the truth, even. No matter how much the Nilurae hated me now, it was nothing compared to what would happen if the people found out the Hellbringer was in their midst.

I nearly chuckled thinking about it. A queen couldn't unify our people, but a common enemy just might.

When I didn't reply, Jac shook his head, allowing his eyes to drift closed. I wondered what he was holding back. "I'm not physically capable of doing this for much longer, even if I did want to. Moping in bed isn't an option anymore. Get off your ass and go find the scholar."

He turned to leave. "Jac," I called. My brother hesitated, arms crossed. "I'm sorry. It was unfair of me to ask this of you. I mean it when I say the truth will come out once the treaty is signed. And then you're free to live your life. I won't ask anything more of you."

My eyes burned, but I didn't want to cry in front of him. I massaged my temples, hoping to push back the emotion until he left. My head throbbed. But when the door didn't creak open, I glanced up. "What—*oof.*"

Jac's arms wrapped me in a hug so tight, I could hardly breathe. He was still taller than me without his disguise, but it shocked me to discover my feet dangled a couple of inches from the ground. Had he grown that strong, or was I truly wasting away so significantly?

"You can't do this by yourself," he said. His words were shaky, and when I wrapped my arms around him to reciprocate, I wondered if a stray tear was making its way down his cheek, too. "We're all on your side. But we can only help you if you let us in."

I nodded, pressing my face into his shoulder. After a long moment, he set me down and stepped back. The transformation took over him again, and Halvar smiled down at me. "Go find the scholar before he gets bored," he said, ruffling my hair as he strode to the door. "The man must have read our entire library by now."

10

Revna

IN THE FIRST DAYS OF MY REIGN, WHEN I'D BEEN CONFINED TO my bed healing from the injuries on my face, Volkan had declared he was going to read to me. He'd returned from the library with a sour expression, then told me with disdain, "Your kingdom's library is abysmally small."

I hadn't seen any other libraries, so I believed him. But now, looking into the room of books as Søren had left it, it became abundantly clear just how small it must be in comparison to a typical library.

The shelves were empty. The plush rug on the ground was nowhere to be seen. Instead of its usual dust-covered, practically untouched state, every book had been placed in disorganized piles on the ground.

Søren was bent over the table in the center of the room, which was also entirely covered by books. Several were flipped open to various pages. As I watched, he ran a finger along a line of text in one, mouthing the words silently to himself as he read. Apparently unsatisfied, he pursed his lips, flipped it closed, and then tossed it across the room. It let out an echoing *thud* where it landed.

It was the most content I'd ever seen him.

Still, I furrowed my brow. Was this really the same man who had spent a significant portion of the last seven years living in an abandoned prison, the organization of which was utterly pristine? There, everything had its place.

This was utter chaos.

You don't really know him, I reminded myself, bringing a hand up to rub against my chest at the pain the thought caused. *You knew two versions of your enemy. Both of those versions were masks. He's a good actor.*

I tightened my grip on the dagger I held. The carvings in the wood handle grounded me when I ran my thumb over them. They were the same weapons he'd made for me all those weeks ago. Given to me as a gift. I couldn't bring myself to get rid of them, but I'd convinced myself it was because they were so perfectly balanced. Not for any other reason.

Learning from him—*again*—was the last thing I wanted to do. Especially knowing why he had killed Frode. Perhaps he'd told me the truth because he thought it would bring me closure, thought I would forgive him. The opposite was true. No motivation could be enough to justify his actions.

I bit my lip. Maybe stabbing him was the easier route after all. Maybe the treaty was too far gone to be worth this salvage attempt.

The thought of Jac's and Volkan's expressions if they discovered I had killed the man had me sheathing the weapon again.

Søren was perusing a perilously tilting stack of books on the other side of the room. He picked one up and blew, a cloud of dust falling from the cover. He didn't look over to me as he called, "Are you going to stand there skulking forever, Princess?"

I gritted my teeth. *Do not stab him. No matter how badly you want to.*

"It's 'Queen' now," I said. "You will refer to me as such."

He raised a single dark eyebrow. "Whatever you say."

I stepped around the books until I reached the table, pulled out one of the unused chairs, and sank into it with my arms crossed. "You've been busy." The words carried all the bitterness I felt.

Søren shrugged, flipping through the pages. "Yes. So have you, it seems."

My face heated. "I have a kingdom to run. I can't spend every moment at your beck and call."

Why did his smirk have to be so damn devastating?

"What are you doing?" I asked, hoping the interruption would distract me.

"Researching," he said. "I mentioned finding information about a place in the wastes that might be able to show us the prophecy you spoke of. And I have a theory about it."

When he stopped, I raised a brow. "Care to share?"

"Well." He sat back, intertwining his fingers. "Assuming this place truly exists . . . What if the queen knew about it, too? And what if she went there?"

I had no idea where he was going with this. My expression must have given it away, because he continued when I didn't reply. "She could have heard this prophecy, too. And if it's a prophecy about you and me, then it may have made mention of your Lurae."

"How likely is it that this place is real, though?" I frowned. "Magic in the wastes is unheard of. We are people with magic—there have never been magical places."

"According to us. But the priests used to teach about them, though the doctrine seems to have been phased out over time." He pulled a book from a stack behind him. "This is a volume I brought from Kryllian. We don't have much information on Bhorglid's history there, but it's mentioned occasionally in this volume."

He held out the book to me. I didn't move. *Think of everything he's done,* I reminded myself. *Why should you trust him?*

Finally, he pulled it back and set it on the stack again. "Should I assume you're here to train, then? Or is the plan to let your Lurae continue to fester and hope the queen doesn't notice when she arrives?"

The very Lurae he mocked me for surged with my temper. Gods, training with him was going to be miserable. But Jac's fury looped over and over in my mind, so I bit my tongue.

He tossed the book he was holding in the direction of the other he discarded earlier, then opened another to begin flipping through its pages. The familiar furrow between his brows spoke to his concentration. The only other times I'd seen that expression were when he was cooking and when he was between my—

No, I ordered my thoughts. *Don't even start.*

The determination that had pulled me from my bedroom mere minutes ago was swiftly transforming into irritation. I was remembering all over again what a terrible idea this was. This man, no matter how innocent he looked without the mask, had murdered my brother. He'd told his ruler of our forbidden relationship, simply to gain the upper hand over me.

My knee bounced beneath the table and I crossed my arms. "Are you going to teach me anything, or am I going to spend all afternoon watching you desecrate literature?"

Søren closed the book abruptly. "First, the majority of what this library contains is utter garbage. Very disappointing. Second, there's something we have to do before we can begin working on your Lurae."

He paused, waiting for me to ask. I narrowly avoided rolling my eyes. "What's that?"

I expected him to say something about traveling to the wastes.

After all, he'd been insistent the other night that we would find answers there. But instead, his grin held the edge of the predator I'd come to know. It lurked beneath his surface at all times, no matter how innocent he looked.

"We spar."

◆ ◆ ◆ ◆ ◆

THE COURTYARD WAS FRIGID. WIND WHIPPED A FEW ESCAPED strands of my braid in front of my face, but I held steady. Aloisa's hilt felt like home in my palms, the steady weight of the blade slowing the song in my mind. I stared at the unmasked general across from me, holding his own weapon—though the sword was different from the one he kept on the battlefield—with a single purpose fueling me.

I was going to kick Søren's ass.

He lunged into motion, slicing a direct line toward my face. I brought Aloisa up in a quick parry, spun on the ball of my foot to get out of range of his swing, and then stepped inside his guard for my own strike. From there, we moved seamlessly into the dance of war.

My mind quieted, the only thing inside me the desperate need to *win*. He'd spent every second of our relationship holding the upper hand thus far. Even when I'd finally become nearly his equal in fighting capabilities, he still had his secrets.

It was my turn to be the one in power.

I swung, forcing him to parry over and over. My arms burned from the effort. But no matter how many times I tried, I couldn't put a scratch on him.

I gritted my teeth. The next time our blades collided, I stepped in closer and kicked out sharply with my foot. He jolted backward, barely escaping a boot to the groin, and huffed out a shocked laugh.

He's laughing at you, my thoughts snarled. *He thinks you don't stand a chance.*

The lullaby's opening notes strummed.

"When you start training your Lurae," he said, still managing to block each of my strikes as he spoke, "you'll learn that the rules of using magic are much the same as the rules of swordfighting. And the first is one you should already know: never fight angry."

I scowled, my anger only increasing. How *dare* he tell me not to be angry? I'd been through far too much. If anyone had earned the right to their fury, it was me.

I struck again, speeding up. The song in my head took on a swift tempo, one I matched with every swipe. But while my arms screamed and sweat poured down my face in rivers, Søren barely appeared winded.

The first flakes of gentle snow peppered his hair. "Seems to me," I snarled, my next strike far more heavy-handed than the ones before it, "I'm the only one who's as angry as they should be."

Silence followed, interrupted only by the clash of blades and the song. It built and built, the pressure in my head nearly unbearable. Finally, Søren stepped back, shaking his head and letting down his guard. A signal that the battle was over.

"Your anger is a shield," he said softly, running a hand through his hair. "It's easier to be angry than it is to be hurt. Than it is to be sad. But your anger makes you volatile, Revna. It will be your downfall if you aren't careful—if you let your anger remain a shield instead of using the blade of what you really feel."

My Lurae erupted.

Threads spiraled, and with a single tug I had Søren on his knees, his head tipped back to the sky, exposing his throat. My hand shook with rage as I held Aloisa's sharpened edge to his neck. "Stop it," I hissed. "At least my anger gets me out of bed in the mornings. At least it keeps me from falling on my own sword."

He opened his mouth to speak but I shook my head sharply, silencing him. "You think I'm volatile?" I demanded. "It doesn't matter if my magic destroys me. Because you *already did*."

For a long moment, he didn't answer. When he finally dragged his eyes to mine, he said, his voice low, "I just don't want to see everything you've worked so hard for destroyed. You nearly died for this throne."

My breaths came in sharp gasps. My lungs refused to fill fully.

"You can kill me if you need to," he whispered. The snow on his face had melted, leaving a thin sheen of wetness across his cheekbones. "It's okay if you do. I understand."

The thread connecting us moved, slithering up his chest to wrap around his throat.

Pull, the song crooned. *Snap his neck. Make it quick. Or suffocate him, force him to die slow.*

I stepped back. Aloisa's blade thudded against the nearly frozen ground. Frode's face flashed behind my eyes.

He would tell me not to. He would want me to control my Lurae.

Frode would remind me that so many had died for me to sit on the throne. That I'd lost a part of myself trying to become queen, too. He'd say the scars on my face meant something, but only if I kept living.

Only if I kept trying.

Slowly, painstakingly, I pulled the thread back from its vise grip on Søren's throat.

He relaxed and I stepped past him, back to the castle. "Meet me out here in the morning," he called after me. "Not for sparring—we can start working on your Lurae."

I paused, not turning around when I called out, "Why did you bury him?"

Silence.

"Nobody deserves to waste away out there," he said finally. "Least of all a good man."

I made it to the solitude of my bedroom before the shield of my anger shattered. And the blade of my grief and loneliness left me curled in the fetal position on the floor, gasping for breath between my sobs.

11

Søren

When Mira sat down next to me on one of the bigger pieces of rubble that used to be Bhorglid's main temple, I heard the frown in her voice as she asked, "What, exactly, did that statue do to you?"

I huffed a laugh and rubbed my eyes. The dark circles had become more pronounced in the week since arriving in Bhorglid. Sleep had been difficult to come by in Kryllian and on the front lines—it was nearly impossible to sink into slumber here. My thoughts spun circles in my mind at all hours, stretching from Sonja to Revna to . . .

I swallowed and looked back up at the statue.

There had been more sculptures before the rebellion, I knew. The rubble contained a fair number of disembodied heads, lone hands, and single eyes staring into nothingness. But the one in the center, of the goddess Aloisa, still stood.

And I recognized her.

When I'd come to Bhorglid on surveillance missions before, I'd seen the towering figures. But my focus had always been elsewhere, never on the details of their faces. When I'd come out three days ago to meet Mira in the city center for my first report to the queen, I hadn't been able to stop staring at the carved stone.

It had to be a coincidence. That was the only way this was possible. Goddesses weren't real, and even if somehow they were, they didn't waste their time with lost little boys wandering around in the isolation of the northern wastes.

"Do you think they modeled those after real people?" I asked. Mira raised an unimpressed eyebrow and I sighed. "I knew someone who looked just like that statue once."

She studied my face, then moved her gaze to the tall mass of rock in human form. When she looked back at me, her eyes narrowed. Mira was unreadable to most, but I'd known her long enough to see what she wore so clearly on her face: concern. "Probably. Would be difficult to sculpt a face from nothing."

I nodded. The woman I saw in Aloisa's face had likely lived here at one point. That was the only explanation. Perhaps she'd been close with the sculptor, and they'd chosen to model the goddess of the soul after her.

Didn't make the experience any less eerie, though.

"Report?" Mira asked, bringing the conversation back to safer territory.

I stood. "Let's walk while we talk."

There were plenty of people out and about tonight, just as there had been three nights ago. People we didn't need overhearing our conversation. The surge of nighttime activity still puzzled me, despite Volkan's explanation. "They think it's *warm,*" the prince had groaned, wiping a faux tear. "A true tragedy."

He was right—it wasn't warm, not at all. But Mira and I were still forced to cut down the occasional alley, making my report choppy and far longer than usual.

"You say Revna is making progress," Mira said. "What does that mean? The queen is going to ask me for details."

I ran a hand through my hair. The queen would be displeased if she knew how little I'd been working with Revna. After our disastrous sparring match the other night, we'd moved into simple breathing exercises, intended to help her learn to calm her mind, while I waited for her to decide whether it was worth traveling to the wastes to look into my lead on the prophecy. She was taking well to the practice.

But the queen would expect her to be nearly a master by now. Clenching my teeth did nothing to relieve my frustration. What had the woman really expected? Choosing me for this role was nothing more than a way for her to exert her dominance over me. But Revna hated me, and learning to use your magic from someone you didn't trust took far more time and energy than necessary.

"Tell her Revna is making the expected progress necessary to have her Lurae suitably mastered in two weeks," I said.

Mira scowled. "Søren. I can't keep covering for you on everything. You know that."

I crossed my arms. "You can, and you will. I know you told the queen about my relationship with Revna."

Mira blinked, her eyes widening slightly before she managed to school her expression into her typical glare. "So what if I did?"

"It wasn't your information to give." I tried not to let my voice slip into a snarl, but gods it was difficult. "She's using it against me, you know. It's the whole reason I'm here and not in Kryllian."

"I was doing the right thing." She crossed her arms. "You were distracted. You stopped paying attention to the people around you. She isn't good for you, Søren. You should be thanking me."

I curled my hands into fists, nails biting into my palms. "You know the queen is using us both. We've been her pawns throughout the war. I treat you like a sister—I'm loyal to you. Was it too much to ask you to come to me first?"

"You don't treat me like a sister," she scoffed. "You'd never truly disobey orders for me. Not when Sonja is out there somewhere."

Guilt struck me like an arrow. She was right. Sonja had been my priority for years, even though she wasn't present. Only now, when Revna was furious with me and Mira's words felt like a slap to the face, did I realize the full scope of the fallout of my actions.

Mira was losing faith in me. Revna had lost her favorite sibling at my hands. I'd done horrible things at the queen's command. All because I couldn't stand the thought of being responsible for Sonja's demise.

Still . . . I was doing as much as possible to find my sister. Mira didn't know that, though. She couldn't know, not unless I wanted to put a target on her back. And after she'd told the queen about my relationship with Revna . . . well, I certainly needed to treat Mira better, but it wouldn't stop me from being wary of sharing sensitive information with her in the future.

I cleared my throat. "Maybe you're right. But being angry at me isn't a good enough reason to put other people in danger."

We stood silently for a few moments, refusing to make eye contact. "Tell the queen her expectations aren't realistic. Training Revna shouldn't be my responsibility in the first place, but asking me to do it in three weeks is just insulting. It's nearly impossible to train anyone to use their magic without years of innate experience behind them."

Mira's shoulders slumped. "You're right. You aren't the one who will suffer for it, though."

I stiffened. "What is she doing to you?"

She shrugged. "The usual. Adding more responsibilities to my list, sending me on pointless errands and acting like the world will fall apart if they aren't completed instantly. Withholding the occasional meal."

If the queen was here right now, I would kill her. The thought was the only thing keeping me sane. Because even if Mira had told her about my relationship, it wouldn't be an issue if the queen weren't holding a noose around all our throats. The reminder was enough to make my frustration with Mira calm for the time being. "Is she still traveling to Bhorglid?"

"Yes." Mira wrapped her cloak more tightly around her shoulders as a gust of wind carried through. "On a near daily basis now. I've been teleporting her to a spot out west, in the hills."

"By the prison." I turned my gaze in that direction, brow furrowed. The buildings around me obscured the prison from view, but it grounded me to imagine it there. "Is there anyone out there with her?"

"Not that I've seen. I drop her off and then she orders me to leave and return at a certain time to bring her back." Mira scuffed one boot against the cobblestones. "It's lonely at the palace without you."

My shoulders sank. "I'm sorry. I'd be there if I had a choice in the matter."

"I know," she said. "It's not your fault."

Silence stretched between us. Perhaps any other friends would have embraced in this moment, but I knew Mira would likely stab me if I tried. So we stared at the sunset-streaked sky above us instead.

Finally, she cleared her throat. "Anything else before I go?"

"I won't be able to report in for a couple of days. Making a trip out of the city for Revna's training." *Hopefully,* I didn't add. *If I can convince her.*

Mira studied me for a long moment. I waited for the inevitable follow-up questions. But instead, she merely said, "Okay. I'll check back in after four days, but won't worry until six have passed."

She teleported away, and once I'd gathered myself I continued my stroll. The palace was warm, but night had fallen. I didn't want to spend hours staring at my borrowed bedroom's ceiling again. The castle was surprisingly devoid of ghosts, though there was one irate former king holed away in the library. So far, he didn't seem to care whether I could see or hear him, which I was grateful for.

What I really needed to do was ask another spirit about the archway. Then, next time I saw Mira, maybe she'd agree to take me back to the wastes. I could figure out what had happened to cause it to disappear for Frode—maybe help him pass on. Burying him didn't feel like quite enough to honor his memory, not when I knew he was stuck out there.

My thoughts continued to wander. When I passed the tavern where Revna had gone months ago—the one where I'd sat in a booth at the back and surveyed the scene as her asshole of an ex shared he'd been conscripted and Freja had been arrested—I wasn't sure what possessed me to push through the doors.

The room bustled, just as crowded as I remembered. Musicians played in the corner, and a few people danced. I recognized their steps as those Revna had taught me one of our nights together in the prison. I turned away.

The man at the counter looked surprised to see me. I ordered a beer, studying him as he prepared it. He was tall, with a graying beard and salt-and-pepper hair pulled tightly back. A few of the strands were braided. "You're Revna's friend, right?" I finally asked.

He chuckled, handing me the frothing mug. "One way of putting it. And you're the scholar." I raised an eyebrow, and he waved a hand dismissively. "The queen has me helping with . . . a lot of things. Says I have a better pulse on the Nilurae sentiment than most people."

I hummed and took a sip of the drink. It took all my effort not to wince at the watered-down taste. "Good to see people looking out for the Nilurae," I offered.

"Someone has to," he said, filling a mug for another customer. "Happy to help her out. Otherwise, the war would still be going and we'd all be starving. Can't have the beer tasting like shit forever."

I laughed.

"Halvar," the man introduced himself, shaking my hand. "Why don't you have a seat? Next round is on me."

I turned to survey the open seating, and my eyes landed on a familiar face. I sat down in a booth, facing Volkan. "What brings you here?"

He smiled. "I could ask you the same thing."

I shrugged. "Just finished making a report to Mira about Revna's progress and wandered in. I know Revna likes it here."

Volkan hummed before taking another sip of beer. He didn't meet my eyes when he said, "She doesn't come around much anymore."

I narrowed my eyes at his tone but couldn't parse it. He offered no clarification. "I'm here keeping an eye on that one," he added, subtly flicking a finger to my left.

When I knew I could do it without seeming suspicious, I turned. Arne was there, bent down over a table, muttering to the two men sitting with him. I held back a groan. "I assume he's telling everyone what a monster Revna is and how I'm not to be trusted."

Volkan set his beer down with a *thud.* "Exactly right."

Halvar stepped up to our table, mug in hand. "Here you are," he said, setting it down in front of me. He glanced at Volkan, stern mouth lifting at the edge. "No interest in mingling with commoners, then?"

Volkan's jaw dropped. "N-no! That's not it at all, I'm trying not to interrupt—"

Halvar barked out a laugh. "I'm just giving you a hard time. Made me chuckle to see the only two foreign nobles hiding out here by yourselves."

He strode back to the counter, wiping his hands on the rag thrown over his shoulder. I eyed my fresh cup, wondering if it was worth drinking. Instead, I said, "Didn't know you had a thing for older men."

Volkan groaned and put his flushed face in his hands.

Halvar's voice joined the fray again. This time, though, he sounded furious. "Can't believe everyone believes that *impostor.*"

I raised a brow at his hostile tone. I hadn't heard him come back to the table. I looked up . . .

And locked eyes with a very incensed ghost.

I froze. The ghost in front of me was Halvar—the same man standing at the counter and whistling while he wiped down glasses. My eyes shot from the ghost to the living man over and over, trying to make sense of what I was seeing.

The spirit realized I had heard him. "You can see me," he whispered, stepping closer. "Can't you?"

Slowly, I nodded.

"Søren?" Volkan asked. "Everything all right?"

"Fine, fine," I said, waving a hand. Something strange was happening here—maybe even sinister—and I needed to figure out what it was. Especially if one of Revna's most trusted friends was involved. Did she know the man behind the bar was a fraud? "I'm going to head back. The noise in here is giving me a headache."

When I stepped around the side of the building, the ghost was waiting for me. I crossed my arms. "How are you here," I demanded, "while you're also in there?"

Halvar scowled. "How can you see me?"

He didn't know who I was—I often forgot when dealing with spirits, since most of the ones I encountered were from people I'd just killed with my helmet on. But it was strangely comforting to know that this man, despite being a confusing contradiction, had no clue I was the Hellbringer. "It's my Lurae," I told him. "Now what the hell is going on?"

He crossed his arms. "The man in there is a fake. A shapeshifter posing as me. And I was murdered by the liar who calls herself queen."

Wait. Revna had killed Halvar?

The pieces all fell together. Surely the one posing as him was Jac, her missing shapeshifter brother. If Revna had killed a friend, it would never have been purposeful. Likely an accident. I tried not to wince at the realization. I was more than intimately familiar with such mistakes. Her failing confidence, her anger—of course, it was all justified. But she was angry at herself. Not just at me.

Halvar continued to rage as I thought. "And no one recognizes the priests are still plotting. They sit in booths and whisper. Plotting to take back their power. But they aren't caught because they can blend in without the veils."

"The priests?" My attention snapped back to the spirit. Alarm built beneath my skin. "What exactly are they plotting?"

"None of it makes sense." Halvar kicked at the side of the tavern, his boot passing through the wall. "They talk about Callum and Arraya—the two who founded Bhorglid on lies—and say they're going to return somehow. The priests are waiting on something, but I can't figure out what."

Volkan had mentioned there was an assassination attempt on Revna the day before their delegation arrived in Kryllian. Perhaps this was related. I tucked the information away mentally. For now, I needed to ask him about another suspicion I'd been harboring. "Are you here because you want to be, or are you unable to pass on?"

The man scoffed. "I wouldn't know how to pass on if I tried. I'm stuck here—can't seem to find any way out."

I swore under my breath. This confirmed my suspicions. The streets of Bhorglid were dotted with dozens of spirits, more than what I'd seen during the days I'd spent here a few months ago doing reconnaissance.

My mind spun. I needed to get back to the library, see if I could find any information on Callum and Arraya that might explain what the priests were waiting for—or perhaps a book with theories on why spirits were unable to pass on.

“I have to go,” I said absentmindedly.

Halvar hollered after me as I rushed back toward the castle. “I want to see the queen pay for her lies, understand?”

I clenched my jaw. A shame my Lurae could get rid of only living people and not spirits.

12

Revna

AFTER ANOTHER SLEEPLESS NIGHT, I WASN'T SURE IF I dreaded seeing the morning light streaming in through the windows or welcomed it. Still, the breathing exercises Søren was teaching me were surprisingly helpful. My Lurae was silent for the first time in recent memory as I descended the staircase and moved toward the castle doors on my way to another session of training with him.

Freja, Astrid, Volkan, and Halvar stood in the foyer. They cut their signing short when they caught sight of me, Volkan's eyes wide enough to tell me whatever I'd walked in on wasn't going to be pleasant.

The silence in my head ended as swiftly as it had begun. "What's going on?" I asked, signing while I spoke.

It could be any number of things, but I had my suspicions. Upon returning from Kryllian, we'd established a new tax law—one that treated all the citizens as equals instead of favoring the richest of the Lurae and no one else. No outright pushback had happened yet, but

Jac had reported whispers from some of the more influential Lurae in the city. Had they finally organized enough to strike?

But my hunch was incorrect. Volkan scratched the back of his head. "Halvar was just telling us that the Nilurae are . . . unhappy with the news that you are using your Lurae more often."

I heard the truth behind his statement: Arne had been telling everyone what happened at the ball in Kryllian.

I didn't anticipate the realization would sting as badly as it did. I'd expected it, after all. When Halvar frowned, I knew my wince must have been more obvious than I wanted. "They're afraid, Revna," he said gently. "They've been put down by the people in power for so long. They don't know what to do with the little freedom you've given them. They think it's going to be taken from them in an instant, with no warning."

Freja interrupted. "It's time to take this to your father's office."

I followed her gaze behind me. Søren had entered, his steps nearly silent. Now he raised a brow and stepped up beside me with a smirk. "Don't stop the gossip on my account."

His hands moved with his words. I raised a brow. He'd never mentioned knowing sign language.

Freja scowled and crossed her arms. Astrid took a step closer to her. "He's fine," I said. "The queen already knows there's unrest. There's not much more he can take to her that will make things look worse than they already do."

"Debatable," Volkan muttered under his breath.

But Søren spoke up before I could acknowledge the prince's statement. "Revna and I need to make a trip out to the northern wastes anyway. Why don't we take a few days out of the city and train her Lurae while we're gone? Accomplish two things with one trip."

I blinked at him. Volkan said, "What could you possibly need to visit the wastes for?"

"Søren has a potential lead on Valen's prophecy about me . . . and the Hellbringer." I swallowed down the strangeness of speaking about him like he wasn't there, even knowing the truth of the man beside me. I'd been hesitant to agree to such a trip when there was so much work to be done here, in the city, but perhaps Søren was right that a few days away would calm the rising tensions. "The one they told me about before they left to join the other Seeing Ones."

Part of me hoped the mention of Freja's other friend from prison would soften her a bit, but her shoulders grew more tense. "You want to just leave? The Lurae will see it as an opportunity to organize an attack."

Halvar scratched his beard. "I hate to say it, but I agree."

The song in my head sharpened. I threw my hands in the air. "Then what do you want me to do? I'm stuck with this Lurae. There's nothing I can do about that. Either I learn to control it or we have another incident like the one in Kryllian—or the one from the day before. Or—"

Or the one where I killed Halvar. Those were the words threatening to burst from me. I barely managed to hold them back, but the close call sent a strike of pure fear through me.

The threads appeared.

For the first time, though, the sight of them wasn't a stranglehold attempting to drown me. Instead, I noticed the gold and slowed my breathing, forcing my shoulders and my jaw to relax. I instinctively moved into counting a steady rhythm and inhaling along with it.

The way Søren had taught me.

In moments, the threads cooled, their color already lighter. The song in my head dimmed. I tuned back into the conversation as Volkan said, "—be wrong. The Lurae are upset about Revna's rule, but a few days won't create enough of a vacuum for a coup. Especially if we give all of them something to occupy their time."

"What could possibly entertain a city's worth of bored, angry

Lurae?" Astrid asked. She frowned, but I had the sense she was more genuinely curious than upset.

"They're soldiers," Søren signed. "Make them fight."

Freja scoffed. "That's a terrible idea."

"Maybe not," Halvar said slowly. Volkan nodded, running his palm over his mouth. I heard Jac's strategic expertise when Halvar said, "Can we get them to . . . I don't know, compete? Have them spar to keep their training fresh?"

"And only one can be the true victor." Volkan nodded enthusiastically. "You're brilliant."

Halvar's face flushed, but I didn't dwell on it because Freja stomped her foot. "We're going to treat them like children? They have the power to kill us all if we aren't careful, and your solution is to give them a game to play?"

"I know it sounds strange, but they're used to having a routine," I said with an apologetic look. "If they're bored, they'll plan an attack. If they're too occupied with small things to realize the changes we're making are for the better, they won't fight back. There are certainly some who crave power, but most of the Lurae are followers. They care more about feeling secure than anything else."

The next moment happened so quickly it caught me off guard. I reached out to put a reassuring hand on Freja's shoulder.

She flinched away.

My hand froze midair. The next two seconds felt like an eternity of stillness and silence and anguish. The lullaby, once quiet, now roared in my ears like the rush of a river.

I lowered my hand, and the moment passed like a heartbeat. I wondered if I was the only one who had truly witnessed it.

"You really think there's information about this prophecy in the wastes?" Volkan asked.

Søren leaned back against the wall, hands in his pockets. "It's just a hunch, but I feel it's worth looking into. Revna told me the queen knew she had a Lurae even before the Trials, and if she somehow had access to this prophecy it might explain some things."

"Why do you care?" Astrid asked, eyes narrowed. "Anja is your ruler. Shouldn't you care more about pleasing her than anything else?"

Søren offered a serene smile. "I am a scholar. While I live in the queen's court and abide by her rule, I worship only one god—knowledge."

If I hadn't been drowning beneath waves of hurt, Freja's reaction playing on a loop in my mind, I would have rolled my eyes. It was, somehow, the haughtiest thing I'd ever heard Søren say.

"And if you're killed?" Freja asked me, her voice almost as stiff as her posture. "If your scholar is more foe than friend, and you're murdered and left in the snow, what then?"

Had she used that imagery on purpose? Frode's face, frozen in death, flashed before my eyes, and my hands curled into fists so tightly, I wondered if my fingernails had made my palms bleed. But even as the song gained momentum and the threads gained substance, I forced myself to breathe through it.

My body calmed. My magic calmed.

My fury, however, did not.

I knew the grin stretching across my face did nothing to hide the way I was feeling—hurt and frustration and betrayal simmering just beneath the surface. They could hear it all when I snapped, "Then pick some strangers off the street, toss them into the arena, and make them kill each other until the last is crowned queen. Or put the crown on your own head and call it a day. If I'm dead, it won't be my problem anymore."

My best friend and I stared at each other, and when I saw the resentment lurking beneath her façade of indifference, my breath stuttered.

Watch them turn against you, my thoughts whispered. *You've committed to being better and it isn't enough. Freja already hates you.*

"Sorry." I forced a chuckle, looked away from her, put a palm against the back of my head like I could wipe the sinister thoughts away. "Sorry."

"It's settled then," Søren said. "We'll leave first thing in the morning."

⬩ ⬩ ⬩ ⬩ ⬩

THE OTHERS HEADED BACK INTO THE CASTLE, BUT I LEFT THROUGH the front doors. I took my time descending the mountain path until I found the familiar patch of slightly trampled foliage that marked the way to the small clearing where Arne, Freja, and I had once practiced our swordfighting together.

Every step weighed more than the last as I replayed the moment stuck on repeat in my mind. When Freja had flinched away from my touch.

She was afraid of me too, now. They all were.

And they should be. These thoughts weren't tainted by the too-quick breaths and flickering threads of my Lurae. They were entirely my own, plucked from a place in my chest that ached and ached and wouldn't stop. *You're afraid of yourself.*

I stumbled into the clearing and fell to my knees. The afternoon sun cast its pale glow over me. Was there no way to sink beneath the surface of the earth until everything had gone dark and quiet? Couldn't I suffocate the part of me with a Lurae until I was myself again?

The earth was still damp from the most recent snowfall, though it had all melted away now. I dug my fingers into the dirt, watched handprints appear.

The brush filled with the sound of crashing footsteps and loud swearing. I forced my expression to neutrality and stood up, dusting my palms off as I did. The clearing was no longer my secret—Søren had insisted we needed to train somewhere off the castle grounds, where I wouldn't be distracted by the occasional ogling passerby. I'd begrudgingly agreed.

So we practiced here.

And afternoons were our practice time. I'd been headed this direction anyway when I ran into the group in the foyer. It made sense he had followed me here.

Finally, the Hellbringer pushed through the last of the foliage. Søren glared. "The moment we get back, I'm clearing that path."

Right. Because in the morning, we were leaving for the wastes again. The thought made me nauseous. Several days alone with the Hellbringer. Here, his presence was bearable. We were nearly always surrounded by people, our training the only real time we spent alone. And it was easy to think of practicing my Lurae as nothing more than a professional collaboration.

Solitude in the wastes was another story entirely.

I didn't have the energy to fight with him. "Sure."

"Before we start, there's something we should discuss," he said. "I heard a concerning rumor when I was down at the Sharpened Axe last night."

I narrowed my eyes. "What rumor?"

Søren glanced around, despite already knowing we were alone, then lowered his voice. "That the priests are still in the city. They're unrecognizable without the veils, and apparently they're meeting in the tavern, plotting something."

I stiffened. "We ran the priests out of the city."

But even as I said it, I wondered. I hadn't been there when Halvar led the charge that sent the Holy Order running for refuge. What if some of them had split off and taken shelter, stripping off their robes and becoming as innocuous as the other Nilurae?

I would never have known.

Søren shrugged. "It was only a rumor. I didn't see or hear any of them myself, but the person who mentioned it seemed quite convinced."

I frowned. "Who spoke with you about it?" The Sharpened Axe was a Nilurae haven, and most of the Nilurae were suspicious of newcomers.

"Halvar."

My stomach sank. Jac had told Søren of these rumors, but not me.

Jac doesn't trust you, my thoughts insisted. *And why should he? You've forced him to play this charade for too long. He asked you to tell the truth and you refused.*

Søren spoke softly. "The pub was busy. I'm sure he would have told you himself if he could."

I cleared my throat and tried to wipe the expression off my face. Søren could read me like an open book, and I didn't need anyone else knowing the secret of what had happened to Halvar. Better to keep him in the dark for as long as possible. I pasted a faux smile on my face. "I'm sure you're right. Let's start training."

When we settled in our usual position, cross-legged on the ground and facing each other, I readied myself for the breathing exercises he'd been teaching me. Gods knew I needed them right now. We ran through them over the course of half an hour, and the tension slowly left me. The threads felt close, like they always did, but far less volatile.

But when I moved to stand and leave, Søren shook his head. "Time to take the next step in your training."

My throat tightened. The breathing exercises were simple, easy. They helped take the edge off my Lurae. I hadn't lost control again since we sparred in the courtyard four days ago.

But the queen wanted my Lurae mastered in two weeks. Maybe it was manageable now, but it wasn't mastered. Despite the nerves clawing at me, I nodded. "Okay."

"The first rule is to not fight angry." Søren stretched his long legs out and leaned back on his hands in the grass. The wind caught his hair, and for a moment I wanted to lean forward and run my hands through it. "The second lesson is similar—power is not worth having unless you can control it."

I clenched my teeth until my jaw ached. But before I could snap a retort—because honestly, no insult could have been more pointed than this one—he spoke again. "Most Lurae struggle to control their gifts when they first manifest. It can take years to hold true mastery over them. I'm sure you can remember plenty of instances when your brothers fumbled with their new magic."

"Jac went through a phase where anytime he saw an animal, he'd turn into it on accident. He'd get so excited to see a cat or a dog . . . It was even a chicken once." As I remembered a disheveled young Jac, head hung in despair, cheeks covered in grime after transforming back from being a kitten for several hours, a smile tugged at the edges of my cheeks. "He started covering his eyes when we visited the local farmers as a family that spring, worried he'd see a cow or a duck and be stuck like that for a while."

Søren's chuckle resounded. "I've read records of other shapeshifters having similar issues. Any other instances you recall?"

Memories cascaded through my mind. Finding nine-year-old Björn in minutes during a game of hide-and-seek because the cabinet he hid in had started smoking. Erik breaking Frode's arm during a training session by mistake. Jac transforming into my father while the two of them were mid-argument.

The first time Björn had reached for me, his too-hot palm searing my skin, he had apologized. Less than a year after that, he'd groaned, "Am I just never supposed to touch you again? Grow thicker skin, Revna." Father setting things on fire when he grew angry, the castle workers knowing to keep a full bucket of water in every room of the castle at all times.

"Plenty," I said, not elaborating further.

Søren didn't push. "Right now I want to work on actively choosing to use your Lurae without letting it take control. We're going to practice sensing the heartbeats around you."

I frowned. The nervous edge had brought back the faint hum of the lullaby. Trying to use my Lurae scared me, but besides that . . . "I can sense heartbeats?"

He shrugged. "You should be able to. Your magic is attracted to blood, right? It would make sense. Every Lurae is different, but there are a few basic things they all have in common. For those who can manipulate already existing matter, the simplest task is awareness—sensing that matter in the near vicinity." When I didn't respond immediately, he probed. "What?"

I studied him. "How do you know all of this?"

Søren wouldn't meet my eyes. Were his cheeks turning pink, or was I imagining things? "The scholar title isn't *all* a façade. I've been researching magic for nearly fourteen years. When you used your Lurae on me, after the Trials, I returned to Kryllian and did some research."

I shifted my weight. "The only heartbeat around to sense is yours."

"Yes."

"And what if . . ." My voice trailed off, the steadily increasing tempo of my pounding heart warring to be heard over the song in my mind. If I had a choice in the matter, I'd hand my Lurae away in an instant. The last thing I wanted to do was use it.

As I watched, he lifted a hand, reaching it in my direction before halting it suddenly. When he clenched his fist over one leg, his knuckles were pale.

I opened my mouth and inhaled sharply, the icy air against the back of my throat steadying me. "And what if I kill you?"

I waited for him to smirk, to act like he was immortal. But he didn't. "You won't. I trust you."

I laughed. "A mistake on your part. Can't we just . . . wait until I feel ready for this?"

"You won't ever feel ready." His voice was gentle and I hated it. "We're not manipulating any of the magic yet—just using your Lurae to listen to what's around you. It's entirely safe."

"I get it," I snapped. "But I don't even know where to start. Until now it's been holding everything back until it explodes."

"Start by relaxing and closing your eyes. And then let yourself feel. Your Lurae will naturally guide your awareness to the living things around you."

Relax? Not likely. Not when the thought of feeling the threads connecting me to every living thing around me sent a chill down my spine. *Think of the treaty,* I told myself. *You're doing it for your people.*

I closed my eyes, my surroundings becoming darkness; the only sensations remaining were the cold ground beneath me and the rustling of the wind through the leaves. I took a deep breath in, then let it out slowly.

"Good." Søren's voice was a quiet murmur. "Now allow your Lurae to show you what surrounds us."

I struggled not to tense up again. His voice made me hyperaware of his eyes on me. My mind threatened to slip into the familiar ease of imagining the time we'd spent together in the prison—his arms wrapping warmth around me, his lips on my neck, his low voice in my ear. The lullaby pounded in my head like it sensed my anxiety.

My eyes flew open. "I can't do this."

I pushed to my feet, unsteady. My breathing was fast, like I'd just run a mile, every exhale accompanied by a brief cloud.

I can't do this. I'm going to kill him and it's going to be just like Halvar and then two people I love will be dead by my hand and—

The next thing I knew, the castle stood before me again. Søren was behind me, calling my name, but I ignored him.

You can't do it, my thoughts hissed. *Don't even bother trying.*

I shut myself in my father's office for the rest of the day, grateful for the lock on the door. No matter how many times Søren, Volkan, or Halvar called my name from the corridor, I was able to ignore them.

13

Revna

IT TOOK ME LONGER THAN IT SHOULD HAVE TO REALIZE I WAS hearing two voices coming from the stables.

At first, I genuinely thought I might be hallucinating. My night had involved very little sleep, as usual—but the dream of the boy falling through the ice had returned with a vengeance. Every time I woke from it, I'd calmed myself and managed to go back to sleep. Only to be woken by the same exact dream again. The face of the boy reaching out in desperation before he slipped under haunted me, vivid and bright.

If I wasn't dreaming, I found myself spiraling, caught in the choking fear of what my Lurae was capable of. And knowing I couldn't avoid using it forever if I wanted to do right by my people.

Even now, thinking about trying again had me stiffening. I forced my feet to move, one in front of the other.

But the voices in the stables were not figments of my waning sanity. Despite the early hour, the sun barely peeking over the hills, Søren was not alone in the paddock. I stepped inside in time to see him finish hitching saddlebags to a slate gray mare. The hinges of the door creaked as it swung back into place. Volkan grinned at me from where he leaned against the wall, listening to Søren talk.

"—left to go back to Faste and Sonja waxed poetic for over an hour about how much she hated you," he was saying.

Volkan put a hand over his chest. "I am *wounded*. I did nothing to her!"

"I find that story unlikely," I said. The words escaped before I had the chance to vet them, and I wondered why I felt comfortable inserting myself in what was clearly an attempt to reminisce on better times—times I hadn't been part of. But Søren reached out a hand for my pack and my sword, the smirk he wore so familiar it made my heart stutter, and I relaxed slightly.

Volkan sputtered. "When have I been anything but the pinnacle of decorum to you? And now you're out here insulting me."

"It's far more fun that way," Søren offered, double-checking all the straps on the saddle.

I caught myself staring for too long, the shape of his ass grabbing my attention, and cleared my throat. "I'm sure she was justified. What did you do to her?"

"It was a harmless prank. Emphasis on the word 'harmless,'" Volkan said. His eyes glittered despite his overexaggerated frown.

"Volkan changed out her soap," Søren offered. "Put some kind of dye in it. She was blue for a week before she managed to get it out of her skin."

I couldn't help it—my mouth fell open and I gaped at Volkan. "You call that harmless?"

He threw his hands in the air, rolling his eyes. I could tell he was smothering a grin. "For the record, I was only twelve. How else was I supposed to show off to the pretty boy I'd just met? Thought I was doing him a favor by tormenting his sister on his behalf."

Søren chuckled, and I forced myself not to look at him. I knew his smile like the back of my hand, and was fully aware how quickly it would wipe away the animosity I felt for him. Even now, listening to his voice, falling into the cadence of his teasing, I struggled not to forget the things he'd done.

"Well, how did it end, then? Were you able to convince her to forgive you?" I couldn't say her name aloud—it felt like the first step on a slippery slope of questions I wanted the answers to but had been barred from the right to ask. Anyone hating Volkan felt like an impossibility, though.

But to my surprise, the prince's face fell. "No. I wasn't."

Søren had stilled, hands poised to tighten the saddle. I glanced at him, twisting my hands together. Talking about Sonja, about Volkan and Søren's past relationship and their friendship . . . it was all new territory for me. But in the silence, it was easy to tell I'd made a misstep.

When Søren spoke up, his voice was stiff. He didn't look at either of us. "Between that visit and the next, Sonja became a prisoner."

Volkan clapped me on the shoulder, startling me before I could speak. "I'd better be going. The two of you stay safe, all right?"

I nodded, brow furrowed at the abrupt change in subject. "Of course. Don't let all the soldiers kill each other, okay?"

Søren stepped up next to us and the two men embraced. I turned away, unsure if they wanted a moment of privacy for their goodbyes. Volkan muttered something in Søren's ear. I thought I caught the words *fix things* but it was difficult to tell—either way, Søren just grunted in reply.

When Volkan departed, I looked to Søren. "Is this mount yours or mine?"

His raised eyebrow made my heart sink. "This trip isn't for fun. We can't train if you can't hear me talking to you, so we'll share a mount."

He swung up into the saddle, and my cheeks heated. I turned away. If I didn't look at him, then he couldn't distract me. "That won't be necessary. I'll be able to hear you just fine."

Søren huffed a laugh, devoid of any humor. "You'll also be able to run away from me if you decide you don't like hearing what I have to say. We share the horse or content ourselves with not hearing the prophecy. Your choice."

Heart in my throat, I swallowed. The sound of hooves against the wooden floorboards alerted me to Søren's approach. I didn't turn around, even when the mare pushed her nose against my hair. My hands clenched into fists.

You've already let him teach you magic, I thought. *If you let him step even closer, he'll think you've forgiven him.*

But . . . I swore internally. I needed to know what the prophecy said, and we had no other leads. If my future was intertwined with Søren's, if the queen was using the prophecy against me to sway the treaty negotiations, then gaining knowledge was the best weapon available to me.

Silently, without meeting his eyes, I accepted Søren's outstretched hand and pulled myself up to sit in front of him.

The moment I settled in the saddle, felt him warm against my back, I stiffened. His hands came around me to grab the reins, and I pulled my arms into my chest to keep from touching him.

My traitorous body was more than content. I bit my lip hard until the pain and the copper taste of blood shook me from thoughts of leaning back, resting my head on his shoulder. Relaxing against him, the way I would have a month ago.

Søren had mentioned yesterday that this journey would take us two days of riding. And truthfully, I didn't know if I was capable of remaining strong and resisting his embrace for that long. Not when I was exhausted and frazzled at the edges from lack of sleep and the argument with Freja yesterday.

Have you forgotten the sight of Frode's body, lifeless in the snow? The logical part of my brain was intent to keep me staunchly away from the general behind me. And the other half of my mind asked, *Wouldn't Frode forgive you for letting Søren back in? Wouldn't he understand how desperately you need someone who is on your side and no one else's?*

"Revna." Søren's voice was low and quiet, his breath brushing hot against my neck. "This arrangement is a necessity, nothing more. I will not take advantage of it."

My exhale shuddered through me.

"You're in control here," he continued. I was keenly aware of where the backs of my thighs brushed the insides of his; where my tailbone met his pelvis. I regretted braiding my hair back tight to my scalp—convenient for the ride and baring my neck to his lips. "I won't touch you in any way that isn't necessary unless you ask me for it. Understand?"

Somehow I brought myself back to my right mind. I was grateful for his promise but refused to show it. "If you're anything but a gentleman, I'm perfectly capable of sticking a dagger where it hurts."

The huff of his laugh vibrated slightly in his chest, and I felt it through my entire body. He nudged the horse into a canter.

I pursed my lips. This was going to be a long ride.

◆ ◆ ◆ ◆ ◆

WE SPENT AN HOUR IN TENSE SILENCE BEFORE SØREN FINALLY spoke. "Ready to try listening for heartbeats again?"

I gritted my teeth. "No. Not when it puts your life at risk. And the horse's life, for that matter—what if I kill her by accident and we're stranded in the middle of the wastes?"

"Unlikely." I heard the smile in his voice, and irritation crept up my throat. "But not an invalid concern. We still need to practice, though, so . . . what if I made you a wager?"

I furrowed my brow. "This isn't a joke."

"I'm not joking."

The utter unfairness of the situation hit me like a shock of lightning. I was barely managing to hold my kingdom together at the seams. The man who killed my brother wasn't just my teacher, but my singular traveling companion. I hadn't slept more than three hours a night in weeks. And he had the audacity to offer a *wager* and think it would be enough to tempt me into using my magic?

Hell no.

I twisted in the saddle to face him, seething. "Fuck you."

Søren's lips tilted up into an infuriating smirk. "I did say you would call the shots on touching."

I wanted to pull my hair from my scalp. Jump off the mare and run into the woods. Anything to get away from him.

"This is *not funny*."

"I didn't say it was."

"My Lurae is *dangerous*."

"I know it is."

"I've killed people, S—you asshole!" Gods be damned, why were my eyes filling up with tears now?

His eyes, the dark gray irises still more beautiful than they had any right to be, softened. "I have, too."

That stopped me. My breath hitched in my lungs. I couldn't—*wouldn't*—let myself cry. Not in front of him.

He took my silence as an invitation to keep talking. "Any Lurae can be dangerous. But to have one that manipulates life and death, the way ours do?" Søren shook his head. "I understand more than you think. I'm not trying to force your hand. But three weeks is not nearly long enough to accomplish what the queen has demanded of us. Especially considering the other political duties you have to attend to.

"Hiding it away and refusing to acknowledge your Lurae would be far easier. But the only way you will learn is by practicing. And we have to start now if we are to have any hope of making the treaty possible."

How did he still have the ability to take a single glance at me and know everything I was thinking? While he spoke, my shoulders had inched higher, knowing he wasn't going to let this go—he was determined to see it through.

I wanted him to give up. To call me a lost cause, the way everyone else had. The way I had.

But he wouldn't.

As I wallowed there, unable to move or summon a scathing retort, movement in my peripheral vision made me frown. I glanced down at the mare, who had settled into an ambling gait while we spoke.

That's when I saw it—the faintest thread stretching from her heart to me. And when I listened close . . .

The faint *thud, thud, thud* of her heartbeat.

I chewed my lip. "Tell me more about this wager, then."

14

Revna

"THAT'S NOT A WAGER. THAT'S BLACKMAIL."

Søren laughed, the sound so genuine I scowled. "You have a fundamental misunderstanding of what blackmail is," he said between chuckles. "This just raises the stakes. Makes it more entertaining. True blackmail would be putting your sword into my hands, pointing the blade at your chest, and demanding I tell you something true."

In the pointed silence, I resisted the urge to elbow him in the stomach. It would be so easy from this position. A pointed jab would be perfect payback for the smirk in his voice as he reminisced on our early time together in the wastes, when I'd done exactly what he referenced.

He'd suggested that every time I sensed a heartbeat successfully, I could ask him a question—one he'd have to answer truthfully. I'd been fully on board with that idea. I had plenty of things I wanted to ask about: What had really happened to his missing sister? Why had he told the queen about our relationship?

"It will go the other way, too," Søren had continued, a hint of something indistinguishable in his voice. Nerves, maybe? Anticipation? "If you give it your best shot and are unsuccessful, then I get to ask you anything. And you have to give me a truthful answer."

Hence, my accusation of blackmail.

"And if I refuse?" I shot back. I was grateful I couldn't see his face. Remembering how annoying he was became far more difficult when I was confronted with our height difference, with the way his hair sometimes swept across his forehead if he was too concentrated, with the pine and smoke smell of him. "What then?"

"Then we do the exercise anyway, and you don't get to ask me any of the things you're wondering."

I was wary. He had the upper hand—my Lurae was wild, often uncontrollable. And there were things I didn't want to tell him.

But when I considered every curious thought I'd had over the past week since seeing him again . . .

"Fine."

"Excellent. I earn a question when you become too frustrated to continue practicing that round. Shall we begin?"

I glanced at the empty path ahead of us, the shadowed copses of trees on either side. "What if there's no wildlife around?"

"Then you can try sensing my heartbeat, or the horse's. But don't forget, I can sense the living things in the vicinity, too. There are rabbits everywhere."

The reminder startled me. For all the time we'd spent together and all the stories of his battle prowess, I had no idea how his Lurae worked.

Sense a heartbeat, and you can ask him.

Less than two minutes later, I was wishing for a training dummy. Stabbing something was becoming awfully appealing. "*Fuck.*"

"Harder than you thought?" I heard the smile in his voice when he spoke.

"Yes," I grumbled. The thin thread connecting me to the horse had vanished since I felt it last, her heartbeat now a silent mystery to me. When I had started to lose patience, I'd considered lying to him. But despite it all, the thought of sullying our *tell me something true* ritual with my bitterness felt wrong. And focusing for too long on the task was making my head throb. I needed a break. "Ask a question."

I waited, grinding my teeth, for him to ask something invasive. Maybe a question about my past. *How many people had you slept with before me?* Or one that stoked the flames of his betrayal. *How did it feel when you watched the life leave your brother's eyes?*

He'd even earned the right to a truthful answer to the worst question of them all. *Do you still care for me?*

But instead, he simply asked, "What does your Lurae feel like to you?"

My expression twisted. "My Lurae?"

"Yes. Do you feel a physical sensation when you use magic? Does it speak to you? That's not uncommon, actually, though there's no true evidence that a Lurae is sentient."

"It's . . ." I hesitated. For all the chaos of gaining magic so late in life, no one had ever asked me for any specifics about how it felt to me. Everyone simply watched me kill people and then thought of me as a monster. I chewed on my answer for a moment. "It manifests in a few different ways. I do think it speaks to me, sometimes. And I see threads connecting me to people. Their blood."

"Interesting." His reply wasn't pandering, but genuinely curious, like the scholar in him was rising to the surface. "I see threads, too. I can't manipulate them, only sever them."

I frowned. "Is that uncommon?"

"Not necessarily. There are very few descriptions of how individuals experience their Lurae. It's a topic I'd love to do more research on at some point."

We lapsed into silence. I debated not telling him about the lullaby but mentally shook myself. If I expected him to answer me honestly then it was the least I could do. Telling the truth about the song wasn't enough to make it more dangerous. "Do you remember the song I sang when you took me to the hot spring for the first time?"

"Of course." Was I imagining it, or was his voice suddenly rougher than before?

"That song is in my head." I rubbed a thumb over the leather of the saddle horn. Saying it out loud sounded bizarre. "Well, not in my head. It's a real sound. But no one else can hear it. And when it gets too loud, I know my Lurae is going to snap."

He hummed softly. "Let's start the next round then."

I was startled. That was it? But, too afraid to push him, I obliged.

By the time I sensed my next heartbeat, Søren had asked me two more questions. How and when I met Freja—Halvar had introduced us when we were both eleven—and when my Lurae had manifested for the first time.

"Immediately after the Trials. When my father stepped up to try and kill me."

"Are you sure?" he pressed. "There was never any inkling of magic in you before that moment?"

Irritation sparked. "Seriously? You still think I was hiding my Lurae this entire time?"

"No, nothing like that. I've just wondered if it was truly as sudden as we were led to believe or if there were signs it was going to happen." I felt him shrug. "Knowing might help me in my research. But it isn't a big deal. Try again to hear a heartbeat."

I closed my eyes, intending to do just that. But my mind wouldn't settle. Something nagged at me. The idea that my Lurae might have been present before that moment when I killed my father was absurd.

Wasn't it?

I sucked in a breath, my eyes flying open. "When you sent me to spy on my family . . ." I began slowly. "Frode snuck up on me in my hiding place. I broke his nose. Blood was everywhere. Later when I was talking with him, I thought I heard the lullaby. When I asked Frode about it, he told me that part of the forest was rumored to be haunted, so I brushed it off. Do you think that was my Lurae?"

He hummed. "It's entirely possible. Hard to be sure, though. Let me know if you think of any other instances."

An insidious thought wormed its way in alongside the lullaby beginning its careful path through my mind. *Did you have a Lurae all along and you were too naive to know it? Are you chasing down a prophecy just to learn it doesn't mean anything at all?*

The idea was like a knife to the gut, but I shoved it aside. There were only a couple of hours left before we would camp for the night, and I'd be damned before I arrived without having asked him a single question.

I closed my eyes, took a deep breath, and settled back slightly in the saddle—

My back connected with Søren's chest.

Faster than an arrow flying through the air, I straightened my posture, putting as much distance as possible between us once more. My heartbeat thundered.

When Søren's lips brushed the shell of my ear, his breath hot against my face, I shivered. "You can lean on me," he said softly. "I don't mind."

I mind, I wanted to scream. Or at least, I wanted to mind. Logic dictated that I should be disgusted by his nearness, but even as I tried to convince myself that denying him was the best course of action, my thighs gave a pitiful throb. My shoulders were aching, too—weeks of sitting hunched over my father's desk, studying recorded legislation late into the night the clear perpetrator.

And, in a move that defied all sense, my body longed for him.

I remembered exactly what it felt like to rest against Søren's broad chest. How his warmth would seep into me no matter how frigid the temperatures became. I could imagine in vivid detail exactly how his chin would rest on the top of my head.

A moment of rest, I told myself. *Nothing more. Only what is absolutely necessary.*

Slowly, slowly, I adjusted my weight once more until I was leaning back against him. I was careful to put no more of my weight on him than was essential. He adjusted his hands on the reins to better support me on either side.

I hadn't been wrong about his chin resting lightly on the top of my head.

He took a deep breath, like he was going to say something. I felt it through my bones when he let the air leave him without a word.

Instead of pushing him to speak, like I might have done a few weeks ago, I chewed my lip, closed my eyes, and settled my mind once more.

After my second attempt, Søren had suggested thinking of the lullaby if it didn't come to me directly. I began to imagine the sound of the notes, the cadence of Mother's voice when she'd sung it to me as a child. Søren's chest was warm, keeping me from drifting afloat in a sea of nothingness.

There was a firm, strong anchor at my back, grounding me.

My Lurae's song began, joining in with the part I was getting to. But when my heartbeat spiked with excitement, it vanished once more.

I pursed my lips. I hadn't wanted to hum the song aloud, not in front of Søren. I was trying to guard myself. He didn't deserve to bear witness to this intimate part of me, of my magic. Especially not while I was still discovering it myself.

But we were going to be riding for a while yet. *He's already heard you sing it. It doesn't matter.*

I steeled myself and hummed the first note. My voice cracked slightly, and I cleared my throat before beginning again.

Søren did not speak. He simply waited.

The song was familiar in a way that was both comforting and nerve-wracking. Once, my mother had cared for me. Once, she had seen me as precious.

And I had killed her.

The melody swelled at the chorus, and I felt the moment my Lurae resurfaced once more. This time, I was careful, treating it like an easily startled animal. I focused instead on the notes. And on the steady presence of Søren at my back.

With my eyes closed, I could not see the threads. But I felt a gentle tug in my chest as my Lurae connected me to Søren.

When I heard the steady *thud, thud, thud* of his heartbeat, my lips curled into a satisfied smile.

"What's your question, Princess?"

I wondered whether the pride in his voice was my imagination, then told myself it wasn't worth mulling over. Instead, I needed to decide what I wanted to ask. Something about his sister? I knew what it meant to love a sibling and lose them—and of course, Søren would speak about Sonja that way.

But he had killed Frode to spare her. And that knowledge ached like a tender bruise. Talking about her would only remind me of my own loss.

So instead, I asked a question I'd been chewing on all week. "Which of your personas do you identify with the most?"

When the silence stretched on in the wake of my question, I turned to glance at him. He was staring at me, brows furrowed, eyes wary. Our eyes met for only a brief second before he glanced away. "You'll have to clarify."

I faced forward again, careful to hide the smile threatening to emerge. Only one question in and I'd already managed to unsettle him. Finally, for the first time since his arrival in Bhorglid, I had the upper hand.

"Well, the Hellbringer is not the same man as Søren the scholar," I said, willing to elaborate if he was going to insist. "One is a general, easily able to command armies, an expert on war strategy, and the queen's right-hand man. You, on the other hand—or at least, the you you're pretending to be right now—are a man of knowledge, far more likely to be found in a library than on a battlefield. You're an ambassador. Someone who loves your country and finds no fault in its leadership.

"The Hellbringer once told me he feels differently."

"The Hellbringer and the scholar are both loyal servants to their queen in any way she so requires," he snapped. I watched his grip on the reins tighten, wondered if his knuckles were blanched white beneath his gloves. It seemed I struck a nerve.

Good, I thought. *Now he knows how uncomfortable it is to feel like I don't know him at all. Like any moment together from the prison could have been a lie and I might be in the dark about it.*

He sighed. "The Søren you came to know during our time together in the prison is . . . neither the Hellbringer nor the scholar."

I wasn't entirely sure I believed him, not when the Søren I'd known so intimately had obviously been hiding things from me. But the version of him who had agreed to tutor me in magic was different, too. I wasn't sure how I felt about it. For now, I was at least grateful to know not *everything* we'd experienced together had been a lie.

"And which version do you relate to more?"

"What a question." His tone was dry, but I felt no remorse at asking him a question far more uncomfortable than the ones he had leveled at me. If he chose not to pry any deeper than the specifics of my Lurae, that was his choice. This was mine. "I suppose the truthful answer is that the Hellbringer and the scholar are both masks. Versions of myself I use for protection. Each one holds pieces of me, and each represents a different set of rules I have to follow. I don't know that I would gravitate toward either of them as being more honest than the other—you are more aware than most how the need for survival can change a person. Warp them into someone they aren't."

The question escaped before I could stop it. "Then who are you really?"

The heaviness following his answer evaporated like fog, his answer belying the hint of a grin. "Hear another heartbeat and I'll happily tell you."

◆ ◆ ◆ ◆ ◆

WE MADE CAMP FOR THE NIGHT AS SOON AS DARKNESS FELL. I built a roaring fire and Søren hunted, then cooked us dinner. We ate in silence until snow began to drift down from above.

"Let's set up the tents," I said, pushing to my feet. My thoughts had drifted to Frode, and my mood reflected it.

Søren moved to the supplies, which he'd unloaded earlier to allow the mare to graze. She huffed at him from her spot near the tree line and he chuckled. But then he turned to me, uncertainty on his face. "Did you move the other tent?"

I stiffened. "No."

He ran a hand through his hair, not meeting my eyes. "Ah . . . well, we only have one tent then. I don't know what happened to the other. Maybe it fell off while we were riding."

I tried to muster up enough energy to be angry, but I didn't have it in me. Not when a barrage of memories buffeted my mind and the sorrow lingered. Frode was gone, and here I was gallivanting into the wastes with the man who had killed him.

"Just set it up." My voice was monotone.

Sharing a tent with the enemy? my thoughts whispered. *Your friends are right not to trust you. You're keeping so many secrets from them. Maybe you're not a good person at all.*

Søren was silent, and I found myself turning to the breathing exercises he had taught me. The poisoned thoughts running through my head didn't feel entirely *mine*. Like a foreign entity had placed some of them there.

My magic, maybe. Perhaps this was my Lurae speaking to me, the way Søren had mentioned earlier. It built inside of me if I didn't use it sometimes, and often the only way to calm it was with violence. It made sense that it would try to turn me against my friends, try to make everyone who loved me my enemy.

The acknowledgment didn't ease the burden of the thoughts, though. If anything, they weighed heavier. Did I have any hope of controlling my Lurae if my own mind was fighting me?

Søren cleared his throat. "It's ready. I set up the bedrolls."

I stepped inside, removing my boots at the entrance so I didn't track in mud and slush. The tent was tiny, intended for one person, but two bedrolls managed to fit. I suppressed a sigh. This didn't seem like a purposeful attempt to cajole me into forgiveness. Søren looked more uncomfortable than I felt.

We settled down, and I willed my body to relax.

"How are—" He stopped, clearing his throat, uncertainty slowing his careful choice of words. "How are you . . . feeling?"

Did he mean about him specifically or in general? I didn't know the answer to the first, but the darkness made the answer to the latter slip from me without a second thought. "Sad. I miss him."

Several long heartbeats of heavy silence passed. Then, tentatively, Søren asked, "Will you tell me about him?"

I hadn't shed a tear since our journey began. Instead, my sorrow had sealed over while I dealt with the problem in front of me. But now the dam burst, and I gasped, air refusing to enter my lungs.

"Revna?" My name sounded far away as I threw off the blankets and forced myself to my hands and knees, trembling.

I heard the rustle of Søren's blankets tossed aside and a wave of pure panic whited out my vision. "No," I forced out. "Stay back."

"Are you sure?"

"It will only be harder if I can see you." The truth was harsh, but the moment it spilled from me my shoulders relaxed a bit. The sounds of Søren moving stopped, and I changed position to sit cross-legged, arms wrapped around myself. I said the first thing that came to mind. "Frode was the worst gossip. Always spreading secrets. Not far enough to be hurtful, to cause harm, but I know far more about the servants working in the palace than I should."

The memory hit me like the crush of an avalanche. I waited for the tears to burn behind my eyes, but it never happened. Instead, the strangest sensation overwhelmed me until—

I laughed.

It was a short, quiet thing. More a breathy chuckle than anything else. But I couldn't remember the last time I thought of Frode without dying inside. It still hurt, my chest throbbing dully as I recounted the memory, but it was easier when the pain lived alongside happiness.

My panic faded slightly, replaced by curiosity. I tried again. "When I was young, we would play hide-and-seek. I was at quite the disadvantage, as I'm sure you can imagine. But I made him work for it. I started climbing the trees on the mountainside and hopping from branch to branch, so he could hear my thoughts but not see me. And he had to see me to win, so."

No chuckle this time, but a wave of fondness settled over me instead. "He was so mad when he found out I cared for you. I couldn't keep myself from thinking about our time together, and he gave me the silent treatment for several hours after I was rescued."

"Rescued?"

"Mira wouldn't have told you, but she dropped me in the middle of nowhere instead of taking me back to my family before the Trials."

A growl of frustration. "I'm not surprised in the slightest by that information, sadly. I'll speak with her about it later. Continue."

I found I had no interest in griping on about Mira's mistreatment of me. Not when the recollections of happier times were both calming my breathing and pooling in my stomach like a well of neverending sorrow that would ache for the rest of my life.

"The front always made him so depressed. Every time he returned, we would ride to the prison and pretend we were doing security checks for a few hours. Really, though, he would bring a saddlebag full of blankets and take a nap in an empty cell. The silencer guards had no idea they were helping him so much. We knew if Father found out we would both be punished."

Finally able to breathe again, I curled up beneath my blankets once more. Søren was so quiet I wondered if he had fallen asleep. For several long minutes, there was only the sound of our breathing.

His silence made me bold. I assumed he'd fallen asleep. It had been several minutes of no words between us when I finally murmured, "Do you ever regret meeting me?"

"No."

I froze. His answer had been so instantaneous he might as well have been reading my mind. I had expected to be met with nothing, for the version of him living in my imagination to admit that yes, he did regret our time together. And that would have been the end of it.

But the unshakable note of stubbornness in his voice startled me. There was no hesitation, and I couldn't help but wonder if maybe he was lying. After all, someone had to do the smart thing. Someone had to look at the past and see the mistakes we'd made by growing so close and feel the guilt of it all.

"I do," I said, staring at the ceiling. "Wouldn't this all be easier if a stranger had killed my brother? If the only thing I wanted was revenge for what you'd done? In another world, you would have killed me without a second thought if your queen had ordered it."

"Revna." His voice was ragged around the edges, and I could

hear that he had turned to look at me. "If you want to regret what we had . . . I can live with that. I have some regrets, too."

Something inside me tightened. *He* was *lying*. My fingers curled into the blankets, and I reminded myself that it was a good thing for him to feel this way.

"I regret how long it took me to open up to you. That it was four weeks of pretending to hate each other, pretending I didn't want to take my mask off and bare my face to you."

Now it was my turn to listen silently, startled by his earnestness.

"If I could go back, I would do it all differently. But not in the way you think. I would dance with you more. Touch you sooner. Make you laugh again and again. And kiss you the first time I considered it."

I stared at the top of the tent until the darkness felt surreal. Søren hummed a half chuckle as he continued, "Can you imagine? If you'd walked into the forge to find me shirtless *and* maskless? If I'd let my thoughts become reality and pressed you into the wall so I could taste your beautiful mouth the moment I realized I was gone for you?"

He rolled over onto one side, the sound of his voice quieting as he turned away from me. "You can hate me forever, if you like. Those six weeks we spent make it bearable. At least I have the memories."

He fell silent again. I rolled over too, and desperately hoped I was not the only one restless until the night sky began to turn light once more.

15

Revna

THE SOFT DRUMBEAT OF A HEART SOUNDED IN MY MIND. "There." I pointed into the woods, following the thread leading to the heartbeat's owner—a small creature, based on the speed. Maybe a rabbit or a squirrel.

The thread pulled slightly in my chest, and I watched the opposite end shoot upward to the top of a pine tree. I adjusted my pointing finger to follow it. *Definitely a squirrel.*

A brief silence, while Søren checked the validity of my find. He finally nodded. "First question of the day is yours, then."

I chewed my lip and considered what to ask him. Once again, I found myself lingering on the question of Sonja. I felt connected to her somehow. Her life came at the expense of Frode's, and while I had no intention of ever forgiving Søren for his choice, it made me curious about their relationship.

"Tell me more about Sonja. Do you know where she is now?"

Søren stiffened behind me. We rode farther than I expected to before he finally answered. "Sonja is . . . well, the way all older sisters are, I assume. She spent most of our childhoods annoying me while trying to look out for both of us. We became adults long before any child should have to, and it took its toll on her. But the thing I remember most is how much of a comfort her Lurae was to both of us when we were trying to make a new home in an unfamiliar palace."

I realized I didn't know—"What is her Lurae?"

He didn't comment about it being an extra question. "She can make anything grow. Any flower blooms, any seed sprouts, any withering plant rejuvenates in her presence. Her room at the palace was filled entirely with green."

Was that a smile in his voice? I wished there was some way to turn around and surreptitiously glance at him. Smirking came more naturally to Søren in this scholar role, but I missed the genuine joy that took over his entire being sometimes.

No, you don't miss anything about him, I told myself, attempting sternness.

"She absolutely despised Volkan," Søren chuckled, oblivious to my internal monologue. "I think because she thought he had it easy. Which you and I know isn't true. But he's so happy all the time, and it grated on Sonja."

"Can I ask what exactly . . . *happened* to her?" I ventured. "When we were in the prison together, you told me the queen threatened to torture Sonja if you stepped out of line. That she knows Sonja's location and that's how she threatens her, even though Sonja isn't in the palace. So where is your sister now?"

His knuckles paled where they gripped the reins. He'd left the gloves in the saddlebag today. "I don't know where she is. The queen kept growing more possessive of her as the war continued, realizing I would do just about anything to keep Sonja safe. Eventually Sonja was even put in the dungeon, behind bars, to keep me obedient. But at some point—I don't even truly know when, if I'm honest—she escaped."

"And the queen knows where she went," I finished. "Likely has eyes on her still."

"It's how the queen keeps her collar around my throat," he said. His voice was thick with anger. "I don't even know where Sonja might have gone. I'm doing my best to rectify that, though."

I glanced over my shoulder, curious. "You are?"

He exhaled sharply, warmth on the back of my neck. "Another heartbeat and you'll have your answer."

This time, hearing one came easily. In fact, I pinpointed three small wildlife at once. All without losing control. *Maybe the training is working after all.*

I didn't ask a question this time. "You're looking for your sister."

"I am. I've hired someone from Kryllian to search for her. I met with him while you were at the palace, actually. He seems to have a solid lead."

Oh. I couldn't help but chuckle. "That's who you snuck out to see."

"Yes," he confirmed. "Why were you out there that night anyway?"

I ignored the heat on my cheeks and shrugged. "I wasn't about to stay in my rooms after Arne found out you'd been training me."

"He had a problem with it?"

I definitely wasn't imagining the smirk in Søren's voice. I rolled my eyes. "Of course he did. And apparently the others take issue with it, too."

We lapsed into quiet silence for a few moments before another question came to me. "Why search for Sonja now?"

Søren pulled the reins slightly, and the gray mare followed along the path. The road was barely visible with snow covering it in a perfect, unblemished blanket. "I don't like what the queen is doing. And I'd prefer not to be her puppet forever. It's not a good feeling to have to choose between the safety of someone you love and what you know is right."

He let out a shaky breath and continued, "I also just . . . miss her. I hope to discover that she's safe, make my apologies, and then see what kind of relationship she wants in the future. We spent our childhoods fighting to survive in many ways, even if we weren't on a battlefield. We deserve a chance to discover who we are without a threat hanging over our heads at all times."

It was the perfect answer.

It made me want to heave my meager breakfast in the snow.

Because why did Søren get to see his sister again, work hard to make his amends and heal their relationship, and I was alone? One day he might have a reunion with his sister. He might have the chance to tell her he was sorry.

But Frode would never hear me apologize for not stepping in front of him that day.

Erik would never roll his eyes while I told him I hoped he could be better than the hypocrite our father had made him.

And Björn . . . he'd been kind, once. Long ago. I missed the young boy who'd played games with me all day while our older siblings were too busy for us.

The next round of listening for heartbeats, I was unsuccessful. Thoughts of my brothers swirled in my head like flakes in a winter storm. Memories I could barely grasp before they were ripped away. The slow and steady ache of their loss throbbed through me. As did the memory of plunging my dagger into Björn's chest.

The lullaby returned, too. I shuddered, then swore. "Ask," I demanded.

One of his hands left the reins, lifting toward me. It stopped in midair, hung frozen for a moment before curling into a fist. He reached it behind him and ran it through his hair.

His words were slow and soft, like he'd thought them through carefully but was afraid to hear my answer. "What are you thinking right now?"

My lungs refused to expand all the way. It was the only explanation for the shortness of breath I experienced. My body had betrayed me once already—in the arena all those weeks ago, when the Lurae buried deep within me was allowed to burst forth. It made sense my flesh would betray me again, allow my lungs to fail me now.

And while I struggled for air, my mind spun in dizzying circles. The words I spoke were not carefully considered, the way they should have been. They were far, far too honest.

"I'm thinking about how unfair it all is." The admission choked me, and I pushed back the tears burning behind my eyes. "You're a monster. You betray and destroy and devour. You lie."

He interrupted. "Perhaps I do all those things. But not to you."

"You don't get to decide when to be the good guy," I snapped. "You don't get to choose how I feel about what you've done. So stop trying to force me to let go of my anger when you deserve it."

We lapsed into silence.

Are you angry? The voice in my head was Søren's, so convincing I almost wondered if he'd gained a second Lurae somehow. But no. It was just my imagination, my mind so full of him that he followed me everywhere. *Or are you afraid?*

Of course I was afraid. The thought of letting that fear go was unsettling. I'd spent years of my life fighting to help the Nilurae. When that was no longer a possibility, I fought for the crown instead. But despite winning the Trials, achieving what I set out to do, I wasn't happy.

All my life had been spent fighting. When the fighting was over, when it was all done . . . who was I? At least if I was fighting, I remained in the battle. At least then, I wasn't another casualty.

The moment I allowed myself to think about what I would have done in Søren's situation that day—how I would have chosen if

Frode's life had been on the line instead of Sonja's—was the moment I'd have to reckon with something deeper than my hurt. I wasn't ready to acknowledge that maybe he wasn't the monster I wanted him to be.

Because if he wasn't, then what did that make me?

Something worse.

There was no point in distinguishing my own thoughts from the voice of my Lurae anymore. As the weight of the past days began to settle on me again, I realized perhaps they had been the same voice the entire time.

◆ ◆ ◆ ◆ ◆

"THE FORGE?" I KNEW I SOUNDED AS INCREDULOUS AS I FELT. "I thought you said you knew a way for us to hear the prophecy."

The mare slowed to a stop at the edge of the woods and Søren dismounted. He held out a hand to help me down. My pride didn't allow me to take it. Instead, I put up with my screaming legs, sore from so much riding, as I swung one over and landed with a grimace in nearly a foot of snow.

Søren began walking toward the mouth of the cave, and I followed, sullen. It had been a few hours since our last round of truth-telling, but we'd spent all of them in silence. I'd relied on my breathing exercises to keep Mother's lullaby at bay. It was the most chaotic my Lurae had been since I blew up on Søren while we sparred the other day. And seeing my progress move backward was disappointing.

It became easy for the thoughts to creep in. *You spent your entire life disappointing your parents. Then you disappointed Freja and Arne when you trained with the Hellbringer and entered the Trials. Now you're queen and you're still managing to be a disappointment to everyone around you.*

"We're not going to the cave," Søren said, his hands shoved deep in his pockets. His cloak lifted behind him, following a gust of wind. The towering pines offered a patchwork backdrop of green as he glanced over his shoulder at me. I refused to acknowledge how nicely the color complimented his dark hair and gray eyes.

"Then where?" Trudging through the snow was terrible, and I was glad my boots were high enough to keep the cold from sneaking into my socks. But it was nice to be moving. The soreness in my legs screamed with every step, but at least blood was flowing again. "We left our weapons with the horse. Should we grab them?"

He shook his head. "No. Here, look."

We stepped up past the cave entrance, around the side. Søren pointed through a gap in the trees. It wasn't far before the pines disappeared into nothing but a white plain.

I swallowed. I knew exactly what I was looking at, because I'd dreamt of a similar place so many times. "A lake."

When he glanced at me, he appeared pleased. "Exactly."

Surely this wasn't the same lake I'd been dreaming of. It couldn't be. *Calm down,* I told myself. *There are dozens of lakes in the wastes. They likely all look identical. You can dream of a lake without dreaming of* this *lake.*

Søren hadn't clarified what he meant yet, and I tapped my foot. Finally, I said, "If I'd known you thought ice fishing was the way to discovering prophecies, we could have stopped at the lake on the outskirts of the capital and made this a much shorter trip."

He rolled his eyes. "We're not here to fish."

"Then how can this lake possibly help us?" I threw my hands up. "I can't believe you made me trek all the way out here for . . . nothing."

Søren stepped in front of me, blocking my view of the endless, snow-covered ice. His eyes held every ounce of deadly seriousness I knew him to possess. And then, he said something utterly absurd.

"There is something magical beneath the ice."

Silence fell over us, so profound I didn't dare break it. Only when the weight of his words settled over me did I reply, "What is it?"

"I don't know, not exactly." He ran a frustrated hand through his hair. "But there are records of strange happenings here that go back generations. You heard the queen's story, about Callum falling into the ice and Aloisa diving in after him. I believe this is the same lake."

The dream flashed before my eyes. The surge of panic I felt watching the boy swallowed up by the freezing water sent a shudder through me. "Why do you think it can reveal the prophecy to us, then?"

With a sigh, he unlatched his cloak and spread it down over the snow like a blanket. "Sit," he said, gesturing. "This is going to take a while to explain."

Warily, I did as he asked. When we were comfortable, he turned to gaze out over the lake and began.

"When Sonja and I were young, we tried to escape Kryllian once. We made it out of the castle, snuck our way onto a ship in the harbors, and set off for what we thought was Faste. But the queen had seen us leaving. She paid the merchants who owned the boat a hefty sum to take us to the farthest port from 'home' and drop us there with nothing."

I frowned. "The farthest port? In the Fjordlands? Isn't that . . ."

He closed his eyes, like he saw it stretched before him. "Kølig. The tiny village on the northernmost coast of Bhorglid. The captain said he'd been sent with a message. Told us that when we grew tired of playing house on our own, he would be there to take us right back to the palace. We were kids, and we weren't thinking straight. So when no one offered to help us, we walked out of town and into the wastes. At the time, it seemed a better option than returning to Kryllian."

I gaped. "How are you *alive*?"

"I shouldn't be. Neither should Sonja. But just as we started to consider that we'd made a huge mistake, we ran into a woman. She told us she was a wanderer, but that she had a place we could stay to warm up for the night until we were ready to go back."

"She wouldn't take you in?"

"No. And rightfully so, I now understand. She was living alone in the worst place in the Fjordlands. It was no life for two young children."

I bit back my argument. If he'd forgiven the woman, then far be it from me to dissuade him. *Besides, it's not my job to protect him anymore.*

"This is where she brought us." He glanced over at the cave, and I saw the fondness hidden in his eyes. "She spent several days teaching me how to forge and letting Sonja go wild with growing pine trees. It's why there are so many around here compared to the sparser areas of the wastes. But every night, I'd wake up and wander out to the lake. It was summertime then, so the water was still frozen over but not nearly as thick as it is now. I'd sit at the edge and wonder about . . . everything.

"One night, the wandering woman found me. She came to me and asked what I was thinking about. And I told her the truth about my Lurae. I was only twelve, so I hadn't come into my magic that long ago, but I already hated it. I went on and on about how no one understood me. There was no one else I'd been able to find in the history books who could cause death with their Lurae.

"She said I was wrong. And then she told me a story." He tilted his head to me. "Can you guess what the story was?"

"The one the queen told us," I murmured, chewing my lip. "About Aloisa and Callum."

"Exactly," he said with an approving nod. "But the wandering woman's version had far more detail. According to her, there is a god living in the lake."

"A god?" I snorted. "And you seriously believe that?"

Søren shrugged. "I don't think it's a god necessarily, but there are a couple of other accounts that mention this place specifically and claim it as a site of powerful magic. Perhaps the wandering woman had some experience of her own with the lake."

"You said her story had more detail," I said. "What details?"

"She claimed Aloisa had spoken with the god in the lake when she dove in after her friend. The god had told her the people were ready to receive magic, but it would require a sacrifice. If she was willing to pay it, then her friend would live again."

I didn't need Søren to tell me what Aloisa had done. I would have chosen to sacrifice for my friends, too. "What was taken from her, then?"

"The wandering woman didn't say. She merely said that within the lake is 'the fabric of the past and the threads of the future.'" His lopsided grin sent my heart galloping. "Incredibly vague, I know."

I leaned back on my palms. "Well, if the 'god' lives beneath the ice, have fun on your swim."

Søren raised a brow. "I don't think so. Maybe this prophecy involves me, but you're the one who needs to hear it." He stood and stretched, then held out a hand to me. "Come on. Time to see what all the fuss is about."

For a long moment, I chewed my lip and looked at his hand. "If you're trying to kill me, this is a terrible and uninventive way to do it."

He laughed, the sound wholehearted in a way that made my stomach flip. "It's also incredibly more complicated and time-consuming than it's worth to kill you by convincing you to jump in a lake. Besides, you can swim. You have nothing to lose."

I took his hand.

16

Revna

SØREN SPENT THE NEXT HOUR PREPARING. HIS WORDS, NOT mine. I thought we were wasting time.

He insisted on going into the forge and lighting the fire. Bringing in our saddlebags and unpacking a dry change of clothes to heat up while we were gone. The mare was covered in a thick blanket to keep her comfortable, but Søren allowed her to roam free so she could graze to her heart's desire while we were occupied. He even grabbed his knives and pulled out some of the leftover game we'd brought with us from last night, ready to cook when we got back.

Meanwhile, nerves scratched up around my throat like long fingers. "Stop it," I finally snapped. "If we don't do this now, we aren't doing it at all. Come on."

Now we stood on the ice, snow cleared away and our reflections staring back at us. I couldn't help but glance back in the direction of the shore. I almost expected to see a shadowed figure waving at me, like I had in my dreams.

When Søren hefted the serrated blade he'd unpacked from the saddlebags earlier, my mind flashed to the boy I'd seen falling beneath the surface. The metal bit into the ice, severing it easily. The sound shouldn't have been familiar.

"I dreamt about this lake, I think," I murmured. I didn't expect Søren to hear me over the sound, but I needed to say the words. They'd lived too long alone in my mind. The thought threatened to lap over my head like a frigid wave of water.

But Søren's movements stopped briefly before starting again. "You have?"

Water lapped over the edge of the ice, where a small gap had been created. "Or a lake just like it. I don't know." I shook my head. "The dreams are the same story—Callum falling in and Aloisa diving after him."

"Huh." He grunted as he pulled the knife through the last part of the ice, leaving a floating mass of ice in the center. I watched him take out another instrument, one with a hooked barb on the end, and use it to pull the floating ice out. "That's . . ."

Søren ran a hand through his hair, breathing heavy. I tried not to stare as I said, "It's strange. And everything feels strange right now."

"Yes," he said. "Makes it difficult to know if there are things we should be paying closer attention to or if it's all in our heads."

I took off my cloak, then stooped to unlace my boots. "Perhaps I'll ask the god when I meet them."

He didn't miss the wry note in my voice. "I hope that woman wasn't lying," he said, laughing. Probably at the absurdity of the situation.

"How far do I need to swim before I'll see it? Will I only have a few seconds to speak to it?" As I spoke, my teeth began chattering. I undid my braid and wrapped the hair into a tight bun, securing it with the same strip of worn leather as before.

Søren didn't answer immediately, and when I glanced at him, his mouth hung slightly ajar, the gray of his eyes nearly disappeared into dark pupils. I looked over my shoulder, wondering what he'd seen, but there was nothing there. He cleared his throat. "Sorry. I'm not sure, honestly. If the story can be believed, then Aloisa had plenty of time to speak with it. Swim as far as you can and see what you find. I'll keep my eyes on your soul threads and pull you out. Ask the important questions first, just in case."

I shook my arms out, as if that would help the nerves or the cold. It didn't. I stepped out of my boots and pulled off my gloves. I wasn't willing to strip all the way down in such frigid temperatures—or with Søren watching. Just before I steeled myself to launch into the dark depths, Søren grabbed my arm.

I raised a brow. The expression on his face was some combination of panic and desperation. But he gritted his teeth and released me. "Be careful."

I didn't want to think about how much I longed for him to pull me into his chest and warm me up again. Didn't want to ruminate on the fire he'd lit to make sure I'd be warm when I returned from speaking with a possible deity. And I definitely didn't want to linger on the way his fingers had wrapped around my arm with a crushing grip and yet still managed to convey care instead of anger.

I hate him, I reminded myself instead.

And then I dove.

◆ ◆ ◆ ◆ ◆

ANY LESS DISCIPLINE AND MY BREATH WOULD HAVE ESCAPED ME entirely the moment my body connected with the water.

Every inch of my skin screamed. My fingers and toes were numb instantly, and my heartbeat sped, working overtime to keep me from freezing immediately. Muscle memory kicked in swiftly, and I pulled my hands through the water in front of me, forcing myself down into the depths.

I couldn't see anything. How was I supposed to be on the lookout for something magical, other, godly even, if nothing was visible? My eyes stung with the rush of water, and before long I closed them, telling myself I'd open them to peer into the depths. As the seconds ticked by, I began losing what air I'd sucked into my lungs. Fear gripped me. I forced myself to keep swimming down even as my arms and legs stiffened. I couldn't feel my fingers or my toes. At this rate, I wouldn't be able to continue swimming for much longer.

Maybe Søren is *trying to kill me,* I thought. *This is a terrible way to die.*

I forced my eyes open for a moment and looked around me. And still, nothing but darkness. No mystical presence, no all-knowing being.

Did I trust Søren's absurd story enough to keep going? Did I want to know the truth of the prophecy *this* badly?

Just as I was about to turn around and force myself upward to give him the chastisement of his life, the water vanished.

I blinked. One moment I'd been fighting for my life in the cold darkness. And the next, I was warm and dry and standing . . .

Where the hell am I?

I looked around, uncertain what exactly I was looking at. There seemed to be endless nothing stretching around me in every direction. My feet rested on a solid surface, but the area had no walls or roof. There was no ceiling visible, but also no sky—just white expanse.

I was utterly alone.

"Hello?" I called. My voice echoed slightly, and I frowned.

Blinding light began to gather in front of me. It collected in a small pool of gold at my feet, pulling in on itself to grow taller and taller. I stared for as long as I could before my eyes began to burn and I was forced to shield them.

"Hello."

The voice was one and yet many, everything and yet nothing. I separated my fingers to peek out at the thing standing before me. It was shaped like a person, but made entirely of threads, just like the ones that connected me to the heartbeats I heard. The same strings I used to puppeteer my victims.

It stood with its hands behind its back, head tilted slightly. It was the exact same height as me, no taller or shorter, and it had no defining features—faceless, expressionless.

My plans for asking questions flew from my mind. The only thing I could think to say was, "What *are* you?"

It took a small half bow, sweeping out a hand. "We are the Tapestry."

I crossed my arms, suddenly wary. "And what does that mean?"

"It means we are everything that was and everything that is," it replied simply.

Not helpful. "Are you a god?"

It sounded amused. "We suppose it depends on your definition of 'god.'" Before I could interrupt, it continued, "'God' is the closest word you have for what we are. But we are short on time, and there is little point to arguing semantics. You are here with questions, are you not, young Bloodsinger?"

I stiffened. It knew who I was. But Søren's reminder to ask the most important questions while I could echoed in my mind, and I pushed my hesitancy aside. "There is a prophecy. About me, and a man called the Hellbringer. It was given by a Seeing One named Tam hundreds of years ago. I need to hear it."

"And what do you intend to do with the knowledge once you have received it?" The Tapestry sounded curious.

I answered honestly. "I'm not sure. My hope is that it will provide some answers about why the Queen of Kryllian has taken an interest in me and reveal how she came to learn of my Lurae before I did."

I waited for the follow-up questions, but the Tapestry had none. Instead, it simply said, "We can sense the truth in you, Revna Bloodsinger. And we will grant your request."

The Tapestry disappeared, and the emptiness around me flooded with color.

It was like my dreams. Instead of watching from a distance, I existed in the vision. My traveling clothes had been replaced by older, thicker ones, clearly handcrafted. Cold scratched at the edges of my awareness, but I was too focused and too eager to pay attention to it. I paced back and forth, torches illuminating the room around me. What were a few frozen fingers when compared to the culmination of everything I'd spent years working toward?

I tried to gasp when I recognized where I was, but the body I inhabited didn't move. *The prison. Where I spent all that time training with Søren.*

In the vision, it looked far different from the version of the prison I'd known. Torches flickered from their places on the walls, and there was no dust on the floor. The cell bars were polished and new, rust nowhere to be seen.

Who am I? I wondered. But I had no control over this vision. I experienced the world in front of me like I was her, whoever she was.

Someone coughed weakly from within the cell before me. I stepped forward and wrapped one pale hand around a bar. The frigid metal bit into my palm. "Well?" I barked. My voice was haggard and rough from disuse. I knew intrinsically how rarely I spoke to others these days. "Are you ready to speak the prophecy?"

A guard stepped up next to me, holding a torch. His uniform was unfamiliar to me, but the person I was in the dreamlike world was confident in his trustworthiness *because* there was no clear sigil on the right side of his chest. The flickering flames illuminated the prisoner: a Seeing One was strapped to a chair, head lolling. Bruises and dried blood covered their face, and their arms and legs were emaciated. Every breath they exhaled was a wheeze.

"Yes," they finally whispered. "I'll tell it."

My fingernails scraped along the metal, and excitement leapt like a living creature in my chest. *Finally,* I thought. *After endless days of torture, they've finally broken.*

I realized with a jolt whose body I inhabited. This was Arraya, Callum's wife. I remembered what Valen had told me—that Arraya had taken Tam hostage and forced them to be her personal Seeing One. When she discovered Tam had a prophecy they did not share with her . . .

She had tortured Tam until they succumbed.

Dimly, I was aware of existing in my own body still, too. I swallowed.

Arraya gestured to the guard, who opened the cell door. Tam made no attempt to escape or even fight back. They were too weak for either. Arraya moved forward and knelt next to Tam. "Prophesy," she commanded.

Tam exhaled a rattling breath. Their eyes lit with dim, glowing silver, and they began to speak.

Old gods will rise
To meet the new.
When the Weaver meets her end
By her own creation—
A guardian divided—
Her heirs shall rise.
Him, harbinger of forebearers' doom.
She, born of brothers' blood.
Hellbringer. Bloodsinger.
Dawn of new threads, with uncertain ends,
Stained souls awakened once more.
Beware: weaving is a careful art.

Those fragile threads
Care not for unwinding.

Tam fell silent once more. Arraya turned to the guard, who held a sheet of parchment, scribbling frantically on it with an inked quill. When he reached the end, he handed it to Arraya.

She studied it for a moment. I knew she was committing the words to memory. I was doing the same, after all.

There would be time to interpret it later, she knew. But for now, there was a promising amount of detail here. Tam had seen the future before, but never given a prophecy like this—one told in riddles.

"You don't have anything else?" I asked them.

Tam shook their head. "Nothing."

"And you don't know what it means."

"No."

I stood once more. The ink on the paper was dry, and I folded it in half. "Best put you out of your misery, then." I pulled a dagger from the belt at my waist and slit the Seeing One's throat in one smooth motion.

Then I turned to the guard. "You did well these past weeks. What is your name, soldier?"

The man stared straight ahead. His jaw trembled. Perhaps he knew what was coming as well as I did. He opened his mouth to speak, but before he could, I buried the dagger in his throat, too.

I stepped out of the cell and surveyed the scene. No other witnesses. That had been the plan. The parchment had bloody fingerprints on it now, but it was still more than readable. The perfect text to study as I formulated my plan.

"Callum." The name echoed in the prison hallway. A violent ache tore through me. He was gone. But the parchment I held brought me a bit of hope.

"I am coming for you, my love."

◆ ◆ ◆ ◆ ◆

ON MY NEXT INHALE, I WAS MYSELF AGAIN. I STOOD IN THE ROOM of nothingness, the Tapestry exactly as it had been before the vision. My gaze went directly to my hands—clean. I exhaled with relief. My stomach roiled at the memory of the tortured Seeing One. At Arraya's thoughts, so clear about it having been months since they were captured.

"What was that?" I demanded.

"A memory," the Tapestry said smoothly. "You asked to see the prophecy, and so the prophecy you have seen."

But an intuitive sense deep within me told me I didn't yet know everything I needed to. There were still pieces of the puzzle missing. The prophecy had been almost illegibly vague. Even if the Queen of Kryllian had somehow gained access to it, how would she have known about my Lurae?

Suspicion took root. "How do I know you aren't just showing me what you want me to see?" I took a step back. The whole experience had been . . . eerie. I didn't appreciate feeling like a stranger in my own skin. It reminded me too much of my nightmares, filled with imagined people and all-too-vivid emotion.

Maybe they aren't imagined people, part of me whispered. *Maybe the dreams you're having are memories, too.*

I shoved the thought aside. Impossible. "You could be lying to me about everything," I accused. "All of it."

"Perhaps," it said. Despite the ordeal I'd just witnessed—one the Tapestry must have seen also, at some point—its layered voice remained neutral. "If it is proof you desire, then one of your own memories should serve well enough."

The emptiness filled again, this time with a scene I knew intimately. I was back in the prison, but now it was occupied by someone else's belongings. Søren, dressed in full Hellbringer regalia, walked into the room. I paused in my swordplay practice, sheathing Aloisa and pushing a damp lock of escaped hair off my forehead.

"You're back early," I said.

He pulled the mask off, set it on the table. The frown lines on his forehead were more pronounced than usual. "Long battle today," he said by way of explanation.

Everything was the exact same as it had been when this moment truly happened. Months ago. This was one of the last nights I spent in the prison with Søren, when we had finally confessed our feelings for each other and decided being together was worth the pain that would come from being apart. Distantly, I felt mounting dread in my gut, realizing what was coming next in the memory. But when I tried to say *Stop*, my past self paid no mind.

Of course she doesn't, I realized, nausea taking over. *She doesn't know I'm watching this.*

In the memory, I wished his words didn't send a twist of fear through me. A long battle for him meant Frode or Jac might have been injured or killed. And if not them, then certainly my people had experienced casualties.

But that was our lot in life—the risk I'd come to terms with when I kissed him for the first time. I strode over to him, winding my arms around his neck.

"Forget what's out there," I said softly. "You're here now."

His eyes softened and I pulled him down until his lips met mine. The kiss was slow and sensual, deep and all-consuming. His arms wrapped around my waist, and he lifted me off the ground slightly, pulling a laugh from me.

Teeth scraped against my lip and a rush of butterflies swarmed.

I tried to pull back. The me living the memory did not oblige my silent command.

"Stop," I said, and I heard my voice echoing somewhere distant. "*Stop.*"

The scene faded, and the Tapestry appeared before me once more. I wrapped my arms around myself, grateful for my regained autonomy. "Was anything amiss?"

I stared at the being before me. Not a single thing had been off about the vision. It even included details I'd tried to forget. I'd experienced the moment like I was living it all over again.

"What *are* you?" I whispered.

It extended its arms. I watched the threads it was made of swirl, forming minuscule images that changed as quickly as they formed. "We are all who have come before," it said. "We see all. But there are many paths before you, and to tell you too much would be to choose your fate before you choose it yourself."

"I don't trust you." I didn't mean to admit it, but it was the truth. "Whose side are you on?"

"Ah," it said. "You wish to know where our loyalties lie. We are not tied to the whims of mortals, young queen. Our ultimate desire is for the Fjordlands to thrive."

I paced back and forth, wringing my hands. I was filled with too much nervous energy to stand still any longer. "Do people worship you?"

Its laugh was cacophonous. "No. It would be foolish to worship any being."

"What do you . . . do?" I ventured. "Why doesn't the world know of your existence?"

This god was not like anything I'd pictured. The statues in the center square of Bhorglid's capital were larger than life, not my height—they towered, and in their towering they *commanded*. Obedience, respect, blind deference. This Tapestry didn't seem to be asking for anything of the sort.

It did, however, seem to be all-knowing. A terrifying prospect.

What makes a god, then? I wondered.

"The Fjordlands are older than other places in the world, but they will only continue on if those with ill intent are not allowed to weave the threads in the ways of destruction. This is our purpose—to ensure that when the threads risk becoming tangled and broken, a person rises to keep them intact." As it spoke, it waved a hand and threads split off into a true tapestry behind it, winding together into bigger, clearer images: villages filled with people, bonfires in the center of dances, a red-haired girl and a blond boy holding fishing poles and standing on a lake of ice.

"Wait," I gasped, throwing out a hand. "Those two children—the girl and the boy. You know them."

It hummed. "We do."

"They're real." Tentatively, I stepped up to the woven image. It looked like intricately sewn fabric, but the threads emanated a small amount of light and warmth. I reached up but didn't allow my fingertips to connect with the picture. "I've been dreaming about them."

"Yes," the Tapestry said. "Such things are to be expected now that your Lurae has fully awakened."

"Fully awakened?" I felt like a child, repeating everything the Tapestry said. But so much was unclear, and I had endless questions.

"Your Lurae has lived inside you, dormant for your entire life," it said. "Only when the timing was right could we allow it to wake."

It waved its hand and the woven images changed. I watched the scene from my dream of the frozen lake begin to play out in front of me as I tried to wrap my mind around this new information. "Aloisa was indeed real. She is the girl you've been dreaming of." I watched Callum begin to saw at the ice. The Tapestry murmured, "Best to show you the ending, we think."

This time, when Callum fell into the water and Aloisa dove in after him, I didn't wake. I stepped closer to the Tapestry's threads, twisting into the scene. Aloisa materialized in the same space I now occupied. Her expression was one I understood—wariness and confusion. I stretched my fingers out to brush against the threads making up her image. They were warm and featherlight, almost the same texture as powdered snow.

In the vision, the Tapestry appeared before Aloisa. After she asked many of the same questions I had upon arriving, she crossed her arms and held her chin high. “What will happen when I wake? Will Callum be all right?”

The Tapestry—the version of it from the memory—seemed regretful. “Your friend has passed on, I’m afraid. You may not survive this experience either.”

The girl was silent for a few moments before she said, a hint of sharpness in her voice, “You could save us both.”

The Tapestry nodded. “We could, but we will not.”

Her hands curled into fists. “That’s ridiculous. You’re a god—save him!”

“We will not save him,” the Tapestry repeated. “But you can. If you are willing to accept the cost.”

Aloisa’s face changed, relief warring with uncertainty. “Should I assume you will not tell me what the cost will be?”

“That is correct. But be warned: it is great.”

She didn’t hesitate. She held her head high when she answered. “I accept.”

The weaving in front of me transformed once more, and I watched her emerge from the lake, gasping and hacking for air. A long cut stretched over one eyebrow, and I wondered what she’d hit her face on. A jagged edge of the ice, perhaps. She pulled Callum to shore behind her, dragging his deadweight. His eyes stared unseeing into the distance. Someone else, someone I couldn’t see, screamed.

The Tapestry standing next to me murmured, “I am afraid this part only makes sense if you see it through Aloisa’s eyes.”

Color flooded my world again. My fingers, wrapped around Callum’s frozen wrist, were nearly numb. But with every blink, threads began to appear in the air around me.

I dropped my friend's hand. The threads now formed a tapestry, woven in front of me and stretching out in either direction. I knew, intrinsically, that no one else could see it. Including my sister, who sobbed loudly behind me.

Threads, I thought, and noted one different from the others—it was bright but loose, the end not yet tied off. Tentatively, I reached out for it.

There was a corresponding tug in my gut as I moved my fingers with the intent to manipulate the thread.

My own thoughts broke through the haze of Aloisa's. *She has a Lurae.*

She treated the thread as gingerly as one would a fallen baby bird. It was slow, painstaking work, but eventually, the entire thread unraveled from the tapestry until she held it in her hands. Then, she guided the light into Callum's unbreathing body.

I held my breath. Counted three, four, five heartbeats of stillness.

Callum's chest moved as he inhaled, then turned onto his side to vomit up water.

I sank to my knees. Tears of relief fell from my eyes. My sister's small hand grasped mine. "What happened?" she asked, wonderous. "How did he come back?"

I couldn't look at her, not when I was so busy staring at Callum. But when I glanced down at our intertwined fingers, I noted the glow of threads living beneath her skin, now visible to me as well.

Shaking my head, I wondered when I would find out the cost of what I'd done. "I don't know," I said. "I don't know."

The room of nothing materialized in front of me once more. I rubbed my forehead. An ache was beginning to form there. The deity claimed to be answering my questions, but I now had more than when I'd started. "Aloisa was a real person. How did she come to be worshiped as a goddess?"

For a long moment, the Tapestry studied me. "You have many

questions," it said finally. "Such is to be expected. There is not enough time to answer them all now, however."

My heart sank. Whether the Tapestry was a god or not, it had information I needed. I hadn't even asked what it meant when it said my Lurae had been dormant for most of my life. Did it know what the queen had planned?

"But we reside elsewhere, too," it continued. "Your Lurae is more complex than you realize, child. And between yourself and the Hellbringer, as you called him, there is much ahead of you. Work together, and you will be able to speak to us outside of our physical realm in the lake."

"What do you mean?" A note of desperation slipped into my voice. "I don't understand."

"The threads of your future hold endless possibilities," it said, placing a gentle hand on my shoulder. I was surprised to find the touch comforting. "You have been chosen for a vital task—one influenced greatly by those who came before you.

"Study the prophecy," the Tapestry said. "It will reveal more than you expect. Trust your companion. He has gained new responsibilities as well, and they will grow even more vital in the coming weeks. The more you use your Lurae, the easier it will become to connect with us. You will learn to see the threads of the past and recognize them."

More training with Søren, then.

"Even now, he paces on the ice," the Tapestry continued. "Watching your soul threads with the keenest eye, ready to pull you from the depths."

"He needs me alive."

"Is that the only reason he cares for your well-being?" The Tapestry stepped closer to me once more.

I ignored the question and replied with my own. "How do I speak to you outside of this place? There is more I need to know."

Especially about my Lurae.

"We will come to you in dreams when we are able. Otherwise, continue to practice using your Lurae. In tandem with your Hellbringer's abilities, you can connect with us. Your magic will guide you when the time calls for it."

Before I had the chance to say anything else, the Tapestry disappeared. And when I opened my mouth to call out for it, water flooded in.

17

Revna

PANIC OVERWHELMED EVERY OTHER SENSE. IT FLUSHED OUT the cold, even. Because I couldn't breathe.

My eyes stung with water, nothing but blurry shapes visible. Thinking was impossible—my limbs flailed of their own accord, desperate to reach air.

I'm going to die. The thought rang as clear and true as when I'd lain on my back, Björn carving up my face with his knives. *I'm going to die.*

A strong hand wrapped around my arm and pulled.

I coughed and retched, water pouring from my mouth as the lake surrounding me disappeared. Every limb shook with exhaustion and shock and cold. But there was solid ground beneath me.

After a few minutes, my desperate inhales slowed to shaky breaths. I became aware of fabric draped over my shoulders, pressure beneath my knees and my back. When I blinked, the sun through the pines threatened to blind me. The world around me bobbed, sending nausea spiraling all over again, and I closed my eyes once more.

My left side rested against something solid and breathing. Gods, I was so *cold*. My teeth chattered and I leaned into the warmth. My muddied thoughts swept every which way. The Tapestry, the prophecy, Tam, Aloisa and Callum . . . it all swam around me in hazy waves.

"Hey, stay with me, Revna. Can you hear me? Don't go to sleep, Princess. The forge is right here, let's get you warmed up."

I recognized Søren's voice, but it made something itch at the back of my mind. There was something I needed to tell him. Something I needed to remember.

The light burning through my eyelids, a harsh red, softened to full darkness. And the blissful numbness that had overtaken my body was beginning to be replaced by sharp, stabbing pain. A whimper escaped me.

"Can you open your eyes?" Søren asked. Awareness trickled back in slowly. I managed to force my eyes open, though everything around me remained blurry and dim. "Perfect."

He set me down, right next to the fire. The light stung my eyes but the heat *burned*. My teeth clacked together and my muscles tightened so hard it hurt. Søren swore. "You're not going to like this, but I need to get you out of these clothes."

"N-n-n-no," I managed.

His expression went from worried to dangerous in an instant. "I promised I wouldn't touch you unless you asked me to. Unless it was necessary. I've wronged you enough already, and I refuse to sit here and watch you get hypothermia while you shiver in a puddle of lake water. So choose, Princess—are you stripping down yourself or am I doing it for you?"

I wanted to cry, and I hated it. My options were both terrible, but I could barely move my limbs. Getting out of these clothes myself wasn't a possibility. I gritted my teeth through my shudders. *He's seen it all before anyway.*

"Fi-i-i-ne."

Gods, but I hated how gentle his hands were as he put an arm behind my back to lift me into a sitting position. The cloak he'd wrapped around me fell from my shoulders. I felt nothing when he slipped his fingers beneath the hem of my shirt and lifted it over my head. The soaked fabric peeled off my skin, leaving goose bumps behind in its wake. Once he disentangled it from my arms, he moved to the waistband of my pants, hoisting me up and supporting my entire weight with one arm while he pulled the thick pants from my legs. My underwear and breastband came next, and I shivered naked by the fire, begrudgingly trembling less than I was before.

Søren kept his eyes averted as he hung the clothing up to dry. I watched him reach for the fresh cloak he'd set out earlier, along with a thick wool hat and matching socks and mittens. They were huge and somewhat lumpy. Handmade, perhaps. Did Søren knit?

He draped the cloak over my shoulders, and I relaxed almost instantly. The inside was lined with thick fur, and I relished the sensation. He tugged on each of my ankles until I could extend my leg and allow him to put the socks on. The mittens were next. "D-don't put the hat on," I said, curling in on myself to try to contain the limited body heat I'd regained. "My hair is wet."

Søren eyed the tight bun I'd wound earlier. "Let me take it down. Then it can start to dry."

I tensed but offered no argument when he knelt behind me and pulled out the leather tie softly before unwinding my hair to cascade down my back. The locks were cold against the backs of my ears and I made an involuntary sound—something like a moan of sadness at the chill.

"How's that?" he asked.

"Better." It was the truth, too. Every part of me hurt, worse than when he'd carried me back after I'd spent hours wandering the prison halls once. But the pins and needles were a good sign, I knew. It was enough.

He stood and set some meat to cook over the giant fire. "Did you meet it?"

"The god in the lake?" The acknowledgment of what had happened weighed heavy on my tongue, and if I wasn't speaking to someone who believed in its existence, I would have convinced myself I imagined the entire thing. "Yes. It calls itself the Tapestry."

Søren looked at me over the flickering flames. "And? What did you learn?"

I sighed and pulled the cloak tighter around myself. "I heard the prophecy. Do you have paper and something to write with? I think I still have it all memorized, but I'm not sure it'll stick around if I fall asleep."

Ever the scholar, he procured a notebook and writing instrument from his bag. He dutifully copied down every word I spoke. When I finished reciting the prophecy, he was silent.

"Any idea what it means?" I asked.

He shook his head. "No. It's so vague."

Søren's lips moved soundlessly as he read over the words again. I forced my gaze away. Studying the shape of his mouth was a quick way to more unwelcome thoughts—ones I couldn't afford.

Frode made his own choice, my thoughts whispered. *Maybe you can make yours.*

No. I didn't care what decisions Frode had made in the heat of the moment. He didn't have to die, and forgiveness was too much to ask of me. I dug my fingernails into the edge of the cloak wrapped around me, hoping the sensation would ground me. Instead, it lent my thoughts to the familiar smell infused there. Pine, snow, and smoke.

Søren's next words interrupted my thoughts. "'A guardian divided,'" he read aloud. "If you're 'born of brothers' blood,' then it makes sense for me to be . . ."

He hesitated, and I frowned. "'Harbinger of forebearers' doom'?"

He glanced up at me. "It's a long story."

Søren's tone was a firm boundary not to ask about it again. Chilled as I was, I didn't think to snark at him the way I usually would have. Instead, I thought of my own horror stories, kept from my closest friends, and nodded. Whatever it was, he would tell me if I needed to know.

He cleared his throat and changed the subject. "But that begs the question of what—or who—this guardian is."

"Was," I corrected. "It said they met their end by their own hand, right?"

"Hmm." His brow furrowed as he studied the paper. "You're right, it does seem to imply that the Weaver and the guardian are the same person. A woman."

"Aloisa, maybe?" I ventured. When he offered me a puzzled look, I explained the dreams I'd been having, including the full vision the Tapestry had shown me of Aloisa's past. "It said she was a real person. That what it was showing me was a memory. When she received her Lurae, she could see threads, the same way you and I can. Maybe she was this . . . Weaver."

"It's entirely possible. I wish we had more than just these vague things to go off of." Søren ran a hand through his hair, looking at the flickering flames. "'Old gods will rise to meet the new' is soundly unhelpful, especially when we only know of a single actual god."

I chuckled a bit at that. "I know. Even if the queen had the prophecy, it seems like a stretch that she would know what it meant. Or that it could have provided any real information about my Lurae."

"Her cunning might surprise you," Søren said. "She's more conniving than she seems. And don't you find it odd that she's the one who named me the Hellbringer, and that same title is given in the prophecy?"

I hadn't even considered it, but Søren's mouth twisted in a self-deprecating smile, and I knew he was right. The queen had absolutely heard the prophecy already. Before she even met Søren, it seemed.

Valen had been the first to call me Bloodsinger. I wished we had asked the Seeing One to stay in Bhorglid longer instead of rejoining their caravan. Maybe they had answers we so desperately needed.

"The god—this Tapestry being—it said we would be able to speak to it without diving into the lake again," I said. "That we would need to use our Lurae together to summon it."

"Did it say how exactly we do that?"

I shook my head and huffed a laugh. "Of course not. Could it be a god if it wasn't making things overly complicated?"

Søren chuckled. "Do you think it is a god, then?"

"I'm not sure." A wave of exhaustion overtook me. Logically, I knew the sun hadn't even set yet, but my eyelids began to flutter, weighted down more with every blink. "It's an incredibly powerful being. It can access memories from the past, all of which seem to be correct. But what makes a god, really?" I lay down, curling up on my side. The hard stone floor didn't matter. Not when I just wanted to rest.

Still, through a yawn, I managed, "So what do we do now?"

Søren's reply was the last thing I heard before I lost consciousness. "I suppose we go back to the castle and keep searching for answers."

18

Revna

"THE THIRD RULE OF MAGIC: IT IS AN EXTENSION OF YOURSELF."

I chewed my lip, studying Søren. He appeared totally at ease, like he wasn't obsessively thinking about having to strip me down yesterday in order to save my life. The circles beneath his eyes betrayed his lack of sleep, but otherwise he was calm.

I, on the other hand, couldn't stop thinking about it. I refused to feel awkward—he'd seen it all before, and preventing my hypothermia wasn't the least bit sexual. But it nagged at me.

Maybe because you think he's a monster, and yet he never acts like one around you. The thought was involuntary but not fear-ridden like the other thoughts I'd had influenced by my Lurae. It felt more true, too. Søren had done monstrous things. That could not be denied.

But did it make him a monster at his core?

I wasn't sure.

"So, like my sword," I said, forcing myself back to the conversation at hand.

"Exactly." He sounded pleased I'd caught on so quickly. "At

first, when you learn how to spar, the sword can be too heavy—almost unwieldy. It's easy to feel like the weapon pulls you in the direction it wants. Like you have no control. But once you've used those muscles enough, you become master of your weapon."

The words settled in me, the familiar comparison like the spark of a struck match in the dark. "That makes . . . an absurd amount of sense."

The Tapestry had said continuing to train with my Lurae would help me contact it again. Would allow me to see more of the past *without* diving to my near-death in a frigid lake. And we needed to understand the intricacies of the prophecy we'd discovered. So despite my wariness, despite the strange tension now living between Søren and me, training wasn't something I was willing to set aside.

"Then let's get started," he said.

◆ ◆ ◆ ◆ ◆

"I HATE THIS."

I snarled and sat down hard in the snow, dropping my face into my palms. After two hours of relentless practicing, I was still unable to coax my magic to obey my commands at will. The occasional successes soured after dozens upon dozens of failures.

Colors bloomed behind my eyelids in the darkness, the pressure from my hands blocking out the white landscape, desolate in every direction. *At least when he was teaching me how to fight with a sword it came somewhat naturally.*

Søren perched on an old stump. The wood let out a creak, and I peered between my fingers to watch him lean forward and place his elbows on his knees. "Do you know how my Lurae manifested?"

I didn't move. Why did his question feel like a trap? I was rabidly curious, itching to know the story. But would he have offered if it wasn't meant to . . . I don't know, teach me some kind of lesson? Prove a point?

"Do Kryllians have a ceremony?" I asked. "We do—or used to, I guess, in Bhorglid. I stood on their temple steps for almost an hour waiting for my Lurae to show up. Frode only told me later, but it was all a ruse. They wouldn't hold the ceremony until the child started displaying signs of a Lurae and then they encouraged them to pretend it had arrived in that instant."

He huffed a laugh, no amusement in it. "No. We don't have any kind of ceremony, thank the gods."

Silence fell for a few seconds. *Maybe he doesn't want to tell me after all,* I told myself. *And maybe I don't want to know. Maybe allowing him in will crack the protective barrier I keep up for all the right reasons.*

I lifted my head and crossed my arms, resting them on my bent knees. He wasn't looking at me—he stared back at the forge, rubbing the edge of his hand-sewn cloak between his thumb and forefinger.

He turned to glance at me, and our eyes caught. I rested my chin on my forearms. Søren was unsettled, and I knew him well enough to know he would stay that way until he said what was on his mind. A fragment remaining from our shared and shattered past.

Hesitantly, I asked, "How then?"

He swallowed. Averted his eyes. "I had been nine for almost two weeks," he began. "No magic had manifested yet. Mother and Father were gently trying to convince me it wasn't a problem for me to be Nilurae. They were right, of course, but I was young. Everyone else in my family was Lurae—Mother could conjure illusions, Father was a healer, and Sonja only needed to think in the direction of the nearest seed and it would grow at her command."

I hummed softly, an assurance I was listening. With every word, the towering, often sullen man faded away until I was only able to see the dark-haired visage of a nine-year-old boy nervously rubbing the edge of his cloak.

"We lived in a tiny village along the coast," he continued. "The year before Sonja turned nine, our crops failed. We lost many people. So when they realized she could make anything grow . . ."

"They revered her," I murmured. They had revered Björn and my father, too—their Lurae offering heat in our freezing wasteland.

"Of course they did." He didn't sound bitter acknowledging it, shrugging at the obvious conclusion. "And I thought my sister was the most impressive person to walk the earth. She was full of raw power. The thought of not having a Lurae made a young boy incredibly upset."

A few heartbeats of silence followed. Within them, I felt the dread of what was coming. Søren waited, mouth open but no words coming. The trees, solemn guardians of the forge, twisted in their seats to listen. The wind ceased.

"I argued with my parents. It became heated quickly." Nausea crept in. I knew where this story was headed. "You're well aware of how magic surges when you're angry. One moment I was yelling at them, the next I looked around and they . . . they were dead."

I said nothing. Søren's foot tapped an impatient beat in the snow.

"I ran. Sonja found me hiding in the fields behind our house. She realized what had happened, but she had heard the townsfolk talking of chasing down the murderer. While I waited there, she returned to the house and pointed them in the wrong direction. Then she closed our parents' eyes for the final time, packed two bags full of supplies, and we left."

When he looked at me again, I saw the boy—gray eyes filled with tears and whispering, *I didn't mean to.*

The prophecy's identification of Søren suddenly made a terrible amount of sense. *Him, harbinger of forebearers' doom.*

The tightness in my chest returned. Søren took a deep breath, likely preparing to put on the airs of someone well-adjusted, and in a burst of unfiltered thought, words flew from me.

"I killed Halvar."

There were dozens of things Søren could have said. And somehow he managed the one I least expected.

"I know."

I blinked, heart faltering. "What—what do you mean, *you know*?"

Panic filled me. If Søren knew, did the others? Had Freja discovered the truth and managed to hide it from me? Is that why she was so argumentative with me all the time now? Shit, had I been forcing Jac to live a lie for no reason—

"Revna."

I breathed in and saw Søren kneeling in front of me. His palm was outstretched tentatively toward me, but it never connected. Instead, he pulled it back. Sheepishly, he ran the hand through his hair. "There's something I've been meaning to tell you. My Lurae involves more than just killing people at will. I can also see ghosts."

The revelation startled me from my panic. "Are you serious?"

"Yes. I ran into Halvar's ghost a few days into my stay in Bhorglid. Made the mistake of going into the tavern after I gave Mira my latest update."

I remained frozen. My emotions couldn't decide the best course of action. Did I need to panic? Accuse him of lying? Demand more information? What was the right thing to do?

And most important—how was he being so calm about this?

"Will you tell me what happened?" Søren's voice was far more gentle than it had any right to be, and it pierced through my rib cage like a blade.

I didn't want to resist anymore. Besides—he already knew the damning part. What was the admission of a few more sins?

I took a deep breath and began to speak.

Søren

The story spilled from her in fits and starts. How Halvar declared her a traitor, believing her to have hidden her Lurae. The argument, a culmination of every stress Revna carried that day and the abandonment of her father figure. The burst of power taking on a life of its own.

The aftermath.

"Volkan found me," she said. I knew from observing her she was in a place far from me. Her eyes were unfocused, her voice quiet. She curled in on herself a bit more with every word. "Helped to . . . dispose of the body. Clean the tavern. Said he'd known you long enough to understand what was happening to me."

A rush of affection for Volkan warmed me. He remained as steady as ever, the Fastian prince. "Volkan is one of only four people who knows what I did to my parents," I told her. "He's been nothing but the most trustworthy confidant through the years."

She nodded, but her stare remained far away. "I never wanted this," she whispered. "I didn't mean to hurt him. And now I'm stuck in the most complicated lie."

Maybe, I wanted to tell her, *but did you ever consider how brilliant you are? How much stronger than I've ever been? Has anyone told you yet that you'll make it through this, even if it's bruised and bloody?*

"When Freja finds out—and she will, Jac is getting tired of the ruse—she'll hate me." Revna said it with such certainty. It seemed to bring her back to herself a bit. "Arne already hates me, and he'll make sure Freja never speaks to me again. All of this started because I wanted to save her, and now I'm the one who will ruin her life."

For a moment, I debated killing Arne—the bastard—when we returned to the city. It would be worth it, even if it meant I blew my cover. But it would cause too many problems for Revna, so I stowed away the idea, vowing to return to it when the political schemes had calmed and everything was more settled.

Revna hadn't stopped talking while I thought. "Volkan is getting tired of it, too. He keeps telling me I'm in over my head. Says I need to tell her now. But no one understands how crucial Halvar is to the Nilurae's support and—" She shook her head. "I'm just rambling now."

Keep rambling, I wanted to beg her. *Talk at me until we're old and gray, until the ice covers our bones and we're so sick of each other that you can't help but travel on to the next life.* But I kept my mouth shut, unwilling to yield my position as her confidant.

"When they see me . . . *really* see me and discover who I am . . . they'll leave." Every word was a whisper. "I'll sit in the castle, Queen of Bhorglid. And I will be entirely alone. Being ruler wears on me already. I thought this was what I wanted, what I needed. Now I'm not sure if I fought for the right thing."

I stood and approached her, extending my hand to help her up. For a long moment, she merely looked at me. "I know what it's like," I told her carefully, "to have your responsibility weighing on you. To see the inevitable coming like a winter storm approaching in the distance. But I can also tell you it is worthwhile to hope."

Her frigid fingers were dwarfed by my hand as she accepted my offer to pull her up. "Sorry," she said, tugging on the end of her braid. "I just . . . I can't stop thinking about what I've done. What it says about me."

"All it says is that you made a mistake. And that someone who should have cared for you decided to be an asshole about something you couldn't control, instead of offering you support and comfort."

"It's not his fault," Revna said, her gaze trained on her boots. "And maybe it was a mistake—but not the kind that can be forgiven. People don't come back from the dead, Søren. Lurae like ours have consequences."

"And the consequence of your actions is being alone? Forever?" I pressed.

She nodded. I wasn't sure whether I imagined the glint of sun on a fallen, frozen tear in the snow.

"Maybe your friends deserve more credit than you give them, too." I rubbed a hand over the back of my neck nervously and cleared my throat. "Halvar isn't the only ghost I've seen as of late. When I went and retrieved his body, I spoke to Frode."

I held my breath. I had no idea how Revna would feel about me speaking to her brother. She might be thrilled, but she might also be angry. I braced myself for whatever reaction she landed on.

Her brow furrowed. "And . . . what did he say?"

"That he was proud of you for winning the Trials. He was glad you were safe and hoped you were happy."

There were several long heartbeats of silence. Revna nodded, taking it in, but didn't say anything more. I glanced up at the sky. Thick clouds loomed in the north. "There's a storm on its way here. We'd better leave now, else we risk being stuck in it. I'll go pack up our things—join me whenever you're ready."

My footfalls were heavy as I left her to think over our conversation. I hoped she wasn't watching when my hands curled into fists. *I will never leave you,* I swore silently. *If everyone else abandons you, I will be by your side. There is nowhere you can travel where I will not follow. Even if it means I crawl to you on my hands and knees through the depths of hell.*

I spared no glance backward as I entered the forge. If I did, it would have taken more restraint than I possessed to keep myself from pulling her into a tight embrace, making the promise aloud, and crushing her mouth to mine.

◆ ◆ ◆ ◆ ◆

WE MANAGED TO MAKE IT MORE THAN HALFWAY HOME BY THE time we stopped to make camp. Originally, I'd considered riding through the night. We kept just ahead of the storm, the heavy precipitation easy to see falling in the distance. But as darkness fell, the mare showed signs of exhaustion. As did Revna—she kept dozing off, utterly spent from yesterday's ordeal and the effort of training her magic so extensively.

Her head resting back on my chest was a sensation I treasured. If she were awake, I knew she'd be furious about the show of weakness.

She won't forgive you, I reminded myself. *She's known the truth for ages now, and it hasn't changed a thing.*

I knew things between us would never be the same. Had accepted it long ago, when I made the decision to end Frode's life. It made me all the more eager to hold on to the small moments—her acceptance of my hand this morning after she shared what happened with Halvar; clutching her half-frozen, shivering, sopping form to my chest and sprinting for the forge, desperately hoping to warm her up in time; and now, when she trusted me not to let her fall despite her exhaustion.

But the horse needed a break. Reluctantly, I tugged on the reins and shook Revna's shoulder. "Wake up, Princess. We're taking a short rest."

She stirred, blearily. "We are? What about the storm?" She rubbed her hands over her eyes.

"It's a couple of hours behind us. Don't worry, we won't stay long."

Once the tent was set up, Revna fell almost immediately back into slumber. I once again resisted the urge to wrap her in my arms. The few nights we'd shared a bed during our time in the prison had been the best nights of sleep I'd ever had. Seeing the soft, golden thread of her soul just out of reach now, knowing she didn't want me any nearer, was torturous.

For years, I'd dreamt only of Sonja. It was part of why my insomnia was so terrible. Even sleep was torture. Only after meeting Revna had my dreams changed—her fiery personality kept me company when I managed to truly slumber.

Now that was torture, too.

But tonight, I didn't dream of my sister or of my princess. Instead, I dreamt of the wandering woman who taught me to forge.

I watched from a distance as the red-haired traveler stepped through the woods, into a small grove of trees. A warped, petrified tree stump stood among the rest, and she ran a gentle hand over it. The woman looked exactly how I remembered her—even with the scar that ran across her face. She unsheathed a golden sword from her hip, a weapon more beautiful than any I'd seen before. It felt vaguely familiar, but the part of my mind fully slumbering couldn't put a finger on why. Then, she laid it down in the snow and called, "I know you're here. There's no point in hiding any longer."

Footsteps announced the arrival of a newcomer. In my dream state, I didn't care that it was the Queen of Kryllian—my subconscious creating an unfamiliar scene with bits and pieces of different parts of my life.

The queen's blond hair tangled in the wind like the soul threads stretching between the women. "That's it?" she said with disdain.

"You aren't even going to fight for it? After they revered you for nearly four hundred years—goddess of the soul?"

The woman shook her head. "I've spent so long fighting. So long chasing you. I cannot hold that responsibility any longer."

The queen stepped forward slowly, picking up the blade and examining it. *That's where I know it from,* I realized. *The queen had that sword with her the day I buried Frode's body. She hasn't relinquished her hold on it since.*

Hunger shone in Anja's eyes. She laughed, and a flock of birds scattered into the air. "Oh, Aloisa. I've been looking forward to this."

She plunged the blade through the woman's abdomen.

20

Revna

WHEN I STEPPED THROUGH THE CASTLE DOORS, THE ONLY thought on my mind was how quickly I could fill the bathtub with hot water—that, and Søren's dream. Thoughts of what he'd seen had eaten away at me all day while we rode, discussing the possibilities.

There was something about the red-haired woman he described, the one who had saved him and Sonja when they were children, that felt familiar. When I asked him to describe her appearance, there was a detail that sent chills down my spine.

The woman had a scar through her right eyebrow that descended down over her cheek. I thought back to the memories the Tapestry had shown me—blood running down Aloisa's face from some kind of impact when she returned to the surface and pulled Callum back from death.

"Do you think," I had ventured, "there's any way you may have met Aloisa? The same Aloisa I've seen visions of?"

I'd waited for his laugh, his blatant refusal to accept the impossible. It was what I wanted to do, after all. So when he'd tensed behind me, I expected I knew the answer.

I hadn't thought he would say *yes*.

"Strange things seem to be following us," he'd sighed. "We're the subjects of Tam's prophecy; you met a mystical, divine being at the bottom of a frozen lake; the spirits of the dead can't pass on. What's one more to add to our list?"

There was no time to dwell on his words now, though. Including the news that the dead were trapped in our world. Søren had promised we would discuss it in more detail later, then gone to change clothes before heading into the city. "Mira is likely waiting for me to give a report," he'd explained.

Honestly, I was glad to keep busy and distracted from everything that had happened in the wastes. The news that Søren could see Frode weighed on me, and I wasn't sure what to make of it or whether to trust that he was telling the truth about what my brother's spirit had conveyed. Frode had never been an angry person, but part of me still expected him to hold a grudge for my part in his death.

I couldn't brush it away. The thought looped endlessly, forcing me to confront it again and again with no relief, until something bigger arrived to take its place in my mind.

Thankfully, at home, an ambush was waiting for me.

Freja and Volkan moved to walk in step with me before the doors even closed, one of them on each side of me. I blinked, surprised. "Freja. Volkan. How are you?"

The set of Freja's furrowed brow worried me. "Not well. The Nilurae are growing restless. People are not pleased with the small amounts of rations they're receiving."

Was I supposed to be filled with dread the moment I returned to my day-to-day life? Not for the first time, I wished fervently that being queen involved more swordplay and less . . . politics.

"With the army home now, we can increase daily rations a bit," I answered, slowing my pace. The bath I'd been daydreaming of wasn't going to happen anytime soon, and I swallowed my disappointment. "And maybe we can send a few hunting parties into the hills, see what game they can bring back. Do we have enough rations for that?"

"I think so, but I'll need to double-check. That isn't all, though."

"What else, then?"

She sighed. Volkan picked up where she left off. "There have been some . . . incidents since you left. Our competition between the soldiers kept most occupied while you were gone, but not all. Some of the Nilurae shopkeepers are now refusing to serve Lurae—which is their right, but the Lurae have been lashing back as a result. One shop was burned down by an angry fire wielder."

I inhaled sharply. "Was anyone hurt?"

"No," Freja said, "but only due to pure luck. The man responsible was arrested and put in prison."

I pressed the heel of my palm into my temple as Volkan continued. "Many of the Nilurae were still tentatively on your side, despite your Lurae manifesting, but with the powerless now so outnumbered in the city . . ."

"They worry they will be overpowered," I finished. "Their voices too, not just in a physical sense."

The prince nodded. His hands clasped behind his back. I found myself wondering what he'd said when Søren told him the truth about accidentally killing his own parents. Volkan had known Søren only after the fact—not like when the prince found me, immediately after killing Halvar.

I thought of Søren's insistence that the priests were hiding in plain sight, waiting to launch their own coup. Was the burning house a move by them? The assassin who'd come after me probably was.

Unless the man responsible confessed, there was no way to know. For a moment, I considered telling Freja and Volkan about the potential of the priests' return.

But I held back my words. I didn't want to cause more panic, more problems, right now. Astrid had proven herself trustworthy, though. Maybe she could look into it quietly.

"So?" Freja's impatient voice pulled me from my thoughts.

A huff of irritation left me. "I pulled the army home *because* it would give the Nilurae more food. And now they're complaining about it. I understand their frustration, but it's not like I can send the army back out to war."

Freja glared. "Well you can at least do *something*. Ever since you were crowned, they've been waiting for you to make a move guaranteeing their freedom. And instead, you're—"

I stepped forward, toe-to-toe with her. Anger smoldered like hot coals. "I'm what? Thinking critically about the situation from every angle? Refusing to act rashly and make a move that condemns us all?"

She scoffed. "No. You're sitting on your ass, letting your magic take the blame for your inaction and pretending it's enough."

"Stop it." Volkan grabbed my shoulder with one hand, Freja's with the other, and pulled us apart. But it wasn't enough to stop the lullaby from beginning its sickening melody in my head. Or to stop the hurt from spreading through me, radiating from my chest like I'd been stabbed. "Now is not the time for petty arguments."

He turned to Freja. "Revna is doing everything she can. Just because it doesn't look the way you want it to doesn't detract from her progress mending the rift between your people."

Before I could settle from anger into surprise, he faced me. "Freja is upset because these people are her life. It's something you can only partially understand, no matter how much you want to. Your life in this castle robbed you of it. She is passionate and she pushes for you to do more because she loves them. And because she loves you and sees what incredible things you've accomplished in the past.

"Now." He took a step back, both of us staring at him, wide-eyed. "I have an idea. Care to hear it?"

21

Søren

I DECIDED TO CHANGE INTO FRESH CLOTHES BEFORE I WENT INTO the city to meet with Mira.

I opened the door of the bedroom I was staying in and lit the lamps, only to swear. Mira lounged on my bed, kicking her feet off the edge. "What are you doing here?" I asked.

"The queen wants to see you. She's impatient, too—was pretty upset when I returned to her with the news that you'd be gone for a few days." She turned her head to face me. "We need to leave as soon as possible."

I bit back my angry thoughts. Mira didn't deserve to be the recipient of my wrath. I wondered whether the queen had continued to withhold meals from her—whether Mira still thought she'd done the right thing by telling the queen about me and Revna.

Where did the teleporter's true loyalty lie? I hoped it was with me but worried I was wrong.

"Who does she want to see—Søren or the Hellbringer?"

Mira sighed. "The masked menace, of course."

"Not even sure why I bother asking anymore," I said, striding to open the hutch doors. Mira did me the decency of turning around while I changed. The moment my boots were buckled and the last latch on the helmet was in place, I faced her.

"Let's go." My distorted voice nearly startled me. How long had it been since I was the Hellbringer? The scholar mask was innocuous, innocent. I was relieved to wear the face that didn't require me to hide my displeasure at . . .

We appeared in front of the Kryllian palace. My thought finished itself. *Everything.*

◆ ◆ ◆ ◆ ◆

WHEN THE QUEEN FINALLY ALLOWED US TO ENTER HER THRONE room, my patience had worn thin.

My boots made a satisfying sound on the tiled floor with every step, the familiar weight of my sword heavy on my left hip. The nobles leaving as we entered stared unabashedly, their murmurs echoing through the giant room. I ignored them, stopping only to snarl at one who reached out with tentative fingers, as if to touch me.

The sound was terrifying with the voice distortion. Mira's expression of disgust told me everything she thought about the occurrence.

The doors slammed shut behind us, and the queen laughed. Her high-pitched tittering glanced off the myriad embellishments adorning the walls. Unlike Bhorglid's throne room, which was stark and purposeful, the palace was a show of power through wealth. It made sense. The mines in Kryllian made the rich even richer. The people the queen needed to impress were flush with wealth. The show of gold and precious jewels was an intimidation tactic, just like the austerity of the throne room in Bhorglid.

"Welcome back," she said, leaning forward on her throne to study me. Her voice was cheerful, but I knew where to look to see her real mood—and her eyes were full of fury. "I am disappointed in you, Hellbringer. You have yet to bring me any real news of the princess's abilities. I gave you a single task, and you still manage to fail me."

Mira can give the same damned report just fine. I gritted my teeth and forced my tone to smooth, a false layer of calm over my anger. It matched the queen's, fire for fire. "Like I'm sure Mira has attested, the Queen of Bhorglid is progressing well in her training. Her Lurae only rarely reacts to her emotional state now, and for the most part, she is in control of her magic."

"Not good enough."

My head snapped up, and the queen hissed aloud at my defiance. But I refused to bow again. "You gave me three weeks to get her Lurae under control. I've done the best I possibly could."

She stood from her throne, towering over me on her dais. "I require nothing less than *perfection*."

"It takes most Lurae *years* to fully master their abilities—"

The queen drew her sword—the same one I'd dreamt about, that she had taken from Aloisa—and marched to me. She thrust one sharp edge against my throat. "Your insolence will not be tolerated, Hellbringer. Will she be capable of using her magic when I arrive to negotiate the treaty or not?"

The unspoken threat lingered in my mind, as it always did. *Sonja*. Her life was on the line until I found her and brought her to safety, away from the clutches of the queen. Every part of me wanted to cower in the face of her and this knowledge. On any other day, I would have.

But just yesterday, Revna had trusted me. She'd confessed what happened with Halvar. She'd leaned on me and drifted to sleep while I brought us back to Bhorglid. I knew she would never forgive me, but she also never failed to make me feel like a man instead of a monster.

And now this tiny woman whom I'd never even seen use a Lurae wanted to use the woman I love for her own gain. She was desperate for Revna to master her abilities. But why? Did she want access to the Tapestry? Or something else entirely?

Either way, I knew Revna was only a means to an end for the queen. And it made me furious.

I wanted to snuff out the life in front of me. Take the soul and *rip it from her body* until she lay lifeless on the floor. Better yet, I wanted to draw my own sword and plunge it into her stomach.

I held myself back. *Not yet. You need to keep Sonja safe, and Revna needs that treaty signed. Neither of those things can happen if the queen is dead.*

Curling my trembling hands in on themselves, I answered her question with one of my own. "Where," I said slowly, savoring every roughhewn word, "did you get this sword?"

The reaction was instant. Her eyes widened and the blade shook. A slight motion, but one I inevitably noticed, considering the weapon was pressed to my throat. I felt a drop of blood descending from the shallow wound there and swallowed a depraved thought about Revna's tongue tracing the same path. The blood in my veins was a roaring river in my ears.

But the queen's surprise slowly morphed into a predatory gleam. "You want to know about this blade? It has the potential to rend the future in two. Now tell me whether the little bitch will be able to control her magic fully in one week, or it will rend *you* in two instead."

The entire war between Kryllian and Bhorglid raged inside of me in the span of a second.

I gathered the sharp blade of my magic, ready to sever the threads that bound the queen's soul to her body. They glowed and trembled, like her very essence could sense my intention.

And then I thought of Revna. *I can't make things worse for her.*

The queen knew it, too. She knew I still cared for Revna, and she was using my emotions to manipulate me. Anja had me backed into a corner, one I saw no escape from. I pulled back on my Lurae, calmed my breathing, and told the queen what she wanted to hear.

"The Queen of Bhorglid will have complete mastery over her Lurae by the time you arrive for negotiations."

◆ ◆ ◆ ◆ ◆

I WAS DRESSED LIKE A SCHOLAR—EXCEPT FOR THE SWORD AT my hip.

As I arrived in town, the palace spires rising above the forestry, anger beat a furious tempo in my chest. My weapon of choice was my sword, but I knew what kind of attention it would draw if I pulled it on someone here. Swords were the weapons of soldiers, not scholars. Not townsfolk.

Daggers, though? No one would bat an eye if I threatened someone with a mere knife. The one sheathed on my forearm practically begged me to pull it out, but I resisted. Not yet.

I'd taken a circuitous route, worried the queen would have spies tailing me. It wouldn't be the first time. I hoped the cloak I'd swiped from a clothesline on my way into town was enough to disguise me from any lingering eyes. The path to my destination was one I had memorized by now. The village was laid out messily, and no signs denoted the proper direction of any buildings. After all, most citizens in Kryllian couldn't read.

When I arrived at the small home, I rapped my knuckles on the back door and waited.

The instant the man opened it a crack, I shoved my hand in to grab him by the front of the shirt and haul him out. His garbled cries of panic went unheeded as I slammed him against the side of the building and held the point of the blade beneath his chin.

"What news do you have?" I said through gritted teeth.

He'd stopped thrashing when he recognized me. Likely not the first time a client had come demanding answers. "You're threatening me?" His scowl embraced all of his features, distorting them into distaste. "At my own home? Foul of you—I've been waiting for you to show up, you know."

"Why?"

"For an update, you jackass."

I pressed the blade against his skin a little harder. "Then *update me* before I kill you."

"Gods! I found the woman you're looking for, all right? If you want more than that, you have to let me go."

Blinking, I released him. "You found her?"

He pushed my dagger away, an easy feat with me so shocked. As he brushed himself off, he grumbled, "Don't look so surprised. It's what you paid me to do, isn't it?"

The desperation of the afternoon faded like morning fog in the sun. Now I was frantic. "Where?"

The man sighed. "Sonja Anselm. She's traveling with a caravan of Seeing Ones. When I caught wind of her ten days ago or so, they were in southern Faste. Headed toward Kryllian, from what my informants said."

The information registered slowly, but when it sank in, I couldn't breathe. *She's alive, she's alive, she's alive.* Despite the queen's assurances and threats, I'd long wondered whether Sonja had perished after escaping the Kryllian palace dungeons.

"Did they say anything else?" Even I heard the desperation in my voice. "Is she well?"

The man shrugged. "Well enough. They said she looked happy—she had a wedding ring on and a baby on her hip, though it's not certain whether the baby was hers."

Safe. Sonja is safe.

I didn't thank him, only shoved the bag of coins I'd put in my pocket on the way out of the palace into his hands.

I walked back to the palace in a daze. My hands itched for something to do. Did I leave now and go to Faste?

No. No, I wouldn't abandon Revna. Sonja's location and safety were the queen's bargaining chip. While I couldn't guarantee my sister would remain safe, at least I knew where she was. At least I knew she hadn't been killed by the queen.

I had to make a choice. My battles had been divided, two fronts before me. It was the worst thing that could happen to an army, a general. I knew from firsthand experience how hopeless things became when you split your focus this way. When a general was forced to make a sacrifice.

But I could not be everywhere at once. I did, however, know where I was needed most. So when I arrived in the garden to find a scowling Mira waiting for me, I held out my arm and said, "Take me back to Bhorglid."

22

Revna

WHEN SØREN AND I HAD ARRIVED BACK AT THE CASTLE, EVENING was falling. Now, as Volkan, Freja, and I finished our meeting in my father's old office, yawns stretching our faces to their breaking points, the sun's early rays glowed over the mountains.

I sighed. My stomach growled. And I wished for a bath.

Freja chuckled. After spending so much time together brainstorming solutions, our earlier argument could almost be forgotten.

Almost.

Volkan clapped me on the shoulder. "I feel good about this. Do you?"

Freja had proposed an idea to rebuild failing structures and roads in the city. "With more tax money coming in from the Lurae, we can focus on uplifting the infrastructure on the Nilurae side of town. Repair the roads, remove any uninhabited buildings, and help the businesses improve their look."

"That's brilliant," I'd told her. "We can start a few projects as soon as the festival is finished. We've only got six more days until then."

Freja had been thrilled. "Can we start making a list of ideas?"

Despite my exhaustion, I'd obliged her. It was nice to spend time thinking about the people I led instead of the prophecy I was supposed to make sense of.

"You're good at this, Freja," Volkan had noted as we prepared to leave. "If you ever want to be a politician, we could use you in Faste."

"Not unless you're in charge," she'd said with a grin. "Volkan, they really need to let you run your own country one of these days."

A halfhearted laugh. "If only."

I smiled up at Volkan. "I feel good about it, too."

"And how did your trip with Søren go?" he asked. "Were you able to find record of the prophecy?"

"We were. There's a magical . . . being of some kind living in the wastes." I still wasn't sure what to call the Tapestry. *God* didn't feel quite right, and I was hesitant to offer the power of such a word to a thing I didn't fully understand. "It calls itself the Tapestry. It showed me the memory of the prophecy being given."

"What did it say?" Freja asked.

I rummaged through my bag and pulled out the sheet of paper Søren had transcribed the words onto. "You can read it for yourselves. It's pretty vague, but Søren and I discussed it and we think the queen could have reasonably guessed that I was Lurae based on the information it offers."

We were silent for a moment as they read, scanning the paper. Volkan frowned, mouthing the words to himself as he absorbed them. "It sounds," he finally said, "like you and the Hellbringer have now taken the place of this Weaver."

I frowned, peering down at the paper myself. "How do you figure that?"

"I see it, too," Freja said. She pointed to the fifth line. "'A guardian divided' is followed by a description of you and the Hellbringer. Perhaps you two now bear whatever responsibilities the Weaver had."

"I think you're right," I said slowly. "Huh. I didn't pick up on that at all before."

But what had Aloisa's responsibilities been? What was she guarding or weaving? I thought back to the vision I'd seen, where the Tapestry appeared before her after she emerged from the water. She'd pulled a thread from it, placed it back into Callum, and then he'd come to life once more.

I needed to talk to Søren about this.

Volkan made for the door, bidding both of us good night—"Or good morning, I suppose; either way, I'm about to sleep for the next eight hours"—and ambled off. Freja moved to follow him, but I called after her.

"Wait."

She paused, looking over her shoulder and raising an eyebrow. Exhaustion was showing on our faces, and I saw it in the way her posture slumped slightly.

"I was wondering," I said, "if you would take a formal position as my counselor." When she didn't say anything, I hurried on. "You don't have to, of course. You're just . . . Volkan wasn't lying when he said you're good at this, Freja. I managed the conquering, but I'd be lost without you both. You deserve to be acknowledged for your work, and I hoped offering you a formal position might be enough to—*oof*."

She wrapped her arms so tightly around me I lost my breath. "Of course, you idiot. There's nothing I'd want more. Thank you for asking me."

My heart was lighter when I ascended the stairs to my room.

◆ ◆ ◆ ◆ ◆

IN THE PAST DAY AND A HALF, I'D SPOKEN WITH A POWERFUL, INhuman being who showed me memories of the past so vivid, I hadn't been able to distinguish myself from the person whose eyes I viewed them through. But even that couldn't rival the strangeness of what waited for me outside my bedroom door.

I came to a stop at the top of the stairs. For a moment, I considered I might be hallucinating. But no, there they sat—Søren and Astrid, on the floor on each side of the door, glaring at each other.

As I drew closer, I amended my original thought. Astrid was glaring, and if her looks could kill, then Søren would have long gone cold. Søren, on the other hand, smirked. He leaned against the wall, cross-legged, a dagger on the floor in front of him. With one finger, he reached out and spun the end of the weapon. It twirled round and round. He didn't even look at it.

Oh, gods, I thought. *What did Astrid possibly do to bring out the Hellbringer?*

Because this powerful, haughty man bore no resemblance to Søren the gentle scholar. No—this was a standoff, one that the Hellbringer intended to win. I rushed up to them.

Signing and speaking at once, I asked, "What the hell is going on here?"

"You can sign," Søren said, his hands moving in tandem with his words. "No need to accommodate me."

The words held a deadly undertone. He didn't move his eyes from Astrid. With a heavy sigh, I turned to her. "What's going on?"

"He's lurking." Her lip curled in disgust. "I am your bodyguard, so I am supervising."

"Astrid seems to think I cannot be trusted to speak with you privately." Søren didn't take his eyes off the teleporter. "Despite having spent the last several days alone with you in the wastes."

"You work for the enemy," she fired back. "For all I know, you could be planning to assassinate Revna."

"If I wanted to assassinate her," Søren managed to drawl even when he signed, "don't you think I would have done it already?"

Astrid actually growled, and I stepped between them. "Stop it, both of you. Astrid—before Søren arrived, what were you doing here?"

She frowned, as if surprised I didn't already know. "Waiting for you to return. After the unrest in the city while you were gone, it's clear there could be another assassination attempt."

"And Søren?" I turned to the Hellbringer, whose mask of arrogance faded with every passing moment. "Why are you here?"

"I—" He paused for a moment, hands hovering in the air, and I wondered whether he was telling the truth. Finally, he settled on, "I wanted to make sure you were safe."

But his eyes wouldn't meet mine or Astrid's anymore. I noted the dark circles under his eyes. Had he slept at all? How long had he been sitting here, in a standoff with Astrid?

"All right," I said. "Thank you both for your concern. I do appreciate it. I doubt there will be an assassination attempt tonight—or, I guess this morning. Søren, if you want to speak to me, then wait in my room. I have a matter to discuss with Astrid privately first."

Astrid glared as Søren closed my bedroom door behind him. "It isn't smart to allow him to get close."

"I know." It was the truth. I was more than fully aware of how tempting the man was. "But I'm not here to talk about him. I need a favor."

She perked up. "Anything."

"You must keep this a secret from everyone. Even Freja." I raised an eyebrow. "Can you do that?"

She didn't even hesitate. "Of course. My duty and my relationships are separate, and one will not get in the way of the other."

Oh, how I envied the confidence in her reply. Still, I nodded. "There is a rumor that the priests are still in the city, but in hiding. Some have begun organizing. I think they might be planning a coup."

At this, she grew deadly serious. "Do you want me to kill them?"

"Not yet." It wasn't a bad idea, though. "For now, I'm not even sure how much truth there is to these rumors. My source is . . . emotionally biased." *Considering I killed him.* "Spend some time at the Sharpened Axe, and keep your eyes peeled for anyone who looks suspicious. New faces that no one seems to recognize, people who spend time with only Lurae companions. Or anyone who sneers at the Nilurae. I don't want to act until we have proof, but I'd feel far better if I knew you were keeping your eyes on the situation."

"Of course. I'll report back with anything I find out."

"Thank you. Now, go get some sleep." She raised her hands, ready to protest, and I held up a palm. "No arguments. You've been here all night. Your dedication is appreciated, but you need to rest. I need you at your best if you're going to continue being such an excellent bodyguard."

She sighed. "And what about him?"

I glanced at the closed door to my room. "I have a private matter I need to discuss with him before I send him back to his quarters."

Astrid raised a suspicious eyebrow. But she acquiesced, nodding farewell and heading back to the stairwell. I watched her go, wondering whether she was headed back to her own quarters or Freja's.

I entered my quarters to find the lamps lit. Søren was busy closing the curtains. He glanced at me when I stepped inside. "What are you doing here?" I ventured.

For a long moment, he continued readying the space in silence, adjusting my blankets and then shoving his hands into his pockets. "Mira brought me back from Kryllian an hour ago. Made a report to the queen. I wanted to see you afterward," he confessed. "To debrief, of course." The last part was added on in a rush.

I studied him. After spending four days together in the wastes, I hadn't expected Søren to seek me out. Especially when I'd made it clear I had no interest in forgiving him. "You wanted to see me."

"Is that such a crime?" The wry note in his voice fell flat. When

I didn't answer immediately, he turned pleading eyes to me. "Only for a few minutes. Just to talk—I promise."

I hadn't doubted him at any point, but the show of such desperation startled me. "All right."

Søren settled in the armchair. I pushed away the memory of him sitting there in full Hellbringer gear, waiting for me to awaken after the Trials. My scars itched. "What's on your mind?" I asked, stepping into the bathing room attached to my chambers and pulling the privacy screen closed over it.

I eyed the bathtub with longing, but . . . now certainly wasn't the time. My treacherous mind thought differently, and for a moment I pictured Søren pushing back the flimsy screen and pressing me up against the wall, rucking my shirt up over my breasts and—

"The queen is restless."

His voice pulled me from my lusting thoughts, and I inhaled sharply. What in the world was I thinking? This man was responsible for the death of my brother.

But you would have done the same thing. My thoughts snuck in, but I didn't try to push them away. Whether it was my Lurae or myself thinking it, I found myself listening instead. *If Frode's life had been on the line, and Søren's too . . . you would have killed Sonja to try to save them both.*

The realization settled in my stomach like a weight. I wasn't sure what to do with it. Regardless, it wasn't a good idea to fall back into Søren's arms. We'd grown too far apart and had missed our chance to make things work between us.

"What do you mean?" I asked, hoping he couldn't hear the breathy note in my voice. I stripped off my tunic and pants, still filthy from the days of travel. I hadn't even had the chance to change clothes before Freja and Volkan pulled me back into politics again.

"She's insistent that you be a master of your Lurae by the time she arrives next week," he replied. This time, his voice was closer. Almost like he stood directly on the other side of the thin privacy screen. I finished unwinding my breastband, fully aware of the goose bumps traveling along the length of my arms. Gods, even his voice made me *want*. "She doesn't care about civil unrest in Bhorglid. A few unhappy Lurae don't matter in the grand scheme of things. There must be another reason why she wants you so powerful. Maybe your Lurae is what she's after."

I was exhausted. It was the only explanation for the way my body was reacting—nipples peaking at the thought of Søren's hands. Hurriedly, I grabbed a clean breastband off my shelf and busied myself putting it on. "I shared the prophecy with Volkan and Freja earlier. They think the 'guardian divided' means that you and I are now the ones with Aloisa's . . . power? Responsibilities? I'm not entirely sure."

Footsteps sounded. He paced back and forth, no more than a few feet from me. "That would make sense to me, I suppose. We both see threads, and you mentioned that Aloisa saw them, too. Do you know what she was guarding?"

"No. I'm wondering if I might have another dream tonight. I can't control them at all, but it might help me understand."

"We also need to work on using our Lurae together to summon the Tapestry." For a moment, there was silence. "I want to know why the queen killed Aloisa, too. And why is she so possessive of Aloisa's sword?"

I had no idea what the queen would want with a sword, so I focused on the first of his questions. "You think the dream you had was a memory, then? Sent by the Tapestry?"

"Yes." He sounded certain, and it was easy to picture his facial expression—the determined set of his jaw more familiar than it had any right to be. "I rarely sleep. When I do dream, it's never so vivid. And it sounds very similar to the dreams you've been having. It must have been the Tapestry."

"The wandering woman who saved you all those years ago was Aloisa." We'd discussed this on the ride home, but only now, when we'd had a moment to truly process it all, did it feel real. "Was Aloisa truly a goddess, then? Or just a woman?"

"Well, if she's lived for nearly four hundred years, she certainly isn't human."

Tucking in the end of my breastband, I opened my mouth to reply as I reached for a clean shirt. Only to realize . . . "Shit."

"What?"

I sighed. "The laundry maid put my clean shirts in the wrong place, I think. Could you grab one for me? They'll be in the chest near the bed."

"Shouldn't they know where your things go?" His voice, which held only genuine curiosity, moved away. I heard the click of the chest's latch, and he began rummaging.

"I organize my room differently than the rest of the castle's occupants. Typically the chests are used for clothing and there are no shelves in the bathing room." I leaned against the wall and eyed the shelves I'd hung haphazardly in the days following my coronation. I'd taken them from the weapons room in the cellar of the Sharpened Axe—a forceful reminder to myself of what I'd done to the man who practically raised me.

The chest thunked closed. "I grabbed the first shirt I found. Hope it works."

I reached up over the screen and he handed it to me, our fingers brushing in the exchange. For a moment, we both paused. The world was still on its axis, and I knew with my next breath it would all shatter like glass. But the warmth of his hand and the thought of us facing each other while I was undressed and he was vulnerable made me shiver.

Søren drew his hand back, and I wondered whether I was the only one of us who was disappointed.

I finished changing and stepped back out into the bedroom, undoing my braid as I walked. "So the queen killed Aloisa and took her sword. That means the blade is important, but what is it used for? Was Aloisa doing anything in particular with it?"

He was sitting in the armchair again, elbows on his knees, foot tapping away. "She didn't even use it when I met her in person. But I do remember her having it."

"Do you think the sword is . . ." I hesitated, almost afraid to ask the question.

"Special? Magical in some way? I genuinely have no . . ."

I glanced up, combing my fingers through the hair on my scalp to undo the last of the braid. "No what?"

Søren stared at me with the strangest expression on his face. Like he'd seen something he desperately wanted just out of reach. *Longing.* He shook his head. "You're beautiful."

I froze.

"I'm sorry. I don't want to make this into anything it isn't, I swear to you. It's just that I've been thinking of you all day and missing everything about you for . . . weeks, really. And I wanted to be able to say it to you, even if it's for the last time." His throat bobbed. "Because I still care for you, Revna. If you don't want me to, then I'll never speak of it again. But I needed to let you know."

"Søren . . ."

"I also owe you an apology." His gray eyes were so earnest, and I didn't know what to do. "I told you the truth of what happened that day, but I never apologized. And I hope you know how sorry I am. I've spent my entire life ruining everything I touch, but I want to be better now. For you."

"I don't know that I can forgive you," I said softly. "Not when Frode is gone."

"I know."

Was it terrible to wish I could give him more? To search for a scrap to toss him, so he wouldn't look so sad? "Thank you, though. For telling me the truth."

The words were honest. Letting Frode's death go . . . a nearly impossible task. One I didn't trust myself to try pursuing. But learning of Søren's motivations for his actions, understanding the desperation of trying to keep one's sibling safe at least soothed the storm building within me.

The real enemy was the queen.

"Don't lie." The corner of his mouth tipped up. "Not to me, Revna."

I stepped up to him, arms crossed. "And don't accuse me of lying when I've only ever been honest with you. *Too* honest, truthfully."

He frowned. "You're really grateful? You don't wish I'd allowed you to go on hating me for all of it?"

"I don't."

Since Søren had told me the truth, I'd been nothing but angry at him—and the inevitable way we drew together like magnets. Like the other times before, though, my anger was a shield. One I'd put up to keep myself safe.

I wasn't sure whether it was serving me anymore, though. Especially when my mind had started to make peace with the idea that Frode made his own choices that day, too.

I didn't want to fall into Søren's orbit again. Not when it would make me more vulnerable than ever before. But perhaps friendship wasn't out of the realm of possibility. I could offer him my understanding. Mercy. Compassion.

Fighting the pull—the way I desperately wanted to tell him everything and trust him with the frustrations and failures plaguing me—was too difficult. Everyone was going to leave me when they discovered the truth. It was knowledge I carried constantly, a heavy weight in the pit of my stomach, the awareness of how my few friends embraced me a temporary relief. A bomb with a lit fuse, like the ones Halvar had taught Freja to make last year. Before it all imploded around me.

Søren, though? Søren had listened to my confession—that I'd killed Halvar—and handed me his own. He understood my monstrosity and didn't run from it.

I leaned forward and rested my palms on the armrests, bringing my face dangerously close to his. My heart sped and I was startled to feel the thread of my Lurae tying me to him, tempo accelerating with the beat of his pulse.

I wasn't the only one affected, then.

But I told myself it was harmless when I looked into his eyes and said, "I may not forgive you, but I don't hate you either. Not anymore. Not when I would have done the same thing, were I in your position."

His pupils bloomed, the black eating away at the gray until I knew desire encompassed him. The string between us, only visible to me, pulled taut. This time, though, I knew it wasn't a sign of terrible things to come. Instead, my magic saw its reflection and begged me to close the space between us until the few inches separating our faces fell away and we finally, *finally*—

"No." I pulled away from him, gasping for breath. "No, I—that isn't—we can't—"

"Revna." He sounded as breathless as me but managed to put a note of confidence in his voice despite it. "I don't want anything from you that you're unwilling to give. I told you before and I'll tell you again now: I will not touch you unless you ask me for it."

My hands trembled. I couldn't face him, but I stared at the windowpanes, the glass reflecting his outline as he rose.

When he spoke next, he was directly behind me. His reflection raised a hand, hovering it over my shoulder for a long moment before he dropped it. "And please, don't ask unless you mean it. You could break me, if you really wanted."

And then I was alone, a chill seeping into my bones as I tried to convince myself there was no idea worse than loving the Hellbringer.

23

Revna

NO AMOUNT OF AWKWARDNESS COULD KEEP ME FROM ATtending training the next morning.

Secretly, I was growing to enjoy our time spent practicing together. During each session, Søren managed to be relentless and patient all at once, the man who taught me how to win the Trials right at the surface of his persona. The scholar and the Hellbringer both disappeared when we'd sit cross-legged in the mountainside clearing.

Søren ran me through the paces of breathing exercises again before moving over to using my Lurae. And through it all, I forced down the echoes of what had been.

Every time our eyes caught, every time his mouth crooked into a smirk, every time he told me how well I was doing, my pulse sped and the memory of our almost-kiss hovered in the forefront of my mind. I reminded myself what a terrible idea it was—trusting him, caring for him, believing it was possible for him to escape the queen's spell.

Rationale was not enough for my heart.

You're lonely, I told myself. *Preparing for the inevitable moment when everyone else leaves you. Because he's seen your mistakes and hasn't cowered.*

We took a break between exercises, and I decided it was time to dig more into what we'd discussed on the journey home yesterday. "Tell me more about the dead not passing on."

Søren huffed a laugh. "It's about as straightforward as it sounds." He went on to tell me the spirits he'd spoken with recently were no longer able to see the archway others had described to him in the past.

"And you think it's related to everything happening with us?" I asked. "The dreams and the prophecy and Aloisa?"

"Possibly." He shrugged. "Or, it could be something entirely different. Right now it doesn't seem to be causing problems for anyone but me, since I'm the only one who can hear or see them. Obviously some are impatient to continue on. But I think keeping our focus on the prophecy is our best bet. Once we have your Lurae figured out and we've solved our issues with the queen, we can look into the problem with the spirits."

His reasoning made sense. "I like that idea."

Break finished, we moved back into our training regimen. Once I'd proven myself still capable of sensing heartbeats adequately, I said, "So . . . what's next?"

"Learning to actually use your magic," Søren replied. He stretched his arms over his head, and I forced my gaze away from the strip of bare skin showing below the hem of his shirt as it moved upward. "Manipulate it and control it without it spiraling out on you."

I tapped my fingers against the cold ground. The snow had melted a considerable amount, leaving slush behind. I was laundering two cloaks a day at this point, considering I had to sit on something that wasn't muddy ground when we practiced. "What about summoning the Tapestry? We need to discover more about what Aloisa's duties were. What she used her Lurae for."

"Well, if the Tapestry is to be believed, we'll both need to use our Lurae together in order to summon it. Right now you can sense things with your Lurae, but I think the process will require more than that."

He caught my glare and held up his hands. "You're getting better every day. It's undeniable. But the queen will be here in five days and you need to have your magic as mastered as possible by then."

Søren was right, but it made me restless to think about more days of the same training regimen over and over until a final test of my prowess arrived. Especially when the test came from the queen—and her motives were still unclear.

"Tell you what," he said, after a few long moments of my silence. "Let's practice your magic. When we're finished for the day, if you have enough energy left and things have gone relatively well, we can try to summon the Tapestry. If not, it'll be the first thing we do tomorrow morning. Deal?"

"Deal." The plan loosened some of the uncertainty clawing at my rib cage.

He grinned at me, the expression blinding. I remembered suddenly how much I'd cherished every smile he offered when we were in the prison together. Each had felt like a gift.

This one felt like a gift, too.

But something seemed to snag his attention. His eyes flickered past me to a point I couldn't see. I waited for him to give me instructions, but he was quiet. I turned to look over my shoulder, but there was nothing—only the same spread of foliage that usually spanned between the clearing and the mountain trail. Finally, I mustered my courage. "Søren?"

He blinked back to awareness, then rose and jogged over to one of the bushes. I followed, keeping my distance. He stared at a flower, newly blooming after the worst of winter had finally dissipated. Its lavender petals stretched out, rounded at the ends, the entire thing smaller than my fingertip. "I didn't know hellebores grew in Bhorglid."

I frowned at the emotion in his voice. "Are you all right?"

"Sonja loves these flowers," he said softly. I watched as he bent down on one knee, brushing gentle fingers against the blossom. "She would grow them everywhere when we were younger. Our house was nearly covered by them."

I didn't say anything, only waited to see what he would offer next. Part of me was more than willing to listen if Søren needed to talk. The other part of me was stalling, afraid to progress to the next part of my training. I knew how to destroy, how to take. I didn't know how to be gentle.

Finally, he rose, studying me for a moment before he said, "I've located Sonja."

"Are you serious?" His expression told me everything I needed to know. "You—gods, where? Where is she?"

"In Faste, apparently." Søren meandered back to where we'd been sitting earlier. He left the flower where it was, but I caught him glancing at it once or twice more. "With a caravan of Seeing Ones. The person I hired to find her said they were heading toward Kryllian. I'm not sure why. But she's safe and healthy. Married, even, if my sources are to be trusted."

He's going to leave, I realized. *To go and find her.*

It made sense. As the queen's guard dog, Søren was a liability—anything we attempted to do would be halfhearted at best when the queen could turn and order Sonja killed at any sign of rebellion. Finding Sonja would relieve him of that burden.

I swallowed. "Do you think it will take you long to find her? Or will you be back in time for the negotiations to continue?" He frowned at me, but my thundering heartbeat kept me rambling. "Volkan probably knows about the movement of the caravans within Faste's borders. We don't get many Seeing Ones here, since my father hated them, but I'm glad they're headed to Kryllian. If you aren't able to find her in Faste, you won't need to look far. Maybe Volkan would even go with you? If you're not here when the queen returns, I can come up with some kind of story to tell her—something to keep her out of the know while you search and get her to safety. Astrid could teleport you, since we don't have plans to go anywhere soon—"

"Revna." My name was a melody on his tongue, his affectionate smile like a balm. "I'm not leaving."

I paused. "You're not? Why?"

He shrugged. "Right now this is where I'm needed. Training you and helping things stabilize before the queen arrives. Sonja is safe. She can wait until things are calmer before I go to find her."

The logical part of me wanted to argue. Wanted to make all the points that had run through my head moments ago, aloud. But the other part of me, the part that craved his presence and couldn't stop thinking about him . . .

That was the part that won.

"Thank you," I said quietly. "For staying."

Training was one thing, but with the queen's arrival drawing ever nearer, so was the moment when I'd have to tell Freja what I'd done. The fallout from that moment would leave me scarred and bruised. And as much as I had tried to hate him until now, I didn't want anyone but him there to pick up the broken pieces of me.

My jagged edges couldn't hurt him. He'd proven it over and over again.

"Of course." His voice was gentle, like a caress. "But back to the training at hand. I want you to try and manipulate me with your Lurae."

I blanched. "Like control your movements?"

"Yes. Or slow my heartbeat. Whatever kind of manipulation you choose."

"No." I crossed my arms. "I won't."

He tilted his head. "Why not?"

"Because I'll hurt you."

"You don't have to hurt me."

I glared. "I don't always have a *choice*, Søren."

The scholar stood, picked up his cloak, and set it back down to touch the edge of mine. He indicated for me to sit and then sat down himself, close enough that our knees nearly touched. "And what if I said I trust you not to hurt me on purpose? And that I don't mind if you hurt me on accident?"

My vision swam. I looked away. "I've killed people on accident. Friends. I don't think I could handle it if you . . ."

"Just try," he encouraged. "If things feel out of control, we can stop. I promise."

I counted the seconds in my head, each one agonizingly long. When I got to ten, I forced myself to exhale. "I'll try."

Beneath my closed eyelids, the world was dark. The only sounds were the wind through the trees, Søren's quiet breathing, and my own heartbeat. The budding trees and the last remnants of snow smelled crisp and fresh. I forced myself to relax.

And then, I grasped for the thread tying me to Søren.

Even with my eyes closed, I saw it—sensed it. It was gold and thin, but not as flimsy as the other threads I usually saw. I decided I would try to make him curl his hand into a fist and then relax it. Simple enough.

Slowly, calmly, I closed my fingers around the thread and gave the tiniest experimental tug.

His whole body lurched to the left, and he let out a grunt.

Instantly, my eyes flew open. I didn't remember standing, didn't remember picking up my cloak and dashing for the hidden path to lead me back to the castle. I did remember the panic, so all-encompassing it felt like it might rip me in two.

I came back to myself when his hand caught my shoulder. "Rev—"

"No," I snapped, well aware I looked wild-eyed, but incapable of calming myself. "No! Søren, I can't kill you. I can't. I'm supposed to hate you still. I told you the other night that I don't want to be anything but friends. It—I—I lied, okay? In just a few days I'm going to be entirely alone except for *you*. I can't afford to lose that. I can't afford to lose you!"

I clapped my hand over my mouth, the realization of what I'd said filling me with dread. *I shouldn't want him. I shouldn't care for him. But I can't stop myself.* Søren's eyes were wide, his mouth agape. Tears ran down my face, but I paid them no mind.

"I *can't*," I repeated again. Equal parts of mortification and dread and panic filled me, and this time, when I tore from his grasp and ran, he didn't try to stop me.

◆ ◆ ◆ ◆ ◆

I SPENT THE REST OF MY DAY HOLED UP IN MY FATHER'S OFFICE, planning for the festival. Freja was thrilled to have my help, and Volkan didn't turn it down either. He'd shown up late, a knowing smile on his face, and I knew Søren must have said something to him.

When I finally retired to bed, I was utterly exhausted. I'd run the entire encounter over in my mind again and again, and it never ceased to be mortifying. I half expected Søren to be sitting outside my bedroom door, but the hallway was empty. Perhaps he saw fit to give me my space.

Gods knew I needed it.

And when I wasn't thinking about Søren, I was mulling over Frode's spirit. Stuck in the northern wastes, assuming Søren's assumption about spirits being unable to move on was accurate. Wondering what I would say to my brother, if I had the chance to see him again.

Surprisingly enough, the only emotion still embedded in my chest was pain. The fury I'd felt toward Søren for so long had faded when I wasn't paying attention. I hadn't forgiven him, but I did understand his reasoning a little better. And knowing the truth had taken the jagged edges of the gaping wound and sealed them slightly.

Still, my mind was a crowded place. The last thing I needed was another vivid dream—presumably from the Tapestry. But I didn't exactly get a say in the matter.

I watched from a distance, thankfully, as a teenage Aloisa stood on the bank of the lake. She appeared the same age as when she'd first dived in. The scar over her eye was still puckered, like the ones on my face. It couldn't have been more than a couple of months since my first vision of her.

She tapped her foot, looking out over the ice. The weather must have warmed, because the lake was no longer solid all the way through. The edges of the water were covered by only a thin layer of frost, and a bit lapped at the shore.

For several long minutes, she simply stood, deliberating. Then, much like I had mere days ago, she stripped off her top layers, left her boots in the snow, and then stepped out over the edge.

The ice shattered with a *crack* so sharp, I jumped. She waded out as far as she could, teeth chattering, and when it was finally deep enough, she submerged herself entirely and swam into the depths.

The scene didn't change immediately. It became clear why mere seconds later, when Callum—panting, hands running through his hair with dismay—ran up to the water. He took one glance at Aloisa's things sitting there and shouted, "No. *No.*"

Then he began stripping as well. Soon enough, he took his boots off and waded into the water, too.

I frowned. This was the same Callum who had tried to bring the godforsaken into submission, who had created the Holy Order of Priests I spent most of my life trying to thwart. But he was also . . .

Just a boy.

It unnerved me.

Before I had time to think too far on it, the world around me blurred and re-formed into the space of nothingness again. Aloisa stood before the Tapestry once more, and she looked even more furious than the first time around.

"What have you done to me?" she demanded. "I thought the price I'd have to pay was my own life in exchange for Callum's. Not . . . whatever *this* is." She threw her arms wide, and I frowned. Did she mean the threads she'd seen since bringing Callum back from the dead?

The Tapestry tilted its head, but she barged on before giving it a chance to reply. "The ghosts are everywhere. They keep asking me to help them pass on. Every single one! How am I supposed to do that? Why me? There aren't ancient spirits following me, so surely they were passing on their own just fine until you changed me."

There was a loud *thud* and Callum appeared, landing hard on the ground next to Aloisa like he'd fallen from the air. She gasped. "I told you not to follow me!"

He glared, brushing himself off as he stood. "And I told you not to come back here."

"Children." The Tapestry spoke in a voice so commanding they turned to listen immediately, both wide-eyed. "The world is changing. The Fjordlands are ready to receive magic, but they cannot do so unless there is a keeper to hold things in balance. And Aloisa . . . you volunteered to be that keeper."

I leaned forward, listening intently. Perhaps this was the answer to what Aloisa's responsibilities as a guardian had been—responsibilities that had apparently passed on to me and Søren.

She blinked. "Me?"

"Yes. That is the cost you chose to pay when you asked to save your friend." It gestured at Callum. "Humanity is ready for *more.*

With the addition of magic to your world comes more responsibility. A firmer framework, to prevent it all from running amok. This means someone must now aid spirits in passing on. The threads of the soul must be cut from your world and woven into the fabric of ours." With a wave of its hand, the same weaving I'd seen appeared behind the Tapestry. It stretched endlessly, the images on it moving and changing like the flow of water.

Everything clicked into place. The Tapestry was made up of souls of the dead. And it seemed capable of accessing a vivid array of memories from those who had already passed on and those who still lived.

"And you." It turned to Callum, likely taking advantage of Aloisa's momentary stunned silence. She didn't seem the type to let the Tapestry get a word in edgewise. "There must be one to hold the balance of the magic as well. That responsibility now falls to you."

"What—" Callum swallowed nervously. "What does that mean?"

"Aloisa's gifts will allow her to pass on the souls now woven to your plane of existence," it said. "Your gift will allow you to remove magic from those who misuse it. We have looked into your soul, Callum. It is pure and good. You are fit for this role."

He bowed his head. "Thank you. I will do my best to be worthy of this responsibility."

I furrowed my brow. Callum—the godforsaken's biggest enemy—was *chosen* to be the first Silencer? I shuddered at the idea of a man who could steal Lurae directly from the people who possessed them. As a young girl, I remember wishing Callum had used his gifts for good, to level the playing field between the Lurae and Nilurae.

The hardest part of watching the past was knowing what history held in store.

Aloisa spoke again, her voice quiet and timid now. "How do I help them pass on?"

The Tapestry sounded like it might be smiling, if it had a face to do such things with. "You will learn how to summon us and we will teach you how. Do not worry—when you emerge from the ice, you both will find yourselves changed. Time matters not to your mortality anymore. You cannot be killed, and you will never die."

The two teenagers looked at each other. Maybe the Tapestry missed it, but it was plain enough for me to see the weight of this new information on their shoulders.

Aloisa and Callum had become immortal.

24

Revna

I FINISHED STRAPPING ON MY ARMOR AS THE SUN BEGAN MELTing down over the horizon.

It had been a long day. I'd convinced myself to attend training with Søren despite the mortification I felt after yesterday's session. Thankfully, he hadn't made mention of anything that happened—in fact, he'd held up his end of the bargain he made, and we'd tried to summon the Tapestry.

We'd had no success, though.

I'd revealed my dream from the night before to him. It felt important to keep him up to date, especially since the Tapestry had finally revealed to us what Aloisa's purpose had been.

"Passing on souls," Søren had mused, picking at the grass. "And it offered no explanation of how to do such a thing?"

"It told Aloisa the same thing it told me. If she used her Lurae and learned to summon the Tapestry, it would teach her. I suppose that's the first step."

"Now I understand why spirits haven't been passing on," he said with a sigh. "When Aloisa was killed by the queen, there was no one left to take on that responsibility."

I'd spent all my free time lately reading the prophecy over and over, hoping to scrape new meaning out of the words. The paper we'd written it on was worn and soft from the press of my fingerprints. The words echoed in my mind. *Dawn of new threads, with uncertain ends.*

They felt particularly apt. "And it's our responsibility now." The words weighed in my mouth, incomprehensible. The two of us had been thrust into this duty without being asked whether we wanted it. Taking on the mantle of Aloisa's power felt like too much to bear. Especially with my kingdom on the verge of collapse and Søren so close to the queen still.

When we finally returned to practicing, we didn't try much else. After a few minutes of attempting to summon the Tapestry, the thought of reaching purposefully for my magic frightened me and I departed with the excuse of a headache.

During my afternoon meetings working on legislature, Volkan had suggested I join the soldiers in their sparring matches every evening. At first, I'd hesitated—after all, these men were soldiers in my father's army once. Now we pitted them against each other in friendly combat with the hopes it would drain them of the energy to commit crimes against their fellow Nilurae citizens. The winners were exempt from taking a shift guarding the city during the festival at the end of the week.

I questioned Volkan's idea, but the prince of Faste had made some good points. "The goal isn't to rule with an iron fist, like your father did," he'd said. "It's to earn their respect. And for the soldiers, that respect will be earned by showing your combat prowess."

"And if one of them manages to kick my ass? What then?" I'd scoffed.

Volkan shrugged. "Congratulate them. And then try again." He turned to leave before calling over his shoulder, "Or make sure whoever you fight first is someone you're confident you can beat."

Now I approached the courtyard with Søren at my side. He'd kept close to me since dinner. When I realized there were nearly three dozen Lurae soldiers waiting there for a chance to try their luck against me, I stumbled. Søren slowed his pace to match mine and murmured, "Only one of the people here has trained with the Hellbringer, you know."

It hit me that every single one of them would cower if they realized who the man standing next to me was. Not one of them would have survived those six weeks alone with him in the abandoned prison—much less emerged stronger from it to drive a dagger through Björn's sadistic heart.

The thought gave me the confidence to step forward into the ring. Whispers rushed through the crowd, but I kept my demeanor light. "Who's up first?"

A woman in her late thirties stepped up and bowed. "Your Highness. My name is General Raunstrup. I'll be sparring with you first." She quickly explained the rules—no harm was to come to either candidate, three strikes against your opponent made you the winner, and Lurae was absolutely forbidden.

As we arranged ourselves to fight, she leaned toward me and whispered, "Can I be honest? I've heard tales of your winning the Trials. I know many don't support your rule, but I look forward to seeing what a monarch with new ideas can bring to our country."

Her words startled me, mostly because the expression on her face was sincere. In fact, I was so taken aback I barely managed to parry against her first strike.

The fight was quick—General Raunstrup laughed as she conceded, admitting her strength was more on the strategic side of things. "But gods above. I haven't felt so alive in years. You're a force of nature, Your Highness."

And then another Lurae took her place, and a few minutes later, they conceded a win to me as well.

On and on and on.

By the time darkness had fallen fully, someone had lit a bonfire in the courtyard to offer us more light. Several of the spectating soldiers held torches. The mood had changed drastically. When I first arrived, I felt their stares and judgment like blades pointed at my back. Now their wariness was tinged with the first hint of respect.

"All right," I managed through my labored breathing. The last opponent had made me work for the win, and I'd enjoyed every second. "Let's call it an evening. We can reconvene tomorrow if anyone still wants to spar."

"No," a voice called.

Heads turned to the dissenter, and I kept my face carefully neutral when Arne pushed through the crowd, stepping into the ring. "You're not done yet, *Your Highness*."

Quiet laughter followed, but not as loudly as I expected. In fact, most of the observers frowned. I held back a sigh. "We can spar tomorrow, Arne."

"We spar *tonight*," he spat. "Unless you're too much of a coward to face me."

I wondered briefly whether anyone in the crowd—besides Søren—actually knew what had happened between me and Arne. He was furious with me. Was it because of how poorly our relationship had ended? Or because I'd admitted to him that I trained with the Hellbringer? I hadn't seen him since we'd returned from Kryllian, but he'd been more than happy to sow discontent among the Nilurae. He wasn't going to leave me in peace until I'd beaten him.

This was personal. So I shrugged. "Sure. What's one last match for the evening?"

There was a sinister edge to Arne's smile as he raised his sword. "Shall we?"

A hand gripped my shoulder. Freja. "Promise me you won't kill him," she muttered, too quiet for anyone else to hear. After a heartbeat, she added, "Or maim him."

I hadn't even realized she was watching. Caught off guard by her sudden appearance, I nodded. "Of course."

The general, who had been moderating the matches, caught my eye to make sure I was ready. She called, "Begin!"

For a long moment, we circled each other like birds of prey. I studied Arne's form, his grip. They were improved from the sloppy ones he'd taught me so long ago. Apparently I wasn't the only one who had trained since we last sparred.

But when he stepped forward, swiping his blade toward me in a wide arc, I parried easily. I held back a grin as I remembered the first time I had attempted to spar with the Hellbringer and realized Arne was slow in comparison.

But instead of moving to swipe at me again, he leaned his full weight into the crux of our met blades. I huffed in amusement. Søren was lean, but pure muscle—and he'd won our matches with this same move more times than I could count. Arne, though? He was wiry and thin. The unfortunate result of food shortages, but now, an easy advantage for me.

For a second, I let Arne believe the move was a success. I allowed his momentum to push the blades down, subtly guiding them with my grip until I stepped swiftly to the side, disengaging from the hold entirely.

Arne stumbled forward. I stretched my blade out, quick, to rap him on the back. General Raunstrup shouted, "One to the queen!"

The crowd of soldiers murmured. I stepped back, allowing Arne to catch his balance. It would have been easy to move in and catch him off guard, to throw two haphazard final taps in and win the match.

But this wasn't just about winning.

So I waited, keeping my breath steady, as Arne whirled back to face me with a scowl so furious it seemed to rend his face in two. My Lurae hummed softly, present but patient. I held it back—I intended to follow the rules of this game.

Arne steadied himself and I studied him. "You've improved," he noted. "Last time we sparred you were nothing but a girl pretending she had power."

I raised an eyebrow. "And now I'm a woman who could kill you in an instant."

"Is that a threat?"

I caught the disgruntled murmurs of the crowd. Probably not the best idea to threaten a soldier, even if I wanted to confirm that yes, it was absolutely a threat. I still couldn't resist a bit of a pointed jab, though. "Of course not. I have no need to threaten my loyal subjects."

He lunged without warning. When I leaned back, out of the path of his sword, I heard the sweep of metal through the air.

I steadied myself. He knew better than to pull his blows now.

Two quick steps and he was on me again. I spent my time parrying, learning his weaknesses. He slashed again and again, the fury in his eyes lending to his strength.

But not his precision.

Each swing was wild, simple for me to block. This was no challenge. After several minutes of allowing him to rage, I made my move. The next time our blades clashed, I leaned my weight into the swords before he could move away—the same move he had pulled on me mere moments ago.

Arne's eyes widened. My own narrowed. I watched as he put all his focus into holding me back, his muscles straining. Then I took advantage of his distraction, bringing my knee up to hit him directly in the stomach.

Air whooshed from him, and he couldn't resist the instinctual urge to curl in on himself. I batted away his halfhearted attempt at a parry, slipped through his defenses, and my blade crashed against his armor once more.

"Two for the queen!"

Before I had time to even pull my blade away, sharp pain lanced down my leg. I stumbled backward with a hiss, felt my Lurae reach out as if to pull the blood back in. Confident I was far enough from Arne to be safe momentarily, I glanced at my thigh.

The wound was long but shallow. It would be a pain in the ass to bandage with how close it came to my hip, but I could finish the fight. Straightening, I looked to Arne, who now held a small dagger in his nondominant hand—covered in my blood.

He grinned. "One for the soldier."

The discontented murmurs of the crowd permeated the quiet place I'd retreated to in my mind. Raunstrup's face was troubled, and she looked to me with a question in her eyes. I nodded and she confirmed, "One for the soldier."

In the back of the crowd, a voice hollered, "*One for the cheater!*"

Cries of disgruntled affirmation followed. I was stunned. The soldiers were . . . on my side? I hadn't realized such a thing was even possible.

Arne began to circle me again, and I matched him step for step. I knew Søren was in the crowd somewhere, watching, but I refused to search for him. Not when I needed all my concentration for this moment.

I wanted to smack my past self. *Why did you promise Freja you wouldn't maim or kill him?*

"As a reminder," Raunstrup called, "no party may attempt to seriously injure the other."

Arne chuckled darkly. I scowled. Fine—if he wanted to play rough, who was I to deny him?

I lunged.

Weeks of training with the Hellbringer followed by weeks of drowning the call of my Lurae by sparring for hours on end made me strong; made me fast. Most important, they made me lethal.

The first clash of our blades caused him to stumble slightly. The second strike, immediately after, made his eyes widen. My feet swept into the dance of battle and knew instantly: this was no equal partner.

Arne parried every strike. Because I allowed him to. We fought, and through it all my Lurae hummed beneath my skin but remained where it was, content as a cat curled by a fire. I leveled blow after blow after blow, each one just restrained enough to keep from truly injuring or even killing him.

When the first bead of sweat rolled down his forehead, I moved for the takedown. My next strike pushed him into another half stumble. My boot was there, waiting—he tripped, rolling as he fell to make sure he didn't gut himself on his sword in the process. *Shame.*

I swept my blade across his and he lost his grip. The weapon tumbled into the grass. The momentary panic slowed him for half a second; the perfect amount of time to plant my foot on his chest and shove him down with all the force I could muster.

His head thudded against the grass. I pointed the tip of my blade at his throat, just shy of touching skin. "Yield," I demanded.

Fingers scrabbled at my boot, attempted to shove me away. I was immovable.

"I said *yield*."

"Tap me with your fucking sword and end it!" he snarled.

I laughed in his face. "No. Yield to your queen."

"You are *not* my queen."

I leaned down, allowing my sword to follow the movement and press gently against his Adam's apple. He swallowed, finally daring to show nervousness, and the motion put a nick in his skin. My threads, pulsing from the cut in my thigh, reached for his.

I pulled them back.

"If I am not your queen," I whispered, softly enough that no one else could overhear, "then you do not belong here."

His eyes widened. "You would—"

"Exile you, yes." I studied him. Gods, it was delightful to see him fear me. About damn time. "Freja is the only reason you are still alive right now. Did you know that? You owe her your life."

In a last desperate bid for escape, he stretched up and hit me, slamming his knuckles into the cut he'd made. Over and over he scrabbled, hoping to find the threshold of my pain tolerance.

My Lurae, so carefully contained all evening, screamed. The threads lit between us, mine branching out to light every vein in his body. I wanted nothing more than to *pull*, to force his limbs in unnatural directions, to snap him like a twig. *He deserves it,* the magic seemed to scream. *Kill him, kill him, kill him!*

I pushed my blade into his throat with even more pressure than before, forced my voice to remain steady despite his abuse, and called, "Yield."

Arne muttered it so quietly I almost didn't hear. "I yield."

I sheathed Aloisa, stepping off him. The crowd around us was silent and still, no one daring to utter a sound. The sun had sunk closer to the distant horizon, tingeing the sky blood red. Arne pushed to his feet.

I watched him retreat to the crowd. A small group of former soldiers took him in, some shooting glares at me as they did. But they were few in number. The vast majority left without looking back, eager to get home to their spouses and children.

They didn't consider me an equal. Not yet. But I was shocked at how well Volkan's suggestion had worked.

A hand brushed my shoulder. "You need to clean and bandage that cut," Søren said. "Before it gets worse."

I sighed, looking down at it. Weariness plagued me. Defeating my spiteful ex-lover and putting him in his place had been satisfying, but . . .

I missed Arne. The one who'd been my friend and confidant for so long, who'd kept a careful and even balance between my and Freja's fiery personalities.

"I'll take care of it," I told him softly. "I'm fine. It's not deep."

"Maybe not, but it will most certainly have a bruise beneath it in the morning." Was I imagining the scowl I heard in his voice? A glance up confirmed I wasn't, and I stifled an affectionate smile. But then his expression grew deadly and we locked eyes. "I wanted to kill him. I *should* have killed him, Freja's wishes be damned."

I pressed the side of my face into his chest. He stilled, and both my Lurae and my ear pressed against his rib cage confirmed his speeding pulse. "I'm glad you didn't. Because one day, when he's truly earned it, I'll kill him myself."

Søren burst into surprised laughter, and the sound echoed through him. I grinned. Once, I'd struggled to decipher even an ounce of humor from the fearsome Hellbringer. And now, he laughed in my arms.

He curled an arm around me, then hesitated. "Come on. Let me take care of you."

I was too tired to argue. When he moved his arm from me, I reached out and grabbed his wrist, holding it in place to keep his arm around my shoulders. My temple was still pressed into the fabric of his shirt, and I inhaled the smell of pine and snow that followed him everywhere.

Gods. I missed this. The familiarity of his warmth, of his body pressed to mine, was already calming me. Was I drunk on the victory of putting Arne in his place?

Maybe you're just happy for the first time in months, I realized. And when I was happy, the person I wanted to be with was . . . Søren.

He was the only one whose eyes I could meet without thinking of all my mistakes and all the pain I had caused.

We came to his door and he opened it, guiding me over to an armchair similar to the one in my own room. "Sit," he ordered.

I obeyed, and the stretch of my muscles sent fire up my thigh. "Maybe you were right," I admitted with a chuckle. "Bandaging this isn't a bad idea."

He looked over his shoulder to raise an eyebrow at me from where he rummaged through a hutch. The lamps glowed softly, stretching into the shadows to reveal a familiar helmet and armor stored there.

Søren followed my line of sight. "I keep it locked."

"I'd be concerned if you didn't."

He stood and approached, hands filled with a roll of fabric bandages and a small pot. I eyed it suspiciously. "It's just a salve. Volkan left and went into the city earlier; otherwise, I'd make him patch you up."

Volkan in the city? I tucked the knowledge away, planning to ask the prince about it later.

I watched Søren kneel before me. The sight filled me like a heady drug. When I reached out and brushed the hair back from his forehead, I wasn't sure what I was doing. But his eyes closed, and his throat bobbed in a swallow, and for the first time in days, weeks, months, I had the kind of power I really wanted.

I pulled my hand back and exhaled shakily. "I'm going to have to take my pants off for this, aren't I?"

I hoped the note of wry humor in my voice came through, but based on the way his lashes fluttered open to reveal his pupils, still huge and dark as his gaze scraped over me like the rough pads of his fingertips—hesitating in all the places I wanted, wanted, wanted—I guessed he had barely heard me.

Søren's voice was rough when he whispered, "Yes. You will."

I reached for him and he grabbed my hands, tugging me forward and up. I bent to unbuckle the light training armor I wore, one greave after the other, before pulling off the thin metal covering my thighs. And all the while, Søren stared.

I didn't try to stop him. Not when I wanted him to look—wanted the reminder of how I affected him. My pulse pounded, and I unceremoniously pushed down the pants I wore.

He didn't move until I sat back down on the edge of the armchair and hissed as the wound stretched. The sound pulled him back to the moment, and he cleared his throat as he moved to examine it.

"It's not deep, but there's quite a bit of blood. Most of it's dried now. And I'm sure it hurts more than it should considering—" Søren bit off the end of his sentence, and I watched with fascination as a muscle in his jaw flexed. "Are you sure I can't kill him? It would, unfortunately, be painless. And quick."

"I'm sure," I murmured.

He looked up at my face and blinked, startled by whatever he saw there. Were my feelings so obvious? He'd always been able to read me like a book, so I supposed they were.

When he returned to the task at hand, he smeared a thick handful of the salve over my wound. I jumped at the sensation. It was frigid, and after a moment, it *stung*. "What the hell is that?"

"I told you, a salve. It's going to speed the healing process."

"Well it *hurts*."

I caught the edge of his smirk. "I've never seen you balk at pain before."

He was right. Begrudgingly, I settled back into the chair and waited for the sensation to subside. Søren wiped his hands on a towel, then wrapped his arms around his bent knees and watched the slow process of bruises blossoming beneath my flesh.

"I still remember watching you hit the wall in your room as hard as you could," he mused. "It was the same night after I saw you for the first time. Made me wonder what could possibly have happened at that short dinner to make you feel so *much*."

"Were you *in* my room?"

He huffed a laugh. "No. There's just enough of a ledge outside your window that someone with a lot of patience could balance there and see inside."

I sighed. "Not the best first impression, then."

"Not a bad one," he countered softly. "I watched you and thought, 'She knows exactly what it means to hurt like I do.'"

The words hovered in the air before us until they sank in, sending a shuddering breath through me. And it was a bad idea, a terrible idea, but I didn't stop myself from placing my palms on either side of his face and pulling his lips to mine.

Søren's mouth was warm and familiar. He surged up to meet me, hands wrapping around my waist. The kiss was raw, desperate, wild—when his tongue brushed against my lower lip I shivered and he groaned.

My legs spread and he fit perfectly between them, our faces almost level with him kneeling. Our first kiss had been like this: with me sitting on his lap, I'd been just barely taller. I loved it as much now as I had then.

Teeth scraped my lip as he pulled me closer, so tight against him that every inch of our bodies touched. The pace grew faster, headier. My Lurae quieted to a whisper, my mind empty of everything but Søren, Søren, Søren—

The Hellbringer.

I forced my eyes open and looked past him, to where the mask watched us from the closet.

"Wait," I gasped, my desire souring into something rotten, a rock in the pit of my stomach.

He pulled back instantly, breathing heavy. "Are you . . ."

Søren didn't finish the question. I couldn't force my eyes to meet his. "What are we doing?" I whispered, panic setting in. "I shouldn't have— Why did I—"

I stood, and almost collapsed. Swearing loudly, I managed to catch my balance enough to sit back down and glare at him. "Why is my entire leg *numb*?"

"Salve." He waved the question away. "Can you stand up? I need to put the bandage on."

He was . . . acting like nothing had happened. Warily, I stood, balancing all my weight on my left leg. Søren carefully wound the fabric over my thigh. The closeness made me stiffen. But his hands never wandered, and he remained focused on his task.

When he finally tucked in the end, he looked up at me. I swallowed at the sight. A supplicant kneeling in prayer before his goddess.

"What do you need?" he asked softly.

I kept myself from crumpling. Still, my anguish must have shown on my face. "I don't know."

The truth was too heavy, so an excuse would have to do. There was no way to be honest. No way to say, *I need my brother back. I need to be with you like I need to breathe. I need, I need, I need. And I don't know how to reconcile it all.*

An answer finally came to me. "I need . . . to not be alone."

His eyes lit up, and I wondered whether I should feel guilty. He wanted more than this. Being together was the worst idea—especially when I still had a kingdom to pull together and he was under the influence of his queen.

Maybe, I thought as he tugged me toward the bed, holding back the blankets while I clambered in, *we're together in another life. If not this one, surely the next.*

When he settled behind me, wrapping an arm around my waist, I wanted to cry. My eyes remained dry, though. Once, I would have pushed him away, snarled at him. I knew I *should* do those things.

But instead, I counted myself lucky to have even this small comfort: Søren's warmth, his heartbeat in tandem with mine.

"Good night, Revna," he whispered into the dark.

I settled, deciding that worrying would not help me tonight. "Good night, Søren."

25

Revna

WELL," FREJA SAID, STEPPING BACK AND DUSTING HER hands as she surveyed her handiwork, "it's better than I expected."

We stood in the town square. The bright sun cascaded over the shops surrounding the open space, which was decorated for the festival tomorrow. All of us—myself, Freja, Astrid, and the others who were helping us to set up beforehand—dutifully ignored the pile of rubble on one end, where the temple had once stood.

We were in high spirits, despite Arne. He had walked by earlier, raising his voice as he recounted the story of me losing control at the ball in Kryllian to the people he walked with. I'd tensed, refusing to make eye contact, but Freja had pulled Arne aside and scolded him. I wasn't able to hear her, but from the few glances I had at the conversation, he seemed thoroughly chastised by the end.

I shielded my eyes from the sun as I looked up at the brilliantly intricate garland of woven flowers and paper lanterns that now extended from one corner shop to another, stretching over the road. "It's beautiful."

Astrid nodded in response to my spoken and signed sentiment. "It truly is."

Freja beamed, clasping her hands together in front of her. "Thank you both for helping. I'm so excited for the celebration. Can you believe it's been seven years since the last one, and we weren't even invited because we were godforsaken?"

I scoffed. "I can believe it."

I remembered the year vividly. My family had left me behind, Frode rather reluctantly, and in a petty attempt to irritate them all, I'd snuck Freja and Arne into the castle, where we had our own party. Now I looked at Freja to see fondness in her eyes.

"I remember," she signed. Astrid saw but didn't pry. It was clear the gesture was meant for only Freja and me. "We've come a long way since that night."

We had. Those rebellious children had gone on to see tragedy and loss; to fight for their freedoms; and now, to rule a kingdom.

Freja turned to converse with Astrid, and I held my breath like it would freeze the moment forever. It didn't, though. Halvar, or rather Jac, locked eyes with me from across the square where he was setting up his own decorations.

Tomorrow, we would celebrate. And then I would sit Freja down and tell her . . . everything.

Dread made my stomach roll, but Freja's voice pulled me from my moroseness when Freja turned to Astrid. "I'm going to the Sharpened Axe for lunch," she told Astrid. "Care to join me?" I smothered a smile. Freja's words were tinged with nervousness.

"You go on ahead, and I'll meet you there in a few minutes," Astrid said. "I want to help Revna finish up this part first."

Freja wandered off and I tensed, unsure whether Astrid wanted to give me a report or . . .

Maybe she's figured out the truth. The thoughts slipped in, smooth as practiced thieves. *She sees you for what you truly are.*

My Lurae swirled in my veins, but instead of allowing the fear to grip me, I took a deep breath. The thoughts didn't fade—because after all, they could be true. But it kept me from succumbing to them and making a rash decision before any words had been spoken.

Or maybe, I countered, *I'm allowed to hope for the best. Including friends who see the good in me.*

Astrid glanced around, keeping her hands low when she said, "I've spent time in the Sharpened Axe lately, looking for leads on the priests."

My heart leapt in my throat. "And?"

She shook her head. "Signs point to them having met there before, but they stopped just before I started looking into it. I talked to Halvar." She held up a hand before I could interrupt. "I was subtle. He mentioned there was a small group of newcomers who became regulars shortly after your coronation, but he hasn't seen them in about a week."

"Do they know we discovered them? Why else would they have moved on?"

Astrid shrugged. "I'm not sure. I'm going to keep looking for signs of them. I'll let you know what I discover."

"Thank you." Part of me relaxed, a part I hadn't realized was so tense to begin with. "It's a relief knowing we have you on our side."

Her gaze flickered past me, and her mouth curved into a tight frown. "Look who's on his way."

My head turned so quickly my neck popped. Sure enough, there was a figure clearly moving toward us from the other end of the street. The confident set of his shoulders made it obvious it was Søren, despite the cloak pulled over his head.

I eyed Astrid as she took a deep breath and forced her scowl away. "I'm off to catch up with Freja." She tucked her hands in her pockets and jogged across the square.

"When did that happen?"

I turned to Søren. His face was flushed from the walk, and a single drop of sweat trickled down his face. *It's unfair,* I thought, *how full of life he is.*

Realizing I was ogling him without shame, I panicked and blurted, "What?"

His smirk told me he was fully aware of what I'd been doing, but he didn't mention it. "Freja and Astrid. How long have they been romantically involved?"

I glanced over my shoulder to where Freja had emerged from the Sharpened Axe and was excitedly tugging Astrid into a shop I knew served warm pastries. "I don't know." It was the truth. "I probably should have asked, but . . . I'm going to tell Freja everything tomorrow, after the festival. I've been preoccupied, thinking about it."

Søren didn't say anything. When I swallowed the lump in my throat and gathered the courage to meet his eyes again, they held no pity. Only understanding.

"Thank you," he finally said, "for staying the night."

I blinked, well aware of the heat flushing my face. "I think I'm the one who should be thanking you."

He chuckled and took a step closer to me. We stood nearly toe-to-toe, and I was forced to tilt my chin up to maintain eye contact. My heart thundered. His arms wrapped around me, his hands pressed along my spine—it had been the best night of sleep I'd had in weeks, even with the dream I'd had.

I wanted him. Badly.

Despite everything, he was working to get out from under the queen's thumb. He was helping me learn to use my Lurae. He was patient with me, endlessly waiting for my forgiveness; even with the knowledge I might never give it.

Søren leaned forward, the tilt of his mouth belying his thoughts. He pressed a palm to the wall behind me, hair falling forward to frame his face. I stared, unable to look away from his lips.

But you shouldn't want him, part of me insisted.

It didn't stop me from imagining his mouth on mine or his hands gripping my hips.

"Revna?" he asked softly, breath warm against my temple. "Where'd you go?"

I shook my head slightly, pulling myself back to the man in front of me. "Sorry. Distracted."

He pulled back, allowing a gust of cold air to flow between us. My stomach swooped with disappointment, and I swallowed. "I want you, Revna. I think you know that. But we do this on your terms." His mouth lifted in one corner with the hint of a smile. "I think you know that, too."

I knew my whole body was flushed, but Søren appeared nonchalant as ever. He gestured to the ladder Freja had been standing on to hang the garland. "Let me help with the ribbons."

I held the base of a ladder as he scaled it, ribbons in hand. Slowly, my heartbeat decelerated and I found myself more calm. Still though, the itch to reach for him, to brush my fingertips over his skin, was overwhelming. I decided it was best to distract myself and change topics. "I had another dream last night," I called up.

His face furrowed with concentration as he began to tie the ribbons to a lamppost next to the building. "What about?"

I glanced around, confirming no one was within earshot, then explained. "Aloisa was on a battlefield. She was older, an adult this time. She had soldiers with her. They were fighting Callum and his army—I saw a lot of priests in the crowd. When they fought each other, every blow they gave healed almost instantly."

Søren shook his head. "They really were immortal, then. It must be how Aloisa lived so long. But what happened to Callum?"

"Well," I continued, "Aloisa begged Callum to fall back and put down his weapon. Said if he surrendered, they could be done fighting. He refused. And so she pulled out a second weapon—the golden sword you saw in your dream. The one the queen killed Aloisa with. Aloisa told him he would be 'marked for eternity' with evidence of the blood he spilled. Then she used the sword to kill him."

Søren stilled, alert now. "He was immortal. But the golden sword could kill him."

I nodded. "I heard Aloisa call it the Soulcleaver. I had another dream about it a few weeks ago. I'd forgotten about it, with everything happening. She forged it with her blood."

His lips moved silently as he mouthed the sword's name. "A weapon that can end immortal beings. If the queen had tried to kill Aloisa any other way, she wouldn't have died."

"Exactly," I said. "But why is she so possessive of it now? If Aloisa and Callum are the only other immortals and they're dead . . . what could she possibly do with such a weapon?"

"Maybe she doesn't want anyone else getting hold of it? Or she likes having the reminder of killing a goddess?" He paused in his work, wiping a bead of sweat from his forehead. "I wonder what happened in between the first vision you had and this most recent one. To make Callum lose the desire to be worthy of the responsibilities the Tapestry gave him."

"That's not all." I gripped the ladder more tightly while Søren adjusted, leaning out farther to reach a particularly distant tie point. "Once Aloisa killed him . . . all the priests in Callum's army bowed down to her."

"Are you serious?"

"They started saying 'the strongest rules all' and other strange things." I shuddered at the memory, the dream still visceral. "They said she was their true goddess now. Aloisa wasn't having it—kept telling them there is no one true god to be worshiped. But the priests didn't seem to understand what she meant. They asked her to stay and rule over them, but she refused." I blinked against the bright sunlight when I looked up at Søren. "She walked into the trees and didn't come back."

"That's . . ." He sighed. "Depressing, maybe? I'm not sure what to make of it."

I was ready to respond when he reached just a bit too far and lost his balance.

Søren hit the ground with a *crack*. He landed hard on his extended arm. The limb bent unnaturally, bone tearing through the skin. His head slammed into the cobblestone, opening a waterfall of blood over his face.

It all happened within a split second. My heart stopped in my chest as blood began to pool around Søren, his eyes rolling back. A jolt of utterly indescribable fear took hold of me for a moment, the threads of my Lurae extending toward him.

An injury like this was life-ending.

I need him. The thought was as desperate as the rest of me, slamming into my fear like a battering ram. *I cannot lose him.*

I didn't think when I reached out with my Lurae. My left hand extended toward Søren, gathering the thread between us—startling in its golden hue, still the easiest to distinguish from the dozens of lives gathered in the square—and moving to his head to slow the bleeding there. And the other stretched toward the Sharpened Axe, where I'd seen Volkan enter earlier.

Come on. I shuffled through the threads until I found the prince's—familiar and calm. Then I tugged it softly until I could feel him moving of his own accord in our direction. I applied gentle pressure so he knew where to go.

I turned my full attention back to Søren. If I could stanch the blood long enough, Volkan would make it in time to heal him. The golden threads pulsed with Søren's heartbeat, and when I studied them closely, the light they were made of flowed. A true connection to his blood. To his life.

An eerie calm descended over me as I stared at him. Keeping him at arm's length suddenly didn't seem to matter nearly as much. I'd lost Frode so quickly—at Søren's hand, too. And while my feelings surrounding that were still complex and tangled, I begged whatever gods might be that I'd have the time to sort them all out.

It was only a few moments later when Volkan arrived, panting. But it felt like it had been hours. "Revna? What—*oh*."

He knelt before Søren, and I released my Lurae from its hold on the prince. "Head first. I'm slowing the bleeding but can't hold it any longer."

Volkan nodded, then traced careful fingers over the gash on Søren's temple. I watched, fascinated, as flesh knit back together. Søren groaned, gritting his teeth against the pain. When the skin was sealed, I allowed my Lurae to drop his thread, too.

A wave of tiredness overtook me, and I sat down in the street. Volkan spent a while repairing Søren's arm—"The bones have to be set just right; otherwise, I'll make things worse," the prince explained to me—and Freja and Astrid had joined us by the time it was done. Finally, Søren sat up.

I reached for his hand, grabbing and squeezing it without thinking. "I'm so glad you're okay. It's lucky Volkan was nearby."

"Yeah . . ." Volkan said slowly. "It's very lucky. Especially lucky that I was dragged here against my will." He frowned at me. "Was that *you*?"

"And did you say you were stanching the bleeding from my head wound?" Søren added.

I blinked. I hadn't even realized how monumental it was. It had been second nature, born of desperation. "Yes. I did both of those things."

Søren's face broke into a smile and he laughed. Freja jumped up and down and signed, "You can use your Lurae! Just in time for the queen's arrival tomorrow, too."

I stared at my hands. For once, they had been helpful. Instead of bringing destruction and death, I'd helped an injured Søren. "Huh."

"Good job." Søren's praise was quiet, but I heard the pride in it all the same. "I knew you could do it."

26

Revna

When I knocked softly on Søren's bedroom door, night had fallen and the castle lay suspended in stillness.

In the few seconds of waiting, my heart thundered. *It doesn't have to go farther than you want,* I reminded myself. But I was fully aware the true problem lay in how much I *did* want.

The door swung open. Søren, backlit by the firelight, was swathed in shadow. He reminded me of the now-crumbled statues that had once stood in front of the temple, depicting the pantheon of gods. Men molded from stone, chiseled to perfection by careful artists' hands.

He stepped back, and I crossed the threshold.

"The preparations for the festival look like they're going well," he said, sitting carefully on the edge of the bed.

Was he as nervous as I was? He was certainly thinking about the same things as me. Standing in the center of the room, I wrapped my arms around myself. "I can't imagine them going better," I said, pulled from my momentary uncertainty by the thought of all the dancing and food planned for tomorrow. "As long as everything goes right and the treaty negotiations go smoothly . . . we'll be on our way to seeing some actual change happen around here."

"All thanks to you," he said softly. I looked up to see the corner of his mouth lift. "How's your leg?"

"Stings a little if I stretch it too much, but it's not bad. The salve you put on it really helped." I was glad he hadn't mentioned Volkan. The prince would have dropped everything to heal me. But each time I'd thought of seeking him out, part of me had cradled a tiny hope that I might be able to return to Søren tonight and ask him to tend my wound again. "How is your head? Any lingering effects from your fall?"

"I'm fully healed. Want more salve?" He raised a brow and stretched his arm out to grab the jar where it rested on the windowsill.

His words from earlier ran through my head. A declaration of desire and a reminder that I was in charge. I controlled how far things went. He wouldn't push me if I didn't want him to.

And suddenly, the idea of having everything I wanted wasn't so terrible. Not anymore.

Thoughts of the ointment gone, I stepped forward into the open space between his thighs. He inhaled sharply. With tentative fingers, I combed my hand through his hair.

"Revna." Søren's voice was rough. "What do you want?"

"Does it matter?"

My hand slowed its path, and I stroked down his face to cup his jaw. Restraint warred with desire in his expression. "Yes," he said vehemently. "Yes, it matters."

"I'm . . ." Hesitantly, I pulled my hand back an inch. For a half second, he lurched as if to follow the movement before stopping himself and allowing the space to hover there. "I'm not entirely sure exactly what I want. If that's not enough for you—"

"Princess." His voice turned gentle. "Of course it's enough. I ask because the things I want to do to you, *with* you, right now . . . I don't want to cross a line. I don't want to push you further than you want to go."

Oh. I relaxed, the tension leaving my shoulders, and returned my hand to the slight stubble on his face. He groaned, a sound so faint I wasn't sure he knew he'd made it, and nuzzled deeper into my palm until his lips grazed it.

"Can I worship you, love?" Firm hands wrapped around my waist, and his eyes opened to plead with me. "Can I show you every depraved thought I've had since the last time we fucked?"

I was hyperaware of his eyes on my flushed cheeks, the column of my throat. Of his grip tightening on my back, the warmth pooling in my stomach. Of the way my nipples, now hard, brushed against the fabric of my clothing, desperate for more, more, *more*.

And still, my mouth curved into a smirk as I said, "Say please."

The gray of his irises shrank as his pupils dilated. I waited for him to grin, but he grew more serious. The fingers on my back crept around to my stomach, tracing dancing lines over the sensitive skin just above the waistline of my pants. His voice was deeper than I'd ever heard it before, and I memorized the shape of his lips as he begged. "*Please*, Revna."

We crashed into each other like an avalanche, the build finally too heavy to resist the pull of gravity. As his tongue parted my lips, pushing into me, a high-pitched sound of desperation escaped. It broke something in him. His arm banded around my waist, and he pulled me down onto the bed beside him before rolling overtop of me.

"Søren." His name was a fervent prayer, gasped between kisses. This was more divine, more holy, more ordained than any god. "Søren, Søren."

"My princess." Every word was carried on the edge of a growl, half feral with desire. "My queen."

My hips bucked up into him, pelvis grazing against the hard length in his pants and eliciting a hiss. Gods, why was I so addicted to that? "Say it again."

Søren's wicked mouth moved to my jaw, my throat, my shoulder. "My queen."

I pushed at his shoulders and he rose onto his knees immediately, panting and flushed. I tugged at the hem of his shirt. "Take this off."

No hesitation. A quick movement of arms and the clothing was discarded, leaving him bare from the waist up. And while he lifted my own shirt, I studied him. *I wish I were an artist.* The thought hit me suddenly as the ropy scar over his shoulder caught the flickering firelight and the stretch of his frame canted over me as he muttered, "Work with me, love," until I sat up slightly and goose bumps danced across my now-bare skin that had nothing to do with the temperature.

He coaxed me up to sitting with gentle words and gentle touches and gentle presses of his lips against my collarbones, the bright fire of our first touches now simmering heat. I raised my arms and allowed him to carefully unwind the fabric around my breasts until I was bare before him.

Søren kissed me, mouth roving over mine with a hunger I matched. His arms wrapped tight around my torso, pulling us chest to chest and skin to skin. He gasped and I shuddered against his mouth. "I missed you," he muttered.

I pulled him back on top of me, lying on the bed again. One of his arms remained banded around my torso; his other forearm braced next to me as he kissed down my throat, down my sternum, over the tops of my breasts. When he pressed his teeth gently down over my nipple, I tightened my fingers in his hair and pulled.

He soothed the spot with a lave of his tongue before moving to the other side. By the time he paused to bury his face between my breasts, I was a lit fuse, desperate for release. My body clenched on nothing and I'd now turned beggar. "Please, Søren. I need—I need—"

Moving back and pulling my pants and underwear down my legs, he murmured, "I know, sweetheart. Just let me love you for a little longer. You're so beautiful, I can't stand it."

Reverent hands cascaded down my sides, and I opened my legs to him. Waited for him as he looked and looked, palming the bulge in his pants. The cool air on every oversensitive part of me made me throb. "*Søren*."

The finger he slid inside me in reply only keyed me up more, and I whined, reduced to a wanton thing at his hands. "I haven't even touched your clit yet, sweetheart," he said, and I could hear the smirk through my closed eyes. It was infuriating as always, and I wanted more of it. He slid another finger in alongside the first, and the slight stretch was heavenly.

Lying down on his stomach, he used two fingers to pull my lower lips farther apart. He muttered something unintelligible as his eyes turned predator again. I opened my mouth to ask him what he was doing, why he wasn't giving me what I *needed*, when warmth closed around me and I arched my back, the sensation overwhelming in the best way.

He had his mouth on me. His *mouth*.

Our one night together in the prison, he'd talked about wanting to do this—but we hadn't ended up with time. As the minutes dwindled away from us, I'd cared far more about whispering to him in the dark, feeling the warmth of him solid beside me. Especially not knowing if I would see him again afterward.

Thoughts of that night disappeared beneath his touch. Fingers in his hair, feet scrabbling against the blankets. He opened his mouth to lick softly over my clit. "Søren you don't—you don't need to—"

"Of course I don't *need to*," he scoffed in between caresses. "You're my queen." Laving tongue. "I worship you on my knees." Teasing taps. "The way you deserve."

Who was I to argue with that?

Not that it would have been possible. My thoughts were nothing but swirls of pleasure, the rush building and cresting after only a few more strokes of his torturous mouth against me as I lay spread open on the bed—his personal feast. He carried me through it, pulling away right when I became too sensitive to take any more, my breaths coming in heaving gasps, my mind sated and silent.

I tugged on his hair, a silent request for him to clamber over me once more. I wrapped my arms around him and rolled us onto our sides, intertwined so intimately it was a wonder we weren't one.

"How was it?" he asked, his smile content.

Every inch of me still buzzed. I huffed a laugh and buried my face in his chest, the dusting of hair soft against my cheeks. "I think you know exactly how incredible that was. You really didn't have to, you know."

A finger tapped against the underside of my chin until I looked him in the eye once more. My face warmed thinking of how incredible the last several minutes had been. But his expression held no judgment. "Has no one ever done that for you before?"

I shook my head. "I never wanted to ask. And I wasn't sure I'd enjoy it. You certainly proved me wrong on that front."

He hummed, nudging his nose against mine to kiss me deeply once more, then again and again, leisurely. Like we had all the time in the world. "You came quicker than I expected."

I shoved him playfully. "Well, it's been a bit since we last had sex. Besides, it's your turn now." Allowing my voice to turn sultry, I rolled him beneath me and ground down over the pants he still wore, waiting to feel him hard and ready.

Nothing.

I frowned. "Do you not want . . ."

"Revna." Søren pulled the last sound of my name out into a groan and threw an arm over his eyes. An adorable pink flush danced across the tops of his cheeks. "I do want. So, so much. Which is why

I came at the same time you did, just watching you arch beneath me and feeling you tighten around my fingers."

I blinked. "Really?"

He moved his arm to smile self-deprecatingly at me. "Really."

And now I was wanting all over again. "Why are you embarrassed? I'm flattered. To think I could possibly have such an effect on you is . . . intoxicating."

"I can tell." The teasing tone returned, a smug grin forming on his lips. I realized I'd started grinding down against him, slowly working myself up once more.

"Sorry," I mumbled, already lost to the feeling. He was warm and real and, for the first time in ages, I felt safe.

"Don't you fucking dare apologize. If you want to come again, I'll see to it you do."

My eyes had drifted lazily closed, but I opened them. "Even when you're not getting anything out of it?"

"Who said I wasn't getting anything out of this?" Søren's hands wandered, skimming up my sides to cup my breasts once more. "Watching you pleasure yourself on me is more than enough."

He rolled my nipples between the pads of his fingers, and I moved faster, every ounce of pressure echoed tenfold through my body.

"Do you want to come like this?" he asked. "Or can I use my fingers or my mouth on you? *Please*, Princess, let me—"

A single nod and he was lying on his side, curled around me, fingers replacing the rough friction of fabric with something softer, more lovely. My mouth fell open and gods, was I truly going to orgasm again? Right after I already had? It seemed more than likely.

He watched my face carefully as he pressed the pad of one finger onto the center of my swollen clit, exactly where I was most sensitive. It was almost too much, but I liked it. Liked the threat of pain at the edge of my pleasure. And it showed, because a sound escaped me—high-pitched and vulnerable, dissolving me into a needy creature. *His queen.*

"Perfect," he sighed, lids growing heavy. "Just like that. Let me tip you over the edge. Gonna make me come in my pants again, you're so beautiful when you're splayed open for me. When you let me touch you and lick you. So good, sweetheart."

It was like a string was tied directly to my pleasure and those last words delivered it a sharp tug. His finger continued to move in steady circles, and I couldn't help myself, I wanted him to—

"Say it again," I begged. I didn't recognize my own voice. I ignored the way my eyes stung, how directly connected the sensation of tears was to my impending crest. "Please? Tell me—"

"That you're good?" Søren's eyes held more sincerity than I'd ever before experienced. "That you're so good for me?"

The orgasm was nearly instantaneous. I cried his name and clutched at his forearm while he stroked me through the waves, kissed my temple gently while I caught my breath, wiped a stray tear from my cheek.

I closed my eyes as the pleasure faded into contentment. "I don't want to talk about it," I said the moment I was capable of speech again.

He knew what I meant. "And we don't have to."

As we embraced in the quiet, my thoughts wandered to places I didn't like. *Did he mean it? Or was he lying, the way everyone else has lied to you before?* My Lurae song started, growing faster with my agitation.

"Stop thinking," Søren chided softly. "Remember, I don't lie to you. Ever. If you ask me for something and I give it, it's because I wanted to."

I opened my eyes to stare incredulously at him. "Are you sure your Lurae isn't mind-reading?"

He laughed, the sound sending a thrill through me. "I wish. But no. You just have a very expressive face."

I fidgeted with the fabric of his pants, rubbing it between my thumb and forefinger. "How do you think tomorrow will go?" Here, in his arms, was the only place I felt comfortable asking for a truthful answer.

"It's impossible to know exactly what will happen," he said. "But as far as your preparation, you've done everything you can. She'd be lying to herself if she refused to sign the treaty because of your abilities—you're more accomplished than any other Lurae I know who's had so little training."

I raised a brow. "Ah, yes, more accomplished than any nine-year-old you know. I'm flattered."

"Not what I meant," he chuckled. "There are people who take years before they've mastered their far simpler abilities at the level you've mastered yours. I'm proud of you."

I pressed my face into his chest. "I couldn't have done it without you."

"You could have, if you'd been given the time."

And thus, thoughts of the queen resurfaced once more. I sighed. "If she were a fair, just ruler, I wouldn't be so worried. But . . . we cannot afford another war. The treaty must be signed. Kryllian has the power to annihilate us."

"What she wants has something to do with your Lurae," he said grimly. "She won't get that if she starts another war. Think of when you forced your way into the Trials. It worked so effectively because your father had made you the necessary pawn in his plan. It didn't work without you. The moment you refused to follow through with it, everything fell apart and he was forced to concede his hand. I have a feeling tomorrow, when we're able to get a better sense of just what she believes your magic can accomplish, will be much the same."

"I hadn't even considered that," I said. My thoughts still spun, but his logic made an absurd amount of sense. Even my Lurae song was quiet. "We have more power than I thought."

"I am still at the queen's bidding tomorrow," he said, arms tightening around me. "But please know no matter what—my true allegiance lies with you. I promise you."

The haze of drowsiness settled over me as my breathing calmed. Contentment was heady as a drug, and I basked in it. When was the last time I'd been this gratified? "Wake me up when you want a turn," I mumbled, wrapping my arms around his waist and squeezing tight.

Søren's breath rushed from him. He carded a hand softly through my hair. The world was quiet and still. "We'll see." He hummed softly, and I felt the brush of his lips against the crown of my head. "Rest well, my queen."

And I did.

27

Søren

THE KRYLLIAN DELEGATION ARRIVED IN BHORGLID'S CAPITAL city right on time.

Revna stood, shoulders straight, her red and gold gown the perfect combination of casual Nilurae celebration attire and queenly garb, the matching crown on her head pinned to her intricately braided hair to keep it from slipping off. She was stunning, but more than beauty, she radiated *power.*

It made me want to fuck her again.

I shook the thought from my mind. Now was not the time to lose focus—not when the Queen of Kryllian appeared across the small courtyard, her arm intertwined with Mira's for a moment before the teleporter departed again to bring the rest of the delegation.

I'd barely seen Mira over the last two weeks. My report given in person was the last time we'd truly spoken about more than just my work in Bhorglid. Where did she stand on all of this? When I broke my ties with the queen, when I found Sonja, would Mira come with me? Or would she stay?

I didn't know the answer. Not for the first time, I hated having to keep Mira in the dark on all of this.

I put on my practiced scholar smile. The one I wore at events with nobles, on the few occasions I was allowed to blend in instead of be shown off in the mask. The expression was entirely cordial and entirely fake. As the queen approached, I stepped forward and bowed. "Your Highness. It's lovely to see you again."

"Rise," she commanded. Her gaze was a sharp assessment. When she studied me like this, I always felt like she was looking for something beneath the surface. What it was, I couldn't be sure.

My own eyes, on the other hand, went straight to the sword at her hip. Aloisa's sword. I held in my grimace at the memory of my dream: the queen running her sword through Aloisa's middle with no regard. Blood spilling on the snow as the woman—goddess—fell limp.

The queen noticed and raised a brow. Before she could reprimand me, Revna stepped forward. "Welcome to our home. The spring festival begins today, and we'd love for you to join us there once you've settled. There is no better opportunity to take in the sights of the city. Our people are excited for the war to come to an official end."

Revna began walking back toward the castle doors, shepherding the queen and the two other nobles who had arrived with her. "Allow me to show you to your quarters, Your Highness."

But the queen laughed, high-pitched and falsetto. "Kind of you to offer, but I'd prefer Søren show me the way. After all, he's due a report of your progress to me."

To Revna's credit, she hid her distaste for the change of plan well. I was confident only I saw the way the set of her shoulders tightened slightly—her otherwise demure disposition remained unchanged. "Of course. Søren, Her Highness will be staying on the second floor, the room at the end of the hall on the east side."

"Of course. If you'll follow me." I started for the castle without checking to make sure the queen was following. We wound up the spiral staircase, and I began a stream of casual conversation in an attempt to avoid whatever interrogation was coming. If she wanted me alone, it wasn't going to be good. "Queen Revna has put together a most excellent event down in the city. I hope you and the others are planning to join in the festivities."

She sounded bemused. "Certainly, if we have the time. There are negotiations that must be completed first, of course."

I couldn't decide if her words were promising or ominous.

I opened the door to her room and she stepped inside. I followed closely behind, already knowing there was no way to get out of this—even when I desperately wished I was at the festival dancing with Revna. The sooner I dealt with the queen, the sooner this would all be over.

And maybe this was my chance to discover what the queen truly wanted with us. The prophecy echoed in my mind.

"Report," she snapped, and I straightened automatically.

It's just an act, I reminded myself. *You know where Sonja is. The moment these negotiations are over, you can go search for her. And then you'll be off Anja's leash.*

The thoughts steadied me. "My report is much the same as last we spoke. The Queen of Bhorglid has mastered her abilities. She will no longer be a liability in the case of a treaty between our nations."

"What can she do with these newfound abilities?" Anja asked, examining the room as she spoke. She ran a hand over the bed linens, peered into the washroom, and took in the view from the window.

"She has the ability to sense heartbeats," I said. "She can control the blood in people, make them move if she wishes. If someone has a cut, she can slow the bleeding—but not stanch it entirely. That would require a healer."

"Anything else?"

She was digging for information. Did she know of the Tapestry's existence? Certainly, unless she'd somehow accessed the prophecy a different way. Did she want to know whether we had discovered how to access it or how to weave the souls of the deceased?

I resisted the urge to slam my fist into the wall. The queen held her cards so close to her chest, manipulating us all like pieces on a chessboard. But unlike when Revna's father had attempted to do the same with her, the queen kept her endgame a secret. Begrudgingly, my strategic side respected it. I would have done the same thing, were I in her position.

If she wanted us to be able to access the Tapestry, she was out of luck. We hadn't been able to do it anyway. So I told her what was technically the truth. "Nothing I've noticed. Her Lurae is blood. I doubt it can do much else."

"Hmm." The queen smiled, and it had a sharp edge. "Interesting."

"If that's all," I said, moving for the door, "then I really must insist you join us at the festival."

"Oh, there is one more thing."

I paused, hand over the knob.

"I have an errand I need you to take care of for me. Before the negotiations can proceed."

Her shoes clicked against the floor with every step she took toward me. I remained frozen, a sudden sense of dread filling me. She reached my side, and her whispered words sent an unearthly chill through me.

"Find a shovel. You buried something here a few short weeks ago. I find myself in need of it now."

28

Revna

MUSIC AND DANCING WERE IN FULL SWING IN THE SQUARE and my heart was full.

I took a bite of boller, a cardamom bun filled with chocolate, made by one of the Nilurae bakers I frequented before the Trials. Booths from all the locally owned shops lined the plaza, the sweet scents of sugar and fruit mingling with the aroma of freshly cooked meats. The bright blue sky held no clouds. True to the changing of the seasons the festival celebrated, it was the warmest day we'd had this year.

The baker, Linnea, smiled at the obvious bliss on my face. "It's been years since I had one of these," I said through a full mouth.

She laughed. "That's what we're all saying. Thank you for making it possible, Your Highness." I nodded graciously, but before I could reply, she leaned in and lowered her voice to a whisper. "I'm not sure how you did it, but the Lurae are being *cordial* to us these days. I didn't think it was possible."

"I'm so glad to hear that." My instinct was to reach for her hand and clasp it, but I held myself back. Maybe Freja wasn't flinching away from me anymore, but the rest of the Nilurae were still wary of me. I saw it in their eyes—they watched me carefully, but the moment I turned to face them, they flicked their eyes away.

Fear is a powerful thing, I reminded myself. It would take time for that fear to fully leave them, considering Arne's commitment to sharing what I'd done at the ball in Kryllian.

But I could be patient.

The moment I finished the last bite and wiped the chocolate from my fingers, a hand snagged mine and tugged me into a twirl. My skirt flared slightly, dark hair twisting around my head. By the time Freja stopped me, the world continued to spin.

"You look nice!" she said, raising her voice to be heard over the music. Feet stomped in unison, the square itself seeming to shake under the pressure. "I didn't get to tell you before the delegation arrived. I don't remember this dress."

Steady once more, I held out my arms. "I commissioned a Nilurae seamstress to make it for me. I wanted something more casual for today."

While the dress was more traditional than my usual garb as queen, no one would describe it as *casual.* The red and gold fabric landed mid-calf, the skirts made up of several overlapping layers while managing not to feel or look heavy. The bodice hugged tight, sleeves slipping off my shoulders and cinching around my wrists. A brown leather corset laced up my back with gold ribbon, intricate golden patterns woven into it with delicate embroidery.

I'd asked Søren to help me lace the corset this morning. The activities that followed nearly made us late to welcome the Queen of Kryllian.

"Your hair is incredible, too," I told Freja. Her usual curls were woven tight to her scalp in a beautiful knotted braid that cascaded down her back.

"Thank you! My mother did it for me."

We shared a smile as we looked out over the crowd. Despite the occasional tense exchange, it was clear the people were intermingling far better than would have been possible mere weeks ago. I readjusted the crown on my head, checking to make sure it was still carefully pinned in place. “You did it,” I said, nudging her with my shoulder. “This is incredible. And it was all you.”

“I know,” she said, hands clasped together. “It feels like everything is truly beginning to take a turn for the better.” She scanned the crowd, then frowned. “Where is Søren?”

I shrugged, my fingers twisting together. “I’m not sure. I waited for him at the castle, but whatever report he’s giving to the queen must still be going. He’ll come down when he’s available, I’m sure.”

Truthfully, worry threatened to tie me in knots. What could the queen be asking of him that would take more than an hour? He’d been reporting to her regularly since our training began—surely there was nothing new left to say.

But I had to trust him.

I began to run through one of my breathing exercises. Despite my nerves, my Lurae song hadn’t flared up. Perhaps it was saving all its energy for later, when the queen would likely demand a demonstration of my control.

“Well,” Freja said, “hopefully it just means the queen is preparing a treaty as we speak. Perhaps she needed Søren to write down all her incredible ideas for cooperation between our countries, so she wouldn’t forget them in the meantime.”

We stared at each other for a long moment. Then a laugh burst from both of us so forceful it nearly brought me to tears.

When we had finally calmed again, I watched the dancers spin, locking arms with their partners as the music crested. A flash of red hair caught the corner of my eye, and for a moment so minuscule it didn’t even last a heartbeat, I turned excitedly, expecting to see Frode there.

The face of a nameless stranger was a knife to my gut.

He would have loved this. I was certain of it. The thoughts of the crowd would have overwhelmed him quickly, and he would have left to nurse a splitting headache—but he would have shown up and danced for as long as he could. At least here he would have been overwhelmed by happy thoughts. A stark difference from the thoughts of the dying that had plagued him incessantly on the war front.

I wanted him back. The knowledge hung heavy in front of me. I had everything I wanted except for Frode. Even Søren and I were learning to trust each other again, moving past the impossible hurdles keeping us apart. But it didn't make up for the hole in my chest.

"Revna?" When I turned to look at Freja, it was obvious she'd said my name multiple times.

The sympathy on her face made it clear she knew where my thoughts had gone. For a swift, short moment, I wished she was queen instead of me. I didn't want to be here, negotiating treaties and making speeches. I wanted to curl up in bed and tell Søren all my stories of Frode again. I wanted to run away and leave all my responsibilities behind. Søren could take me to the wastes, where my brother's ghost resided and where we could have a chance to speak again.

Freja looped her arm around mine. "Join me for the next dance. I'm teaching Astrid, but she should learn the steps from you. You're a far better dancer than me."

My instinct was to refuse. Freezing felt easier, sinking into a corner and denying that life moved on around me. Especially considering how much my worries threatened to drown me. But I swallowed and forced myself to nod. "Yes. Let's dance."

I lost myself in the music and the rhythm, the familiar steps that had guided my childhood and teenage years into rebellious adulthood. At first, it took all my concentration to keep from slipping back into the uncertainties and sadness. But by the third dance, I managed to anchor in my muscle memory.

The festivalgoers were mostly Nilurae. While some Lurae lingered at the edges of the event, not many had stepped fully in. I caught a glimpse of Volkan laughing at something Halvar—Jac—said. Freja giggled when Astrid stumbled and got turned around next to us, gently putting her hands on the teleporter's shoulders to realign her as the music continued.

The song came to an end and we paused, everyone breathing heavily. I caught sight of a little girl, no older than ten, standing nervously at the edge of the dance floor. One of the musicians stood on his chair, cupping his hands around his mouth and announcing, "Up next, we'll play the bygdedans!"

One of my favorites—and a simple one to get the hang of. Freja and Astrid were occupied, the former trying to explain a dance step to the latter with a complicated series of made-up gestures that had no real sign language equivalent, so I stepped over to the young girl.

Her eyes widened as she recognized me, noticing the crown I wore, and she wrapped her arms around herself. I bent down to reach her height. "You look like you want to dance."

She peered up at me between her lashes and nodded. "I don't know how, though."

Maybe she was Lurae and hadn't grown up learning, the way most Nilurae did. Maybe she just hadn't had the chance. Either way, I shrugged and beckoned for her to follow me. "This one is easy. I can teach you."

"But—"

I glanced back at her. She appeared befuddled. "You're the *queen*."

I laughed. "I wasn't always. And I'm also just a person."

My words seemed to steady her. She set her shoulders and followed me into the crowd just as the music began.

The musicians played, and the dancing began. With every crescendo we spun, skirts flaring in a brilliant burst of color. The girl

I'd pulled into the dance caught on quick, and soon Freja and Astrid had her laughing and learning bits and pieces of sign.

Another hour passed. The Queen of Kryllian arrived, two of her guards flanking her. Freja and Astrid escorted her to a shaded, open tent set up for her to observe. When she and I made eye contact, I offered her a cordial smile.

And yet, still no sign of Søren.

The festivities continued. Slowly, the Lurae began to join the fray. A few stood along the edges, watching with wary eyes—the soldiers who hadn't been impressed when I defeated them in sparring. Arne stood among them, arms crossed. There were others who refused to participate, too. Faces I didn't recognize. Perhaps soldiers who had declined the offer to spar.

I stepped away from the dancing and went to the queen. "How are you enjoying things? Can my people get you some food?"

Her gaze was piercing. She leaned her chin against one hand, surveying the dancing. "I'm not sure how you've managed to bring these people together, but I'm impressed."

I choked on my breath. Impressed? Suspicion doused any excitement at the thought. "I am queen of all my people. Not just Lurae or Nilurae. Once they began to see that in my actions, things started coming together."

"I can see that." A breeze caught the hem of her long skirt, purple fabric fluttering in the wind. "You've become quite a good investment, Your Highness."

I wasn't sure how to respond to that. "I'm glad you think so. The treaty between our nations is the highest priority."

The queen's mouth tipped up into half a smile. "Then perhaps we should begin negotiations today instead of waiting until tomorrow."

A hand landed on my shoulder. "May I steal you for a dance, Your Highness?"

Søren's voice settled something in me, and I turned to smile at him. "In just a—"

But he tugged on my shoulder gently, his eyes urgent. Was that dirt beneath his nails? "Her Highness can wait one song."

Shit. Something was wrong. I turned to the queen. "If you'll excuse me—let's meet back at the castle after this song and we can begin negotiations."

She stood. "No. We'll begin now. There will be plenty of time for dancing later." Søren's hand tightened its grip, and the queen's eyes flickered to it. She raised an eyebrow. "Unless you'd like to take back what you said before, about the treaty being your highest priority."

We must act the part today, I told myself. *When the treaty is signed, we can find Sonja and finish this.*

I forced myself to nod. "In that case, let's return to the castle. Mira?"

The teleporter grabbed my arm and the queen's and pulled us away.

⬩ ⬩ ⬩ ⬩ ⬩

"YOU HAVE MY HELLBRINGER ON QUITE THE LEASH," THE QUEEN said as we arrived in the throne room. Mira disappeared without a word, and Anja brushed her skirts. "It's impressive."

I tensed. This woman had a way of knowing exactly what to say to throw me off my guard. I was saved from replying when Mira rematerialized in the throne room, Søren at her side. He stepped forward. "Do we need the others?"

"No," I said, waving a hand. "Let them celebrate." Dealing with the queen was the least I could do. Freja would be furious after I sat her down and gently told her the truth of what had happened to Halvar on my coronation day. This way, she'd spend as much time before then happy and carefree.

"Good." The queen clasped her hands. "Mira, you may return to the festival."

The teleporter bowed her head, but before she vanished, Søren placed a hand on her shoulder. He leaned down and whispered something to her. Anja cleared her throat. "Leave us, Mira."

Søren removed his hand, and Mira's eyes flickered to me briefly. Without another word, she left.

Søren and I were alone with the queen. The throne room, despite its decor making it the most lavish room in the castle, felt hollow. My heart thudded ominously as I waited for the queen to reveal her hand—to finally demand what she truly wanted.

And there was no chance to ask Søren what was wrong.

"Revna," she began, "I sent my scholar to spend three weeks with you, while you learned mastery of your Lurae. Today there is one last test I would have you complete before we move forward. One to ensure we are both getting the most out of this treaty."

I pasted a smile on my face and forced my voice to coolness. "Of course. What did you have in mind?"

She gestured to Søren. "Show her."

His hands clenched, knuckles whitening. He wouldn't meet my eyes as he turned away, striding into the hall. My pulse thundered in my ears. What was he so upset about? What had gone wrong? Would there be a chance to find out before everything imploded?

Søren returned, a body in his arms.

I stood frozen. The body hung limp, covered in a white sheet. Søren's jaw trembled, and I turned to the queen. My once calm demeanor turned to ash and I snarled, "You killed someone? One of my citizens? This is a peaceful negotiation, not a battlefield."

Søren stepped to a table that had been set up next to the dais of thrones. I hadn't even noticed it when we arrived, too preoccupied with the queen and her abrasive comments. He laid the body down gently, almost reverently, and when he turned back to me there was undisguisable panic in his eyes.

"No one has been killed today," the queen said, waving her hand as if it would brush away all my concern and anger. To Søren, she said, "Lift the sheet."

He pulled away the sheet to reveal a shock of red hair and a pale face covered in dirt. I took a step back. "Frode? You—" My anger knew no bounds. The threads of my Lurae writhed in my peripheral vision, and I clung to them, trying to hold them back. "You dug up my *dead brother*?"

"But, Revna, don't you see?" the queen said. Her eyes shone with a fervor unlike anything I'd seen in her before. "Your Lurae can control blood, certainly. But more than blood, it controls life itself. *Souls.* You are the prophesied heir of Aloisa's power—well, one of the heirs. Søren here is the other."

She moved toward me, and I stumbled, tripping over myself in an effort to get away, away, away. Away from the horror of my brother's dead body staring at the throne room ceiling. Away from the madwoman who had taken everything from me. Away from the past as it choked me, fingers tight around my throat.

My Lurae song began to echo.

"And as her heirs, you can do anything Aloisa could do." Still, the queen advanced toward me.

Søren appeared between us like a phantom. I hadn't even seen him moving. "Stop," he demanded, holding out a hand until the queen stilled. "Revna doesn't want you any closer. If you have something to say, then say it. Without moving."

My breaths had become shaking gasps, and it was a struggle to stay upright. But everything froze when the queen uttered her next words.

"Together, the two of you can raise the dead."

29

Revna

SØREN WAS THE FIRST TO SPEAK. "YOU'RE LYING."

The queen laughed. "No. Haven't you noticed there's more than blood to Revna's Lurae? She can sense heartbeats, stanch bleeding—and see the threads of souls themselves. Just like you, Søren. Because her Lurae is life and yours is death."

My hands shook. I tried to keep my eyes from flicking over to where Frode's body lay, but it was impossible.

"The story I told of Aloisa is truth," the queen continued. "Aloisa pulled her friend from the lake, and when she emerged, she had a Lurae. But that isn't all. Callum had perished, and Aloisa used her abilities to resurrect him."

If what the queen said was true . . .

"Why would you want me to resurrect Frode?" I demanded. "What does my brother being alive do for you?"

She put a dainty hand over her heart. "You wound me with your presumptions, Your Highness." I raised a brow, waiting. Finally, she sighed. "The idea was a trade-off. I have told you about the ability you possess, and now your brother's body is here, ready to be revived. In exchange, I only ask that you first help me raise someone I have lost."

Søren stepped back to stand at my side. "You haven't lost anyone."

"And how would you know?" she snapped. Her demeanor changed quicker than I thought possible, like she'd been hiding her anger just beneath the surface, where it waited to snap. "I had a husband once. Someone I would have done anything for. And just because you don't know about it, I must be lying?" She tsked with disgust. "I thought you of all people would understand the pain of losing those you love."

I wrapped a hand around Søren's wrist to keep him from lunging. He certainly looked like he might. "So what if we're Aloisa's heirs?" I argued. "It doesn't mean we're actually capable of resurrecting anyone."

"You haven't tried." She set her mouth in a firm line. "I ordered one last task before I sign our treaty. Resurrect my husband—prove you're capable. Then, and only then, will I agree to peace with your country. And afterward?" She gestured to Frode's body. "Consider what a gift my tutelage will have been. You can resurrect anyone you want."

Once again, Bhorglid was used as a bargaining chip against me. If it were anything else being offered to me in return, I'd scoff. But . . .

Frode.

"I had Søren dig up your brother here as an offering." The queen didn't move her eyes off me, gauging my reaction. "Assuming bringing my husband back to life goes smoothly, you could resurrect Frode immediately."

I thought about Jac, exhausted from pretending to be someone he wasn't. Of Volkan, who'd been pestering me to tell the truth since the beginning of my ruse. Of Freja, who had lost her real father to the man standing next to me—and her adopted father figure, too. She didn't even know. Not yet, at least.

I thought of running a country alone when this was all said and done. When Søren was off on his journey to find Sonja, Volkan was back in Faste, and everyone else was sick of me. Would Astrid stick around to prevent another assassination attempt? No; she would go with Freja.

The crown was heavy on my head. Not for the first time, I wished I could take it off—wished I could leave the expectations and the needs of everyone around me and disappear into the wastes until I was ready to return.

I didn't have that luxury, though.

I squeezed Søren's wrist. Saw a muscle work in his jaw. He knew what I was going to say, what I was thinking. I found myself wishing I could communicate mind-to-mind with him. Reassure him that I wasn't interested in doing anything else with our combined Lurae abilities. No hidden fairy-tale villain lived within me—once Frode and the queen's husband were breathing again, I was content to leave the rest in their graves.

He ran his free hand through his hair and said, "Fine. How do we even go about it?"

The queen beckoned us over to Frode's body. I approached, staying carefully at the end of the table near his feet. Any closer and I would have to close my eyes or be forced back to the last time I saw him.

Søren glanced at me, concern written on every one of his features. I knew what he was trying to ask: *Are you sure?*

I nodded and hoped he understood my silent answer. *Yes. I've never been more certain.*

"The prophecy spoke of threads," the queen began, her eyes alight with an excitement I'd never seen in her before. "Each living being is made up of a soul thread. You have been manipulating them. Søren's Lurae allows him to cut soul threads and see threads of those who have passed on. All you have to do is access the amalgamation of threads from those who have passed on, identify the thread of the person you're resurrecting, and bring it back to this world."

"Simple," Søren muttered.

"Can you do it or not?" the queen asked coolly. "If not, I can find a new general to help us decimate Bhorglid."

"When were you married?" Søren replied, crossing his arms. "You took the throne of Kryllian twenty-six years ago, at the age of eighteen. Were you wed in childhood? There are no records of a king consort during your rule at any point."

"You don't believe me." She pursed her lips. "I kept my husband secret to allow him some semblance of privacy. Surely you understand that."

"Then how do you know so much about soul threads? The prophecy wasn't detailed enough to tell you all of this. And I'm a scholar—I've studied every book in the Kryllian palace library and have seen nothing describing this kind of magic so thoroughly."

The queen wore a pitying expression. "Oh, Søren. Of course you've read all of the available manuscripts. But I would never be foolish enough to allow you unfettered access to everything. I've removed volumes many times over the years."

Søren opened his mouth to argue, but I laid a hand on his bicep. The deeper we dove into the semantics of it all, the more I worried the queen would change her mind at any given moment. I understood his endless questions—I had my own. But my heart pounded with the surety that the longer we waited to begin, the further Frode's life was slipping from my fingers. "Maybe we figure out if resurrection is even possible before we get caught up in the details. There's a chance this doesn't work at all."

The queen narrowed her eyes but didn't say anything. Søren nodded, his wariness easy to see. "Step away," he said. "We need space to work."

Anja clenched her jaw but acquiesced. "As you wish. Records of

Aloisa's life speak of all the threads being golden. My husband's soul, however, is red. That is the one you'll want to bring with you. I'll be on the other side of the room."

Her heels clacked on the floor as she left. Søren leaned down to whisper in my ear. "The prophecy. Was it about this?"

I took a shuddering breath. "I think so."

Beware: weaving is a careful art. Those fragile threads care not for unwinding.

We stared at each other for a long moment. This was a crossroads, I knew. But I was also certain of the path I had to take. Regardless of any ominous warnings given generations ago.

Søren must have seen it in my eyes. He didn't press any further. Instead, he said, "We need to reach the Tapestry if we have any chance of this working."

"I know." I grimaced. "I want to try. Even if it doesn't work."

"Do you see any threads? In Frode's body or anyone else in the room?"

I took a deep breath and focused, pushing away my worry and stress until there was room in my mind for nothing but calm focus. Deep within me, my lullaby began to sound. I opened my eyes.

"I see yours and Anja's threads, but that's it," I said to Søren. "I'm assuming you don't see any either? No ghosts nearby?"

He shook his head. "I'm not sure how to use my Lurae with yours unless I'm killing someone." His eyes flickered toward the queen, and despite the circumstances, I suppressed a smile.

"Maybe . . ." I chewed my lip. "This will sound strange. But your thread has always seemed different than the others to me. I wonder if it's possible to take part of your soul thread and use it to weave the Tapestry?"

Søren blinked. "Yours looks different to me, too. It's worth a shot. You try it on mine first—your Lurae will have less dire consequences if something goes wrong."

I wasn't sure about that, but for Frode I would try. I reached out tentatively with my Lurae, the thread of awareness stretching from me to Søren. Instead of tugging it in one direction or the other, I put all my focus toward unraveling it. I turned it over in my hands, examining it for a separation point.

There. I narrowed my eyes, leaning forward to brush the thread with my fingers. It parted slightly and I exhaled with relief. Just as I'd suspected, it was two threads twisted together. I unwound it, pulling one part over the other again and again until the threads were nearly entirely separate.

Søren inhaled sharply. "I can see a thread. Connecting us."

My eyes met his, full of trepidation and wonder. "Just one?"

"Yes."

"Point to it."

Søren obliged me. The thread on my left was visible to him, which must mean . . . "I think that's the one we use to access the Tapestry. The other is your soul thread. I'm going to try pulling it to see what happens."

"Go ahead."

I tugged carefully, wincing as I prepared for one of Søren's bones to crack or for pain to shoot across his face. But instead, the thread fell gently into my hands, pooling there in a puddle of gold. I gaped.

Søren stepped forward, examining it. "It's still attached on your end. I think I need to . . ." His voice trailed off and his face turned concentrated, his hand moving in a slight sweeping motion as he cut it from me.

I held my breath. The thread lifted into the air of its own accord, stretching and twisting around and around, tying itself deftly into practiced knots. Søren and I stared, his fingers winding with mine as we were encircled by gold on every side.

The Tapestry stepped out of the weaving, a humanoid among

moving pictures of unrecognizable figures flitting through behind it. I turned in a circle, awestruck. *Maybe it is a god,* I mused.

It spoke with the same endless cacophony of voices I'd heard from its humanoid version when I went beneath the ice. "You have found us."

I stepped closer to Søren, our shoulders brushing. His eyes were wide, mouth hanging open slightly as he studied our surroundings and the being before us. I realized this was Søren's first time seeing the Tapestry. My explanation of the experience could go only so far. Somehow I knew no one outside of this enclosed space made up of the Tapestry could hear us. "We have."

"Good." It sounded serious. "We know why you are here, child. The fabric of the universe is not to be tampered with."

I held my shoulders back. It had addressed only me, not Søren. "Then you should not have offered me the power to tamper with it in the first place."

It huffed a humorless laugh. "A stubborn one. Very well—the threads of the future tangle for generations at this moment. Your choices here will determine which threads will be pulled into the weaving and which will be discarded. Go forth."

Then all was silent except for the hum of my Lurae song.

Søren turned to face me. "Are you sure about this, Princess?"

"What choice do we have?" I felt the desperation leaking into my voice, impossible to deny. "You said it yourself—Bhorglid cannot afford another war."

"I'm not asking about that." His eyes flickered to the side, where Frode's body rested outside of the Tapestry's cocoon.

I deflated. "I . . . I don't know, Søren. I have to get through this first, see if resurrecting the queen's husband even works, before I think about Frode." Even his name made my throat tighten.

He squeezed my hand. "You're right. One thing at a time."

The pressure building in my chest eased slightly with his confident support. *He really isn't going anywhere,* I realized. Deep down I'd wondered if Søren's care for me had limits—if I could manage to push him away when I grew volatile again. But he'd more than proven his support for me was unwavering.

Bolstered, I studied the Tapestry, stepping closer to the interwoven threads surrounding us. "The queen said to look for the red thread. I don't see it anywhere . . ."

"Why would it be red?" Søren asked, studying the weaving himself. "And not gold, like all the others?"

I raised a brow at the Tapestry's humanoid form, but it remained silent. "No help from it then," I muttered. "I don't know. Maybe we'll understand when we've raised him."

I hovered a hand over the weaving. Nothing happened.

I walked in a circle, examining each section of the Tapestry carefully. When I'd gone almost all the way around, my Lurae song hit a discordant note. I stilled. Extended my hand again. The song grew louder, louder.

Like it was pulling me to one thread more than the others.

I peered at the section of the weaving calling to me. It was layered and complex, the threads twisting in constant motion over one another.

A flash of red snuck through.

"Found it!" I called. Søren was at my side in an instant. "It's beneath this top layer."

Tentatively, I brushed a finger along the threads. They snagged against my fingers, swarming over me. I chuckled and pushed them back, pressing through the top images of weaving until I grasped the red thread. It was taut, but I tugged on it gently and was surprised to find it disentangled itself with ease.

The moment it was fully unwoven, cradled in my hands, the rest of the Tapestry disappeared. But its voice echoed. "You have made your decision. Unwoven the threads of the past in order to weave your future. Now you will see the consequences of your actions."

I blinked and a vision materialized—one clearer than any of the other dreams I'd had before.

Søren stood next to me this time. He frowned, taking in the scene around us.

Aloisa stood, a crowd watching her from a careful distance. She was young, no older than me. A man knelt at her feet, his expression murderous as he glared at her. He was around the same age I'd estimate the queen to be. His hands were tied behind his back, and Aloisa held a thin sword pointed at his throat. They were in the wastes, surrounded by pines and snow.

"Esben," she called, projecting her voice so the nearby crowd could hear clearly. "You are sentenced for your crimes of denying service to Nilurae patrons. We are all human and deserve to trade fairly. What do you have to say for yourself?"

He spat at her feet. "Why should I have to serve them? We have *magic*. Hasn't anyone stopped to wonder why they don't? What did they do to be so undeserving?"

Disgust enveloped me. This man was no better than the priests.

"A Lurae does not make a person better than someone else," Aloisa argued. "Magic is a gift—you should be using it to make the lives of your fellow villagers better."

"Easy for you to say." Esben scowled. "You can commune with the dead. Raise them, even. I know you brought my son back after he perished."

Murmurs rippled through the crowd. My eyes widened. This was Callum's father. Aloisa's eyes flickered to the watchers before she set her jaw and gripped the blade tighter. "Callum, take his Lurae."

Callum stepped up next to her. He'd aged as well, gangly teenage features replaced with budding young adulthood. I waited for him to stretch out a hand. His father was so much like mine—the man deserved his Lurae be taken from him.

But Callum leaned closer to Aloisa, his voice lowered to the quietest murmur. "I don't want to."

She hesitated. "I know he's your father. I can't imagine how difficult this must be. But if he gets away with this, it's only a matter of time before there's a huge divide between the Lurae and Nilurae. We can't have that."

"Why not?"

Aloisa raised a brow. "Do you hear yourself?"

He crossed his arms, frowning. "You and I have been touched by a literal god. That is how we received our magic. We're"—here he moved closer to whisper in her ear—"*immortal.* Without us, there would be no peace for the dead and no magic. Why take people's Lurae when they misbehave? Instead, they should be bowing to us. They need *leadership.* Not whatever this is."

"Callum." Aloisa spoke through gritted teeth. "We can talk about this later. Not while everyone is watching. Take his Lurae. *Now.*"

He looked at his father for a long moment. "This isn't over," he said to Aloisa. He extended a hand and clenched it into a fist until his father swayed and toppled to the side, groaning.

Aloisa sheathed her sword and turned to face the crowd, looking for someone. The weaving changed to show the faces of the watchers. And there, staring back at Aloisa with an uncertain frown, was the Queen of Kryllian.

"Is that—" I started.

But the vision changed, and Aloisa sat outside a closed door, her back against the wall. I couldn't identify the building, but it was likely part of the village—the walls were planks of wood and she was wrapped in a shawl, her breath fogging in front of her although she was indoors. As I watched, she twisted her fingers together and sighed. "I'm not trying to be rude. I'm trying to be a good sister."

A voice sounded from the other side of the door. It was muffled but familiar in a way that itched against my mind as I tried to place it. "Well, you're not."

"Arraya, please."

I inhaled sharply. "Arraya and Aloisa were sisters?" Søren whispered. "How? Not a single record mentions their relation."

"Maybe the records do mention it," I said grimly. "The records the queen had removed from the library."

Søren had no time to reply before Aloisa continued. "You shouldn't marry him. He's going down a dangerous path and . . . I just think that if you give him more time to figure himself out, you have a better chance of a successful marriage, is all."

"More time. What a terrible excuse. You're just jealous. He may have been your friend first, but he fell in love with *me*. Time to stop pining for him."

Aloisa frowned. "No, I'm not jealous. Callum and I have only ever been friends—you know that."

"Do I?" Arraya snapped back. "The two of you have always had a strong bond, that I'll grant you. You raised him from the dead when you were children. Met the god under the ice together—the Tapestry, is that what you said it was called? Now you're both immortal. I suppose if anyone was going to marry him it would need to be you or me."

Aloisa opened her mouth, closed it again, and then finally said, "I would think the most important part of a marriage would be love."

"So you do love him?"

Aloisa threw her hands in the air. "As a brother, yes. But not romantically."

The door opened and Arraya strode out, wearing a long-sleeved white dress and a white fur shawl over her shoulders. She held a bundle of flowers in one hand. "I don't know, actually. Because no real sister would go this far out of her way to ruin my wedding unless she had feelings for the groom."

The images began to fade, but not before I got a good look at Arraya's face.

"The Queen of Kryllian is Arraya." The words fell from my lips, but they couldn't have been true.

And then I opened my eyes, feeling the bite of a blade against my throat, and understood just how big of a mistake I had truly made.

30

Søren

BETWEEN ONE BLINK AND THE NEXT, THE VISION DISAPpeared and the queen rematerialized in front of me. For a long moment, I had only one coherent thought.

Fuck.

Somehow, the Queen of Kryllian was Arraya in the flesh. A fact only further confirmed when my eyes adjusted to the throne room once more and I saw Anja—Arraya—whoever she was—gripping tight to Revna, a dagger at her throat.

Revna swallowed, and a bead of blood trailed down her neck. I stiffened, unwilling to move an inch. The queen scowled, her eyes alight with the same mania I'd seen in them when she forced her way into my quarters covered in blood only a few weeks ago.

"What the hell are you doing?" I growled.

"Getting justice," the queen hissed. "My husband should never have died in the first place, but my bitch of a sister murdered him in cold blood. Simply for creating a world far beyond anything she could imagine."

I put a hand on the hilt of my sword, but the queen shook her head. "I wouldn't do that if I were you. Not unless you're willing to see what your love's throat looks like when I slash it open." My princess's eyes widened slightly, her hands shaking, and I thought, *Oh, I am going to rip that woman to pieces.*

"What do you want?" I demanded through gritted teeth.

"Put the soul in the body," the queen barked. "Now, Søren."

Revna held the bloodred thread loosely in her palms—a thread I now knew belonged to the worst man the Fjordlands had ever known. And I had no choice but to resurrect him. In Frode's body, no less.

I held up my hands in a loose gesture of surrender and moved forward until I was face-to-face with Revna. Her teeth were clenched tight. I didn't need a mind-reading Lurae to know what she was trying to tell me with widened eyes. *You cannot put Callum's soul into Frode's body.*

But what other option did I have? I reached out and cupped my own hands, allowing Revna to pass me the glowing thread she held. My heartbeat pounded in my throat. The soul warmed my palms, and I glanced over at Frode's cold body. The queen hauled Revna to the table where he waited and tilted her head toward it. A gesture for me to begin the process.

I took in a shuddering breath. Was this the right thing to do? Raise a villain from the dead to save Revna's life?

Of course it is. There was no other option. Revna was my light. Even if it meant the world fell into darkness, I would do anything to keep her. I hovered my hands over the body, fear crawling up my spine like ice.

An idea struck me—one so wild I hardly dared consider it.

But we were out of options.

I took a deep breath and made eye contact with Revna. She saw my resolve, and her mouth set in a grim line of determination. There was uncertainty in her eyes, but behind it, the fury she carried with her always. Once, it had been a shield. Now, I knew it was sharp as her blade.

I lunged for the queen.

Her surprise offered a momentary distraction. I grabbed her dagger wrist in my free hand as tightly as I could, creating enough space between Revna and the blade for her to duck away. The queen let out a scream of surprise and frustration as she lost her balance.

The soul in my hand shuddered. I held the queen's arm away from her and pressed the palm of my other hand flat against her sternum, drawing a rush of my Lurae forward as I did so. The red soul thread sank beneath her skin, and my Lurae, rather than killing her, sealed it there.

There was no time to marvel at my newly discovered ability. Anja fell to the ground, convulsing. I didn't hesitate—I pulled my sword from its sheath and slammed it through the queen's stomach, pulling it out swiftly. A deadly wound, one that would end both her and Callum in a single blow.

Revna grabbed my arm. We watched with bated breath, relaxing slightly as blood poured from her. "Is she dead?" Revna whispered.

I opened my mouth to confirm the queen breathed no more . . . but I couldn't. Before my eyes, her shuddering body began to heal itself, the wound sealing in a matter of moments. Horror crept up my body.

Callum's soul had made Arraya immortal, too.

Revna looked around frantically. "Where's the sword? The Soulcleaver?"

For the first time since I'd noticed the weapon, the queen didn't have it on her. "Not here." Dread sank like a stone in my gut.

"We can't fight an immortal," Revna said, shoving me toward the door. "Run! We have to warn everyone, before she decimates the festival!"

We sprinted for the courtyard, the doors slamming behind us. I spotted the mare from our trip to the wastes out grazing and ran toward it, pulling Revna up behind me and urging the horse to a gallop. My mind flashed through the faces of everyone at the festival. Volkan and Mira were there. Revna's friends, too.

I called to her over my shoulder. "We have to tell everyone to be ready to run or fight."

"Fight." Her voice was taut. The sky above us was darkening steadily, a storm blowing in. The weather felt as ominous as the coming battle. "We'll fight."

31

Revna

I COULDN'T KEEP THE PROPHECY FROM WHISPERING IN MY MIND again and again as we descended the mountain path. *Old gods will rise to meet the new.* It felt more like an ominous threat, now that I understood which gods it meant.

Søren slowed the horse enough for me to jump off as we arrived in the square. Already I was screaming, "Soldiers! Raise your arms and prepare to fight! Bhorglid is under attack!"

It took a few repetitions before it caught on. The jovial atmosphere quickly turned to panic, but Freja rushed over with my sword and I buckled the belt around my waist quickly, unsheathing Aloisa and holding her high. "Nilurae, into your homes. Protect those who cannot fight!"

Soldiers rushed forward, all eager for the call of battle. Freja leaned in close. "What happened? Negotiations went *that* poorly?"

"It's the queen," I muttered. A glance up at the mountainside path confirmed a lone rider was making their way down. We had minutes before we were under attack. I pitched my voice to a yell once more. "The Queen of Kryllian is not who she claims!"

A voice rang out above the rest. "Neither are you!"

My shoulders tensed and I turned to find the accuser, but a cry of help pushing through the crowd caught my attention first. A panicked voice—not just any voice, either—growing louder.

I pulled back, alarmed, in time to see a red-haired man in too-big clothes shoving dancers aside to run to me. "Jac?" I breathed. My brother was entirely himself—the façade of Halvar long gone, sweat dripping down his brow. "What's wrong?"

He could barely get a word in between gasps for air. The confused soldiers around us were hushing their neighbors, listening in. All eyes were turning toward us in a steady wave, the momentum building past its peak. Even the fleeing Nilurae, unable to see the coming danger, had stopped moving toward the safety of their homes. Jac managed to get out his explanation. "I couldn't keep—he found—saw me shift and I—"

My heart sank. I couldn't breathe. This was it. This was the end of the charade.

It couldn't have come at a worse time.

Freja gaped. Astrid was pushing through the crowd, seeing the truth unfold before her as well.

No.

Slow claps echoed through the air, and now the crowd was turning. Soldiers parted to reveal the person, like a canyon forming in seconds and not over millennia.

Arne wore his light armor. The same plates had covered him when we sparred only a few days ago. A bulging satchel was slung over his shoulder.

And the audience, which had rushed to the ready at my command only a minute ago, now stared at him. Captivated.

"You've all been deceived," he said, cupping his hands around his mouth to ensure the words echoed. "This woman, your *queen*, has lied to you."

A hand that could only be Søren's gripped my bicep.

Desperation seized me. Freja pushed through to step into my field of vision, twisting to look between me and Arne.

"Stop," I choked out. "Stop, Arne, we have to be ready to fight." But my voice was hoarse, weak. A glance at the path confirmed—Arraya was halfway here. Arne raised his voice to speak over me.

"Halvar is *dead*."

Gasps echoed. Freja whirled to me, her eyes wide and shocked. I held out a desperate hand, said, "Wait, you don't understand—"

"The shapeshifting prince, who never arrived to compete in the Trials, has been posing as the Nilurae's righteous leader for weeks. Months, even."

I lurched out of Søren's grasp to fall at Freja's feet. "Please, just listen—"

"And his killer? Revna Thorunsdotter, the Bloodsinger Queen herself."

Freja screamed, the sound a knife. When I reached for her, she backed away. The crowd was falling back too, horrified shouts resounding. The pastry I'd eaten curdled in my stomach and I heaved in air, trying not to vomit.

All the while, the queen descended.

"Freja—"

"You *killed him*?" she demanded, her horror and anger swirling into something terrible, something life-ending, something with claws. When I only stared, she screamed, *"Answer me!"*

My Lurae buzzed, but I wasn't afraid. I wasn't even angry. Resignation wrapped me in an inescapable embrace, and I forced myself to say it. "Yes."

She slapped me.

The sting bloomed up my face, and I savored it. If she wanted to kill me, I would let her. I deserved it.

But Søren's voice pushed her back. "Stay away from her." I

watched his shadow fall over mine as he stood behind me. "The Queen of Kryllian is on her way *right now*. She refuses to sign the treaty, she wants war—"

"And *you*."

Arne pointed a shaking finger accusingly—at Søren, who scoffed. "Point that finger somewhere else or I'll slice it off you."

But Arne opened the satchel at his back and I glimpsed a familiar carved visage. I scrambled toward him, desperation flaring like unquenchable flames within me.

"The man you believe is a harmless ambassador, a known scholar, is someone far worse," Arne called. "Your greatest enemy brought to life. He's killed your fathers and brothers, your mothers and sisters, your sons and daughters! He—"

I slammed into Arne, pushing him backward onto the cobblestones. His head smacked, and the strings of my Lurae called to me, the threads pulsing with unrestrained fury as my magic called to every vein, every rush of blood through him.

"How dare you," I said. Only later would Søren tell me my voice was hoarse because I had screamed in Arne's face. "You know *nothing* about who he is!"

But the silence was too great, and I paused, looking up. Horrified eyes locked on the street beside me. And there it lay: the Hellbringer's mask, in the open for all to see.

I clambered off Arne, turned to look at Søren. His expression was guarded, no emotions visible. But I knew the way his jaw ticked, knew the way his knuckles tightened. When his eyes met mine, he shook his head slightly. A warning: *I'm not worth it.*

"Your queen has harbored Kryllian's notorious general in our capital for weeks. You all saw the way she looked at him—she has no intention of punishing him for his crimes. No intention of bringing justice to your murdered family members. No, she'd rather fuck hi—"

Arne's voice cut off because he was choking, my Lurae keeping him from breathing. I heard the *thump* of his boots hitting the ground. Søren only stared at me. His mouth moved in silent words. *I'm sorry.*

The soldiers were beginning to murmur, to shift their stances and reach for their weapons. How was I to point them in the direction of the true enemy? Impossible, when Arne had ensured their sharpened blades thirsted for the blood of the wrong target.

I was going to kill him.

I released my Lurae's hold on Arne's throat and used it instead to snap his arm so hard bone broke through skin. He screamed.

The crowd began to rush for the exits—at least, the Nilurae did. The Lurae powerful enough to contend with me, namely the former soldiers, advanced. Thunder boomed, lightning crackled in the now-darkening sky, and the ground beneath my feet rumbled.

Søren took a step between them and me. "I wouldn't touch the queen if I were you."

Surprisingly, several of the Lurae ignored the Hellbringer's threat—including his now-outstretched arm. He really did plan to kill them. Somehow the thought made me want to laugh.

If the soldiers didn't care for their own lives, then maybe they'd care for their comrades in arms. "Step any closer and he dies," I called. Then I broke Arne's leg.

His cries of pain went hoarse. The Lurae didn't dare move, all of them afraid. A bit of relief flowed through me like a trickle of water. *Afraid. Finally.*

I bent down and picked up the Hellbringer helmet, tucking it beneath my arm. No matter what it represented, Søren had carved this thing by hand. He deserved to lay it to rest or keep it if he desired. If it was left here, they would trample it, crack it, crush it.

I cradled it.

Then I stepped closer to Arne, until I was sure he could see me. His gritted teeth held back his groans. "You know," I said, "I didn't mean to kill Halvar. It was an accident. Not that you would believe me, clearly. I was going to take Freja aside after the festival ended and tell her everything. But I deserve this—you, coming here to tell the people the truth. That I'm a monster."

I tugged his strings and, like a puppet, he rose. When he was sitting, I continued. "But you made a mistake when you chose to bring Søren's identity into this. A mistake so horrible, I'll watch you die for it."

"Stop."

Freja stepped into my line of sight. Tears tracked down her cheeks, but her shoulders were set. "You believe yourself worthy to lead these people, and yet you threaten them. Hide things from your friends. Commit crimes in our names. You're just as terrible as your father."

I laughed. The sound was forced. Deep within me, Freja's words struck like a blade. "The Kryllian Queen is on her way here to declare another war *right now*. She's an ancient being with power we don't even understand. This is not the time to discuss whether I'm *worthy* of the throne."

The sound of hooves on cobblestone approached. The queen thundered into the crowd, not slowing her horse until several soldiers were nearly trampled. The Lurae, despite being armed and ready to fight, took hurried steps backward.

Chaos reigned now. Not me. No one knew whose command to obey.

The queen dismounted and turned to glare at me and Søren. Her eyes were bloodshot, her hair disheveled. Søren and I both drew our swords. He took his helmet from me gently and put it on, the voice distortion kicking in as he said, "Anja."

She laughed. "No, not *Anja*. Her name is Arraya. Remember it when she kills you later. But you're not speaking to her, you're speaking to *me*."

The crowd held its collective breath when she said, "Callum."

No one moved.

The queen—Callum—surveyed the scene. "You've gotten yourselves into quite the mess. Do you know what that tells me? That you do not deserve the power you have."

He stepped forward and I lifted my blade, prepared to fight. But Arraya's face split into a horrid grin. "Let's solve that problem, shall we?"

Several of the Lurae soldiers behind me sheathed their weapons, the sound of sliding metal loud in the silence. I glanced back just in time to see one drape an all-too-familiar veil over his face.

The red-stitched, dripping eye stared back at me as he shouted, "Long live Bhorglid's true god!"

Callum lunged.

I sidestepped, but he wasn't aiming for me. Instead, he drew Arraya's dagger and locked it with Søren's sword. At the same time, the priests in the crowd—who'd grown in number—swarmed me.

Caught up in dodging poorly aimed swipes and parrying scythes, I didn't have eyes on Søren when he screamed.

Panic seized me. I reached out with my Lurae, grabbing the strings of everyone in the vicinity and forcing them to kneel with their hands behind their back. It was more power than I'd ever used at once before, and it made my vision blur. But now I had a clear view to watch Callum battle Søren with one hand and stretch out his other, fingers splayed.

Søren's blade trembled against Callum's strength and he stumbled. But Callum didn't go for the final blow. Instead, he backed away, letting down his guard.

I waited for Søren to renew his vigor and strike again. Instead, the masked Hellbringer wavered and dropped his sword before collapsing to his knees.

I dropped my grasp on my Lurae and ran to him. No one tried to stop me, though I kept my sword out and ready for an attack. "Søren," I called, fear paralyzing. "Søren, what—I don't—"

"His Lurae is gone," Arraya's cool voice answered from behind me.

An uneasy murmur ran through the crowd, much of which had dispersed. When I turned to Callum, it seemed the crowd had transformed. Nearly a third of the festivalgoers now wore veils. Had there been this many priests before my reign? Or had people joined the Holy Order once I won the Trials and banished the priests?

Several of the priests held their scythes to the throats of prisoners. Freja and Astrid were each restrained by two priests. So were Volkan and Jac. The hopelessness of the situation hit me in full.

"I am a god," Callum called, stretching Arraya's arms out. "The true being deserving your worship. And after hundreds of years, I have returned to restore the rightful order of things in the Fjordlands."

I reached out with my Lurae, but before I could begin wrapping threads around throats, the world lurched beneath my feet. A piercing pain ricocheted through my head and I cried out, pressing a palm there. My sight wavered and nausea swept over me. Just as everything reached its peak, just as I became physically incapable of feeling more sensation . . .

It stopped.

Dizzy. I was so dizzy.

But Callum's words still permeated through the haze. "And now your Lurae is gone as well."

Søren's chest rose and fell beneath my hand. *Still alive, thank the gods.* But my legs were weak beneath me. The crowd was still and silent, the reality of what was happening finally seeming to sink in. Despite my spinning head, I reached for my weapon. The knowledge that I would likely die to the Queen of Kryllian in a few short moments settled like a stone in my gut.

And like my thought had reminded her—or Callum, whoever was in control of Arraya's body—she called out, "Kill them."

But a loud *crack* sounded. A hand wrapped around my wrist and Søren's and then the square, the festival, the faces of all my friends—everything before us vanished.

I fell into unconsciousness before my eyes opened again.

32

Revna

IN MY DREAM, I WAS VISITED BY THE TAPESTRY. SØREN HAD passed out too, it seemed, because he was there with me.

"We feared this would come to pass," the Tapestry said, not even bothering to greet us. I was just grateful the vertigo wasn't present in this place of nothingness. "You must destroy Callum once and for all. We should never have let her—"

It broke off mid-thought and sighed. Søren and I exchanged a glance. I raised an eyebrow and said, "I wasn't aware you cared about the political state of the Fjordlands."

"Politics are but a second string in this equation," it murmured. "This is bigger. This is about magic. The threads tying the world together. They are all at risk, more now than ever before."

"Because of Callum," I said. Then I swallowed and looked away. "Because I brought him back."

"Yes." There was no sympathy in the many voices. I wrapped my arms around my middle. "But the past cannot be undone. Only the future is still susceptible to change."

"You can see the future. See what happens. Do we manage to defeat Callum? Even without our Lurae?" Søren asked.

I looked down at my palms. Sure enough, I didn't hear the song of my Lurae anymore. The telltale twist of something *more* in my blood was gone. "How are we even here if we don't have our Lurae anymore?"

"So many questions." If the Tapestry had possessed a face, I would have expected to see a wry smile on it. "You are able to be here because you were chosen—selected by Aloisa personally to be her heirs. Your connection to us does not change even if your abilities to manipulate life and death are gone.

"As for your other questions: we can see the future, yes. Every possible future, like rolls of unspooled threads tangled together. But we decided long ago it is not our place to tamper with your choices. They will simply be made or not."

"You can't offer us anything?" I knew my frustration was obvious and I didn't care. "Nothing to help defeat a monstrous dictator? You'd leave us alone to suffer through?"

The Tapestry's voice sharpened. "Need we remind you who withdrew said dictator from our peaceful weaving and restored him to life?"

I scowled. Søren grabbed my hand, squeezing it gently.

But it continued before I managed a retort. "We will offer you the only gift we have to give—the past. In your visions, you will find all the answers you need."

It waved a hand, and the room flooded with color. I blinked and readjusted to the disconcerting sensation of seeing the world through a stranger's eyes.

My hand pushed open the door in front of me. I stepped into the wastes, my boots sinking in two feet of powder. "Boys!" I shouted, cupping my hands around my mouth so I could be heard. "Time for dinner!"

Six small figures rushed over the hill in the distance. One tripped and proceeded to roll all the way down, the snow cushioning his fall. I only chuckled. An older brother helped him up when, with a wave of his hand, the snow beneath the fallen toddler lifted and deposited him directly on his feet once more. Delighted, he clapped his mittened hands together and ran over to me.

I scooped him up in my arms, and he immediately pressed his tiny, cold nose to mine. "Welcome home, Hjalmar." My voice was filled with all the fondness I—or rather, Aloisa—possessed. One by one, the other boys filed into the house and I called them by name.

Somewhere far away, I felt myself breathe in sharply. *Hjalmar. Like the god of fire from Bhorglid's pantheon.* Six sons . . . which meant the rest of them had to be . . .

"Aksel." I ruffled the hair of the oldest. "Asger. Viggo. Elias. Valdemar. Your father needs help setting the table."

She set Hjalmar down, and Asger immediately stooped to help the tiny one take off his fur cloak and boots. *The gods of Bhorglid's pantheon,* I thought. *A mother and her little boys.*

Aloisa moved to step over the threshold also, but then she heard it. I heard it.

A whisper on the wind.

The notes of a familiar melody.

I frowned and murmured, "After all these years?"

"Mama?" Elias said. "What is it?"

"Tell your father I had to run into the woods for just a moment," I told him. "I think I hear an old friend."

I blinked and rematerialized in the woods, staring at the Tapestry. It was identical to the version that appeared to me now. I—well, Aloisa—crossed her arms. "What are you doing here?"

"There is a . . . situation," it said. "We understood your decision to be left alone, but we're afraid someone must interfere before things are taken too far."

I bit my lip and glanced back over my shoulder at the cabin. It was nestled at the foot of a mountain, safely shadowed there. Smoke puffed out from the chimney, and the clear windows were easy to see through—wrestling boys pulled apart by a laughing, patient man I knew was my husband.

"It is the only way to keep them safe," the Tapestry said quietly. "The threads of the future have never pointed in a single direction so clearly before."

She set her jaw. "Where are they?"

I blinked again and found myself in a familiar place—the prison where Søren had kept me, where hundreds of years prior Arraya had tortured Tam. But it wasn't the dank, horrifying place from my last vision. Now it was polished and clean, lit well, and staffed with a dozen guards.

But I barely stepped through the front door before I was intercepted. My sister stood in front of me, her smile too genuine for comfort. I tried to flinch away from Arraya—she looked as young here as she did in the present. Aloisa's body didn't move, though, reminding me once again that I was not the one in charge of this vision.

I realized I still didn't know exactly what Arraya's Lurae was. Something that kept her from dying, clearly. I tucked the question away, thinking I needed to consult with Søren upon waking to see what he thought. I didn't see him anywhere, so I wasn't sure if he was experiencing this vision, too.

"I'm so happy to see you." Arraya wrapped Aloisa in an embrace. I stiffened, and she clearly noticed. She pulled back with a slight frown on her face. "Aren't you here to join us?"

"I'm here to find out more about this . . . movement of yours," I said, adjusting my cloak. "I haven't made a final decision yet."

"Oh." It was strange to see the Queen of Kryllian appear genuinely sorrowful. I knew her only as a cunning leader, carefully holding her secrets to her chest until she held the upper hand. But Arraya perked up quickly. "Callum will convince you. Come sit down and I'll get him. He's been so excited to see you again."

Soon enough, we all sat around a table in a barren room. I glanced around, noting the absence of guards. It was frigid, my breath fanning out in front of my face. Callum's hair had darkened a bit since his resurrection. He wore it longer, falling to the tops of his shoulders, and his face now bore lines of wear. He appeared to be in his mid-thirties now, but I wasn't sure what his age truly was.

Despite the changes in his appearance, my heart ached at the sight of him. He'd been my best friend once. But along the way, he'd decided power was worth more than his responsibility to do right by the people of the Fjordlands.

He drummed his fingers against the surface before him and said, "What do you know of our efforts?"

I shrugged, feigning indifference. "Nothing, really. Only that you're endeavoring to unite the Fjordlands. Rumor has it you're building an army."

"Not an army," Arraya interrupted. "A group of trusted elite."

"To fight?" I raised a brow.

Callum shook his head. "To worship."

Silence stretched. "Worship . . . what? Whom?"

He rolled his eyes, then looked at Arraya. "I told you she was just here to try and right our 'wrongs.' You know the answer, Aloisa. The moment that thing in the ice touched our souls and made them *more* we ceased to be human. We became gods. Letting magic run free is a recipe for chaos. The people need leadership, guidance. Someone to look to in their times of need. Who is better suited for such a thing than us?"

I folded my hands together. "Us? Not just you?"

"No. We need you, Aloisa. You and I are both gods—you deserve the worship you've earned as well."

I bit my lip, knew instinctively that Aloisa was holding back dozens of responses, all of which involved screaming. I managed to keep my voice level when I asked, "And how have you earned it? What are you doing to improve people's lives?"

"Well." Arraya leaned forward eagerly. I realized she looked the same, but it was obvious just how much younger she was in this vision. Time hadn't jaded this version of her. She was no cunning monster, not yet. Just a young woman with a vision and a husband she'd do anything for. "We've built multiple prisons throughout the wastes, and most teleporters are faithful to our cause. Callum goes from village to village and introduces himself. Those who follow and pledge their allegiance are blessed—many choose to join the Holy Order of Priests. Those who don't are shown the error of their ways."

I tilted my head. "You imprison all who do not agree with you?"

"No," Callum said, crossing his arms. "It has nothing to do with us and everything to do with their willingness to acknowledge what is absolute truth: the Lurae are superior to their Nilurae counterparts in every way. And within that hierarchy, you and I reign supreme." He shrugged. "A like-minded people create a productive society. Many villages are relocating to be more central—moving south, to where we've started building a capital city. We plan to name our empire Bhorglid."

"After the lake where we received our Lurae," I murmured. Within, my heart sank. The situation was more hopeless than I had guessed.

He nodded. "The hierarchy does not end with gods. It ends with universes of combined consciousness. With . . ." He gestured for me to finish.

"The Tapestry," I concluded grimly. Aloisa's thoughts spun, mingling with my own horror. "Tell me what would happen if I joined you. What would my role in your revolution be?"

Callum relaxed slightly at this. "You and I will reign as gods side by side. We can divide responsibilities among us. But think of what it would mean for people to know they couldn't move on after death without accepting our teachings first! Your efforts in our cause would be a monumental help."

Arraya chimed in. "Aren't you tired of suffering? Living off the land? We know your home is in the middle of nowhere. Haven't you worked hard enough? Callum's doctrine is clear: the strongest holds the power. In this world, in our lifetime, perhaps for eternity, *you* are the strongest."

My emotions changed the instant Arraya reached across the table and placed her hand gently over mine. *She believes this. She genuinely believes this is right.*

Anger vanished, replaced by a sorrow more bone-deep than anything I'd ever known. Aloisa's eyes filled with tears, her vision blurring as her mind spun. *I will have to kill my sister and my best friend. How? How can I do such a thing?*

I stood abruptly. "Thank you for speaking with me. I need some time to think things over. For now, I must return to my home."

Arraya stood too, and it seemed she did not understand what her sister was feeling or thinking. "Don't let twenty more years go by before we see you again. I want to meet my nephew before he's entirely grown."

Aloisa nearly buckled at the reminder. Arraya had no idea that Aloisa was a mother six times over—no, she knew of only Aksel's birth. It had been shortly after when Aloisa had taken her family away, determined to free herself of the demands her Lurae brought on them all.

She can never know of the other children, I thought fiercely. *I will keep them safe no matter what it takes.*

The scene faded, and the Tapestry's endless space of nothing reappeared. "You are waking. You will not be able to access this place on your own without your Lurae."

I sat with the knowledge. Callum and Arraya were trying to do the same thing they'd done over three hundred years ago. Imprison the Nilurae, force the Lurae to comply, and establish themselves as gods. My voice was empty as I said, "I understand."

The Tapestry disappeared, and the real world greeted me once more.

33

Revna

I PACED ACROSS THE WOODEN FLOORBOARDS OF THE INN, RESTless as ever. My fingers drummed against Aloisa's hilt. Søren, who somehow managed to lounge on the bed, said, "You're thinking too loud."

I tensed. "I'm worried. What if—"

"If today is different?" He sat up, brushing hair out of his face. Dark circles had taken up residence beneath his eyes. He could argue with me about my anxieties all he wanted. I knew he wasn't sleeping through the night either. "Maybe it will be. But we're working on a plan."

"It's not *enough*." I tugged at the ends of my hair, looking anywhere but at his face.

After the disastrous events of the festival, Søren and I had both awoken in the forest just outside the Kryllian palace. The same place where he'd told me the truth about what happened with Frode. Astrid had been in a panic. "I didn't know where else to go," she kept signing, the words repeating again and again as if it would give them substance.

I'd put my hands on her shoulders, which stopped the worst of her shaking. Then I'd caught sight of Søren, still unconscious in the grass. My mind was nothing but white noise. "We need a safe place to stay," I'd managed to sign back. "I know where the village is. Help me carry Søren." Having a task had calmed her somewhat. Søren's teeth chattered and he stirred into consciousness when I hauled him to his feet. "My Lurae." His voice was hoarse. "It's gone."

"I know," I'd said, holding back tears. The names of the people we'd left behind looped through my mind over and over again, along with the fate we'd likely sentenced them to. *Freja. Volkan. Jac. Arne, even.*

There were others, too. The girl we'd danced with all morning. The seamstress who made my dress. The baker whose pastries I'd eaten only a few hours ago. We pulled Søren through the forest slowly. Eventually, he'd managed to walk on his own. Dark circles clung beneath his eyes. "There's an inn," he told Astrid. "Nilurae and Lurae are both welcome there. Can you secure us a room and then come back and teleport us?"

She'd chewed her lip. "Will they understand my signing?"

"Probably not, but they shouldn't be rude about it." Søren pulled from some inner strength to reassure her—a strength I lacked. Inside me there was nothing but a gaping hole. "They'll offer you a pen and paper to write on."

Astrid departed without another word. Only once she was gone did I collapse to my knees, my own shock and devastation catching up with me. In my dream with the Tapestry, I'd been totally coherent and calm. I did not have the same luxury now.

Søren had sat down, leaning back against the trunk of a tree. I'd crawled on my hands and knees until I reached him, curling up beneath his arm and pressing my head against his chest. He let out a laugh, but there was no humor in it. "Did you know this forest is full of ghosts?" he said. "I can't see them anymore. Can't hear them. They're just . . . gone."

Now a knock sounded. The inn wasn't crowded, but it wasn't empty of patrons either. A perfect balance for us to remain hidden as long as we obscured our most defining features with the hoods of our cloaks. Astrid came and went as she pleased, and no one had bothered to stop her. I wasn't sure whether news of our escape hadn't yet reached Kryllian or if the queen had chosen to forget about us. I turned away from Søren, who leaned on one of the bedposts, and rushed to open the door. Astrid slipped in soundlessly, putting down her hood once the door was closed and locked behind her.

"What news?" I demanded.

She shook her head. "The same as yesterday and the day before. Freja, Volkan, and Jac are all being held in Bhorglid's prison, but they haven't been harmed. I presume Jac and Volkan have had their Lurae taken, like the others being held with them. The place is still swarming with silencers."

Relief fell over me like a waterfall, and I was suddenly exhausted. I sat down on the bed next to Søren, who grabbed my hand and squeezed it. "Did you go into town at all?" he asked.

"I didn't get far before I was forced to come back here," she said, grimacing. "There are priests everywhere. No real citizens out and about, except for a few Lurae who seem thrilled with the change in leadership. I wasn't able to speak with any of the prisoners either."

"We need to go rescue them," I said.

Astrid and Søren exchanged a look.

"We've waited too long," I argued. "Callum and Arraya could kill them at any moment. If we want to have any chance of defeating these false gods, then we have to get our friends out."

Astrid shook her head. "I want that more than anyone. But it isn't possible. Not with only three of us. There are three prisoners, and we'd have to get them all quite far from the prison before I could teleport them away. If a single silencer chases after us far enough, then we're fucked."

"The sword then," I said, refusing to think about every other time we'd had this argument, every other time we'd run these scenarios through over the past three days. "We go in, steal the sword, kill Callum and Arraya."

"Revna." Søren's voice was gentle and I hated it. I pulled my hand from his and crossed my arms. "You already know the answer. If we messed anything up, your friends would be killed to punish us. Are you willing to risk that?"

Tears burned in my eyes and I shook my head. "I feel so helpless. I want to be doing something. If it's numbers we need, then let's go find more people to join us."

"I've been looking for Nilurae, whenever I go to Bhorglid," Astrid said quietly. "To see if they have interest in joining our cause. I haven't been able to find anyone yet, but maybe when I travel there tomorrow I'll spend more time in the city proper. If Freja, Volkan, and Jac haven't been killed or slated for public execution by this point, then I think the queen plans to keep them alive—if only to use as bait for you two."

"We can start looking for people sympathetic to our cause here, in Kryllian," Søren chimed in. "But we'll need to be incredibly discreet about it. Otherwise, word of our location might get back to Arraya."

"Word is going to get back to her either way. I don't exactly blend in," I said, gesturing to the scars on my face. I'd barely left the room since we arrived. Mira and Søren brought me any meals, and the one time I had gone out, desperate for a sight besides the plain walls, I'd crept out the window and scaled down the side of the building. Just in case.

"Revna is right," Søren said wearily. "It's time to form a better plan. We can't hide away forever."

I cleared my throat. "Go rest," I signed to Astrid. She was swaying on her feet, the effort of so much teleportation wearing on her. "We can meet again once you've gotten some sleep and some food. Hopefully by then we'll be able to come up with a plan."

Astrid didn't argue. She closed the door quietly behind her and I locked it, then leaned my forehead against the wood and let out a groan.

Søren came up behind me and wrapped his arms around my waist. I allowed it, despite my begrudging mood. The work of rescuing my friends was slow—and all the more tainted by the knowledge that I had caused it this time.

They likely didn't even want me to save them.

He laid his chin against the top of my head. For a long, blissful moment, I simply basked in his warmth, allowing my nerves to settle. He'd given me the space I needed over the last few days, remaining close enough to offer comfort if I went to him.

I knew the loss of his Lurae was affecting him deeply. Neither of us was sleeping well, and I'd caught him staring at his palms and flexing his fingers with a furrowed brow more than once.

We'd also been visited by the Tapestry every night, shown visions of the past until we could barely keep them straight. Arraya, meeting in secret with the priests after I won the Trials, coordinating them for when Callum rose again. They'd been hiding out in the hills near the prison, and she'd been traveling there to visit and speak with them on a near-daily basis ever since. We'd also seen Aloisa and her sons becoming gods to the priests after she defeated Callum with the Soulcleaver—the original Holy Order taking to heart Callum's doctrine that "the strongest deserve the most power."

The priests had been desperate for someone to worship once

their original leader was killed. Aloisa had gone into hiding, and her sons had eventually relocated to Kryllian and Faste. But Bhorglid had held on to a warped idea of them all, using their fiction to create a reality where the Nilurae suffered.

Watching it all had been exhausting. Even though I recognized the importance of understanding what had happened in the past, it made me dread sleeping. Especially thinking of how such terrible things might happen again—all because of me.

"How are you doing?" I murmured, letting myself relax against him. Søren. My anchor, my rock.

"Surviving," he murmured. "Astrid is trying to be strong for us, but she's just as worried as we are."

Guilt dug into me like a blade. "I know. She's thinking of Freja, I'm sure."

"I don't blame her. I'd be rampaging into the prison alone if it were you."

Despite our situation, I couldn't help a fond smile. *Of course you love him,* I thought. *He is the only one who has seen all of you and never turned away, no matter the cost.*

He adjusted his position, lips moving to brush against my ear as he murmured, "What do you want to do when this is all over?"

"What do you mean?"

"Well . . . at the risk of being insensitive, you don't seem to enjoy being queen. And I don't think Freja or the Nilurae will want you back on the throne after all is said and done." I waited for the words to send a chill of dread through me, but they didn't. I regretted everything else that had happened, but the thought of handing over the responsibility of the crown to someone else sounded strangely appealing. "Pretend we've done it all. We've defeated Callum and Arraya. The world is ours. What would you want to do?"

"I've . . . never really thought about it before," I admitted. My next words felt like sacrilege, but they poured out of me. "I wouldn't want to stay in Bhorglid. And I don't think Faste is a place I could be happy either."

Søren perked up. "Maybe we could . . . travel. See the world together."

"That sounds nice," I said. The honesty in my words surprised me. "If we found somewhere we really loved, we could settle down. Otherwise, we could just . . ."

"Keep going." He twisted me in his arms to face him, then leaned forward to press his forehead to mine, and the sincerity radiating from him made my shoulders relax. "But you've had so few choices in your life. I don't want to be another obligation. So be thinking about where you want to go first. Anywhere. I'll follow you. Just say the word."

I pulled his mouth down to meet mine. The kiss was slow and languorous, an anchor in the current of my emotions. "We could decide together. Take turns if we disagree on a final destination." I brushed our noses together. "The world will be ours. We can find somewhere safe, where we don't have to run. And just . . ."

"Be," he finished for me. "Just be."

I relaxed in the cradle of his arms. The exhaustion of the last few days weighed heavy. But tonight, we would sit down with Astrid and make a real plan. The storm raging inside me settled a bit.

"I asked Astrid to grab us both a change of clothes," he said, nodding to the bag she'd left behind.

I stepped out of his hold to examine the contents. Basic pants and shirts for both of us, including new undergarments as well. Thank the gods. Our room had a tub, but our clothes were beginning to feel unclean.

After setting everything out on the bed, I turned my back to him. "Will you help me with the corset?"

He moved behind me and began to unlace it without speaking. I'd been numb and angry since we arrived at the inn, but the simple twist of his fingers through the laces of my corset, an act of mundane kindness anyone might have granted, brought a lump to my throat.

"Thank you," I said quietly, twisting my fingers, "for staying with me."

"I—"

"Please let me finish." He fell silent, went back to the task at hand. I watched his reflection in the window above the headboard, grateful to be on the third story of the building. "I have made many mistakes in my short life. None of them have ever been presented to me as succinctly as they were at the festival."

I took a shaky breath before I continued. "I've lost everything. The crown I fought for. The friends who made me want to fight in the first place. The trust of my people. My home."

By now his fingers were still, the corset loose around my torso. Cool air crept beneath the fabric of the bodice. "I have been a monster. I *am* a monster. And selfishly, horribly, I—I am eternally grateful that you are, too."

"Revna." His voice was low and hoarse. "I am yours. No one can part me from your side. No matter what you do, I will follow you. When everyone else leaves, I will stay. Always."

His hands gripped my waist, and I heard the meaning of his words like a whisper. *I love you, I love you, I love you.*

Søren tugged on the corset until the laces were undone and set it aside. His fingers brushed along the waistline of my dress. "May I take this off?"

I wasn't sure what I wanted, whether doing anything other than changing into clean clothes was a good idea. But my body craved him half as much as my soul, and my answer was inevitable. "Yes."

He pulled the fabric over my head, tossed it to the side with our bags. When he finished his work, I stood bare. I knew I'd savor the memory of this moment forever—naked and vulnerable, exposed and wanting, while he stood behind me still fully clothed.

We barely touched, the only contact his gentle fingertips on my wrists. "Perhaps the world sees a monster when they look at you," he whispered, his breath sending shivers down my spine as it caressed the shell of my ear. "But I see only this. Perfection. A goddess in human form, made for my worship."

I exhaled a shaky breath. He walked around me and sat down on the edge of the bed before pulling me to stand between his knees. It was easy to believe it when he looked at me like this—like he would shove a knife between his ribs if I only asked.

"Can I show you?" he pleaded. "Can I prove it to you?"

I hesitated. "I don't know that I deserve it. Not after everything that happened."

"Fuck what happened." Søren was fierce now, and I knew with a certainty my words had brought the Hellbringer to the surface. My heart pounded in my chest, a harmony to the blood rushing through my head. "You are *good*."

My body shook and I gasped. His hands slid down to palm my ass, grip the backs of my thighs. "You like that? You like it when I tell you the truth?"

I squeezed my eyes shut. "It isn't—"

"Do I lie?" The words held an edge of sharpness, a demand so firm I was forced to answer.

I shook my head. One moment, I stood before him. The next, he'd hoisted me into the air, hands clutching my thighs, and buried his face into the hollow of my throat. I wrapped my arms around his neck, hanging on for dear life as he kissed and licked and nipped at me. The fabric of his clothes brushed friction over my breasts as he walked us over to the wall and pressed me up against it.

"S—Søren," I managed.

"Hmm?" His answer was muffled against my throat, his lips then trailing softly down to the tops of my breasts.

"I love you."

He froze, then looked up at me through his lashes. His pupils were blown, the gray of his eyes barely visible but still there. I watched his throat bob. "I love you, too."

Then his mouth met mine again. The heat was still there, building faster than was controllable, but I found myself surprised that the fire and the secure safety of knowing how he felt seemed to lift each other. One making the other more poignant.

His mouth was warm and soft and, gods, I wanted him. I knew the fabric of his shirt must be wet where I pressed into it, and the thought sent a thrill through me. He loved me, monstrosities and all, and maybe I didn't deserve it.

But I wanted it. And that would be enough.

I nipped at his lower lip, delighted when he moaned. He twisted us away from the wall and deposited me, laughing, on the bed. My eyes drank him in while he took off his shirt, then his pants, until he stood naked looking down on me.

His gaze lit across every part of me, taking his time. He ran a palm over his cock absentmindedly, stroking himself while he looked between my breasts and my cunt, like he was trying to decide where to begin. I stretched, luxuriating in the way his gaze heated, and spread my legs while I ran my hands over my own body.

The predator had emerged. But before he could pounce, I made a decision. Swiftly, I sat up, pushed his meandering hand to the side, and wrapped my mouth around him.

"*Fuck.*" I don't think I imagined the way his knees started to buckle. He gripped the bedpost as I sucked, laving him with my tongue. "You're gorgeous like this."

His praise made my chest hum contentedly. I hollowed my cheeks and moved faster. Søren groaned, and I relished the taste of him. But soon, he was placing his palms on my cheeks and pulling me off him. I caught my breath, frowning. "Was it not good?"

A firm hand pushed me onto my back, and he knelt over me, eyes heavy-lidded. "It was *too* good. I want to make this last, Princess. I can't do that when I'm watching your lips stretch around my cock."

"Oh." I knew he loved me, knew he wanted me, but hearing him say it so succinctly still surprised me. I ran my hands over the planes of his chest, traced a finger over the ridges of his scar. "Well, sometime I want to get you off that way."

His hand trailed over my stomach, teasing before it fell between my legs. "You never have to."

"I said I *want* to," I managed, one of his fingertips circling my entrance. I squirmed beneath his touch, wanting more, more, more. "I might need some practice, though. I've never—"

Søren interrupted me with a kiss, sliding his finger into me at the same time. My mouth opened in a silent gasp, and his lips brushed my ear when he whispered, "We can practice all you like, Princess." I heard the smirk in his voice, even as his quiet words turned rough. "My good girl."

I clenched, and he chuckled, moving back to drink me in again. "You had your turn to make me feel good. Now it's my turn to make you beg."

34

Søren

I WASN'T SURE WHAT I'D DONE TO DESERVE THIS, BUT I SILENTLY vowed to do whatever it took to make sure it happened again and again and again.

Because propped up on one arm, a finger coasting in and out of my princess while she gasped and moaned beneath me, my lips pressed against her sternum, was something I'd happily spend the rest of my life doing.

I watched as her pupils dilated at my words. Gods, her eyes were mesmerizing. Something about having her here, entirely naked on the bed and spread wide for me, was intoxicating. Maybe because she spent so much of her time with her walls up, angry, refusing to let anyone in unless they were willing to break down those walls and earn it. Somehow, she'd decided I had earned her vulnerability. Had earned the right to make her plead for release, to learn her pleasure inside and out.

Somehow, she loved me.

I pushed another finger in beside the first. She was so wet, so ready, but I wanted her to come first before we did anything else. My cock throbbed, and I forced myself to ignore it.

"Søren." Revna's voice pitched to a whine, and I smothered a grin.

"Begging already?" I murmured, casting my eyes down to where my fingers disappeared inside her. Next time we did this, I'd need to put my mouth on her again. Even looking at her—pretty lips spread, her clit swelling and desperate for me—my mouth watered. Maybe she would sit on my face if I begged her. "How badly do you want it, sweetheart?"

Her hands flew up to tug on my hair, and I groaned, faltering in my rhythm for a moment. Gods, how was she able to make me see stars so *easily*? It was entirely unfair, and I relished in it.

She used her grip on my hair to tug my lips down to hers, the kiss all-encompassing. When her teeth scraped my lip, it took all my concentration not to come right then and there. She pulled back, panting. "Stop teasing, Søren."

A thrill settled in my stomach at her frown, but I tucked the feeling away. She loved me, she loved me—we'd have all the time in the world to drag it out later. Right now I was helpless to do anything but what she asked. I brought my thumb up to circle around her.

Revna's head fell back, exposing her throat to me. What the hell was it about the slope of her neck that made her so exhilarating? Every inch of bare skin was another ounce of heat burning in me. She whimpered as I found the right rhythm, determined to have her coming soon.

I ran my tongue lazily over the slope of her breast, pressed my teeth gently into the soft flesh of her nipple. And then she gasped and arched her back and came on my hand. Clenching around me while her toes curled and I held her through it.

"I love you." I couldn't help the words slipping out, even though

I knew she might not even be able to hear me. "Fuck, you're so beautiful."

She panted and I pulled my fingers out of her slowly. My other hand caught hers and I intertwined our fingers, scattering kisses down the inside of her arm.

"I want you inside me," she said, and we locked eyes.

She looked at me like I made up the sky. Like if we were ever separated, she would pull the gods from the lake and make them pay for their sins in blood. "No need to tell me twice."

Revna grinned. "Lie down."

Oh, shit.

I obeyed, rolling over to lie next to her. She pressed a kiss to my knuckles before sitting up to straddle me. I swallowed hard at the sight. Her dark hair was mussed, her cheeks pink, a small bruise blossoming along her throat from where I'd sucked too hard. A vicious possessiveness took hold of me, and I reached up to grab her hips. If she didn't wear a cloak when we went down to dinner, everyone would know what we'd been up to. Would know that she was mine.

Good.

"Søren?" I glanced back up at her. Revna's brow was furrowed, a little smile on her face. "Where did you go just now?"

I bit my lip, ran my hands up her sides. "Thinking about people seeing the mark on your neck. Thinking about everyone knowing what we were doing up here. Thinking about how I'm the luckiest man in this world and the next."

Her gaze softened. "I missed you."

"I missed you, too." The truth of it sent another pulse of need through me. "Will you fuck me now, Princess? Or will you make me wait for you?"

"What would you do if I said 'wait'?"

I groaned but couldn't help my smile. "I'm not a patient man, but I'd become one. For you."

My answer settled something in her. Using one hand to line me up with her entrance, she carefully began to sink down. My fingers tightened their hold on her hips, and I watched with rapt attention as my cock sank into her. When she paused, I said, "Take your time, sweetheart."

She exhaled roughly. "I want to savor this. Last time we didn't get to."

But in the next moment, she descended fully. The sound I made was something raw, something inhuman, and her hand cupped my jaw, thumb tracing across my cheekbone. "I like you like this," she said. "Completely at my mercy."

And by the gods, I liked it, too. My entire life I'd worn a mask. Kept my true self hidden from the world. I knew I was a monster, knew I was powerful, but did it really mean anything? No. Not until she arrived. Because maybe I'd had magic and she had none. But she had a furious determination, a righteous anger I lacked.

At some point, the mask had become a shell. I'd withered away under it. And Revna had brought me back to life.

Fitting then, that she should be the embodiment of life with her Lurae. Whether it was gone now or lived dormant inside her still, it made her radiant.

"I've always been at your mercy," I told her. "Do you want me to beg? I will. *Please*, Revna."

She began to move, rolling her hips as her hands grabbed my shoulders for stability. I lost myself in the pleasure of it. Dark strands fell over her face and she closed her eyes. I moved one hand between us to rub against her clit, determined to make her come again. At the sensation, she inhaled sharply, eyes flying open to watch my face.

"Look at me," I begged, hearing the need in my own voice. "Fall over the edge with me."

Because the pressure between us was building, a fire I dared not smother. I stroked her gently. Her movements grew faster, until her thighs began to shake on either side of me. It was all I could do to hold on until finally, finally, she cried out and pulsed around me.

I came too, calling out her name until the stars faded from my vision and she rolled over to lie next to me. When I'd caught my breath, I grabbed a cloth from the washroom to clean us both up. Then I pulled her to my side, her head nestled on my chest.

"You really love me?" she asked.

I chuckled. "I really do. Always have, actually." *If only I'd had the courage to tell her sooner.*

"I'm glad you didn't leave," she said quietly. "Even when things were hard between us and I needed time to figure everything out. You were still there. And I'm grateful."

I held her more tightly, exhausted and sated, but already dreaming of having her on top of me again.

"I'm not going anywhere."

♦ ♦ ♦ ♦ ♦

THE COMMON ROOM OF THE INN WAS A COZY SPACE WITH SEVERAL tables set up and a roaring fire burning along one wall. It was packed, but I noticed Astrid had sectioned off part of a table so we could join her. Considering how private the room upstairs had felt, I was surprised to see so many people eating and chatting.

"I'll get us some stew," Revna said. She pulled the hood of her cloak tighter around her face, so the shadow of it obscured her scars from view. The last thing we needed was for someone to recognize us.

Reluctantly, I released my hold on her. I knew Arraya and Callum were in Bhorglid, but part of me worried the moment I turned around, Revna would be gone.

It's what had happened to Sonja, after all.

The memory of the day I'd returned from the front and descended down to the palace dungeons, intending to see my sister after two weeks of utter hell on the front lines only to find her gone, haunted me.

This is different, I told myself, forcing my feet to carry me to Astrid. She slurped the broth in her bowl—all that remained of her hearty stew—like a starving woman. *I'm doing everything I can to protect Revna.*

I settled across from the teleporter, keeping my signs close to my chest so the strangers on the other end of the table couldn't glimpse them easily. "Have you surveyed the Kryllian soldiers in Bhorglid at all?"

Astrid raised a suspicious brow. "No. Why, Hellbringer?"

I tried not to wince. Astrid hadn't brought up the secret of my identity being revealed before now, but I'd seen her narrowed eyes when she thought I wasn't looking. She studied me often, maybe searching for a hint of the monster she expected to see. "Because if we need more numbers, I think Mira—the teleporter who worked with me—might be willing to help us."

Astrid drummed her fingers against the table. "Why would she be loyal to you and not the queen?"

Revna appeared at my side, depositing two big bowls of stew on the table. There was no room for her to sit beside me . . . until she glared hard enough at the stranger at my side that he got up and left of his own accord. I hid my smile behind my hand.

Astrid was not feeling as lighthearted, apparently. She caught my attention with a snap and said, "Why should I trust anyone who works for Kryllian?"

"Do you see any other options?" I replied. "We need allies if we're going to rescue Freja and the others. Unless we're willing to try and sneak back into Bhorglid, Kryllians are our only option."

"You want to recruit Mira?" Revna asked, understanding. She chewed her lip. "Do you really think she isn't loyal to the queen? She was willing to tell Arraya about our relationship."

"Maybe," I conceded. "But when I spoke with her about that, she told me she was trying to protect me. I think she'll join us."

Astrid nodded stiffly. "We can try to recruit her tomorrow."

"Why are there so many people here?" I asked as another wave of visitors swarmed through the front doors, all ordering bowls of stew for themselves. "We're in Roskilde. It isn't like this is a travel destination."

Astrid seemed to appreciate the change in subject. She relaxed slightly as she explained, "The innkeeper said a whole caravan of Seeing Ones arrived in town this afternoon. They're setting up to camp outside for the night—near the edge of the forest."

My heart skipped several beats. "Seeing Ones."

Sonja.

I was out the door in an instant, running for the trees. The moment I broke through the last of the houses in the village, I found myself in the midst of dozens of travelers. A circle of tents surrounded a blazing fire, the edges of the camp beginning to encroach on the road a bit. A shopkeeper was having a loud argument with one of the caravan members, a small group worked on preparing a meal around the campfire, and an older person clapped a hand on my shoulder.

I turned to see a wizened face and white hair. "I've been looking for you," the Seeing One said with a wry smile. "*Hellbringer.*"

A few of the caravan members within hearing distance stilled, gaping. I winced, turning away as if hiding my face would be enough to take their words back. "How do you know who I am?"

They laughed and extended a hand for me to shake. "Valen, friend of your Bloodsinger Queen. But that's not important. Follow me."

I didn't know what else to do, so I obeyed. *Is this how things are now?* I wondered. *Does everyone know the man behind the mask?*

The thoughts sent a chill through me. The protection of my anonymity was officially gone. Everyone in Bhorglid's capital had heard Arne's declaration that I was the Hellbringer. And here, it seemed Valen—whoever they were—truly didn't care to protect my secret.

Was I imagining the eyes on me as we walked through the encampment? Or were they truly as hostile as they felt? I resisted the urge to pull up the hood of my cloak. Hiding would be easy, but after I was done listening to whatever this Seeing One had to tell me, I'd begin searching the tents for Sonja.

She could be here. Right now.

The realization sent a jolt through me. Day was turning to dusk in the sky above, orange streaking through gray clouds. The palace spires loomed in the distance, foreboding. And my sister was in the same place as me for the first time in five years.

Valen tapped my shoulder. "You with me, Hellbringer?"

I blinked back to awareness. We now stood in front of a tent, slightly bigger than all the others. Valen pulled back the flap and gestured for me to enter. I frowned. "Why?"

They shook their head, amusement in their eyes. "You'll see."

I was still suspicious, but I didn't think someone like Valen had the capacity to kill me. Even without my Lurae. Still, I kept my guard up as I stepped into the tent.

My eyes adjusted slowly to the dim light. A few lanterns flickered, and a flap in the top was pinned open so the fading daylight streamed down over a small table. A slender woman with light brown hair faced away from me, her elbows resting on the table. "Valen, this map doesn't make any sense. What do all the symbols mean?" She waved her left hand exasperatedly, and a small wedding ring glinted from her ring finger.

Heart in my throat, I opened my mouth. No sound came out.

She turned. "Valen, I said—"

We stared at each other. Sonja looked nearly the same as when I last saw her. Her hair was short now, cut to just above her shoulders, and her cheeks were no longer shaded hollows from being underfed as a prisoner. Her shock mirrored my own, even in the widening of her gray eyes and the way her jaw trembled almost imperceptibly.

She took a half step forward, her hand lifting toward me. "Søren?"

"Sonja." I rushed for her, wrapping her up in an embrace. Tears streamed down my face. "You're real."

"Can't breathe," she wheezed, and I pulled back immediately, loosening my grip. As soon as I did, her palms came up to frame my face, a watery smile adorning her own. "Look at you. The last time I saw you, you were just a boy."

"And you," I choked out. "Married?"

She laughed. "Gods, I'll have to tell you the whole story sometime. But yes. Her name is Clara. She's funny and kind and brilliant. You two will get along far too well for my liking, I already know it."

"What are you doing here?" I asked.

She wasn't able to answer before Revna barged into the tent, her hand on the hilt of her sword. Fury shrouded her, and I found myself grinning. Since our activities earlier this afternoon, she'd seemed far more like herself than before. *There she is,* I thought. *That's the woman I fell in love with.*

Revna looked between me and Sonja once. Twice. Her brow furrowed and her mouth opened slightly. Then understanding dawned. "You're Sonja."

My sister nodded—wary after Revna's entrance. "I am. And . . . who are you?"

"This is Revna," I said, unable to hide the pride in my voice. I moved over to her and wrapped my arm around her waist. "Queen of Bhorglid. The woman I love."

"Well," Sonja said, "it's lovely to meet you, Revna."

Valen entered the tent, too. "Now that introductions have been made and siblings are reunited, it's time for us to make a plan."

Revna frowned. "Why are you here? It's nice to see you again, Valen, but there's a lot going on that you don't know about."

Valen laughed. "I highly doubt it. Last month, I began having visions of the future after more than twenty years without. Sonja and I are fully aware of Callum's revival—in Arraya's body, no less—and we've informed the rest of the caravan that Bhorglid is under new leadership."

Revna winced. I glared. "You couldn't have come to Bhorglid to warn us? Instead of reconvening with us here?"

Valen shrugged. "We could have, but it seemed like the better option to avoid Bhorglid rather than risk what Lurae we do have on our side losing their abilities before we decide what to do next. And here I thought you were supposed to be a brilliant war strategist."

"Valen," Revna snapped. "We don't have time for this. I understand you made your choices, but we have a right to ask why you made them."

"The right to ask, sure," they said. "The time? You're running out. If my visions hold true, then they are going to make moves to begin taking the rest of the Fjordlands in a matter of days. With the priests on their side, they rule Bhorglid with a fist of fear. And Kryllian troops are already en route to the seaside ports."

Sonja stepped slightly in front of Valen. "We came to bolster your numbers. Defeating Callum and Arraya can't be done without help. There aren't many of us, but we're the best option you have right now."

A lump formed in my throat and I nodded. "Thank you."

Sonja's eyes were loaded with emotion, but as Valen had mentioned, time was of the essence. She and I would have to catch up later.

Revna drummed her fingers against her thigh. "Small numbers are good. We can't wage a war, not against a full army. We're better off using stealth to try and gain the upper hand. How many in your caravan are prepared to fight?"

Valen answered. “Thirty-five.”

She nodded. “Perfect. We can send most people in to do a prison break. And then Søren, you and I can steal the sword and, if we feel the timing is right, strike against Callum and Arraya.”

“A sword?” Sonja frowned. “What sword?”

I held up my hands. “Why don’t we all sit down and discuss everything we know? Then we can strategize with every facet in mind.”

I looked to Revna. She sighed and straightened her shoulders. “You’re right. Let me grab Astrid from the inn and then we can begin.”

35

Revna

HOURS LATER, WE ALL EMERGED FROM THE TENT. I RUBBED my hand over my lower spine, wincing. The chairs the Seeing Ones had provided were functional, not comfortable.

Despite midnight nearing, the camping group was just as lively as when I'd first shoved my way through the crowd, desperately following Søren. The campfire now roared, and a group sat around it, sharing stories. I stared, uncertain why the scene called to me so deeply. I wasn't a storyteller by any means and often resented things shared in this way—after all, the priests had used such settings to manipulate my people for generations.

Søren and Sonja were deep in conversation behind me, their heads close together as they murmured. I stood out of hearing distance, trying to offer them a semblance of privacy. Sonja intrigued me, but I didn't know how to feel about her quite yet. Søren was thrilled to have her back, and ultimately, it meant he wasn't under the queen's command in any way now. But the unification of long-lost siblings made my heart ache thinking of Frode.

I'd been promised a reunion with him, and instead I'd created a monster worse than me. Was his body still in the throne room? Had it been reburied or disposed of? I forced the questions from my mind, unwilling to think about the possibilities.

Astrid was already walking back to the inn when Valen came up next to me, bumping my shoulder with theirs. I huffed a laugh. They grinned. "Are you ready?"

I shook my head, thinking over the details of the plan we'd created. We'd drilled down every step over and over again until I knew I'd be dreaming about it. If I wasn't dreaming about Aloisa and Arraya, that is. "We still have a lot to do. Besides, I don't think there's any way to be ready for a revolution."

"Is that what we're calling it now?" Valen sounded bemused.

I shrugged, my gaze still drinking in the group of young Seeing Ones trading stories. One stood, their face covered in the flickering shadows of the firelight, animatedly lifting their arms and their voice as they moved from character to character. "We're trying to kill an immortal king who fancies himself a god. What else should we call it?"

Valen nodded, acquiescing. "True enough."

"There's one part of this I just can't figure out," I said. "How do you suppose Arraya has lived all these years?"

"Lurae are strange," Valen said. "Søren has never seen her use any magic?"

"None."

"She's definitely kept it hidden for a reason. It allowed her to . . . stay the same age, or possibly reverse the aging process on her body as it occurred." Valen pursed their lips thoughtfully. "Magic truly is so vast. Her Lurae could be something entirely unique, or it could be a common power she's learned to cultivate in a new way. It's impossible to tell." They studied me for a moment. "Do you know how she became Queen of Kryllian?"

"No."

"The last queen died suddenly of a mysterious illness. She had no heirs, despite her age. And then shortly afterward, a journal of hers was discovered. It detailed a sordid affair with a courier who visited the castle frequently, and it told of a secret pregnancy the queen had managed to hide. The baby had been born eighteen years ago. A girl was found, matching the birth date and description the queen had left behind. And Anja has been queen ever since."

I gaped. "She assassinated the queen and then laid a trap so the people would believe her the next heir."

Valen laughed. "She's smart, I'll give her that." I mulled the story over, but the Seeing One continued, "Come join the storytellers with me." They wrapped their thin fingers around my upper arm and began to pull me unceremoniously through the fray. There was no way someone so old should be this strong. When we finally reached the group, Valen pushed me down until I sat on the nearest empty log. The current storyteller looked over at Valen, who said, "The Queen of Bhorglid will join our next round, Lykke."

Lykke looked me over with a grin. "Excellent. Your turn then, I take it?"

Valen swapped places with the young seer and stood before the crowd. "The Queen of Bhorglid has some interesting stories, I think you'll find. Make sure to ask her about them when this is all over." I rolled my eyes, but they waved a hand. "There is much, however, that she does not know."

By this time, a small crowd had gathered. At least fifteen people sat within view, with more continuing to trickle in. Valen raised their voice and called, "Today, we welcome Revna to our caravan. She is a temporary visitor, and I am eager to see what knowledge she gains and what knowledge she gives to us during her time here."

Everyone bowed their head in my direction for a moment. It was a clear sign of respect. Nervousness crawled at my throat, but I forced myself to stay still.

"Now," Valen continued, turning to me as if we were the only people around, "the Kryllians and the Fastians keep their history written. Scholars, like your Søren, study that history and record their own. And then it is taught in schoolhouses. How effective do you think that practice is?"

I hesitated, worried my answer would be wrong. "Um . . . very? Søren knows a lot."

"He does," Valen conceded. "He was also raised in the palace, with access to libraries and the education to read books for himself. Not as common in Kryllian as you might believe."

"Not everyone knows how to read?" I didn't bother trying to hide my surprise. "Even Bhorglid offers classes for Nilurae."

The corner of Valen's mouth tipped upward. "You're right. Once, all children in Kryllian were taught in schools. But when Arraya—or Anja, as you knew her—rose to power, she eliminated schooling for lower-income families."

"How is that possible?" I demanded. "Surely the people would have rioted."

"Perhaps. If she had not been so artful about it all." Valen sighed. "Before I came to Bhorglid, to tell your family of the prophecies I had received about your life, I spent my time with a caravan in this very city. During Arraya's early years as Queen of Kryllian.

"The last queen was beloved by the people. Arraya moved slowly, first offering those with more wealth the ability to send their children to private academies. She increased production quota for the miners, which prohibited them from putting their children in school for as long each day. Eventually, she replaced all the royal councilors with nobility. They voted to stop constructing schoolhouses in outlying villages. And the citizens she kept busier than ever, so they didn't have time to riot even if they wanted to."

I rubbed a hand over my chest. It ached at the thought of all the

Kryllians—Lurae and Nilurae alike—who had been used by their ruler. "That's terrible."

"Arraya is cunning." Valen raised their voice, so the small crowd now gathered around the fire knew they were speaking to all of us. "She will not be an easily defeated enemy."

"Why didn't the priests do the same thing?" I asked. "If it was so effective, I don't understand why all in Bhorglid are taught to read."

"Authorities in Bhorglid have never feared the written word—after all, they don't keep their histories written down."

I chewed on my lip. They were right. I'd never even considered how useless knowing how to read had been. Most of the books in the castle library were volumes on war strategy. And even those contained very little history or references to back them up.

"You come from a nation that embraced the oral tradition," Valen said. "Passing down stories and history through spoken word."

It clicked. "The priests."

"Exactly." Valen clapped their hands together.

"They tell the same story of Callum and Arraya's glorious attempt to seize the Fjordlands every ritual day," I remembered aloud. "I only knew it was wrong because my friend Halvar heard the real story from his mothers. And then he shared it with me and Freja." I ignored the pang of remembering Arne had been there, too.

"A perfect example. So you see, Arraya took the power from her people here by removing their ability to read. And the priests took it from your people by removing the histories, the written accounts of events. Both sought to influence the past to their benefit."

Now, the Tapestry's insistence on showing Søren and me the past resonated. Despite Søren's thirst for knowledge and scholarship, so much information from Aloisa's time had been erased—because it all took place in Bhorglid, where access to said information was carefully monitored and prohibited.

Valen continued. "What makes our method unique in the caravans is the encouraged sharing of opinions. We look to each other for stories and history—and then we dissect it together. We acknowledge biases from the teller and the validity of them as a source of information. We do not simply believe. We dig deeper."

"That's great," I said, "but how does that relate to the Tapestry at all?"

"We've all heard stories of the Tapestry here," Valen replied. Nodding heads echoed their words. "During Tam's time, they spoke with Aloisa often. The two met in their young adulthood, and she shared with them the information about the Tapestry. She believed it was the source of our visions, that perhaps we Seeing Ones can glimpse the threads of the past and the future easier than others. We've held these stories close to our chests, never sharing them with others outside of our caravans before now. I wondered if perhaps time dissecting the stories as a group could do you some good."

I wasn't sure this was going to go anywhere. And with the threat of Callum and Arraya's hostile takeover of the Fjordlands on the horizon, it felt like a waste of time. If no one acted, if we sat and did nothing . . .

I couldn't handle more deaths on my hands. Not now.

But Valen laid a gentle hand on my knee. "Regardless of where you think you *should* be," they murmured, quietly enough that only I could hear, "consider that perhaps you are *meant* to be here with us. Would I have had a vision of you convening with us here otherwise?"

Protests weighed heavy on my tongue. But when I caught sight of Søren and Sonja ducking into a tent, both with the same genuine, star-defying smile on their faces, I decided. "Right."

Valen sat back. "Then let us begin. What is the purpose of the Tapestry gifting Lurae to humankind?"

A teenage Seeing One sitting to my right shot their hand in the air. "The Tapestry considers itself a guardian of sorts, responsible for helping humankind progress. Aloisa believed it was a collective consciousness created from the souls of all who have lived and died before us."

A young man not much older than me huffed from across the fire. He wasn't wearing the same garb as the other Seeing Ones. "It may call itself a guardian, but do we truly believe that? Maybe it gave the world magic, but that included Callum. And all the priests. Even the last King and Queen of Bhorglid. If the Tapestry is truly all-knowing, then it should have known not to give such power to so many terrible people."

Valen locked eyes with me and explained, "Rasmus is a refugee from Bhorglid. He joined us a few years ago after the last of his family was killed by the priests."

I turned to the young man. "I'm so sorry."

"He makes some excellent points, too," Valen continued. "Who has thoughts on this?"

A Seeing One raised their hand. "I once heard a story from a distant land, told by a merchant who crossed the sea to trade in faraway places. He spoke a tale of magic's creation that he insisted was entirely metaphorical—it speaks of a weaver who created a tapestry. They worked with only light-colored yarn at first. But when they finished and looked it over, they were unhappy with the result. It was impossible to see the design when all the colors blended together in only a few shades. They took the tapestry apart and began it anew—this time with both light and dark thread. And when they finished . . ."

I picked up the gist. "The design was more beautiful for the contrast. So you're saying the Tapestry gave Callum his abilities on purpose."

"It's possible. But it's also speculated by some in the caravan that perhaps the Tapestry didn't *know* what Callum would become. After all, it can see the future. But can it control our minute decisions? Unlikely. Perhaps Callum took a turn so unexpected even the Tapestry had no idea it placed unlimited power in the hands of a dictator."

"I don't think that's true," I added, surprised to feel so many eyes on me, my new companions listening in carefully. "When I've spoken to the Tapestry, it says there are many threads leading to many different futures. It won't tell me how to achieve the outcome I want, but it's been more than willing to show me the past as I make my decisions. I think it sees all the potential the future holds but refuses to push anyone in a specific direction."

"It won't choose for you," the Seeing One who told the merchant's story murmured.

"Exactly." I nodded. "It does seem quite determined to show me exactly what happened with Aloisa, though. She defeated Callum in battle with her sword, and the priests immediately began worshiping her instead of him."

Valen tilted their head. "Do you not know the story of the first Bloodshed Trials?"

"No."

A woman spoke up this time. "The priests pretend it was a divine order from the gods. But really, they consider Aloisa and Callum's final confrontation to be the first Bloodshed Trials."

The information suddenly clicked in my mind. "The priests thought they were competing . . . for godhood?"

"Yes," the teenage Seeing One said, excitement evident in their briskly tapping feet. "Callum taught them to believe that the strongest were the ones who deserved devotion. When Aloisa was able to kill him, they did exactly what he had taught them to—they turned their devotion to her. So much so that they named her and her six sons their pantheon."

"And that's why they worship the gods while still revering Callum as a revolutionary," I finished. It all made sense now. "Despite Aloisa working for so long to destroy Callum and everything he worked for."

Valen concluded. "When it came time for the first King of Bhorglid to pass the throne on to one of his sons, the head priest at the time remembered what had happened when Aloisa killed Callum. And he suggested the king at the time adopt the same practice with his children. Whoever was left alive in the arena at the end of the Trials would take their father's place on the throne. The people had been coaxed to bloodthirstiness for years with no war to show for it; they were all too willing to accept a battle to the death for succession."

My mind was reeling. "And the priests just . . . pretended this never happened?"

Valen laughed. "They still revered Callum, even if they'd lost faith in his godhood. Telling the truth might have turned some people against their leader."

A hand came to rest on my shoulder. Søren looked down at me, a soft, weary smile on his face. "It's getting late. We need to get some rest before tomorrow."

He was right. I stood, stretching, mind racing with everything I'd learned. "Thank you," I said to Valen and the small gathering of caravan members. "For sharing your knowledge with me."

Valen smiled. "We lift each other up. Rest well, Revna. Tomorrow, we begin the real work."

36

Revna

I STILL THINK THIS IS A STUPID IDEA."

Astrid's dagger-eyed glare was turned on Søren while she signed, and I rubbed my temples. Over the last few weeks, I'd grown to care immensely for Astrid. Her unwavering loyalty, her steady friendship. Her willingness to see past my wrongs to protect our friends.

But she wasn't afraid to be honest. And right now, I was already at my wits' end. I twisted my fingers over and over each other while I paced, and Søren ran his hands through his hair. A gesture I knew meant his nerves were as frayed as mine.

Because the next few minutes could determine whether we won the battle and saved our friends . . . or died without the chance to even try.

"Mira will show. And she'll be alone." Søren's sharp signs communicated just how frustrated he was with Astrid, and I was reminded of the night not too long ago that I'd found them glaring at each other outside my bedroom door.

I glanced at the sun, steadily rising in the sky. We'd told Mira to meet us before midday, but time was running out. "Even if she doesn't accept our invitation to meet, she could simply decide not to show at all," I reminded Astrid. "There's no guarantee she'll betray us. You should hope she doesn't—without Mira, we have to scrap our entire plan."

Astrid glowered, crossing her arms. I continued my pacing, surprised to find myself reaching automatically for my Lurae. It was strange to have it gone. Almost as strange as discovering it was there in the first place.

I flexed my fingers. All my life, people had made assumptions about me based on my abilities. When I was Nilurae, my family assumed I was useless. The other Nilurae assumed I was their champion. Then, when I'd discovered my own magic, some of those I'd trusted assumed I was lying the entire time. Others grew wary of me.

Instinctually, I knew that the lines between Lurae and Nilurae would have to fade if we were to win the coming conflict. Our only hope was to put aside those biases and accept each other as allies to fight a common enemy.

Footsteps sounded. Søren rose, hand on the hilt of his sword. Astrid followed our gazes, her own knives at the ready. I unsheathed Aloisa.

Mira stepped into the small clearing, emerging from the trees in a cloak so dark green she might have been one of them. Søren relaxed entirely; I relaxed slightly; Astrid didn't relax at all.

The teleporter pulled her hood down and studied us coolly. She held up a piece of paper between two fingers. "Got your message."

I sheathed Aloisa and began to sign, interpreting Mira's words for Astrid. When Søren replied to her, he signed while he spoke. "And? Will you join us?"

There was silence for several moments, the only sound the breeze through the leaves and the birds chirping. Finally, Mira sighed. "What kind of question is that? Of course I will, you idiot."

Søren's face broke into a grin, and he pulled Mira into a crushing hug. She grumbled through the entire thing, but I watched how tightly she clung to him and knew she was glad.

Eventually, she pushed away. "Let *go*, Søren. What are you all planning? The queen—or Callum, I guess—is waiting for the Kryllian army to meet them, and then they're planning to march on Faste."

Dread sank like a stone in my gut. Hearing the words aloud was different from discussing them when they weren't a sure fact. "You're positive?" I asked. "We haven't seen the army moving through the village."

Mira shook her head. For the first time, she didn't appear angry to see me. "Callum sent word that they were to use a different port for the journey. Even merchant ships are being ordered to dump their goods and become passenger vessels for the soldiers."

"I'm sure they're thrilled about that," Astrid signed, rolling her eyes.

"They're sacrificing their people's approval to get the army there fast," I mused. "We can fill you in on the plans when we're back at camp, Mira. We should go now to see what kind of success Valen and Sonja have had."

Søren nodded. "Let's go."

◆ ◆ ◆ ◆ ◆

WHEN WE ARRIVED AT THE SEEING ONES' CAMP, MOST PEOPLE were gathered around the fire, eating a midday meal. I scanned the crowd, looking for Sonja or Valen. They hadn't returned yet, so Søren, Mira, and I settled in to grab our own servings of stew.

Mira and Søren chatted for a while, catching up while I listened in. I lost myself in thoughts of the plans we had in place for that night—plans that could easily go wrong.

Most of my stew went uneaten, my stomach clenching.

After a while, Mira turned to me. "Your scars. Do they still itch?"

My fingertips flew to my face automatically, rubbing against the bottom edge of the healed tissue. This felt like an odd topic of conversation. "Yes."

"Well, if we make it out of this alive, there's an apothecary in this village that makes an incredible cream to help." She wouldn't meet my eyes, and my own gaze was drawn to the scar stretching down her cheek and over her neck. I wondered how she'd gotten it.

"Thank you." I would take her up on the suggestion, too. Once the battle for our freedom was over.

Mira nodded and went back to her meal. I studied her for a few moments longer. Not long ago, she'd left me in the snow to die. Even I'd been doubtful when Søren insisted we reach out to her about joining our cause. But it seemed her true loyalty lay with Søren, and no one else.

It was kind of sweet.

"We're back!" Valen's voice echoed through the circle of tents, and all eyes turned to them. Sonja accompanied them—and so did a group of thirty Kryllian citizens brandishing swords, knives from their kitchens, and even pitchforks.

For the first time all day, my anxiety eased into something a little like hope.

The Kryllians meandered, merging slowly with the Seeing Ones. I approached Valen and Sonja. "You did it. What did you tell them?"

Sonja shrugged. "That there was an opportunity to take out the Queen of Kryllian and fight for something better for everyone." Then, she sighed. "Truthfully, it isn't that many people. We spoke to everyone we could in the neighboring villages, but these are the only ones who were willing to join our cause."

"And they were only willing because we told them the enticing truth," Valen said, wiggling their eyebrows.

"I'm almost afraid to ask."

Sonja rolled her eyes. "Valen told them all that the Queen of Bhorglid and the Hellbringer have teamed up to take down the Kryllian Queen. It was enough to turn heads, that's for sure."

Valen grinned. I smiled too, hoping they couldn't see the falseness behind it. I was grateful my and Søren's identities were helpful in recruiting allies. But it also meant word of our location was likely back in Arraya's hands now.

After our move to strike at her tonight, there would be no going back.

◆ ◆ ◆ ◆ ◆

AFTER LUNCH, I PULLED SØREN BACK TO OUR ROOM AT THE INN with the excuse that I wanted to rest before we left this evening. But truthfully, I just wanted to hold him close. Maybe it was selfish of me, but I didn't care.

Søren didn't say anything about it, but I got the sense he understood exactly where my mind had gone. He wrapped me in his arms, and for a long while, I relished his embrace. My thoughts spun incessantly. Would we all make it back? Would we manage to find the sword? Would my friends be rescued, or would our plans be thwarted before we even began?

"What are you thinking?" Søren asked, kissing my temple.

I pulled back, turned to look at him. My hand drifted to his face, tracing the hint of stubble over his perfect jaw. I wanted to smooth the furrow between his brows, but not if it would make him stop looking at me like this—like I was his dawn and dusk, his death and resurrection.

"I know we have to do this," I whispered. "But why do I feel like this is the end?"

Søren's fingers clasped mine, moving my hand from his cheek until it hovered over his mouth. He pressed a kiss to my palm. "I don't know if it's the end. I only know we have to fight. If we ran away from what's ahead . . . we'd be giving up part of ourselves in the process."

A small voice, one that sounded suspiciously like my Lurae's, refused to be silenced. *You can hope,* it chided. *But hoping does not change what will come to pass.*

For a split second, I contemplated repeating those words aloud. Voicing all my fears to Søren, insisting that I didn't want his reassurances and solutions, only for him to listen.

But I couldn't bring myself to say them all. Not when he was *here* and I'd already lost him once before—at the dawn of a battle that felt much like this one.

So instead, I tucked my fear away and demanded. "Kiss me, Hellbringer."

The words alone tore a groan from his throat, like he'd been waiting on tenterhooks for me to say them. Søren didn't oblige me immediately. His own hands came to my face this time, cradling me gently. When his thumb pressed against my lower lip, I obeyed his silent command, taking it into my mouth.

"Fuck." His breathing was already heavy. If my mouth wasn't occupied, I would have told him I loved it when he swore because of me. A heady confirmation I had undone him. "I've spent years wishing I could leave the Hellbringer behind. And the moment you call me that name, you know what I find myself thinking? That I would be him forever if it meant you kept looking at me like *this*."

Then he brought his lips to mine.

It was the same as always, and yet different. More. Our kisses the day before had held an unspoken promise—so did these. Then, it had been *I love you, I love you, I love you.*

And this time, every tug of my teeth against his bottom lip, every caress of my tongue over him devoured. Said *If we are one, then you cannot leave me.*

His fingers buried in my hair, I pushed on his chest until he lay back, pulling me with him until I was flush atop him. If Søren had told me my rib cage suddenly cracked open, I would have believed it. The yawning cavern there could be filled by only him, after all.

He wasn't wearing a shirt. The expanse of his skin called to me, and my mouth made quick work of exploring the slope of his throat. He let out a shuddering breath, and that hushed sound drowned out the rest.

Impatient, he pushed my own shirt up. I pulled back to take it off, my breastband quickly following. His palms snaked up to my shoulder blades.

When Søren buried his face in my breasts, pressing kisses to every inch of skin he could find, a breathless, needy sound escaped. He hummed with satisfaction. His lips met mine again, and we melded together, skin against skin as the rest of the world fell away.

Søren tugged lightly on my hair to get my attention, and I pulled away, gasping. "I need to be inside you," he said. "*Please*, Princess."

The words sent a rush of warmth through me. I stripped my own pants and underwear off, then pushed his hands away from his own clothing. "Let me."

Finally we were both naked. I lifted up on my knees and straddled him. Gently, I took his hand and guided it between my own legs. "You've barely even touched me, and yet—"

Searching fingertips silenced me, sliding through until they found my center, tracing gently around my opening. I watched Søren's eyes turn feral. "You're soaked, pretty thing. All for me?"

I nodded, unable to form words. I knew the heat of my cheeks likely said enough, though. His other hand found one nipple and rolled it between two fingers. The one pressed slightly inside me felt the responding clench of my body, and he shivered. "Can I fill you up here? Would that make you feel good?"

Gods, when had this gotten away from me? I'd wanted to savor this, make it last. Instead, my desperation made it all feel faster than it was. I readjusted my position, gripping the base of him and pulling myself down over him.

From there it was quick. Murmurs of praise and encouragement, panting gasps, gentle fingers. We barely lasted five minutes before we came one after the other.

I lay atop him, resting my head on his chest. His hand went to my hair, brushing through it automatically. The sheen of sweat covering both of us shimmered in the late-afternoon sunlight streaming in through the windows. The sound of Søren's steady heartbeat mingled with the waking crickets coming to life as the evening began outside.

"I love you," I whispered.

"I love you, too," he said. "I won't let them take you from me."

The euphoria wore off quickly, the pit in my stomach yawning ever wider. I tried to force it aside. "Two Nilurae against a powerful resurrected god. This will definitely go well."

Hands clasped my waist, and he rolled until we were on our sides facing each other. Underneath the seriousness on his face, there was a glimmer of mischief. "Why, Princess," he said, brushing our noses together, "did you think my Lurae was my only skill?"

I laughed, the words from the first time I'd truly tried to kill him so emblazoned in my mind that I couldn't *not* recognize them. Out of all the talk and reassurances, somehow this was the only true thing to alleviate my anxiety.

I memorized the shape of his smile again. "I'd never be that foolish."

"Good. It's time. We need to get ready."

Søren's breathing matched mine, and I wanted to hold him back, insist we stay. The what-ifs clamored in my head. But I kept them inside and instead said, "Then what are we waiting for? Let's go kill a god."

37

Revna

THE WEIGHT OF MY SWORD AT MY HIP WAS ONLY A SMALL comfort.

Søren and I walked hand in hand out of the inn. The sun was setting steadily below the palace spires in the distance, warming the day. The Seeing Ones were packing up, most tents already disassembled. Those who planned to fight with us—which was most of the caravan—outfitted themselves with weapons and whatever armor they'd been able to scavenge.

Sonja jogged up to meet us, skirting around some younger members of the caravan who were helping put out the campfire. Søren wrapped her in an embrace. His shoulders were stiffer than usual, the only visible symptom of his own nerves. Sonja offered me a hesitant smile when she pulled back. Maybe she was uncertain about me, too. I wouldn't blame her—as we'd worked out our plan, we'd butted heads several times trying to decide the best course of action.

Namely, she thought she needed to come with me and Søren.

Despite the arguments we'd had, I understood her desperate need to protect the brother she loved. And she'd finally caved, understanding her help would be necessary elsewhere. Now she turned to me. "Take care of him."

"I'll do my best," I promised.

We reached the center of camp. All eyes turned to us, and I hated that I knew some of them relaxed a bit because of our presence. *I can't guarantee your lives,* I wanted to scream. *This might not work.*

But instead, I asked, "Everyone knows the plan?"

Nods of affirmation. "Good," Søren said. "Mira and Astrid will return here shortly to transport us all to Bhorglid. Remember, do not act until one of them returns to give you the signal."

A loud *crack* sounded and Mira appeared, her face cloaked in shadow and evening light. Astrid followed shortly after. She hadn't been thrilled with our plan, but it was our only chance of getting Freja, Volkan, and Jac out of prison, so she was begrudgingly helping us.

"The priests have started riding out to occupy the other cities in Bhorglid," Mira said. "Minimal casualties thus far, and enthusiastic compliance from most Lurae. Still, I think this is our best chance."

"Are we ready?" I turned to look at Søren.

He slid the wolf skull mask on and latched it into place. It changed his voice instantly. "Let's do this."

Astrid pursed her lips, grabbed the two Nilurae closest to her, and teleported away. Mira did the same. A few moments later, both women returned and repeated the process.

This continued until all thirty-five of the capable fighters were gone and only Valen stood with us. The Seeing One turned to me. "We are all with you," they said.

Motion caught in the corner of my eye. I looked up to see all the remaining caravan members, bowing to me. To us.

I may not be queen, I realized, *but fighting for what's right has earned me the respect of the Seeing Ones, at least.*

Mira reappeared, and the world vanished once more.

◆ ◆ ◆ ◆ ◆

WE REMATERIALIZED IN THE HIDDEN CLEARING ON THE MOUNTAINSIDE, where Søren and I had practiced my Lurae. When Astrid and Mira had scouted ahead earlier, they'd checked to see whether the priests or Arraya had discovered it.

Our luck held thus far. I adjusted the sheaths on my upper arms, the daggers Søren made for me secured there. My hand found Aloisa's hilt, and I breathed deeply, forcing my body to calm.

We had to be swift and careful.

"Callum—Arraya—whoever the fuck they are, stays in the castle most of the time. Unless they've managed to sneak away in the last hour, they should still be there," Mira said. She was as jittery as I was, her hands shaking as she rushed through her explanation. "There are at least ten priests in the courtyard, but the rest are all in the city proper. Wait until a few leave before you make a move."

Søren nodded. "We'll be careful. This is a stealth mission, not a battle in the making."

"What about the sword?" I asked. "Do you know where she's keeping it?"

Mira grimaced. "I haven't seen much of the queen the few times I've done reconnaissance here, but when I saw her yesterday, she had it on her person." She glanced between us. "At what point do I come to get you out?"

"Not until all of the people who came with us and the prisoners are safely away," I said. "At that point, you're welcome to come—but be alone and ready to fight."

"I don't like it," she said, hands fisting at her sides. She looked to Søren. "I'm not going to leave you both in there with no escape plan."

He placed his hand directly on her head, a gesture that made me think of Erik. "We won't need a rescue, because we're going to kill the queen. If something goes wrong, we can play it by ear. But this won't work unless everyone does their job. Sonja and Astrid will need help to corral all those untrained fighters—you have real battlefield experience. I need you to keep them safe for me."

"Fine." Mira turned and pointed an accusing finger at me. "Anything happens to him, you're dead."

"I know," I told her.

She hesitated, then rushed to continue. "For what it's worth, I'm sorry for trying to kill you in the wastes. You're good for Søren. I'm glad to see him happy."

Then she was gone.

A few heartbeats passed before I turned to the Hellbringer. "How concerned should I be if Mira thought this was the last chance to apologize to me?"

Søren's reply was light, but I heard the gravity behind it. "She most definitely believes we are both going to die today."

And Mira had been his right hand through the entire war. I took a deep breath, forced my fear down. There was no place for it here. I beckoned him to the thick foliage that obscured the clearing from view of the mountain path. "Hide here, so we can see when the priests leave."

He ducked down next to me. I barely had time to settle in before a *boom* echoed up from the city below, orange plumes of fire billowing from the southwestern temple. They lit up the night, a beacon in the darkness. Smoke began to float through the sky. We waited with bated breath for three, four, five minutes.

They aren't going to leave, I thought, desperation clutching at my chest. *They aren't going to—*

Hooves pounded down the path, and several priests on horseback galloped by, slowing only a bit to take the sharp switchback down to the city. Several of them were shouting a conversation to each other, scythes in hand.

"Nilurae bastards again—"

"Fucking insolent, that's what they are."

"Can't wait to slice their throats like—"

I closed my eyes, squeezing them tight and counting to ten until the urge to follow them and ram my sword into their stomachs faded enough. Then, when all was quiet, I beckoned Søren forward and we began to ascend the path ourselves.

"Only six went by," he muttered as we jogged toward the castle. "That means at least four stayed back."

I huffed. "Inconvenient. My grandfather built this place as if we were going to be under siege at any moment. It's incredibly difficult to sneak up on the castle. This might take longer than we expected."

He glanced over his shoulder, down to the city. "The fire from the explosion is spreading. Hopefully it buys us enough time." I heard the rest, though it remained unspoken. *And hopefully there are no innocent casualties.*

The explosion was the only diversion we'd managed to think of with enough of an impact to pull priests in from all over the city. We needed eyes away from the castle and the prison while we worked. But we'd also known how dangerous it would be. Fear seized my gut again at the thought of someone with no involvement in our plan dying. Because of the decisions we had made.

We reached the top of the path, ducking between trees to stay out of sight. As we studied the courtyard—two hooded figures standing beside the castle doors, scythes in hand—another loud *boom* sounded from behind us. The second half of the diversion, an attempt to force the priests in the city to call for backup from the castle and from the prison guards. More flames flickered to life on the north end of the city right as we arrived at the manor. It was close enough to pull most of the remaining guards from the streets.

"How do we get rid of those bastards?" I murmured.

Søren studied the long expanse of ground before us, no hiding opportunities in sight. "Can you still throw the daggers well?"

I raised a brow. "You doubt me, Hellbringer?"

I heard the grin behind the mask. "Never. I'll start running toward them and see if I can catch them off guard. While they're busy trying to fend me off, you'll have the perfect opportunity to throw your blades and take them out. Hopefully they'll get the attention of the other two, wherever they are, without alerting Arraya and Callum."

I chewed my lip. "It's risky."

"There's no other way."

He was right. The chances of alerting our prey were high, but it was unavoidable now. Mira hadn't known the castle layout well enough to teleport us directly into a spot where we were guaranteed to be hidden. We knew a moment like this might come.

I pulled the daggers from their sheaths. "Let's go."

Søren crept through the bushes lining the path, going as far as they allowed before he drew his weapon carefully and stood, sprinting for the priests. They spotted him almost instantly, and while I couldn't hear their shouts, their waving scythes showed their panic. Even when they certainly knew Søren was without his Lurae, they still feared him. The Hellbringer, omen of death, come to end them.

I kept low, moving up in the bushes. The priests rushed at him, swords raised. Søren blocked their first haphazard strikes, swiping at one of their weapons with the ease of a master. Within moments, he disarmed one man, then stepped aside and out of range. *Perfect.* I rose from my hiding place and hurled a dagger with precision. It spun end over end until it landed with a sickening *thud* in the priest's jugular, blood spilling down his white robes.

Once he was down, I watched Søren move for the other priest. I lifted my second knife, ready to strike once more.

The priest looked directly at me. And then he disappeared.

I blinked. *Shit.* Had he teleported away, or was he invisible?

Søren had stilled, sword at the ready. Every inch of him was tense, like a predator ready to strike. I listened carefully, trying to make out any sound besides the wind. The priests were trained in brute strength, not patience and stealth. If he was invisible, he would out himself soon enough.

Søren sprung into motion, whirling to his left and bringing his sword up just in time to connect with . . . something I couldn't see. In the next heartbeat I moved, sprinting toward the confrontation. Søren kept his movements close and controlled, always on the defense. Suddenly, he froze, then turned toward me. "Look out!"

I heard the priest right before he struck, the *thud, thud, thud* of his footfalls alerting me to his presence. In the split second I had to think, I crouched down and sprang for where I estimated his knees to be. Sure enough, I connected. Wrapping my arms around his calves, I tackled him to the ground. He lost hold of his Lurae, flickering back into my vision, and Søren slit his throat.

Panting, I accepted the Hellbringer's proffered hand. "I hope no one was watching through the windows," I said grimly. "If they were, they've had plenty of time to escape."

"The dark might have been enough to keep us concealed. We'll find out soon." He kept his bloodied weapon out and strode toward the doors. I followed behind him, bending to pull my dagger out of the dead priest's throat. I grimaced as I slid it back into its sheath, wiping my hand on my pants before drawing Aloisa.

We took defensive positions and pushed the heavy doors open.

Stillness and silence.

A few lamps flickered in their overindulgent sconces. Doorways led to other parts of the castle. Stairs to my right spiraled up to another floor. But the entryway was empty. No priests surged forward to battle, no Lurae soldiers demanded our surrender, and no gods or queens smote us down.

I remained in my defensive position. “This isn’t right.”

“Of course it isn’t.” Agitation was abundant in Søren’s voice. “We’ll do a sweep of this floor and then ascend. Agreed?”

Despite it all, having him ask for my opinion was enough to steady me. “Yes. Let’s go.”

The throne room, ballroom, dining room, and kitchens revealed the same as the hall. Empty. The second floor was as well. My father’s office was devoid of people too, but I spotted unfamiliar papers on the desk that gave me pause. I grabbed the lamp hanging inside the doorway and brought it over, Søren standing guard while I did.

“A letter from a Kryllian general,” I told him. “The army is on their way and should dock in the coastal city in two days.” I shuffled through the rest, finding a map of the Fjordlands. “No timeline here, but it seems they plan to solidify their claim on Bhorglid, reinforce Kryllian, and then see whether Faste can be convinced to surrender by . . .” I leaned in, studying the messy handwriting. A chill ran up my arms as I read aloud, “Using the prince as leverage.”

Søren swore. “Of course. They have the entire Fjordlands under their thumb.”

“Will the Fastians agree?” I asked tentatively. “They didn’t seem to care much for Volkan when they came to visit originally.”

“Unfortunately, they most definitely will agree.” Even Søren’s voice was enough for me to know what expression he wore beneath the mask—his mouth set in a grim line. “They’re cruel and callous, and so they view him as an object. A precious gemstone. They don’t want to lose their only heir.”

I cringed just thinking about it. An object. It was exactly how my father had treated me. Only worth his attention when I could benefit him in some way. My heart ached for Volkan.

"Cowards." I moved the map aside, skimming over the other papers. Nothing else caught my eye. I picked up Aloisa from the desk, smoothing my thumb over the hilt. "Let's go before we lose our nerve."

Søren led the way with a chuckle. "I forget you never really were *at war* besides those last few days you spent on the front. You'd find with time that the anticipation and nerves eventually turn into boredom."

I remained alert, following him up the steps, but my mouth curved slightly. I remembered the one real battle I'd fought in for a moment before leaving with Frode. Father had ordered the army to wait for almost an hour before actually attacking. "Lots of waiting for the right moment to strike?"

"Exactly."

We stepped through the doorway and into the second-floor hall. The only warning was a slight *whoosh* through the air before an arrow buried itself in Søren's upper arm, managing to find its way right into the gap of his armor. Neither of us hesitated—when the second arrow darted toward me, I ducked out of its path. It lodged in the wall behind me.

"Hmm," the Queen of Kryllian said. She stared at us from the other end of the hall. Now she discarded the crossbow she held and drew the golden sword—the Soulcleaver. "Pity."

"Go," Søren said through gritted teeth.

I didn't hesitate. There was no time to argue that he was injured, so I should take Callum—Arraya—*both* of them, contained in a single body, on my own now. Our combined battle skills, arrow in the arm notwithstanding, would have to do.

I sprinted across the short distance and swung my blade. Despite the Soulcleaver being far too big for Arraya's petite frame, she hefted it like it weighed nothing, her parry expertly crafted.

When she laughed, it sounded like two voices instead of one. Her eyes were bloodshot and glowed slightly red, the same color Callum's soul had been.

"The poor godforsaken," Arraya tittered, using one hand to block Søren's attempt to slice her in half from the other side. When metal sounded on metal, I realized she wore armored bracers on both arms. Her other hand still gripped the Soulcleaver, holding it steady. Some of the skin on her fingers was blackened, like it had been burned. The scorch marks followed the path of her veins—the same paths I knew souls twisted through.

Holding a second soul in her body was destroying her.

I twisted, adjusting my balance and trying to throw her off so I could disarm her, but to no avail. "Did you think killing a god would be easy?" she snarled.

We danced, the speed of our duel faster than the ones I practiced with Søren most days. Two opponents against one and yet we were unable to gain any ground. In fact, I found myself taking a hurried step back as she twirled her blade with unerring precision. Every strike I barely managed to block with the innate knowledge that a single second of hesitation on my part would have made it deadly. "You sat on your ass through the entire war," I managed between clashes. "How the hell are you suddenly an expert swordswoman?"

Arraya laughed, stepping out of range of my sword and forcing me to follow her. "The godtouch of eternal youth is rare, but not unheard of. I've had hundreds of years to perfect my craft—it's second nature now."

Her words did nothing but invigorate me. If she was relying on age-old knowledge she hadn't truly used in years, then she would make mistakes. I could count on it.

"But I," she continued, her voice changing slightly to take on a lower cadence, "am a *god*. I nearly conquered the Fjordlands once before. I will not allow two insolent children to stop me now."

Søren dove into the fray, renewed. Callum's voice, coming from

Arraya's mouth, chilled me to the core. Were they balancing control of their shared body? Or was there a struggle going on beneath the flesh we could take advantage of?

I stepped back to catch my breath and assess the situation, knowing Søren could handle their combined fervor for a moment. If the two were struggling for control, it didn't show—a chill ran down my spine as I realized suddenly how well and truly fucked we were.

We might not win this.

It felt like the moment in the Trials when I'd understood, the truth a throbbing twin to my heartbeat, that I was going to die.

But just like then, I knew now: I would not go down without a fight.

As I readjusted my grip and moved to jump back in, a grunt of pain echoed through the room. Søren. My eyes flew to him, and my heart rushed to my throat. Søren's left arm, the one with the arrow, hung limp at his side as he battled one-handed, desperately trying to keep Callum at bay. The stranger in Arraya's body wore eerie calm like armor, every swing pushing Søren a half step backward. In the single second I stood still, Callum forced Søren to parry before sliding his blade closer and closer to the hilt—and the hand—of my Hellbringer.

I rushed back into the battle.

Callum twisted his sword in a skillful move I'd never been able to truly replicate, trying to cut off Søren's fingers. But before he got the chance, I lifted Aloisa and swung.

He saw it from the corner of his eye and growled, abandoning his assault to parry. "I will kill you for your insolence," he spat. "I am your god!"

My wrists shook, and I was forced to take a step back against his strength. Relief surged through me. Søren was safe for now, standing behind Callum and catching his breath.

Callum pushed himself to the offensive, raining blows on me. I parried every one, barely managing to keep up with his sheer speed. Before long, sweat dripped down my face and my wrists ached.

With our blades locked together, his eyes flickered over my shoulder for half a second. When they returned to me, his mouth spread in a mocking grin. Then he stepped back, leaving me there.

My breath was heavy, and I didn't lunge for him again. No—this fight would be useless if it was a competition of endurance. Neither Søren nor I had managed to strike a blow against him yet.

And then Callum drew another, shorter sword with his other hand. My heart sank.

"Tired yet?" he asked, smirk sharp as a dagger's edge. "Toying with you has been fun. Perhaps together, you'll prove a real challenge."

Søren stepped up next to me, weapon in hand. He'd broken off the end of the arrow shaft protruding from his armor. I knew the arrowhead was still there, hidden beneath the skin, but he could fight. It was enough.

I took my ready stance. Søren laughed, a humorless sound, and the distortion of the mask made it deadly. Chills ran up my spine. "I think you'll find us more than capable of killing you. Bhorglid will no longer suffocate under the rule of false gods."

As one, we lunged.

Søren and I had sparred against each other over and over. This, however, was our first time fighting against the same adversary together. Callum was a force of nature, his blades seeming to know where we would strike before we even realized it. But we moved as one, each stepping forward through the blaze of silver to take the lead when the other needed it.

Søren's strategic mind stayed ahead of the curve. He blocked and parried, allowing Callum to take the upper hand just long enough for me to scratch him with my blade. Before my eyes, the thin cut sealed itself.

Immortal flesh renewed once more.

For a moment, no one moved. I had drawn first blood—proof that we could win this battle if we played our cards right. And when the resurrected usurper laid eyes on me again, something new had taken residence—something that had lain dormant until now.

Fury.

Callum launched back into battle without a second thought. Two swift moves was all it took for him to disarm Søren and slash his thigh open. Søren tumbled to the ground, and my heart stuttered to a stop. But I couldn't take my eyes off Callum. The moment Søren was no longer his adversary, he rained wrath down on me with every strike.

The wall came up behind me. I tried to get around him, back to the more open part of the hallway, but Callum blocked my desperate swipe and kicked me in the stomach with all his strength.

Air knocked from me, I stumbled backward. My spine collided with the wall, and I barely managed to hold up my blade and cower beneath it while he slammed steel against it over, over, over with his whole strength.

Søren yelled. I didn't hear the words. He'd been forgotten by Callum, who had eyes for only me. My sword's metal bent, threatening to snap, becoming more useless with every hammer against it. Every beat of his blade against mine brought the sharp edges closer to me.

Once again, I knew with a certainty. *I am going to die.*

Callum sneered. Between strikes, he shouted over the din. "The Tapestry thought *you* could best me? You're a disappointment. Both of you—"

His words cut off, as did the deluge, when a black-clad arm wrapped around his throat from behind.

Callum choked on air and stumbled away, dropping the Soulcleaver. I took a deep breath to steady myself. Søren's weight pulled

Callum back toward the center of the hall. Wild swings did nothing to dislodge the Hellbringer, not when Arraya's body was so much more petite than his.

"Revna!" Søren shouted. His mask was gone, discarded somewhere I couldn't see. "Do it now!"

They'd managed to get several feet away while I recovered my bearings, but grim determination fell over me. I pulled a dagger from the sheath on my opposite arm and stalked toward them. Callum would heal from any wound I gave with this weapon, but I could maim him enough to distract him while I grabbed the Soulcleaver. The moment I was in range, I prepared to swing, Callum's eyes turning even more bloodshot from lack of air.

But one of the conqueror's flailing arms caught my right arm in a vise grip. I scowled and tried to pull away. Callum's hand latched around my other dagger, drew it from the sheath, and in one expert movement, thrust it directly into Søren's abdomen. He pulled it out immediately after, a cruel twist on what was undoubtedly a killing blow.

"*No!*" My scream echoed, and I thrust my own blade into Arraya's throat so hard I knew I must have been covered in blood. Søren released the queen, who fell to the ground.

Søren coughed, hard. Blood ran from his lips, and when he stumbled, I caught him with my shoulder, lowering him to the floor. "Shit. We need Mira."

But there was no one coming to save us.

"S-sword," he gasped, one hand clamped over his stomach. "Don't you dare leave without that sword."

"I am *not* leaving you." All the same, I reached out and grabbed the hilt with one hand, dragging the Soulcleaver over to me. Was the wetness running down my face blood or tears? Did it matter? "Stand up," I begged. I couldn't breathe. Maybe I was the one dying. "We have to get you to a healer, Søren. *Stand up!*"

But he pressed down my desperate, tugging hands. There was far too much blood. I knew it. He was going limp, and I had no hope of carrying him out on my own. Silence reigned supreme, nothing but the rush of blood in my ears, the rush of blood pouring from his abdomen.

His eyes locked with mine. Søren studied me, taking me in. He squeezed my hands. And then he relaxed, eyes open wide, dead in my arms.

38

Revna

SOMEONE WAS SCREAMING.

I had a single lucid thought amid them all. *Things were quiet like this when Frode died, too.*

Unthinking, I reached deep within for my Lurae. If I could keep his heart beating, then he would live until we got to a healer. He would make it.

But my magic did not answer when I called.

How unfair. Distantly, I knew the thoughts were mine, not an impostor's. I sent them out the way I would have when Frode was alive. Loud and clear, with the intent of being heard by someone who loved me. *The one time I really could have used a Lurae, it's abandoned me. How unfair that the most beautiful face in the world is covered in blood when life leaves it. How unfair that I would have given it all to save him and it wasn't enough.*

My breath sawed from my lungs, ragged and heaving. With one hand, I clung to the Soulcleaver, unwilling to let it go. With the other, I cradled Søren until he lay on the ground.

Callum spoke. Of course he did. Because the Tapestry had offered him immortality, and now it expected me to give everything, everyone I had to correct its mistake. I didn't register a single word.

"Just kill me now," I whispered, pressing my forehead to Søren's chest, to the armor I'd painstakingly latched on him barely an hour ago. I wasn't speaking to Callum—no, I wanted my voice to reach beyond the line of death. Surely Søren could hear me, if his soul wasn't able to move on. "Take me with you. You promised you wouldn't leave me."

I waited for the blade to fall, wondered if I would feel the wetness of my own blood mingling with the river of tears flooding down my face. *Please.*

But a hand grabbed my wrist. The darkness enveloping me wasn't the sightlessness of death. I gripped Søren's cooling body tighter as my stomach lurched and we were pulled from the castle.

◆ ◆ ◆ ◆ ◆

WHEN MY KNEES HIT THE GROUND, I STAYED SILENT, CURLING OVER Søren. Clutching at his body, at his armor, at his clothes. They had taken Frode away when he died, muscled me back to camp. I wouldn't let them do the same with Søren.

Minutes passed, or maybe hours. And as my muscles stiffened, as hands brushed at my skin and murmurs reached my ears, I clung tighter.

He was gone. Søren was gone and I would never again hear him tell me he loved me. That I was worth it all. Never again would I hear his laugh or see his smile, rest my head on his chest in the darkness and listen to him breathe.

We would not see the world together when all was said and done. We wouldn't travel, leaving our responsibilities behind while we explored new places. We would never get married, never discuss whether we wanted to have children. There were no more chances to *tell me something true.*

The world around me came back slowly. All the while, pressure built in my chest—inescapable, undeniable. The first word I registered was my own name.

"Revna." Mira, maybe. Who cared anymore? "Revna, what happened?"

I said nothing. But the pressure, the unshakable creature clawing its way through my chest reared its head in anger. *I didn't save him. He did save me.*

Another voice, this one Sonja's. "You need to stand up, Revna. Get cleaned off."

And gods, she was so *gentle* about it. Sonja, who'd argued that she needed to come with us, and we'd refused her. Told her it was smarter for us to go alone. She'd even suggested we take Astrid, and I'd insisted we wouldn't put anyone else in danger. How would the tides have turned if we had another person on our team? If we hadn't been so damn stubborn? The what-ifs ate at me, until I was nothing but bone. Hollow, yet filled with too much grief to go on.

Perhaps that's why I pulled my head up from Søren's chest and screamed.

The feet in my line of vision took a step back as the sound, long and drawn out, nothing but rage and anguish made breath, stretched into the silence. And when I ran out of air, when my voice cracked and I was forced to inhale, my sobs echoed.

And that was how they left me. Screaming and sobbing, the love of my life dead on the ground.

I must have fallen asleep at some point. My mind too overwhelmed to let me face the rest. But opening my eyes did nothing to pull me back from the horror of his bloody face and torso, the unnatural angle of his neck.

"I never wanted this." My voice was so hoarse I could barely hear myself. "I only wanted to protect my friends. Keep the people I love safe. I didn't want a Lurae or a crown; I didn't want to be a leader; I just wanted to be equal and—and happy. If this is the cost of revolution, then *I don't want to pay it.*"

I brushed the hair back from Søren's face. My lower lip trembled, and I felt more tears coming when I whispered. "You said you wouldn't leave me."

A throat cleared. I didn't look over. Why should I care if anyone heard me? No one else could possibly understand what a loss this was. The world was afraid of the Hellbringer. They didn't deserve to mourn him, no matter any change of heart they'd had down the line.

But I did look up, blinking to clear the tears from my eyes. Dawn broke, lighting a set of hills on either side of me. *Bhorglid,* the thought registered. *We're still in Bhorglid.*

I was numb to my core, but a single question throbbed in my mind. I called out to whoever stood in my vicinity, my voice hoarse. "Did you get the prisoners out? Is everyone safe?"

Footsteps padded over the grass until a pair of boots entered my vision. "I wouldn't say safe, but we're all alive."

No other voice would have been enough for me to take my eyes off Søren. But Freja's? I stared up at her. Waited for her rage to spill from her again, like it had at the festival. She could kill me right now for everything I'd done. I wouldn't have blamed her.

She turned her impassive gaze away from me and crossed her arms. Through blurry vision, I noted her gaunt cheeks and shaking hands. Had prison been easier the second time around? Or had Araya and Callum made them suffer more?

"Is Jac okay? And Volkan?"

Freja's cold disdain was almost worse than her fury. "You'll have to ask them when you're done here."

I allowed silence to fall. What did it matter if she hated me? I'd known for weeks that this was coming and had chosen to dig myself a deeper grave all the while. She had earned her rage.

It was all my fault. The loss of Freja's trust, my friends' time as prisoners, Søren's death. All of it.

My fault.

"They tortured me and Volkan," she said quietly. "Tried to convince us to tell them where you'd gone. Inconvenient for them that we didn't know."

I blinked slowly, trying to clear my mind of grief and fog for a moment. Finally, I whispered, "We came for you as soon as we could."

She sat down next to me, facing the opposite direction. "So Valen said. You're lucky I believe them. I wouldn't have taken anyone else's word, especially not yours."

"If all you're going to do is tell me I'm worthless, then leave." My shoulders curled in on themselves. "You've already made it clear—you aren't interested in anything I have to say."

She shrugged. "I'm not. But you set out to kill the queen, and you haven't finished that mission yet."

I thought about screaming at her the way I'd screamed at Sonja. Seemed like the only way I was going to get any peace and quiet around here. But before I got the chance, Freja said, "You said you have no interest in being a leader. More than fine with me."

As if I could lead anyone in my current state. Any other day I would have snapped, but the thought of it was too much. "There's no point in being a leader no one wants."

"You can fight, though," Freja said, her lips pursing together. She didn't like admitting this. "And right now, what we need is fighters."

"I don't have any interest in fighting." I slumped back down over Søren's body. It had been hours by now—someone would come to tear me away from him soon.

"Do you have any interest in revenge?"

I paused. Looked up at her. She raised an eyebrow. "We need someone willing to gut Callum with the Soulcleaver, you know."

Revenge.

I let the idea roll over my tongue. *Revenge.* I breathed deeply for the first time since . . .

I nodded. "Revenge will do."

39

Søren

DEATH DRAGGED ME KICKING AND SCREAMING.

The moment the knife embedded itself in my stomach, I knew death had arrived to take me. The pain was staggering. It lit through me like a fire, consuming everything it touched. With every second my lungs had struggled for breath, my heartbeat soon stuttering to a stop. I'd taken Revna in one last time, memorizing her features, twisted in anguish. But when darkness swallowed me whole, I pushed against it.

"Revna!" I shouted so loud my voice cracked with the desperation of it. The suffocating nothingness encroached, unyielding. But in the distance, a pinprick of light shone through—dim and steadily disappearing. I ran to it, desperate to find my way back.

No matter how fast I sprinted, my breathing remained even. And the dim light ahead continued retreating, never drawing any closer. I clenched my jaw and forced myself onward. I knew I could outpace the darkness. I *had* to.

She was waiting for me.

The moment the thought crossed my mind, a glowing golden thread wrapped itself around my waist.

It tightened against my stomach, and I looked down at it, bewildered. I knew far more about dying than I should, a side effect of speaking to ghosts for most of my life. And this was not what any of them had described.

The thread pulled hard in the opposite direction, away from the light. Away from Revna. I scowled at it, but continued moving toward her. The knot in the thread tightened like a noose, but it wasn't enough to halt me. *I have to get back to her. I promised—*

The next tug was sharper. When I glanced down again, the first thread was accompanied by many more. Dozens turned to hundreds, entire swaths of my skin bathed in glowing light.

It's taking me from her.

Panic tightened my chest, sending a chill through me. Not even death would keep her from me—I refused to let it. My pace slowed, but I strained against my leash. I'd lied to so many people through the years, myself most of all—but never to Revna. She made me honest, made me good.

I told her I wouldn't leave her.

Death tried to make me a liar.

Picturing her face gave me strength, and I resisted the pull with renewed vigor. "Revna!"

The next threads caught around my knees and I fell. When my face slammed into the ground, I felt no pain. My arms were covered in threads but not anchored to my sides. Desperate, I scrabbled for purchase. If I still had fingernails, surely they would have broken against the onslaught I leveled. But the ground offered no hold.

The threads, now far stronger than me, pulled again. I slid backward. With a growl, I forced myself to my hands and knees. "I'm not leaving you," I called. But dread sank its claws into the pit of my stomach. I heaved myself forward.

She needs me, I thought, the reminder carrying me through. *I promised I would never leave her.*

I fought the threads. Dug my nails into the nothingness, scrabbling for purchase as they dragged me away. "I WON'T LEAVE HER!"

My entire body was enveloped in gold. I screamed my rage to the darkness when death finally triumphed.

◆ ◆ ◆ ◆ ◆

"YOU," A VOICE SOMEHOW DEEP AND HIGH-PITCHED, AGELESS AND all-knowing, solitary and a hundred voices at once, said, "are quite obstinate, Hellbringer."

My eyes flew open, but immediately watered in the face of so much light. Still, I forced them wide, blinking away the tears and reaching for my sword.

No sheath rested at my hip. So instead, I scrambled backward, trying to put space between myself and my adversary. Slowly, my vision adjusted and the endless expanse of bright white dimmed to reveal a figure standing several yards from me.

They glowed golden—the exact same as the threads that had brought me here. I had seen the Tapestry several times in the past few days, meeting it in dreams with Revna as it showed us snippets of the past.

None of those times had I imagined seeing it while I was more furious than I'd ever been in my entire life.

"You," I spat, adrenaline and anger fueling me to stand on unsteady feet. "You brought me here."

They tilted their head, the humanoid figure somehow managing to radiate polite indifference despite its lack of features. When they spoke, the sound reverberated in my mind, absent any true pitch or accent. "Of course we did."

My hands curled into fists. "Send me back. I'm needed on the other side."

A chuckle. "We know, Hellbringer."

"Stop calling me that." The reminder of my many wrongs, offered so casually by an all-powerful being, sent an uncomfortable chill up my spine. When Revna called me Hellbringer, it was an acknowledgment of everything we'd been through together. When others did, it pointed out my monstrosity, my unforgivable crimes. I waited for my head to throb, but then realized the intense struggle to bring me here hadn't even left me sore. I doubted I could feel pain at all right now. "My name is Søren, and you know it."

"Of course," it said with a nod.

"Why am I here?" I asked, running a hand through my hair. It did little to quell my nerves. "This is not a typical death. My ghost should be back in my world, unable to leave the castle in Bhorglid."

"The circumstances of your life—and therefore your death—are different than most," the Tapestry said. "We chose to bring you here to impress upon you the importance of the responsibility you've been given."

"Responsibility." I let the word settle on my tongue, heavier than usual. "You mean sending souls on to the next life."

It nodded. "Allow us to show you."

It waved a hand and more threads appeared behind it, stretching up farther than I could see. Did they go on forever? The threads swirled together, beginning to form shapes.

"Wait."

The Tapestry paused. I gathered all the courage necessary to demand something of a being far older and more powerful than I could know. While I didn't believe in gods, I wasn't stupid enough to look at the Tapestry and not recognize just how much it had control over.

"You can only show me if you tell me whether she made it to safety."

A heartbeat of pause. The Tapestry's fingers twitched slightly at its sides, like it hadn't expected the demand. But I had to know. Mira had planned to return for Revna, but had she made it in time? Or had the prison break taken too long?

Despite whatever misgivings it had about my request, the Tapestry nodded. "Yes. Revna lives on, safe."

Relief rushed through me, a waterfall of emotion strong enough to bring the sting of tears to my eyes. But I held them back and stepped forward to stand next to the Tapestry. "Then I will see what you have to offer me."

The weaving in front of us moved, taking the shape of a sphere surrounding me on all sides. When I looked toward the Tapestry to gauge whether I should be worried, it was gone. And then, all the golden threads changed color, the image so seamless, it was as if I stood in the wastelands themselves. Only I felt none of the cold.

A woman with long red hair stood before me, frowning. She had a long walking stick in one hand, and she wore layer upon layer of fur. Around her waist was a belt and a sheath, which held a familiar blade: the Soulcleaver.

"Aloisa," I breathed.

But she looked past me. I turned to follow her gaze, inhaling sharply when I saw what she did.

Next to a tall pine was the body of a young boy. He was no more than sixteen, his eyes staring sightlessly. There wasn't a single mark on him. A bow and arrow lay discarded and half buried in the snow next to him.

I knew exactly how this boy had died. Because I'd been the one to kill him.

Aloisa stepped briskly over to the body, surveying his military uniform. Red and white and gold—the colors of Bhorglid—adorned him. My palm moved to rub against my throat as the guilt threatened to choke me.

When Revna had been my prisoner, I'd desperately needed her to trust me. I'd given her what I'd thought was a gift: the chance for her to escape if she truly wanted, but really the chance to speak to her brother Frode, since she missed him so much. The entire time she was gone, I'd paced through the forest, wondering if she would come back to me.

Even then, she'd been brighter than the sun in the sky to me.

She did choose to come back, and in my relief, I wasn't paying attention to my surroundings. The boy, still so young, had been on sentry duty. He'd managed to shoot me with an arrow.

I'd known the danger of being so close to Bhorglid's main camp. But I'd been naive to expect the danger to come in the form of a seasoned, expert soldier.

If anyone had seen me with Revna, our mission would have been for naught.

I had no other choice. It was what I'd been trying to convince myself of since the day it happened. *I had to kill him.*

I hadn't realized he'd been left in the snow and not given a proper burial.

Aloisa examined the body, then reached out to close his eyes gently. She, however, chose to follow the thread of his soul. A single golden string stretching around the body and disappearing into the trees.

Aloisa's face grew determined, and she began to step carefully in the direction of the waiting ghost. It wasn't long before the trees parted to reveal the boy's spirit, the other end of the thread disappearing into his nearly translucent form. He huddled behind a trunk, starting when Aloisa looked directly at him and said, "Hello."

"You can see me?" His voice was timid, still high-pitched. Another wave of guilt wracked me, but I pushed it aside. There was something in this memory I needed to witness, and I hadn't yet figured out what it was. "No one else can see me."

The boy seemed relieved when Aloisa nodded. "Do you know what happened?"

"I died." He swallowed. "The Hellbringer . . . he killed me."

"And now, instead of passing on, your spirit is stuck here. Tied to the place you died, unable to move on," she explained. "I am here to fix that. To offer you peace."

"How?" The boy's voice grew quieter. "I just want to go home."

"Look." She waved a hand, and before them, a golden archway woven from threads appeared. It stretched up, brushing along the branches of the pines with no regard for them. The trees didn't even move, undamaged in the slightest. The threads formed incredible detail, and I leaned forward to study it. The filigree felt similar to the Kryllian palace's architecture, swirls adorned with shimmering light. As it finished, sides touching the snow, Aloisa waved another hand. The boy's soul thread disconnected from the space around his body, floating in the air to flow into the archway.

The boy and I watched with fascination. Aloisa's face, however, broke into a gentle smile. She turned back to him. "This doorway will take you where you need to go. And when you arrive, your soul will be set free."

He fidgeted, trying to twist immaterial fingers around the soul thread. They wouldn't connect, his nervous habit useless in his current form. "Should I be afraid?"

Her gaze softened. "No. You were a soldier. You know what it means to be an essential part of something bigger than yourself, something that offers you purpose. Think of this path as the journey to your next adventure."

The boy steeled himself. And then he ran into the archway, a relieved smile on his face. The moment he breached it, golden light flashed. And when I blinked, clearing my eyes of spots, it had all vanished.

Crossing my arms over my chest, I spoke aloud, addressing the Tapestry. "Aloisa helped that boy pass on. How?"

The image froze, the memory standing still. Flakes of snow hung suspended in the air, and Aloisa did not move anymore. The Tapestry's humanoid form appeared next to me. "Using her Lurae, she constructed the archway. We guided her as she built it, using the soul threads she was able to cut and manipulate."

"Are you . . . also the archway, then?"

The Tapestry nodded. "Yes. We are all who have come before. We reach from this world to yours and gather the souls that are ready to move on."

"Revna and I theorized that Aloisa's death made it impossible for the waiting dead to pass through the archway," I said slowly.

"Correct," the Tapestry confirmed. "It is now your responsibility to pass them on. But you already know this."

"Then . . . how?" I ran a hand through my hair.

I could have sworn the edges of the Tapestry's face moved up, like it was smiling. "And that is why we have brought you here. Because you need to understand why you've been gifted these abilities. Because before you can continue, you must be changed. Made immortal. The archway is gone, unraveled, because Aloisa's soul was the final thread holding it together. You and the Bloodsinger Queen must create a new path for your reign."

"Why do you even need us?" I demanded. Everything the Tapestry proposed sounded much like putting on another leash, only with a holder who professed to be benevolent. I knew as well as anyone how long that arrangement was likely to last. "Why can't you just . . . do it all yourself?"

The Tapestry shrugged. "Even we are limited, Hellbringer. This is how the Fjordlands were created, and it is how they will continue until this world is no more. Humanity was gifted magic when they were ready for more. But this magic is not the end of the progression. One day, when the Fjordlands are ready, there will be even more offered to its people."

I had endless questions. But the one that escaped was, "Just the Fjordlands?"

I heard the Tapestry's smirk. "The world is a complicated place. Don't ask questions you don't have the capacity to know the answers to."

"None of this matters to me," I argued. "There are people back in my world who are waiting for me. Depending on me. If it was so important to you that Revna and I do this together, then send me back to her."

"You have only Aloisa to thank for your Lurae being split between life and death," the Tapestry said, suddenly serious.

I shook my head. Time passed differently here, but I didn't know exactly how to gauge how long it had been since I died in Revna's arms. Clearly the Tapestry intended to send me back, but how much time would be wasted hammering out the details of how to use our Lurae to form an archway? "Once again, I don't understand."

The scenery vanished in the blink of an eye. Now we stood in the grove of trees—so much of the wastes looked the same, but I recognized the warped stump of a petrified tree standing out among the snowdrifts. This was the same place where I'd seen Arraya kill Aloisa in a dream. Stars winked down at us. A fire blazed in front of the goddess. The Soulcleaver rested over her thighs.

And the Tapestry stood across from her, hands behind its back, observing.

"I'm done," Aloisa said quietly. "I have served for three hundred and fifty years, doing my duty to the souls of this world. But I am finished. I am lonely. The Soulcleaver can kill me, and if you do not allow me rest yourself, I will use it." She moved one hand in the direction of the Soulcleaver.

The Tapestry seemed almost hesitant when it replied, "We do not understand."

Aloisa's answering laugh was harsh. "I suppose you wouldn't. Today is the anniversary of my husband's death, you know. Two hundred and eighty-six years ago, he passed away of old age. He lived a lovely, long life. And I am ready to join him."

The humanoid figure across from me tilted its head. "And you would . . . have us pass your duties on to another?"

She sighed. "I am ready to depart, but I hate that you will force me to put this duty on another's shoulders. The same way you forced it upon me."

The Tapestry spoke gently. "Aloisa, you chose this."

"Without full knowledge of what I was agreeing to." She turned accusing eyes to the Tapestry. "You asked a child if she was ready to bear the weight of all humanity. Have you ever considered how unfair that was?"

"Yes."

"And yet you did nothing to change it, and have made no apology to me despite having hundreds of years in which to do so." Aloisa stood, her mouth set in a firm line. "I am here to resign. I have no interest in being the Weaver any longer."

"Then someone must be chosen to succeed you," the Tapestry said simply. "Otherwise, no souls will be able to pass on. You would sentence them all to eternity of hopeless, lonely wandering."

"Sounds familiar," she snapped. "You sentenced me to such a fate long ago. I've stared into the reflection of this blade time and time again since my husband passed. Wishing for the peace of death. I stopped Callum, sent souls on . . . I've done everything you asked."

"And Arraya?" it ventured. "She still lives. Still plots to resurrect her husband, something that will only be possible through your death."

"Let her." Aloisa's exhaustion was the honed edge of a blade, sharp and demanding. "You have asked endless impossible things of me. But I hunted her for years, outwitted by her at every turn. And I have finally decided to tell you the truth: I will not kill my sister."

The Tapestry's voice held no emotion when it asked, "Despite all she has done? Despite the harm she continues to cause? You will not end her?"

"No." She shook her head. "You are all of humanity. All who have come before. If there is anything you understand, surely it is the impossible way emotions cloud our judgment. The way some bonds remain unbroken, despite atrocities."

The Soulcleaver glowed in the firelight. The Tapestry was utterly, inhumanly still, threads ceasing motion. Aloisa pointed the blade at her heart. "If you do not choose another, then I will use it on myself."

"No!" The Tapestry lurched through the fire, so quick my eyes barely followed the motion. Its hands grasped Aloisa's, golden glow atop pale skin.

"I want to rest." Her breathing came quickly. "To sleep. So take my powers and give them to another."

It hesitated. "And this . . . will make you happy?"

"It will bring me peace." Her lip trembled.

My eyes burned watching the scene unfold. Even the cadence of her voice was reminiscent of Revna's. I wondered whether she had seen her sons age, witnessed the end of her grandchildren's lives. Was her red hair a mark that would have survived twelve generations, to Revna's brothers? Were they related, connected by blood and purpose?

"I have only one request," she whispered. "If you are willing to grant it, then I will remain alive until the new Weaver is of age, fully ready to step into their position."

The wave of emotion crashing over me from the Tapestry was wild and chaotic. It radiated, vivid beyond belief. It was grief and longing and sorrow and confusion. The otherworldly being, despite being the culmination of human consciousness, could not comprehend this outcome. "Name your price."

"You will not burden one person with this duty," she said. "Instead, you must split it in two—the Lurae of life and the Lurae of death, separate abilities. And you must choose two Weavers who, according to the infinite futures you see, would fall in love."

If I had a heartbeat, it would have stopped.

"We . . . do not understand," the Tapestry said slowly.

"I will not allow another to suffer in solitude." She shook her head. "You are everything and everyone and all that will be. But I am just a woman. And I have lived nearly two hundred years alone in these wastes, after I hunted down my only remaining family member, trying to convince myself I was capable of killing her. I am tired of killing. Tired of violence. Tired of being *alone*."

The Tapestry reached for the Soulcleaver, but Aloisa clutched it to her chest. It nicked her hand as she did, and blood welled up in the wound. I stared at it for a long moment. The Tapestry did, too.

It did not heal.

"This weapon can kill immortal beings. Regardless of what you have done to my soul, this will send me back into the fabric of you." She gazed down at the weapon with a desperation, a hunger.

I spoke up, interrupting the scene. "So Aloisa chose to give up? Chose to allow us to deal with Callum and Arraya, rather than dealing with it herself?"

The Tapestry hummed. "Would you kill your sister? Your Bloodsinger Queen knows the mark killing a sibling leaves on one's soul. And regardless of what Aloisa chose, she is no longer living. We are not a judge, merely a culmination of humanity."

I threw my hands up, impatience winning over rationality. I needed to get out of here, needed to get back to Revna. But I was also still reeling. Revna and I had unknowingly been thrust into a divine responsibility for the souls of all humanity. A responsibility neither of us had asked for. "You're the cause of this problem. Fix it yourself. Kill Callum. Do what must be done. Why does it have to be me? Why does it have to be Revna?"

"We see all outcomes," the Tapestry said. Its words were slow, calculated. "Some endings are more likely than others. Each is determined by a specific order of events that can change at any time. We do not meddle unless absolutely necessary—unless the very fate of magic, and therefore our existence, is at stake."

I swallowed, thinking of just how deep the Tapestry's hands were in my life right now. In Revna's.

"And now Revna and I are . . . the Weavers." I tested the words, and while I hated the idea of some great obligation, they felt right. True. "Why us?"

"We studied the threads of the future carefully, made note of all possible paths ahead. And when you and Revna were chosen as the Weavers, the threads held the highest likelihood of you falling in love. It's why Revna's Lurae had to be held back until the right moment—if she had manifested her magic at the usual age, then she would have become a far different person. One you may have loved, or might not have."

The scene vanished, and we faced each other in the white nothingness once more. I ran a hand through my hair. The thought of not loving Revna wasn't one I wanted to consider.

The Tapestry stepped closer to me. "The time has come. You must return. We will reconvene with you and the Bloodsinger Queen at a later time, when the battle with Callum and Arraya has reached its end. Then, we can focus on rebuilding the archway.

"When you wake, you will be different," the Tapestry finished. "Remember what you have seen here."

Then it reached out and pressed a single finger to my forehead.

The world went dark again.

◆ ◆ ◆ ◆ ◆

MY HEAD THROBBED. RINGING SOUNDED EVERYWHERE, A NOISE so sharp it made me wince. And to top it all off, my fingers and toes were completely numb.

I remained still, eyes shut tight, as the ringing slowly subsided. Soon enough, sound began to trickle back in. Through the pain in my head, I heard an unintelligible voice. It said something I couldn't hear. Repeated it.

The third time, it broke through the haze. "Open your eyes, asshole!"

Memory came flooding back to me. My death, my struggle to return, and my subsequent interaction with the Tapestry.

I gasped and opened my eyes.

Frode's face stared down at me, suspicious. "I suppose I'm glad you aren't dead."

"Frode?" Confusion made my thoughts muddy. I sat up slowly and looked around: snow stretched for miles in every direction. "How . . . why . . . what am I doing here?"

"I could ask you the same question," he said, crossing his arms. "You literally appeared out of thin air. Fell from about six feet up and landed flat on your back. I've been trying to get you to wake up for several minutes now."

"I can see you." The realization slammed into me, and I sat up. "I can see you. My Lurae, it's back."

And the moment I acknowledged it, the presence of magic in my blood made itself known with a contented thrum. Some part of me relaxed. I hadn't realized just how lost I felt without my abilities, despite wishing I could rid myself of them for so long.

When I reached deep within and summoned the threads of my Lurae into my field of view, I sighed with relief. Frode's soul glowed a gentle gold. The sight was so familiar my throat tightened, and I wished I could sit and watch the shimmering fabric of the world around me pass by for hours.

The steady thrum of my magic heightened, and I blinked against the onslaught of more threads. The pulse of my Lurae was suddenly too much, and I pushed it down so I could focus. Mentally, I made a note to explore the magic later. It felt different now, coursing through me in a way that raised the hairs on my arms. My visit with the Tapestry had been eye-opening in more ways than one, apparently.

But there wasn't time to relish the feeling of my awakened magic.

"I need to get back." I scrambled to my feet, brushing snow off my clothing. The dark pants and shirt were covered in my usual Hellbringer armor. The same thing I'd been wearing when I . . .

Don't think about dying right now.

"Where is my sister?" Each of Frode's words was taut. "What is happening?"

I began to march through the snow, headed for the tree line I knew was to the south. "There's no time. I have to go."

"Hey, wait!"

I didn't turn around, too busy mentally calculating where I might be able to find a horse. Had any been left behind when Bhorglid disbanded their army? It would take a day and a half to get back to the capital on foot. I swore under my breath.

Frode appeared in front of me, and I jumped. "Are you really going to leave me here with everyone? Because the place is getting kind of crowded, and they said they're all waiting for you." He pointed behind me.

"What are you—"

The stretch of open snow behind me was flooded with the dead.

Hundreds, perhaps thousands of spirits stood, drifting among themselves. Soldiers in Kryllian and Bhorglid uniforms, regular people, and even a handful of priests wandered around. The low murmur of the occasional voice floated over to me.

"I don't know where they came from," Frode said while I gaped.

My Lurae forced itself back to the surface, and when the world turned to gold again I sighed. Every single soul was tethered to me.

"Of course," I muttered. I ran a hand through my hair. There wasn't time to send their essences back to the Tapestry now. I wasn't even sure it was possible without Revna here to do part of the work. I needed her if we were going to reconstruct Aloisa's archway. "Looks like you're all coming with me."

But when I looked back at Frode, his own golden thread stretched in the opposite direction. Back to the snowbank where I'd found his body.

I wasn't sure what crossed my face, but it was enough for him to scowl. "No way are you leaving me behind. If the rest of these idiots get to go with you, then I'm coming, too."

"I'm not even sure if that's—" An idea flashed in my mind's eye, and I hesitated. The deeper, newer thrum of my Lurae sounded once more. Beckoning. Inviting.

Frode lifted his hands. "Well?"

"I have an idea," I said with grim determination. "You better hope we manage this without Revna here."

40

Revna

I WENT THROUGH THE MOTIONS OF PREPARING FOR WAR WITH stiff rigidness, both from my sore muscles and from the horror still haunting me again and again. Callum stealing my blade to kill Søren with it. Søren's body being lifted and taken away by people I didn't know—maybe Seeing Ones, maybe Kryllian citizens, maybe Nilurae from Bhorglid who had managed to escape the prison with Sonja and Mira.

Sonja had handed me a change of clothes to replace my blood-soaked ones. I was loath to put them on, to shed any reminder of Søren. *He is gone, he is gone, he is gone.* The knowledge pounded through me like a second heartbeat.

But I forced myself to swallow it down. *You must avenge him,* I reminded myself. *And the best way to avenge him is to do one small thing at a time. Starting by changing into clean clothes.*

Sonja accompanied me to a river nearby. She sat on a rock at the shoreline, silent while I stripped and waded in to wash the death from my skin. I submerged my clothes, let the last remainders of Søren's life wash away. Every movement I made was slow, lethargy eating away at my will with every second. If I'd been any less disciplined, I would have sunk beneath the current and allowed the water to carry me away.

I barely noticed Sonja's presence, but the part of me aware of her chafed against it. Was she here only to keep me from doing something rash to myself? Succumbing to my grief?

Alone is how you're meant to be, my thoughts whispered. All mine now. I couldn't blame these on my nonexistent Lurae. *You deserve this.*

"I should have come back for him."

I was pulled from my haze by Sonja's words, quiet as they were above the river's gentle current. I raised a brow at her, but she didn't seem to see me, staring off into the distance past me at nothing.

Was this her attempt to ask me to assuage her grief? I cleared my throat as it tightened. "I told you not to come with us. If it's anyone's fault, it's mine."

She blinked back to awareness, her eyes the exact same color as Søren's. They really did look like siblings. The same face structure, same smirk, same commanding presence. "No. I mean I should have come back for him years ago. Gotten him out from the queen's clutches and taken him to safety."

I swallowed. I didn't want to tell her I thought she was right.

"I didn't know the queen was using me as leverage for a long time," she said, picking at her nails. I scrubbed my skin while she talked, unwilling to look her in the eyes. "When I finally realized there was a spy in the caravan, and that they'd been sent to watch me specifically, I tried going back for him."

"You did?" I frowned. "What happened?"

"Bad timing." Her smile was bitter. "I'd heard tales of the Hellbringer's brutality, knew that only my brother could be behind that mask, considering the general's Lurae. But I thought they were exaggerating. I tracked him down in the wastes, surprisingly enough. I waited for him to leave camp on a mission and trailed him, trying to get him alone. Before I could, he arrived at his destination: a traveling platoon of Bhorglid's soldiers."

I wondered how long ago this had been.

"He killed them all." Sonja swallowed. "There were over a hundred men, and he wiped them out in less than a minute. I was horrified. I thought my brother had been lost to the violence, the power the queen offered. I didn't know he was only doing it to try and keep me safe."

"You left," I finished. "You didn't even speak to him."

"No," she confirmed. "It's the biggest mistake I've ever made. I'll spend every moment of the rest of my life regretting it."

I wanted to scream at her. *You should. You deserve it, after abandoning him.*

But instead, I thought of my own regrets.

I wished so badly for another minute with Frode. Wished I could undo Halvar's death, be just a little less angry when I stopped by the tavern on the way to the coronation. I regretted killing the assassin who came after me when I first brought the army home—if I'd spared him, we might have known about the threat from the queen long before now and been able to prevent it.

My own mistakes often threatened to drown me. And Søren? He had never judged me for them. Had defended me fiercely despite them all. So I swallowed down my anger and my tears and told Sonja the truth. "He loved you more than you can possibly know. And while you can't change the past, now you know how to be better in the future."

Her eyes welled and she nodded. "Do you . . . want any help with your hair?"

I reached up to the braid hanging down my back. It was matted, tangled, full of dried blood and dirt. "That would be nice, if you're up for it."

I knew what it meant to have brothers. But as she carefully took down my hair, untangled it with her fingers, and washed it clean, I wondered if this was what it meant to have a sister.

◆ ◆ ◆ ◆ ◆

FINALLY, I FORCED MYSELF TO DRESS IN THE DRY CLOTHES AND RE-turn to the small valley where we'd made camp. Freja had explained that we were a few miles away from the prison, past the extent of where she believed the search parties for the prisoners would go. There were so many escapees that she doubted Callum and Arraya would spend the necessary resources to track them all down.

I'd half listened, trying not to succumb to the pain in my chest.

Now Volkan and Jac, both somber, stepped up to me. They had dark circles beneath their eyes, and Volkan bore a bruise across one cheekbone. Vaguely, I realized it hadn't healed—which meant his Lurae was gone.

We stood still for a moment, and I wondered what I should say. What could possibly be enough to express my sorrow for what they'd been through? Nothing would be adequate.

And they wouldn't forgive me anyway. I didn't deserve their forgiveness. I deserved what I had gotten. A lifetime of aching, bitter loneliness.

I stepped back, preparing to go. Jac grabbed me by the arm and pulled me into a tight embrace.

"I'm so sorry, Rev," he whispered.

My arms hung at my sides and I breathed slowly. My chest tightened, my eyes watered. *You can't cry. You can't break down until you've avenged him.*

I untangled myself from his arms. "Thank you, but I don't want to talk about it."

Jac wiped a stray tear from his cheek. I remembered the last time I'd seen him cry—the night before the Trials, when he'd confessed to me that he didn't want to die. My façade trembled, the crack shooting through my porcelain mask threatening to shatter it. But I held firm.

Volkan's face was dry, but I knew he wore a similar shell over his emotions. There were things to do, battles to wage, a war to win. No time for grief. He looked more serious than I'd ever seen him before.

I cleared my throat. "I'm sorry, too. For all of it. Jac, you deserved better than becoming part of a lie so massive. You too, Volkan. There's nothing I can do to truly ever make it up to you."

"You're right," Jac said. I winced but kept my feet planted. "But you're also my sister. And I hope you know I would do anything for you. Even now."

Volkan put a hand on Jac's shoulder. "We both lost our Lurae to Callum, while we were imprisoned. Maybe your actions were responsible for some of what happened. But please don't forget that every single person involved in this made their own choices. Including me and Jac, when we agreed to help you hide what happened to Halvar."

Tears welled, threatening to overflow. I forced them back. I cleared my throat before I said, "Thank you. Do you know what the plan is?"

Jac gestured to the steadily growing camp behind us. The Seeing Ones had been teleported here from Kryllian and were now setting up their tents. My brother explained, "Freja is bringing anyone she can find here. Astrid and Mira are taking shifts sleeping. Whoever is awake teleports Freja into the city. She speaks with as many people as she can, convinces them to fight, and then brings them—and weapons—back here."

Sure enough, when I scanned the expanse, I saw Freja and Astrid reappear. There were two Nilurae from Bhorglid with them, faces I recognized from the Sharpened Axe but whose names I did not know. I frowned when I noticed who accompanied them. "Children?"

"They're trying to evacuate the children before we attack," Volkan said. "The Kryllian army will arrive in the capital city tomorrow evening, so the plan is to attack before then. If we can kill Callum before the troops get here, then we might be able to destabilize their forces enough to actually win this battle."

"You really think making a stand is a good idea?" Jac frowned, looking to Volkan. "Very few of us are Lurae at this point. Do we really stand a chance?"

The campsite was busy, full of life around us. Freja herded children into the tents, Valen was teaching the basics of combat to some of the Nilurae from Bhorglid and Kryllian, and Sonja was taking stock of what weapons we possessed. I even spotted Arne. He had gathered a small group of Nilurae in fighting condition and was teaching them how to hold a shield. We made brief eye contact before he turned his focus back to instructing.

They were all fighting for my same cause. But this battle had become far more personal to me, and I didn't care about anything except watching Callum suffer.

"This is our only chance," I said to Jac. "The Lurae in Bhorglid might worship Callum, but they also live in fear of him. They'd be helpless without their magic. Callum preaches their superiority but threatens to take it away at any moment. And fear is exploitable."

"Callum has to die," Volkan said. He stared at a point past me, his eyes unfocused. I wondered what he felt about Søren's death. The two had been lovers once, and their friendship had endured past whatever parting of ways ended their romance.

"I will kill him." There was no question in my mind, no *if.* "Besides, he isn't expecting capable Nilurae. We were close last time, but . . ."

The mood darkened. None of us wanted to acknowledge where the last attempt had gotten us.

I continued watching Freja, mesmerized. My friend had taken

well to leadership, organizing our forces and heading out into the city when she could. More surprisingly, it seemed everyone in camp looked to her for answers and approval.

Volkan caught my line of sight. "She took charge when we were all imprisoned," he said softly. "If you all hadn't showed, we were planning to break out, actually. Everyone rallied around Freja. She has a fire in her that gives people hope."

"She does," I agreed. And perhaps I was in the wrong for never seeing it. We'd all changed—I had become queen and then realized I didn't want it. Freja had become a prisoner again and stepped into leadership as easily as breathing.

Freja called our names and beckoned us over. She and Astrid stood around a map of the city drawn by hand. "What's this?" I asked.

Sonja joined us, peering over my shoulder. "We're putting together a plan of attack. The biggest issue we're facing is how to lure the queen out of Bhorglid's castle. No one has seen her leave—we think there's a teleporter helping her. She goes directly from the castle to the prison, and even then she's only been to the prison one time."

"To take our Lurae," Jac added bitterly.

Freja raised a brow at me. "So? How do we lure the queen from the castle?"

"Why are you asking me?" I scoffed. "Not even the explosions we planted during the prison break were enough to bring her out. We'd have to blow up the entire castle to force her to evacuate."

Everyone was quiet.

"No," I said, shaking my head vehemently. "That's not what I meant."

"Why not?" Jac asked. "Our grandfather modeled it after the palace in Kryllian. It represents a legacy of corruption and stolen power—oppression, even. And when all is said and done, Bhorglid will have the chance to truly rebuild into something new. Something *ours*."

"He's right," Astrid chimed in. "The explosions from the breakout were passable, a good enough distraction to draw the priests' eyes. But with Freja's knowledge of explosives, we have the chance to do something big. Something that might truly change the tide."

"It might keep more citizens safe as well," Volkan pointed out. "If we begin by bringing the castle down, the queen will emerge and the priests will flock up the mountain. Most of the battle can take place there. It will keep innocents from getting caught in the fighting."

"Then we do it," Freja said, stepping back. She signed in perfect time with her words but didn't bother speaking aloud when she addressed Astrid. "I have explosives stored in the cellar of the Sharpened Axe. Do you have enough energy that you could take me there?"

Astrid nodded, but I noticed her shoulder slump slightly. "It's Mira's turn to sleep anyway."

"And then," I added, signing while I spoke, "Astrid needs to sleep. Our entire plan hinges on her and Mira being able to teleport us all back to the city in the morning. If they aren't rested, we'll set ourselves up for failure before we even begin."

"You're not here to give orders, Revna," Freja snapped. "You're a soldier now, not a queen."

I didn't have the energy to fight with her, so I allowed the aching severity of her words to sink into my bones. Freja may have offered me revenge, asked for me to join her fight. But it wasn't from any remaining crumbs of friendship. Hers was a request of necessity—she knew I would not give Callum's death to anyone else, so she had bargained for it on her terms instead of my whims.

Astrid laid a hand on Freja's arm, her eyes wide with admonishment. "Revna is welcome here," she signed. "This is what Callum and Arraya want. For us all to squabble so much that we lose sight of our common enemy. There will be plenty of time for you to hate each other later."

I fought the sudden urge to laugh. Did no one realize that I harbored no ill will toward Freja? I knew perfectly well who was at fault for the ruins of our friendship. She held no blame here. "What else is left to plan?" I asked, trying to change the topic.

Freja folded her arms, lips pursed. "Everything. I hope you're all ready to fight tomorrow."

41

Revna

THE NEW DAY DAWNED. WHILE EVERYONE ELSE SUITED UP, putting on whatever fragments of armor Freja had managed to scrounge together over the last twenty-four hours, they hugged their loved ones. Said their goodbyes, just in case.

I sheathed the Soulcleaver on one hip—my own blade had been damaged too thoroughly by Callum for me to use it until I had a chance to mend it at a forge—and sat at the edge of the crowd, alone.

My thoughts turned dark, and I let them in. For once, I allowed the anger to fuel me. The need for vengeance drove every impatient tap of my foot.

It was different from the anger I'd carried with me for so much of my life. Distantly, I found myself wondering if Søren hadn't been entirely right when he said to never fight angry. This anger sharpened me, honed my senses. The other anger from before had been nothing but a paltry disguise for my fear.

Now I had lost everything. There wasn't anything left to fear.

A hand fell on my shoulder. I looked up, shielding my eyes from the bright, rising sun, to see Sonja. Her expression was inscrutable, a mask of her own hiding the grief running through her veins. Outfitted for battle, she was regal and elegant, her short dark hair pinned back and out of her face.

"I don't know whether you have any use for this," she said, "but someone passed this to me. Mira grabbed it when she brought you back from the castle yesterday. He would have wanted you to have it."

She extended her other hand. The Hellbringer mask stared at me, all wide eyes and snarling teeth. I took it from her carefully, ran my palms over the wood. "Thank you."

Sonja nodded and moved back to the group of makeshift soldiers preparing for war against a god. Were we all doomed to die today? Was everyone else feeling the same rising sense of dread as me?

Astrid walked by me and signed, "We're heading out in five minutes."

I chewed my lip, glanced around to be sure no one was watching me too closely, and then slid the Hellbringer mask over my head. The world darkened, and my eyes took their time adjusting. Finally, my vision settled. I couldn't see below the snout of the mask without moving my head, but otherwise, it was like I wasn't wearing anything over my eyes at all.

Magic, I thought, curious. *I wonder what kind of Lurae would allow for enchanting objects in this way.*

Volkan came to a stop in front of me, and a little smile lit on his face. "You look fierce, Bloodsinger."

The prince extended a hand, and I allowed him to pull me to my feet. "Thanks." My voice was distorted, just like Søren's had been when he wore the mask. I didn't have the capacity to feel excitement, but my heartbeat sped at the sound. "How are you feeling?"

"About the battle?" He shrugged, gazing at something past my shoulder with longing in his eyes. "Well enough, I suppose."

I looked over my shoulder and followed his line of sight. A small group of archers, including Jac, was gathering arrows for their quivers. I watched Jac lean over to a younger Seeing One—no more than a teenager—and adjust their armor slightly.

I turned back to Volkan. Suddenly, the way he'd spent startling amounts of time in the Sharpened Axe no longer seemed as innocuous as he'd played it off to be. Every excuse for helping Jac keep my secret had been incredibly convenient, especially if . . .

"You care for him." I was careful to keep my voice low.

Volkan didn't even bother looking at me, just frowned while he watched Jac. "Of course I do. How could anyone know him and not care for him?"

"Does he know?"

"No." Volkan scoffed. "I thought I was being obvious, but he's either seeing it and choosing to ignore my feelings or entirely in the dark. I'm not sure which would be worse, to be honest."

I hummed. "Maybe you should tell him. Before we all waltz to our deaths."

At that, his eyes finally flickered down to me. "You're just as pessimistic as Søren was. It's endearing to hear things like that coming from beneath the mask."

My breath stuttered in my chest, a wave of rising grief threatening to swallow me whole. I pushed it down, down, down into the depths. Later. I would deal with it later.

"Stop avoiding the subject," I snapped. When he winced, I softened my tone. "If you don't tell him now, you might never get the chance."

Freja's voice interrupted as she yelled, "Fighters, line up! We're leaving!"

I patted Volkan's chest. "Think about it."

He was still staring at Jac when I walked away to join the rest of the entourage.

◆ ◆ ◆ ◆ ◆

WE WALKED A MILE TOWARD THE CITY BEFORE ASTRID AND MIRA began teleporting us to varying locations. A small attempt to help both women save their energy for the fight ahead. I bounced on the balls of my feet, anxiety and anger flooding my veins in equal measure. I didn't like the plan Freja had laid out—where I arrived last, after the castle had been decimated, hopefully able to catch Callum and Arraya off guard.

It made enough sense that I didn't fight Freja's insistence. Even though I suspected it had more to do with her wanting me out of the way than with logic and careful planning. But the idea of waiting here and missing the beginning of the battle didn't sit right with me either.

Astrid began by taking Freja and Sonja, who were responsible for setting the charges without being spotted. The moment they left, Mira began shepherding our inexperienced soldiers to various locations. Some were going into the city, their job to kill as many priests as possible without being spotted. Others were being stationed in the hidden clearing where Søren and I had trained my magic. They would position themselves on the path to engage with any priests trying to move up to the castle as reinforcements. The rest, including Volkan and Jac, were waiting with me. They would be teleported into the castle courtyard as soon as the opportunity arose.

Jac nudged me with his shoulder. "I didn't get the chance to tell you earlier, but the mask looks good on you."

I found myself turning to him, his approval a relief. After all the harm I'd caused him, this felt like forgiveness. "Really?"

Jac had so rarely smiled growing up, but now his lips curved with ease. "Yes. He would be proud of you. Frode would be, too."

I waited for the sorrow to cover me, weigh me down again. But whether it was because of my adrenaline or for some other reason, it didn't come. Only a vicious determination to be the end of Callum and Arraya. "I hope so."

He and I stood quietly side by side while we waited for our turn to be teleported away. I considered wrapping him in a hug, telling him how glad I was that he didn't die in the Trials for no reason. Considered pretending these were our last moments together—just in case they were.

I couldn't bring myself to do it.

So when Mira arrived and reached her hands out for Volkan and Jac, I patted my brother on the back and let him go with nothing more than a smile and a nod of reassurance. Maybe by pretending we'd make it out of this alive, we somehow would.

They disappeared, and for a long minute, I was alone.

The dangerous thoughts swarmed like flies on carrion. Was Søren's ghost still in the castle? He'd said that souls who passed on were stuck in the place they died. Not even stuck to their bodies. Stupid, that once I'd been able to manipulate soul threads. Maybe then I at least could have brought him with me. Would he be all right when the castle exploded? I shook my head. He was a ghost; of course he'd be fine.

The real question was whether I had the capacity to make Arraya hurt the way I did. Whether I'd be able to give her a slow death; the kind of pain she deserved.

Astrid reappeared, and I took an inadvertent step toward her. She signed, "It's started. The castle is crumbling as we speak."

I rushed to ask, "And the queen?"

She shrugged. "Not sure. But I hope she feels just as scared as I do when I see you in that mask." The teleporter winked at me and held out her arm.

I grabbed hold of her wrist, and then said, "Thank you. For everything. And I'm sorry."

She simply smiled, no hidden malice behind it, no sardonic patience despite my wrongdoings. Only a deep, profound understanding in her eyes. "You're doing everything you can to make up for your mistakes. That's all that matters."

We teleported away, and when I blinked next, the scene around me was utter chaos.

The castle of Bhorglid, once my only home, was imploding. The roof crumbled, the stone caved in on itself, and the tower with the library was on fire. The courtyard shook with the strength of an earthquake, and I bent at the knees to steady myself as the ground rumbled beneath me.

Priests raced away from the impending wreckage, some of which smashed craters into the grass. I drew the Soulcleaver and released Astrid's wrist. The teleporter grimaced as she drew knives from her bandolier, preparing to attack. Fighters from our side of the conflict battled with the priests. Jac was positioned high up in a tree. I watched one of his arrows slam into a priest, just in time for Volkan to step forward and finish the man off.

I stepped through the fray, toward the steadily falling chunks of the castle ruins. The priests were not my responsibility—Arraya was. And she was nowhere to be seen.

The noise of the collapsing building was far greater than I had imagined. The crash of it all hovered over the battle like an ominous cloud hailing a thunderstorm. Only the sky was clear, the sun shining down over us all, glinting on the blades as they crashed together. I stared into the ruins, searching for a glimpse of Arraya. But dust billowed out from the scene, and she was nowhere to be found.

When the sound finally began to fade, echoes the only remains of the explosions that had gone off, I screamed. "Callum! Come face me, coward!"

A haunting laugh came from the dust. I readied the Soulcleaver, dodging a blow from a priest who tried to sneak up behind me and then stabbing him with a fatal wound. I turned back to the wreckage just as the haunting voice of the Kryllian Queen called, "You dare to return here? After I killed your other half?"

The reminder of Søren was like sharp fingernails digging into an open wound. But I stood steady and allowed the pain to fuel my rage. "This time, I have a weapon that will end you."

Arraya appeared through the smoke. She was disheveled and covered in grime, her blond hair coated in a layer of ash. But it did nothing to assuage my nerves. Especially when she grinned, mouth wide enough for me to see nearly all of her teeth. The flesh along her lips was peeling grotesquely, and the scorched marks along her hands stretched farther up her arms now. I tensed, did a quick check to make sure the castle had stabilized enough, and then rushed for her.

She stepped into the crumbled doorway and met my first swipe with her blade. I didn't hesitate—I knew how important it was to kill her early on in this battle. The sooner we could disorient the priests and whatever Lurae fought for them, the sooner we could end this with as little bloodshed as possible. I kicked out, aiming for her stomach.

She—or maybe it was Callum's half—was too quick. She dodged, and then used my recovering balance to catch me off guard when she swung again, now wielding a second, shorter sword in her nondominant hand. I parried and skirted away from every strike, but she wasted no time backing me out into the middle of the courtyard.

The sounds of battle rang in my ears, but I had no space to pay attention to anything but Arraya's fierce attack. After only a few minutes, my breath came in pants. I tried desperately to get the upper hand, but unlike last time, my adversary began the fight without underestimating me. She knew how I fought, knew how hard I was trying to kill her.

Without Søren, I wasn't sure I stood a chance.

But as the first rock of dread began to sink in my stomach, Arraya stumbled. I didn't have time to analyze why, so I swiped with precision, the Soulcleaver's blade managing to draw a thick line of blood from her throat. Not a killing blow, but first blood. I would take it.

She lurched out of the way, and a flood of three priests stepped in front of her. I growled, and while it took less than a full minute for me to dispatch them, it was enough time for her to pull an arrow out of her back and crush it under her foot. *Thank you, Jac.* Blood dripped down her chest for a moment before the wound sealed itself.

"Surrender," I ordered. "Bhorglid will never be yours."

She laughed, and it sent a chill up my spine. "You may wear the mask, but it doesn't offer you any power. You have no Lurae. You are *nothing*."

"I don't need a Lurae to defeat you," I said. "But you do need my Lurae if you ever want to have your body back. It's easy to see the toll two souls is taking on you."

It was the truth, even if slightly exaggerated. Arraya's eyes were bloodshot, some of her movements jerky. Occasionally, her features moved in a way that told me the person making the expression wasn't used to wearing her face. Surely Arraya wanted her own body back. Surely Callum was forcing her to yield her autonomy, taking control more often than not.

But she grinned. "I will take my husband back in whatever form he offers. I will be his vessel in this world until Aloisa's successors are chosen again—since you and the Hellbringer failed so early on. When we control the Fjordlands, nothing will stand in our way. This is what it means to be a god, you insolent child."

"You're not a god," I countered. "You just have a superiority complex."

I stepped forward, swiping at her again, but she stepped out of the way. Didn't even bother to parry. Her change in tactic made me wary, and she used my moment of hesitation to her advantage. A priest appeared at her side, grabbing her by the shoulder. Just before she teleported away, she crooned, “Doesn’t it eat away at you? That you can’t save everyone?”

Arraya disappeared. And a bloodcurdling scream rent the air.

42

Revna

I WHIRLED, SEARCHING THE CROWDED COURTYARD FOR THE source of the scream. Blood covered white robes, bodies strewn along the ground. And then my gaze locked on Freja, eyes wide with horror, a hand covering her mouth. Next to her, Valen clutched at their throat, falling to the ground as Arraya pulled her blade back from delivering a killing blow.

"No." My voice was a croak through the mask. I moved helplessly in Callum's direction, anger fueling me through the desperation. "No!"

Freja attacked the queen, but she was no match for Arraya's superior skill. In a matter of seconds, my friend was disarmed and exposed. Arraya sneered down at her. "No Lurae? Your blood isn't worthy to stain this blade." She beckoned for the teleporting priest to deliver the final strike.

And I was too far away to interfere. Priests continued to step in my way, and when I had dispatched them, soldiers in Bhorglid uniforms attacked. The ground I raced across rumbled beneath my feet until it shot upward, an earth Lurae somewhere manipulating the courtyard to keep me from saving Freja.

I scrambled to the edge of what was now a cliffside. The priest hoisted his scythe, ready to kill Freja. And I knew what would happen next—the priest would teleport Arraya to Jac, to Volkan, to Astrid, and so on until all of my friends were dead. My heart seized. There was nothing I could do to stop it.

But as the scythe swung, Astrid appeared, standing directly in front of Freja. The scythe connected with her crossed daggers instead, the impact ringing through the courtyard. In the split second following, Mira appeared right behind the priest, wrapping her arms around his neck and using her elbow joint to choke him. He stumbled back while Astrid teleported Freja away.

The queen screamed, her rage and fury a howl unlike anything I'd ever heard before. The ground I stood on began to sink back to its usual position, the Lurae responsible now caught up in a battle with a Seeing One. I bounced on the balls of my feet, watching Mira struggle. The priest whose back she was on spun wildly, scythe flailing in an attempt to hit her.

Only a few more feet and I can make the jump down, I thought, impatience gnawing at me. *I can help Mira.*

And then Arraya scowled and ran her sword through the teleporting priest—and Mira.

They collapsed to the ground just as I was able to jump down, my throat raw from the cry of anguish I couldn't hold back any longer. The queen, or maybe it was Callum in control now, laughed as I ran to Mira's fallen body. Her eyes were wide and unseeing, blood pouring down her abdomen.

It reminded me so much of Søren's death. The fury in me made my hands tremble. I stood, stepping up to the queen again, the Soulcleaver raised. Another arrow hit her in the shoulder, and she grimaced before ripping it from her flesh.

"You still believe you have a chance," she sneered. "Aren't you ready to give up yet? Ready to join your other half in the next life?" Arraya lunged, her sword curving down from above, ready to take my head off.

This particular swing was sloppy, easy for me to block. I parried before twisting to level my own blow toward her waist. Pointless, considering how swiftly she matched my renewed vigor and retaliated. I blocked strike after strike, her words ringing in my head, Mira's lifeless body flashing behind my eyes with every blink.

You will watch all your friends die, my thoughts whispered. *Exactly like Mira. Exactly like Valen. And there is nothing you can do to save them.*

My anger faded, replaced by something more familiar. Fear. It dug deep into my bones, impossible to deny. I'd thought when Søren died I had nothing left to lose.

I was wrong.

I dodged the queen's next swipe to strike at her abdomen. Fluid as water, she twisted around it and reached her short sword out to carve a deep wound along my forearm. The pain stung and my hand spasmed—just enough for her to step forward and shove me.

I fell on my ass, losing my grip on the Soulcleaver. The sky flashed with lightning despite being clear of clouds—a sign that another Lurae was joining the fight. A reminder of just how outnumbered we were.

The queen stepped up to me, and I was forced to scramble backward. She touched the tip of her blade to my throat, and I inhaled sharply. "I will savor this," she said. I spared half a thought to wonder who looked at me from behind her eyes. "You and the Hellbringer were nothing but a means to an end for me. And now you will pay. For every moment you attempted to defy me. To defy a *god*."

I spared one last glance around for my friends.

Freja and Astrid were standing back-to-back, swarmed by priests and Bhorglid soldiers. Jac was scrambling down from his perch in the tree, eyes on Volkan, who lay limp on the ground a short distance away. Sonja was lowering her sword to the ground, hands in the air as she backed away from the soldiers who had bested her.

It was the end for all of us. The end of Bhorglid.

Old gods will rise to meet the new. The prophecy took on new meaning, and my hands shook.

Was it worth not interfering? I thought, wondering if the Tapestry could hear me. *Was it worth the end of our work for equality just to meet your own absurd standard?*

And then I allowed the fear to go. I thought of my soul leaving my body, stuck in this courtyard, when Søren's was only a short distance away—tied to the castle. A different kind of eternity than I'd pictured with him, but one I would accept nonetheless.

I breathed deeply, ready to face my end.

Arraya pulled back, preparing to strike her final blow. And then her gaze flickered away from me.

I had just enough time to feel a glimmer of confusion before a black-clad figure leapt off a galloping horse and tackled the queen to the ground.

I knew better than to miss this opportunity. I snatched the Soulcleaver and scrambled to my feet, ready to aid my savior. Whoever it happened to be.

A far-too-familiar man knelt over her, dagger in hand, growling, "Get your fucking hands off her." I froze as I watched Søren—because it was *him*, but *how?*—shove his knife into the queen's throat. She lurched and gurgled, blood coating the ground and mixing with the rain.

I pulled the helmet off my face. Stepped hesitantly toward them. Disbelief colored my voice. "S-Søren?"

He turned to face me, a sly grin on his face. "Hey there, Princess. Sorry it took me so long."

My knees threatened to buckle, but I couldn't afford to fall now. Not when my friends so desperately needed help. But when I looked up—

Sonja's expression of defeat was now a gleam of ferocity in her eyes as she lifted her hands. Vines sprang from the ground, curling outward to haul her opponents away. Freja and Astrid were joined by soldiers. Ones I recognized: they'd been friendly with me during the sparring match here just a few weeks ago. General Raunstrup's mouth was set in a scowl so prominent I hardly recognized her.

Reinforcements. Soldiers from Bhorglid, *Lurae* soldiers, who had come to fight on our behalf. Several aided Arne, who held his blade out to shield an injured Seeing One.

Søren's voice was gentle, despite the violence of him keeping the blade in Arraya's throat, ignoring the way her fingernails scraped against the backs of his hands. "Ready to end this, sweetheart?"

I moved toward him, helmet in one hand and the Soulcleaver in the other. Still uncertain whether this wasn't a dream. Maybe Arraya had killed me and this was some strange kind of afterlife. When I reached him and saw his gray eyes alight with promise, I shook myself.

"You do it." I extended him the Soulcleaver. "She's been your jailer for your whole life. You deserve to be the one who kills her. And her godsdamned husband."

A strained gurgle emanated from below. When I looked down at Arraya, desperately clinging to life, struggling for once, a peace like no other filled me.

His eyes softened. He took the Soulcleaver from me. "You've kept me prisoner all this time," Søren said to Arraya. "You deserve to suffer for *years* at my hand. But instead, all we have is right now."

Then, the Hellbringer turned to me. "She's kept you prisoner, too. Together?"

He switched his grip on the sword and the knife, so the first was in his dominant hand, and I came to his side. I wrapped my hand around the hilt of the Soulcleaver, marveling at the warmth of his skin. *Alive, alive, alive.* The word ran through me like a heartbeat.

"Together," I agreed.

We rammed the blade through her rib cage and into her heart.

I watched the life leave Callum and Arraya's eyes. Waited until her body stilled, not even a twitch of movement remaining. A tingle ran through my fingers, stretching up to my arms and colliding in the center of my chest. I gasped and shook my head, trying to orient myself. When I caught my balance once more, I heard it whispered on the wind.

A lullaby meant for no one but me.

My Lurae had returned. I stared at my hands, but found . . . I didn't really care. There were more important things on my mind. I looked at Arraya again, the Soulcleaver still buried in her chest. Studied her. Only when I was sure she was dead, sure she would never return, did I cup Søren's face in my hands and whisper, "How?"

Søren surged up, pressing his mouth to mine. Tears ran down my cheeks. He touched our foreheads together, and I felt his hands trembling where they rested against my neck. "The Tapestry came for me after I died. And then it resurrected me and dropped me in the middle of the fucking northern wastes."

I laughed because I didn't know how else to express the overflowing emotions running through me. "You're real? This isn't a dream?"

"Not a dream, Princess," he confirmed. "And look."

I managed to pull back from him, and he gestured to the scene around us. Any priests who weren't already dead were on their knees, General Raunstrup moving from group to group and tying their wrists. The soldiers of Bhorglid who had been part of Arraya's takeover were in similar positions, and I watched Astrid reappear in the cluster of prisoners before grabbing two and teleporting away again.

"We won," I said with amazement. "We won."

Søren was snatched from me. Sonja wrapped him in a hug so tight, I wondered how he could breathe. He laughed as she scolded him. "If you ever pull another stunt like that again, I swear to all the gods—"

I stopped listening, scanning the crowd for Jac. When I spotted his flaming hair, I ran over. He knelt over Volkan, clutching the prince's hand in his own. "Volkan," I gasped, relieved to see his eyes open, chest rising and falling. "You're alive."

"My Lurae returned just in time," he said, though he still sounded strained. He had one hand pressed over his side, and from the sticky coating of blood on his palm I knew he had been stabbed. Without thinking, I reached out with my Lurae, slowing the flow of his draining life force while his body continued stitching itself back together.

Jac put his other hand on my shoulder. He was always pale, but now his skin was paper white. I wondered if he was less oblivious to Volkan's feelings than he seemed—maybe even reciprocated them. "Thank you," he said. "Is that Søren?"

I briefly explained what had happened, including his miraculous return, and Volkan sighed. "That bastard can't do anything without making it as dramatic as possible."

I chuckled and turned to look at Søren. My mood fell instantly when I saw him crouched over a small corpse, his face crumbling. "I need to go," I told Jac and Volkan. "I'm glad you're both all right."

Søren clutched Mira's body to his chest, tears falling down his face. I arrived at his side just in time to see him close her eyes. "Araya killed her," I said softly, uncertain what other comfort to offer him. I hadn't seen him grieve before, and after my own experience losing my siblings, I knew how torturous it could be. "Mira jumped on a priest's back and tried to strangle him when he was about to kill Freja."

Søren heaved out a wet laugh. "Of course she did." He shook his head. "She was like a sister to me."

"I know." I gathered him in my arms and rested my chin against the top of his head. "I'm so, so sorry."

He laid Mira gently back down and then took my hands. "Our work here isn't done, Revna. When I spoke with the Tapestry, it told me we need to weave the new path to the afterlife. The old one crumbled when Aloisa died, and without it, none of the spirits can pass on."

I blinked, taking in the information. "How in the world would we do such a thing?"

Søren shrugged. "I think we start by summoning the Tapestry and seeing what guidance it can offer us."

Together, we reached for the thread connecting us and it stretched into the Tapestry. My soul seemed to settle with the use of my Lurae. Unlike last time, it was easier to cast the woven images into the air.

The world turned into a mess of golden threads. And when I turned to face the Tapestry, I instead saw the battlefield flooded with the souls of the dead.

Their golden threads all connected back to one place: Søren.

I didn't miss the two bloodred threads that stretched into the distance, behind a small section of trees outside the courtyard. It seemed Arraya's soul had been marked when we destroyed her and Callum. Whether they were stuck out of sight or didn't want to be noticed by the crowd now that they were helpless was unknown. But I didn't care. They were gone now, and it was time for us to move forward.

Most of the souls I didn't recognize. A few were as familiar as breathing. Mira and Valen stared down at their golden hands, marveling. I caught a glimpse of a salt-and-pepper beard and noticed Halvar eyeing me from a distance. A pang of guilt sank into me like a blade, but it was forgotten quickly.

Because a voice I recognized said, "Can you see us all now?"

I whirled so fast I nearly lost my balance, then choked when I saw Frode standing there, hands in his pockets, grinning widely. "Frode," I gasped. My brother looked the same as the day I'd lost him. Curly hair windswept, two blades sheathed at either hip, his armor gone but the layers that had been beneath it still present. I held my breath for a moment, waiting for him to disappear. But he stayed.

Reaching for him, I let out a shaky laugh. My hand passed through his nearly translucent body. He offered me a wry smile. "Apparently Søren is the only one who gets a second chance at life."

I thought about telling him how wrong things had gone when I tried to secure him that second chance—but I didn't, not when I wasn't sure how much time we had. "I miss you so much." My throat burned from inhaling smoke and holding back tears. "I can't believe you've been here all this time. I should have gone back looking for you."

Frode chuckled. "The Hellbringer beat you to it. Besides, you wouldn't have been able to see me anyway."

I nodded. Gods, if only I could pull him in for another hug. One last time with my arms around him. But . . . even this was a gift. One I would take.

"I'm so sorry." The words spilled out of me, adrenaline from the battle finally receding. "I should have fought harder that day. I should have jumped in front of you—"

"Revna." Frode's expression was equal parts loving and understanding. "I didn't want you to do either of those things. In the moment, I saw no other way to save you. I made a choice, and I don't regret it. I'm sorry it hurt you. But I don't want you to feel guilty about it for the rest of your life."

I swiped away a tear with the back of my hand. "How? How could I possibly forgive myself? You mean everything to me, Frode. Life isn't as bright without you in it."

He smiled. "Forgiving yourself will come with time, but I hope you know there's nothing to be forgiven for. If you can't manage to let the grief go, then instead be grateful, too. Miss me. Tell new friends you make along the way about me. Hold me close to your heart. I hope you'll see the honor in the choice I made one day."

Søren's hand took mine, a quiet show of support. I hadn't realized my hands were shaking so violently. "I do. Of course I do." I swallowed. "I just . . . I wish you could be here for everything. You *should* be here."

"I know." Frode cast his eyes down. "I'm sorry I won't be."

I groaned. "No, stop apologizing. We'll go in circles forever."

He laughed thickly, and I knew he was holding back his own emotions. "You know I'm proud of you, right?"

I nodded. "I do. And you know I couldn't have done it without you, right?"

"Right." Frode looked past me. "Keep an eye on Jac for me. He's hiding more pain than most people realize."

"I will."

We were interrupted by a voice made of endless voices. "Bloodsinger, Hellbringer. It is time to send these spirits on. They should not be made to linger much longer in this world. They have more than earned their rest."

The Tapestry stepped into view, difficult to distinguish from the other souls because the world was awash in so much gold. Søren paused his conversation with Mira, both of them now harboring tearstained cheeks, and turned to the Tapestry to listen.

"How?" I asked. "You've been more than willing to shove this responsibility on us, but you haven't been forthcoming about how we accomplish these things in any way."

I knew my bitterness was obvious in my voice, but I couldn't help myself. How many lives could we have saved if the Tapestry had intervened when I brought Callum's spirit back by accident? Dozens. Hundreds. And yet it hadn't seen fit to help us.

For a long moment, the Tapestry was quiet. Finally, it said, "Aloisa felt much the same way, as the Hellbringer well knows. She accepted the call to this duty as a child, when she did not have all the information necessary to make the best decision for herself. She sacrificed much." It looked up, and if it had had a face, I knew it would have been staring directly at me. "We do not wish for you to feel this way."

"Then what will you do about it?" Søren asked. I heard the wariness in his voice.

A new voice chimed in. "What you need is a purpose."

I stared at Halvar's spirit, uncertain what to say. How to express the depths of my sorrow. Instead, I simply said, "What do you mean?"

His eyes softened a bit. "Everyone has a duty, Revna. Whether it's duty to their country, their people, their family. It's a part of life. But what makes it worth pushing onward is finding a purpose you feel called to in your soul. Something deeper. Something you do because you want to, not just because you have to."

"Like starting a rebellion," I whispered.

He smiled halfheartedly now. "Yes. Though my purpose caused me to make judgments about my friends that I now regret."

Tears traced paths through the dirt on my cheeks. "I never meant to hurt you."

"I know that now," he said.

"It is time to weave the new path to the next life," the Tapestry said gently. "Come now, and we will show you the way."

My chest tightened and I turned to Frode. He watched me with a gentle smile. Pride and peace radiated from him. I swallowed past the lump in my throat. "I don't know that I can let you go. Not again."

"We'll meet again," he said. "There's no place for me here anymore. I need to go. And you need to keep moving forward."

Resignation flooded me. "I love you."

"I love you, too." Frode stepped back.

I took a deep breath. "Well . . . how does one weave an archway?"

43

Revna

THE TAPESTRY SPENT HOURS INSTRUCTING SØREN AND ME ON how to weave the arch. The threads of our friends, our enemies, and all the others who had passed in the days since Aloisa's death came together in my hands, humming with the lullaby while I strung them together.

And behind me, Søren tied the knots and cut the threads. We moved in tandem, every motion as fluid as when we fought side by side. When I finally stepped back to breathe deeply and examine our work, I could barely believe my eyes.

Somehow, we'd woven a brilliant arch of gold. A tall stretch of the Tapestry extended above it, forming a small wall. And on the wall were three images: a crown, a wolf skull, and the Soulcleaver.

Søren had been the one to suggest it. "Like your scars," he'd said. "So that all who pass on remember what happened here today."

No spirits remained, waiting for us. And yet, I knew they were all part of the Tapestry now. The souls made up the arch, and the arch was another facet of the Tapestry itself—the being who had given us our power and who showed us the past. All the souls combined into one essence.

The next time we stumbled across a stuck soul thread, Søren could untie it and I could weave it into the beauty of the archway.

Threaded through the woven sword above us were two strands of red. Callum's and Arraya's souls. There permanently, I hoped. With Arraya gone, there was no one left to trick those who came after me and Søren. My heart settled with the knowledge.

We'd done it. We'd freed the Fjordlands of their worst tyrant.

But my hands shook with exhaustion, and memories of Frode cascaded through my mind like a waterfall. Søren wrapped his arms around my waist, standing behind me to study the arch. "I'm tired," I whispered.

The reality had begun to settle in. *Frode is gone. I am more than human. Søren and I are bound to the Tapestry for . . . eternity.*

When I blinked, my position had shifted. Søren carried me, one arm beneath my knees and the other cradling my shoulders. The Tapestry had disappeared, my magic quiet once more. I laid my head against his chest and closed my eyes. "Then let's go home, sweetheart," he said softly.

Sleep dragged me under, and I did not fight.

◆ ◆ ◆ ◆ ◆

I WOKE IN AN UNFAMILIAR BED, WOODEN BEAMS CRISSCROSSING over my head.

Frowning, I surveyed the space. The sounds of a crowd moving around downstairs echoed slightly, a murmur of noise in the silence. Moonlight streamed in through the window. My belongings—or what remained of them—were gathered neatly on a chair. Armor, swords, boots, cloak.

This must be the upper bedroom in the loft of the Sharpened

Axe. I wondered who was running the tavern now that Halvar—and Jac—was gone. Was it still a hub for the Nilurae?

But the biggest surprise of my surroundings was a welcome one: the warm figure curled up next to me, his height and broadness nearly enough to push me off the side of the small bed.

Søren held me tight, keeping me from falling. My head was pillowed on his bare chest, and I tilted my face to look up at him. His eyes were closed, the tension he usually held in his jaw absent.

When I shifted in his hold, he was instantly alert, gray irises gazing down at me. "Oh," he said, his voice gravelly. "You're awake."

I wrapped my arms around his waist and squeezed. Buried my face in his chest and breathed him in. "It wasn't just a dream. Thank the gods."

I felt him chuckle and clutched him tighter. "I think we are the gods now."

"Are we?" Tension seeped back into me. "I don't like that."

Søren rubbed a soothing hand over my back and hummed contemplatively. "It probably depends on what we believe a god *is*. We're still ourselves, still people. We'll just . . . live longer now. I think."

I pulled back to look at him, raising an eyebrow. "You think?"

For a long moment, he stared at me, a muscle working in his jaw. Then, with a sigh, he sat up. "I have something to show you."

I made room for him to move past me and clamber off the bed. I pulled my knees into my chest and wrapped my arms around them, watching him carefully. His bare back was as enticing as always, but something about him was different. I couldn't quite place it.

He strode to the armchair, where he'd placed his shirt and my clothes in a carefully folded pile. The Hellbringer mask and our weapons rested atop the fabric. He pulled one of my daggers from its sheath, holding it casually.

I forced my shoulders to relax. Forced my mind to picture something other than my hands holding that hilt while his blood poured over them and I desperately tried to stanch it.

His touch on my shoulder brought me back to myself. My breathing had sped up, but his weight sinking the mattress down next to me was reassurance enough to open my eyes.

Søren studied me. "Is it the knife?"

Shame crawled up my skin. I averted my eyes, but nodded. I was incapable of hiding any part of myself from him. I didn't even want to hide anymore. But I couldn't help but wonder what he was thinking. After all . . .

"It was my fault you died."

My voice cracked on the last word, and I held my breath.

"It wasn't," he said, shifting to pull the tie off the end of my braid. He began to undo the twists, running his hands through my hair. Despite my best attempts to fall into panic, his touch soothed me. "It was Arraya's fault. She took your knife. She made the final blow. There was nothing you could have done."

"I—" Panic crawled through my chest, cold as the icy plains of the northern wastes. "I should have been able to kill her."

Søren's nails scratched gently against my scalp. I tried not to think about how long it had been since I'd bathed. But he didn't complain. "There was no winning that fight, Revna. You did your best. I did, too. I'm only sorry you had to witness that." He pressed a kiss to my temple. "Even if a single decision would have changed the outcome, there's nothing we can do about it now. I'm just happy to have you here, with me. That's all I feel now—gratitude that I made it back to you."

I hesitated. "And how *did* you make it back to me, exactly?"

He laughed. "Fuck if I know. But I think it has something to do with what I wanted to show you."

I turned but stared at him and not the knife he held. Until he extended his arm and used the blade to carve a deep gouge in his own flesh.

"Søren! What the fuck!" I shot to my feet, searching the room for a clean cloth to use as a bandage. The lullaby was dim and quiet, but it started up at the sight of his blood. We needed to stanch the bleeding before I went to find Volkan—

I stopped short. Søren flexed his arm, the skin whole once more, flesh unmarred. A bit of blood stained his skin, but even my Lurae had quieted, realizing there was nothing wrong.

"This is what I meant," he said, "when I told you we are . . . more than human now."

"Your body did *not* do that when you had a knife embedded in your stomach," I grumbled, tossing the shirt I was holding aside. "Did the Tapestry do that to you?"

"I think so. And if my hunch is correct, then while you've been sleeping, you were changed, too."

I snatched the blade from him. Without preamble, I pulled the tip across my own flesh. Blood blossomed on my forearm. But before it even began to drip, the skin knitted back together and smoothed once more. Like the wound hadn't even happened.

I glanced in the mirror hanging on the wall and brushed my fingertips over my cheeks and forehead. When I felt the ridges of puckered flesh still there from my scars, I settled a bit. "All this while I took a nap?"

He smiled sheepishly. "You've been sleeping for almost forty-eight straight hours."

"Have you been here the whole time?"

Søren ran a hand through his hair and looked away. "No. I'm sorry. I wanted to—but someone needed to bury Mira. And rebury Frode. Along with everyone else who died in the battle. There was always someone here watching over you—Volkan, Jac, Astrid, and I all took turns."

My chest ached. Sorrow was etched deeply on Søren's face. The battle was won, but we had all lost, too. I took his face in my hands, careful not to nick him with the blade I still held. "Don't be sorry. Mira deserved a proper burial from her brother."

His eyes welled with tears, and he blinked them away. "Thank you. For understanding."

I returned the knife carefully to its sheath before going back to the bed and pushing Søren onto his back. His eyebrows shot up, but I simply crawled atop him and lay down, resting my full weight against him. For a while, we were quiet. Only when he had fully relaxed, his pulse calm once more, did I venture, "We're immortal."

"Maybe. Unless that thing kills us."

I hadn't even realized the Soulcleaver was lying with the rest of the weapons. The sound of Søren's heartbeat beneath me steadied my nerves. "We have to be different than Callum. We can't let this get to our heads."

"Part of why Aloisa insisted that her powers be transferred to two people instead of just one was to combat the loneliness she felt," Søren said. "She spent so much time wishing for company. The Tapestry chose us because it both believed we would be worthy of the power and responsibility, and because of how likely it was that we would fall in love."

I smiled into his chest. For all my anger at the Tapestry, I suppose I couldn't complain about it doing one thing right. "Really?"

"Really."

"So what do we do now?" I asked. "Search for the lost souls that need to be sent on into the Tapestry?"

He sighed, wrapped his arms tighter around me. "I think that's what Aloisa did. She stayed in the wastes for most of the last two hundred years or so, though. She had been hunting down Arraya but couldn't bring herself to kill her own sister."

I snorted. "I wouldn't know what that's like."

"We could live here still, if you wanted." Søren's fingers traced a pattern along my skin. "We could travel, like we talked about. Find souls along the way and help where we can."

"Living in the castle, even a newly constructed one, with all of the memories . . ." I hesitated. "It would be too much. And I worry about what happens now that all of Bhorglid knows we're . . . different."

"Maybe we go to Faste and spend some time with Volkan for a bit. Jac is planning to go with him." I heard the smile in his voice, and tension fled from me.

"I like that idea. Though we might not be able to stay for long. If the tension between them is this palpable now, I'm not sure I want to be around when it breaks."

Søren laughed. "I wondered if I was the only one who noticed. I'm glad they'll have each other for company out there. Volkan won't ascend to the throne for a long time. And the current king and queen have no interest in changing their discriminatory laws."

"Volkan and Jac will find a way," I said. Søren traced a pattern on my back and I shivered. Our bare skin pressed together had become more than a simple comfort now. "We'll just have to see, I suppose."

He hummed contentedly. "It definitely feels like our future is more uncertain than ever, but . . . I can't help but be thrilled to know we'll be together for all of it." Then he grew serious. "I want to write down all the history we've learned from the Tapestry. And everything that's happened with us. Even when we're gone one day, the people of the Fjordlands deserve access to the truth. Not spotty records passed down from person to person indiscriminately. A real, written knowledge of it all."

"Yes." It felt so *right* I had to hold myself back from leaping up and pulling him out of bed to find paper and ink right then. Passing souls on was a responsibility; recording this history was a purpose.

One we chose for ourselves. Halvar's parting advice felt far too perfect now that Søren had spoken the idea aloud. "I'd love nothing more."

Warmth suffused me. I rolled off him and stood, extending a hand. "I'm long overdue for a bath. Care to join me?"

His eyes filled with heat. "Your wish is my command, Princess."

44

Revna

THE HELLEBORES IN THE COURTYARD WERE BEGINNING TO bloom. I tugged absentmindedly on the clasp of my cloak as I double-checked the saddle straps on the gray mare. She huffed impatiently, and I clicked my tongue. “We’ll be off soon enough.”

“You’re sure we can’t entice you to stay?”

I turned at the sound of Freja’s voice. Bhorglid’s new head councilwoman was resplendent in her gown—a flowing style with a functional yet fashionable corset reminiscent of Nilurae clothing. Several other leaders from the provinces to the south, west, and east had arrived the night before, ready to discuss the formation of a collaborative government in Bhorglid. Freja was heading the entire affair, and while she anticipated difficulty, she’d been thrilled that every province sent both Lurae and Nilurae as council candidates.

“Did you sprint all the way here?” I asked. Things were still taut with tension between Freja and me, but I pretended not to notice. “We were hoping to slip away while you were burdened with pleasantries.”

She didn’t meet my eyes, and the tension pulled tighter for a moment. I inhaled and held it close. A reminder of why leaving was the best course of action. Freja had said we were welcome to stay, but it didn't change the truth: she didn't *want* us to stay.

It was for the best. After all, I didn't want to stay either.

"Astrid brought me," Freja explained. She shook her head with a humorless laugh. "I'm still sad to see you go. My heart hasn't yet caught up to my mind, I guess. I thought maybe I'd have something profound to say. Instead, I'm just as lost for words as I have been since the festival."

I didn't say aloud what I knew to be true. That everything we could say had already been said. I'd offered endless desperate apologies in the two weeks since the final battle against Callum and Arraya, but each was underlined with the truth Freja couldn't forgive: I couldn't undo the choices I'd made. Even knowing I shouldn't have kept Freja in the dark wasn't enough. If I were to go back in time, I would do it all the same way again.

Neither of us was ready to let it all go.

"We both need time," I said, wishing Søren would hurry up with the saddlebags and save me from this confrontation. "You're a councilwoman now. I have other responsibilities. The dust needs to settle. There is work to be done."

She clasped her hands behind her back. "Where will you go?"

"Do you care?" I was genuinely curious.

Her jaw tightened. "As one of the leaders of Bhorglid, I believe I should be informed of the whereabouts of the Fjordlands' gods, yes."

I wanted to laugh, but there was nothing funny about the situation at all. Not when every turn of events had manifested this way because of how much I loved Freja. I'd saved her from a lifetime rotting in a cell maybe. Had given her another chance at life. And Bhorglid now had its first true Nilurae leadership.

It seemed the cost was our friendship. I still wasn't sure if it was a price I regretted paying or not.

"I'm sure Volkan told you we're headed to Faste soon," I said. The prince and my brother had returned to Volkan's home country a few days prior. Jac was ready for a fresh start somewhere new, and Volkan had offered him a position there. I knew we would make our way back to Kryllian eventually as well—Sonja and her partner had decided to head back to the seaside town where she and Søren had been born.

In the distance, I saw the castle doors open and Søren step out, arms laden with our supplies. I continued, "We have matters to attend to in the wastes first. We'll likely spend a couple of weeks there. We'll check for messages often enough."

When Søren had explained to Astrid that we were leaving, he'd told her we would build a message box by the frozen lake and the forge—and we'd return to check it regularly. I'd complained about going to the northern wastes so frequently, but the corner of his mouth had lifted knowingly. Søren was perfectly aware that I wanted to make sure we were available for the people we loved.

Just in case.

Even if some of those people didn't want us anymore.

Søren reached us, standing a little too close to me as he glanced over his shoulder at Freja before saying, loudly enough for her to hear, "We really ought to be going, love."

I took some of the bags from his hands. "I'm ready."

Freja took the cue with grace, stepping back and dipping her head. "See you later."

I pulled myself up into the saddle and stared back at the ruins of the castle I'd grown up in. Its mountain perch provided a perfect view of the city. The arena in the distance still stood proud. I thought of the statue of Aloisa in the square, surrounded by temple rubble.

My chest tightened, but not much. After all, I knew it was the truth when I replied, "We'll see you again soon."

Søren and I tugged on the reins and started off.

◆ ◆ ◆ ◆ ◆

"IT WOULD BE FAR EASIER TO DO THIS IF THE ENTIRE NORTHERN wastes didn't look exactly the same," Søren griped.

I pressed a palm to my mouth to muffle my laughter. He was absolutely irate, but I couldn't resist reminding him, "This was your idea, you know."

He groaned. "I'm fully aware. And regretting it more than ever now."

In the two weeks we'd spent resting and recovering in Bhorglid—helping convince the Kryllian army that their queen was dead and they needed to return home being our greatest endeavor during that time—we'd realized one day there had been one spirit in the throng that hadn't been unwoven and reworked into the archway.

"I don't know why she wouldn't have been tethered to me after I spoke to the Tapestry," Søren had mused, "but maybe we should go look for her, just in case."

We'd spent five long days searching the wastes, using the forge as our home base and sweeping the area in one direction each day. Søren had described in great detail the grove he'd seen in his visions. I kept my eyes peeled for the warped stump of a tree he'd described to me, but so far we'd had no luck. Truthfully, I didn't mind. It gave us both a chance to really talk about everything that had happened. Søren explained his time with the Tapestry after he died; I told him about Freja's efforts to lead the rebels.

I didn't mind spending our nights together either. We'd made the cave as comfortable as we could and had happily set out to catch up on all the time we spent apart.

Hour after hour passed. The sky dimmed. "We should go back," I said with a sigh. "Maybe tomorrow."

"Wait." Søren's voice was hushed. "Look."

I followed his gaze into the shadow of the pines. And if I squinted just hard enough . . .

There it was. The glimmer of red between the trunks. *Aloisa was killed by the Soulcleaver, too,* I realized. It seemed the blade didn't discriminate between victims when marking their souls a different color.

"It might not be her," he said as we walked toward it. "There could be hundreds of spirits lost out here."

"True," I said, grasping his hand in mine. The first notes of a familiar lullaby began to sound, and I smiled. Because they sounded different.

They weren't only in my head this time.

We approached slowly and carefully but didn't bother to try sneaking up on the small clearing. A woman's voice, crystal clear and lilting, sang the words my mother had hummed to me over and over when I was a child. A story of loss and love, of power and pride. A melody of peace.

When the song came to an end, Aloisa turned to face us. "I've been waiting for you," she said.

I stepped forward, tugging on Søren's hand for him to follow me. His eyes were wide, and he stumbled a bit but managed to meet her eyes when she rose. After a moment of silence, I took it upon myself to say, "Pleasure to meet you."

She appraised me. "The Bloodsinger Queen herself."

I laughed, and it was genuine. Something inside me had eased since the battle for Bhorglid. "Just the Bloodsinger now. Not queen any longer."

She raised a brow. I didn't know whether she could still speak with the Tapestry as a spirit or not, but if she could, then it hadn't kept her updated on our goings-on. "Well, it's an honor nonetheless."

I nodded and Søren finally mustered words. "Thank you," he

said, "for saving me all those years ago. And Sonja. I owe so much to you."

Aloisa shook her head. "Do not forget you owe much to yourself, Hellbringer. I saved you once, but you continued to survive despite being in captivity for so long. I am proud of you."

Søren's hand clutched mine so tightly I wondered if I would lose feeling in my fingers.

Aloisa continued, "I have lingered too long here. Will you both send me on? I am ready."

"Of course," I murmured.

Søren and I called on our Lurae and summoned the archway. For a long moment, she surveyed the crown, the skull, and the sword. Her eyes flickered from the Tapestry to the Soulcleaver at Søren's hip. I allowed him to carry it. I had repaired my own blade our first day in the forge, unwilling to part with it.

Gently, Søren cut Aloisa's soul thread from the snow and I wove the unspooled red into the fabric of the Tapestry. When it was done, I let out a breath. Finally, it felt like the last chapter of our story—the one full of strife and suffering, Trials and battles—was closed. And now we could begin anew.

Write a story all our own.

I thought of Frode. Of all the laughter we'd shared, of all the tears we'd seen each other cry. I thought of Valen and Mira and Halvar. And of our living friends, too. Volkan and Jac, Sonja, Freja and Astrid. "Do you think the countries might agree to have us speak to their scholars?" I said, leaning my head back against Søren's chest. "We're going to write down all the history we learned, everything we experienced. But why should it stop there?"

He picked up where I trailed off. "Record what comes next, too. Prevent those who come after us from suffering because of the lack of written knowledge."

I nodded.

"There will always be corruption," Søren mused. "But you're right. When we go to Faste, let's speak to Volkan about it. He can convince Freja to implement changes in Bhorglid, too."

"I don't know if Freja will do anything we tell her to."

He chuckled. "Well, we have an eternity to convince her, Princess."

He was right, and the thought made the tension drain from my shoulders. We had all the time we needed to bring about change. Even as queen, I hadn't been able to transform things for the better. I'd thought that when my secrets came to light I had lost my chance to do good. That Søren and I would live a quiet life in each other's company, traveling and sending souls on until immortality began to wear on us.

But maybe . . .

"We have real power now," I said slowly. "Real influence. We can make a difference." Søren's hand reached up to brush away the furrow between my brows, and I spared half a thought for how well he knew me—to know my exact expression without even looking at me.

"No one wants to upset the gods," he said. I heard the smirk and reached up to smack him lightly.

"That kind of thinking is what led to Callum," I chastised. But there was no bite in my words. "We can't let that happen to us."

"We won't." He tugged on my hand, pulling me back toward where we had tied our horses. "Maybe we have power now. But it wouldn't mean anything to me without you here to share it with me."

I cast one last glance over my shoulder. I knew with certainty that we wouldn't come to this grove again—it was a good distance from the forge, and Aloisa's soul belonged to the Tapestry now. Her body would be claimed by the wastes.

Setting sunlight peered through the pines, scattering over Søren's face. He was just as beautiful as the first time I'd seen him without the mask. It stopped me in my tracks, breathless all over again.

I had him forever.

When he realized I wasn't following him anymore, he turned back. The Hellbringer was as serious as I'd ever seen him. "Is everything all right?"

"Yes," I said. I felt the truth of it in my bones. "Everything is perfect."

ACKNOWLEDGMENTS

It's hard to believe we've reached the end of Revna and Søren's story. I first began writing *Blood Beneath the Snow* in 2019, so it's been seven years that I've carried them with me. And now they're yours. Which is why, first and foremost, I'd like to thank you. I've always known I was a writer, but to have people reading my work is the greatest honor I could imagine. I'm grateful you pulled my book off the shelf and gave it a chance.

This book would never have made it off my computer and onto shelves without the tireless work of my incredible literary agent, Bethany Hendrix. Having a champion like you for my work is every writer's dream. These books belong to you as much as they do to me. Thank you.

And of course, my amazing editor, Gabrielle Pachon. Working with you has been the greatest experience. Thank you for loving my writing and my characters. Thank you for seeing the heart of my stories above all else. Thank you for editing with so much care and for pushing me to make these books the best they could be. Here's to many more!

My writing friends carry me always. Sarah Marie Page, thank you for listening to hours upon hours of voice memos from me, going over plot details endlessly until I finally figured them out, and being such a true and supportive friend always. I couldn't have done this without you, and I'm endlessly glad not to have gone through sequel hell alone.

Many other friends offered their support and critiques of early versions of parts of this book. Huge thanks to Shalini Abeysekara, Megan Bates, Mandy Darrington, Madi Ogles, Emily Pearson, and McKenna Thomas for our writing dates and critique nights! To my other writing friends who have become some of my favorite people, thank you for your love and support. This especially includes the Fairytale Trash group—AJ, Chris, Hallie, Marietta, and Valerie. Also Ria Parisi, Jaclyn Rodriguez, and K. C. Woodruff. Annika, a special shout-out goes to you for helping me pronounce all the Danish names I used and for helping me with world-building! Thank you! I'm so glad to have connected with you all those years ago. At least Twitter was good for one thing while it lasted.

My nonwriting friends deserve a shout-out too for putting up with me through the nonsense of deadlines and coming to my book launch. Maci and Katie, I adore you both.

A huge thanks to the authors who helped me promote *Blood Beneath the Snow*. Your kind words have meant everything to me! Ben Alderson, LJ Andrews, Amanda Bouchet, Olivia Rose Darling, Thea Guanzon, Sarah Hawley, Katrina Kwan, Claire LeGrand, Tricia Levenseller, Maggie Rapier, Allison Saft, Nisha J. Tuli, and Demi Winters, I am so grateful for you.

The amazing team at Ace has done so much to ensure these books reach the perfect readers. Kiera Bertrand, Kristin Cipolla, Yazmine Hassan, Stephanie Felty, Lynsey Griswold, Christine Legon, Nick Martorelli, Jessica Plummer, Sammy Rice, and Hillary Tacuri, thank you! And thanks also to Randie Lipkin, who copyedited this book. I'm also grateful to the team at Hachette Children's, who published this book in the UK—thank you! Ellie Gossage narrated Revna in both audiobooks, and I'm incredibly grateful for her amazing performance bringing the story to life. Also thanks to Will Damron, who was the voice of Søren.

I genuinely believe this duology has the best covers of all time. They were designed by Emily Osborne and illustrated by Jason Raish. Thank you for making my cover dreams come true.

To everyone who has posted about my books on social media or even shared them with their friends—thank you. Knowing these books will continue to find their people is the greatest joy. And to every bookseller and librarian who has stocked my books, recommended them, let me come in to sign copies, and helped make my debut experience the best days of my life, please know I am giving you the biggest hug of all time through these pages! The work you do is important and valuable, and I appreciate you.

My family has been my biggest support through the life-changing experience of becoming a published author. To my mom and dad, and to my siblings—Noah, Claire, Sophia, Sam, and Lleyton. And to my in-laws as well! I love you all so much.

Is it weird to thank my therapists? Maybe, but considering I edited this book during what I'm calling "The Great Crashout of 2025," I'm going to thank them anyway. And my psychiatrist. If you're struggling, I hope you get the help you need and deserve.

As always, thanks must go to my lovely spouse. Owen, I couldn't have done any of this without your endless support. Thank you for everything, and especially for being the kind of person who has always believed being an author was a guarantee for my future.

Lastly, to Reeve. You can be whomever and whatever you want to be. I love you.

Photo © 2024 Haili Jean Co

ALEXANDRA KENNINGTON has been writing fantasy stories since she was young. Now she's living her dream as an author of fantasy and science fiction novels. When she's not knee-deep in a world of her own creation, you'll find her reading a book with the enemies-to-lovers trope or obsessing over *Star Wars*. She lives in Utah with her spouse and child.

VISIT ALEXANDRA KENNINGTON ONLINE

AlexandraKennington.com
AlexKenningtonWrites
AlexKenningtonWrites